A family blessed with wealth and power – cursed by a legacy of violent death!

Into their intrigue-ridden lives came exquisite young Miranda, who had known the sting of poverty and abandonment during the Civil War. Now she was eager to share the luxuries – and the destiny – of a family she called her own.

Later, amidst the dazzling opulence of Washington, amber-eyed Miranda learned that the Haversham legacy of prestigious wealth was bedeviled by murder, suicide, and secret financial scheming. And, in order to survive, Miranda must destroy the dangerous heritage of evil that held her prisoner!

D1099596

Also by Daoma Winston

Also in Troubadour paperback

Daoma Winston

The Haversham
Legacy

Futura Publications Limited
A Troubadour Book

A Troubadour Book

First published in Great Britain by
Futura Publications Limited in 1977

ISBN 0 8600 7559 1
Printed in Great Britain by
Hazell Watson & Viney Ltd
Aylesbury, Bucks

Futura Publications Limited
110 Warner Road,
Camberwell, London SE5

With Gratitude to
JAY GARON,
for his constant faith and
FREYA MANSTON,
for her constant help

The Haversham Legacy

Part One

ONE

The word was shouted below within seconds after the derringer was fired and Lincoln's head fell forward and his long body collapsed in the rocking chair. It spread from Tenth Street on the chill, misty April breeze along the wide, sewer-wet avenues, the cobbled lanes, and rutted byways. It swirled through the night, passed in yells and whispers from block to block, over the newly finished dome of the Capitol and the gaslit glow of the White House, around coops and kennels and stables, across vacant fields and wooden bridges, and the massive horse corrals in Foggy Bottom.

But the first that Miranda Jervis knew of what had happened in Ford's Theater was when she heard the angry thud of horses' hooves in the street, and the jingling of spurs, and the immediate swell of questioning voices.

In the week just gone by, Washington City had been celebrating in its various ways the fall of Richmond. She considered that the sounds outside must be more of the same, and sighing at the acts of thoughtless men, she bent

1

her head to take a careful stitch in the worn brown frock she was trying to mend.

The front door banged open. There were cries inside.

Then her stepmother, Susanah Kay, burst into the kitchen gasping, "President Lincoln has been shot! We're going out for news, Miranda. Stay here and mind the house until we return."

Miranda rose up instantly. "President Lincoln shot?" she cried. "Is he dead? Is he dead? What's happened to him?"

"We don't know yet. No one does. But we'll go out and see."

With that, Susanah Kay disappeared into the shadows of the hallway.

The front door banged again. The house was still as a tomb, still as death itself, Miranda thought, her legs melting under her so that she almost fell into the chair.

She was numb. She could not think. The foundations of her world had crumbled. What had seemed firm earth beneath her feet was now revealed as quicksand. She envisioned Armageddon, and great flames lashing across the skies in cresting waves, and mountains rising up in molten lava, and vast chasms yawning where there had been none before. Shuddering, she imagined the Apocalypse, and the four wild horsemen riding in from the ends of the world, leaving trails of famine and disease, death and destruction, in their wake.

The grandfather clock in the foyer chimed, and became a pulse beating within the empty walls of the house. A pulse that beat within her own body, too. It drove her up and out of the chair and into frenzied movement.

She ran into the hall. It was musty and dark. The lights still burned in the parlor. They flickered and jumped, casting long dancing shadows on the bare wooden floor.

She hurried to the window and peered past the curtain, but the angle was wrong. She could see nothing, though she heard shouts and cries and stampings.

She raced from room to room, and saw, from the corner of her eyes, a slender dark-clad wraith come leaping out at her. She gasped before she knew that wraith to be her own reflection thrown at her from looking glass and un-covered window.

She blinked against the hot prick of tears, and caught her brown skirts in both hands as she dashed up the steps to her room. There she lit the lamp on her table, and yellow light fell on the small daguerreotype of Abraham Lincoln. Suddenly weak with disbelief, she looked into his dark sorrowing eyes, and at last her tears came. She wept, and prayed silently, and when there was no more weeping in her, she went to the partly opened window.

From here she could see. There was a crowd gathered at the corner below. She saw the shift and swell of it, and the torches passed from hand to hand. She heard its voice, too, but could distinguish none of the words. It was ter-rible to be alone then, and she wished with all her heart that she dared disobey Susanah Kay and go out to hear whatever news she could.

The pulse of frenzy swelled through the empty house, drumming madly in the silence. Her blood drummed with it.

Her lips firmed. Her dark head tipped up. Her amber eyes suddenly glowed hot with defiant fire. She was no prisoner here. She *did* dare. She *would* go out.

She snatched her black cloak from the wardrobe and went swiftly down the steps.

When she stepped outside, the very air assailed her. Kerosene and horse dung and wood smoke burned through the scent of lilac. And stronger than them all was the thick stench of fear.

She turned away from the canal and hurried uphill to where the corners were clotted thick with people, and was immediately surrounded by the great throng of those who, like herself, were bent on knowing what had happened, what had begun, and what ended.

Candles danced in the windows of the tiny wooden shacks, and at their doorways Negro women stood weep-ing, sobs mixed with prayer, and Negro men watched with anxious eyes, perhaps remembering chains recently broken that might be forged again.

At each intersection there were great huddles of close-pressing massed bodies, and from them emanated small confused snatches of curses and conjectures and prayers.

Horses and carriages jostled in the road, crowding the uneasy pedestrians back against the wooden house fronts and the brick walls of the long warehouses, and enforcing a momentary intimacy which offered comfort.

Women in faded cotton bent their shawl-wrapped heads to the screaming infants at their breasts, brushing the silk-clad ladies beside them. Men in worn laborers' shirts rubbed shoulders with those in fine broadcloth.

It was Good Friday, and the last day of Lent, and all through the day the churches had been filled. But now they were overflowing, and sobbing people knelt on the stone steps before the open doors to pray.

Packs of dogs roamed the lanes, yapping and snarling, and chasing excited chickens. Two goats nibbled a pile of garbage, challenging the pigs that wallowed there.

Soldiers in tattered uniforms, some bearing the bandages of their wounds, and civilians in haphazard dress, asked each other questions, and separated to go on, each unsatisfied by what they had heard.

Miranda, listening, finally knew only that the President and Mrs. Lincoln had gone to Ford's Theater with General Grant and some others to see a play called *Our American Cousin,* and that the President had been shot in his box and carried through screaming crowds, bleeding terribly and perhaps mortally wounded, across the road to a place known as the Petersen house.

Rumor had it that the man who had fired the awful bullet was an actor named Booth, and that he had fled. Rumor also had it that all the government would fall, that cabinet officers had been stabbed to death in their beds, and that Washington City was soon to be destroyed. Rumor had it, too, that a mob had gone wild on Tenth Street, intent on demolishing Ford's, and Taltavul's Saloon next door, and that soldiers, armed and ready, were gathering on Market Square.

The crowd shuffled and shifted, driving Miranda this way and that until, clutching her wrap tightly around her tall slender body, she fought her way to its outward edges and broke free, determined to reach Tenth Street and see for herself what was happening there.

From the shadow-touched roof of a nearby building, three black crows rose up, cawing a mysterious message into the night.

The burning torches behind her faded and new ones flared ahead, just as new crowds, swelling and shrinking, blocked her path. She struggled on, through whispers and questions and oaths and threats.

The whole of the street before the White House was black with people. Here there was a sudden stillness. It was as if every breath was held.

Beyond, though, there were shouts again. Soldiers calling out to each other. Horses racing wildly down the roads, with excited dogs snarling at their hoofs.

The thick, low-hanging clouds were lit from behind by a sudden shower of falling stars, and when that pale silver light was gone the world seemed even blacker.

Miranda shivered and pressed on through the ever-growing crowds, but they moved with her, drawn as she was, to Tenth Street, to the Petersen house, to the place where Lincoln lay.

But there was a point at which they were stopped.

Soldiers were massed. The torchlight gleamed on their grim faces, in their angry eyes. It flickered along the sharp blades of their fixed bayonets, and on their belts and buckles like small flames.

A great wordless wailing seemed to fill the air, to blend with the shouts, the thudding hoofbeats, the echoes of turmoil from blocks around.

Beside Miranda, a legless man in a faded blue Union uniform sat on a small, wheeled platform. His heavy shoulders shook with sobs, and his wasted lined face, eyes fixed beseechingly on the dull sky, was wet with tears.

Miranda put her hand on his shoulder, held tightly to it, and felt his head lean briefly but hard against her knee. Then he took her hand and pressed a kiss on it, and she felt on her fingers his tears, burning like drops of melted wax.

A carriage rattled down Tenth Street, and stopped. Two

men, their bearded faces sober under black silk hats, climbed down. They hurried into the narrow brick building.

Miranda gasped and strained forward. Then that was the Petersen house.

The torches seemed to flare more brightly. The crowd shouted, and argued, and surged, and was thrust back.

When Miranda looked again, the legless veteran was gone.

"The doctors are still coming," someone cried. "There's hope yet! There's hope, I tell you!"

A shrill piercing scream rose over every other sound and hung on the quivering air for a long breathless moment before it faded.

It was a scream of grief, and shuddered through Miranda like living pain in her flesh. She felt tears burn in her eyes again.

She backed slowly away from the massed soldiers and turned and began the slow walk to Georgetown.

Now it seemed that all of Washington City had come into the streets, and there was scarcely room for breath or movement.

As the misty clouds parted and a hazy red moon suddenly glared from the ominous dark of the sky, a single gasp went up. Disbelief, bewilderment, and terror were as palpable as chilled flesh.

The gasp died away into a momentary silence, and then the huddling group seemed to become some huge black animal, crouched to attack as anger seized and inflamed it. Deep rasping voices cried out for vengeance, and tears dried in the heart of rage.

A small black-and-white dog, ears up and tail up, went gamboling down the road and made an excited pass at a soldier's horse. It lashed out in a vicious kick. The dog yelped once. Its broken body sailed through the air and landed in the gutter.

Miranda could bear the scene no longer. She wrapped her cloak more tightly around her shivering body and hurried back to the house.

Just as she stepped into the vestibule the big grandfather clock chimed eleven-thirty. It seemed hours since the others had gone, suddenly, into the night, as if drawn on some irresistible tide. Hours, too, since she had felt the same need and slipped out, alone and shuddering, to wander through the fearsome dark.

She climbed the steps slowly and approached her room. Down the hall, in the back room, there was a faint stirring. She knew one of the boarders, Jake Rooker, had returned, too. If he had been someone else, she would have gone to speak with him, for she yearned to have conversation and company. But she never spoke to Jake Rooker if she could help it, and she didn't want to speak with him even now.

She gently closed the door of her room behind her. Now that she was once more between these familiar walls, she began again to ask herself what further news there was. Had something happened since she hurried away from the torchlit crowds, away from the milling soldiers? Did the President still breathe? Or had the death rattle convulsed his throat? Were others dead as well? What of Seward? What of General Grant?

It was unbearably quiet in the house. She heard the bray of mules, and their slow plodding hooves on the tow-path beside the canal. A bargeman bugled urgently at the nearby lock, and rude shouts answered him.

Susanah Kay seemed to take some pride in the fact that her boardinghouse was situated within sight and sound of the canal. Perhaps that was why she called the dingy, two story red-brick building the Kayhome Arms, and mentioned often on the block that she accepted as boarders only ladies and gentlemen, as had her first husband before her.

Miranda herself would have preferred the scent of country fields to stale garbage, and the smiles of country folks to those she knew here. And to either of these, she would have preferred one of the great mansions that lay just off the main road north, hidden in tree-shaded splendor, and the bows of the gentry who occupied them. That had been the stuff of which her dreams had been made, the bedrock of her convictions. But she had been offered no choice.

She sighed and went to look at herself in the small cloudy mirror that Susanah Kay had grudingly allowed her.

She was seventeen, and even the stains of grief made her look no older. Her hair was dark, glossy, and soft as fine silk, and she wore it drawn back from her brow and secured with a bit of brown fabric from which her thick curls fell. Her face was heart-shaped, delicately formed, with high round cheekbones and a firm chin. It had a patrician cast to it, a look of gentle breeding and blood. Her skin was very fair and smooth. But her eyes were her most remarkable feature. They were set deep and far apart, with long black lashes fringing them. They were the color of amber, and glowed, as if somewhere behind them a light was shining.

She wore now a plain brown dress of heavy cotton. It had long narrow sleeves and a high neck, and brushed her boots when she walked, but even its severity could not conceal the swell of her young breasts, nor the slenderness of her waist. The black cloak still hung from her shoulders.

From below there came the sound of the door opening.

She dropped her cloak and was instantly at the banister, peering down. She was swollen-eyed and shivering and exhausted, but too anxious for news to go to bed.

Two of the boarders came through the foyer, but not Susanah Kay and not Miranda's father.

Nan Cunningham, the very stout, gray-haired widow from Illinois, spoke first. "They said his head was blown clear off his shoulders and his brains poured down gray as muck," she said, sucking over the words as if they were each one small hard candies to be savored.

She was a gross, bawdy woman, with huge red hands and a hard grating laugh. She had once embarrassed Miranda into frozen silence by offering, over the dinner table, to find for her a lusty man to marry, and had seemed put out when Miranda refused to answer her in kind.

"And that he died before he fell upon the floor," Mary Bennett answered. She, too, was a widow, her husband having died at Bull Run. She seemed to delight in Nan's conversation, and trailed her about. She went on, "But some claim he's not dead, nor even near it. They say he's only wounded, or pretending to be, while the soldiers close the city."

"Well, I hope he's gone, or soon will be," Nan retorted. *"Then* let him celebrate the fall of Richmond."

"And what of Grant?" Mary Bennett asked. "He was supposed to be there, too. But now it's said that he wasn't."

"I care nothing about Grant, or where he is, or what he did," Nan replied, and led the way into the parlor.

Miranda watched as the two women disappeared, her slim damp fingers curled tightly around the dusty wood. She knew now why the others had surged out into the night, and why she had followed them. To be with human-kind was to press back the threat of the animal dark. But she felt no call to join the women in the parlor below. Though she had known them for three months, she could never think of them as friends. She had always known that there were many here who held Southern sympathies, but to wish Abraham Lincoln dead in this hour was inhuman. She could not bear the thought.

There was no sound, but a slant of pale light suddenly touched her, and when she looked, she saw Jake Rooker's tall silhouette in his doorway.

She turned instantly and made for her room.

But he was beside her, grinning. He caught her by the wrist, the fingers of his big callused hand closing tight enough to grind the small bones. "Wait," he said. "Don't run away, Miranda. Stop and talk a minute."

She winced with pain and tried to free herself, but could not. She flung her dark curls back and flashed an angry amber look at him. "Let me go! What do you think you're doing? What do you want?"

"Why, you know. At least you're old enough to. And don't try your airs on me. You're only the boardinghouse owner's stepdaughter and not the queen of the realm, whatever you think of yourself."

Jake was twenty-four years old, a tall, gangling, hard-muscled man with wispy red hair and oddly shallow blue eyes. He said that he was a hostler, but at what place in Georgetown he never told, and he kept such hours as made that tale improbable.

Since Miranda had come to the boardinghouse, wan from long months of nursing her grandmother, unwilling to be in that place but having no other to go to, his odd eyes had followed her about. She had learned to evade him, dodging him on the steps as she helped with the chores, remaining in the kitchen with her stepmother while he waited, playing cat and mouse, in the dining room. She had learned to evade his fingers when she served him, to slip away from beneath the covert caresses he offered as he passed her by, coming and going on those errands he never explained.

Now, with his blue collarless shirt open, exposing a great swath of red-furred chest, and his mouth working, he said softly, "There's no need for you to run away from me. You think you're better than I am. But you're not. You're Jervis as well as Haversham, and don't you ever forget it. And more Jervis to boot, I'll warrant, else why are you here in this rundown dump, instead of up at Haversham Square?"

She stared at him in open amazement, forgetting the pain in her wrist, and the need to escape him as well. "Haversham?" she said. The name was a whisper of magic, linked, for as long as she could remember, with her sense of herself, of what she was, and was to be. "What do you know of that, Jake?"

He laughed softly, but with no amusement. "All there is to know."

"Then it's more than I do," she retorted.

"That could be," he told her. "I've worked for John Haversham off and on for years. And lived off and on at Haversham Square." He did not tell her what work he had done for John Haversham, nor that, when he lived there, he had a pallet above the stables and his meals in the cooking quarters. He also did not tell her that he feared John Haversham and always had, and supposed that he always would, though he meant, someday, to change that, if he could.

"But how do you know about me?" she demanded. "I never said . . ."

Again Jake laughed softly. "Don't be such a ninny. It doesn't become you at all. It was your father, of course. I came here by rare coincidence to live, and two days later, old Tom Jervis, needing to shine by the light of his rich relations, told me."

"Oh," she said. "Oh, yes, I see."

It was perfectly within her father's nature, she knew, to boast of the Haversham connection, though that connection was not, in fact, to him.

Jake's grasp at her wrist tightened. He drew her closer. He thought that the house was empty. She was alone. It was what he had waited for since he first saw her.

But she pulled free, hissing like a small amber-eyed cat, and darted away from him, and he dismissed caution and guile as he flung himself after her.

He caught her at the threshold of her room. This time it was not by the wrist that he held her, but by the body, an arm like a clamp around her narrow waist, pulling her body against his, so that she could feel sharply, horribly, the swelling thrust of him at her hip, and the small movements he made while his other hand tore the bodice of her frock and slipped through to fondle her breasts freely, while his mouth, damp and writhing, nuzzled her throat.

She was sickened by his touch, even more sickened, if that were possible, by the timing of his advances. All constraint was burned from her by the searing anger, the painful grief she had felt since she first heard the news. She cried, "How dare you? How can you? The President lies dead or dying, and you—"

"And what's that to me?" he laughed, holding her closer still. "When I care nothing for Presidents, either alive or dead."

Deep hot compelling fury gave her a strength she hadn't known she possessed. Her lithe strong body curled as if in meek compliance and then straightened explosively. It drove him, still clasping her, staggering against the wall.

They stared at each other for a moment, and then she

leaned back from him as far as she could, and brought her fist up and slammed it with all her strength across his face.

He yelled and raised his hand to return the blow, promising himself that pleasure if not another.

But Nan Cunningham appeared at the foot of the steps, peering upward through the gloom from small black eyes. "Who's there?" she demanded.

Miranda cried, struggling still within Jake's vicious grasp, "Is that you, Nan?"

"It's me," Nan answered.

By then, seeing Jake's lifted hand fall, his arm at Miranda's waist, Nan understood. She went surging up the stairs, a woman remarkably agile for all her bulk and breathlessness.

Nan was so quick that Jake had had no time to react. She seized him by an ear, and twisted hard. "Let go, you dim-witted fool, what do you think you're trying to do?"

He swore under his breath, but his arm fell away from Miranda.

She didn't wait. She flashed a quick grateful smile at Nan and fled to her room. With the door bolted securely, she stood panting, until with a sigh she caught her breath.

There came a tap at her door. She stared at it, unmoving.

Nan said softly, "Miranda, are you all right?"

"Yes, I am," she answered, watching the door handle turn but making no move toward it.

Nan laughed. "Locked in, are you? There's a clever girl. But you've no need. I'm here now. And I want to talk to you."

Miranda hesitated, then pressed back the bolt.

Nan brushed by her, sank down on the edge of the bed, causing it to complain loudly, and settled her wide black skirts around her. "Why, you're white as a ghost, child," she said, laughing suddenly. "Don't you know that another time and another place, and perhaps with another man, too, you'd have cursed me for interfering with you?"

Miranda shivered, drew the torn bodice up to cover her breasts.

Nan's laughter faded. She said sympathetically, "But he

did give you a great fright, didn't he? That lout . . . One instant more and I'd have torn his ear off for him, and perhaps his head as well."

"I'm glad you had returned," Miranda said.

"Well, so am I." Nan shrugged her round shoulders under her black shawl. "There was nothing much to see. The crowd are roistering about . . . and soldiers gathering. I don't know why your father and Susanah Kay aren't back yet." She paused, then added piously, watching Miranda's drawn face, "A sad night this."

Miranda, remembering the caustic and unfeeling remarks she had heard below, made no comment but turned her face away.

"That pig-headed fool, Jake Rooker," Nan said. "To think he'd dare lay a hand on you." She paused. Then, "Miranda, child, the truth now . . . he didn't . . . he didn't hurt you in any way?"

"No," Miranda answered. "But he would have. I know he would have, if no one had been about."

"You're right there, I suppose. And he turned pale at the sight of me. His trouble is that he's too stupid for what he wants and too smart for what he can get."

Miranda was silent. She wondered that Nan had so much knowledge of Jake. She had not noticed that the two ever exchanged more than greetings when they met at meals.

Nan rose, breathing heavily. "Go to bed, child. Forget that silly boy. If no harm's been done, then you mustn't brood on it."

"I shan't. But if he so much as looks at me again—"

"You must tell your father and Susanah Kay. They'll see to Jake, believe me. And your stepmother more firmly than your father, if I'm judge," Nan answered. With that she smiled gently, though her avid eyes softened not at all, and left the room.

Miranda re-bolted the door, then sank to the edge of her feather bed, feeling it puff up around her body like cool, comforting arms. She wished that the night were over and day begun.

Below the grandfather clock chimed twelve. She listened, asking herself when there would be more word. When she would know if this nightmare were real.

She rubbed her bruised wrist, remembering the feel of Jake's hard sweating fingers, and the clamp of his arm at her waist, and the rude and intimate probing of his hand on her bared flesh. And at the same time she remembered the sound of his voice when he said, "You're Jervis as well as Haversham, and don't you ever forget it!"

But that wasn't so. It had never been, and never would be. She was a Haversham. The magic of that name had touched her all her life. Even though she had nothing else, she had that.

She had always lived with her grandmother, Martha Appleton, in a western Maryland mountain village called Dealeyton. In the beginning, both her parents had shared the small cottage, too. She remembered her mother as small, with golden eyes and masses of black curls, and a high fluting laugh. One day the cottage resounded with her giggles, and the next it was silent. Bess Appleton ran away with a traveling circus when Miranda was seven. The child did not understand why her mother had abandoned her, why the soft cheek and the warm kisses were gone forever. The wound of it was deep and lasting.

Her father wandered morosely through the too-quiet rooms for several weeks. Then word came that Bess had died of smallpox. He and Martha Appleton had long whispered conversations to which Miranda was not privy. He packed a portmanteau one day and went down to Washington City in search of a job. Within six months he married Susanah Kay. He came to Dealeyton for a few hours to tell about the boarding house called the Kayhome Arms, and to promise that he would soon send for Miranda. He returned only once in the ensuing ten years to see Miranda. He did not again mention her joining him.

Martha Appleton spoke of him rarely, and if Miranda did, the older woman's lips, even then beginning to be blue in color, would tighten, and she would shake her head.

Abandoned by both parents, unloved except by her

grandmother, Miranda always felt different from the other children she knew. She was with them, but not of them.

As she grew up, she saw in the looking glass amber eyes, and a petal-smooth white skin, and black curls. She saw, very nearly, her mother's own face.

The Civil War touched the town. Regiments in gray came through in waves, with prancing horses and rolling cannon, and then, like waves, they receded. On some nights, the thunder of firing roared through the ravines and down the low hills, and the sweet country air seemed touched with the brimstone of hell. Then regiments in blue passed by and were soon gone, too.

Miranda and her grandmother did not much discuss the politics of the day, but they did follow the course of the war anxiously, being for Union and abolition, and Miranda had given her whole heart to the President.

But somehow more real to her than those big events in the shadow of which she grew up was the conviction of her own destiny. She did not remember when she had first heard the Haversham name. She had always known it, and had always known its magic.

Her grandmother had been a Haversham. She had married for love, but not wisely, and had lost contact with her relations. She was determined, though, that Miranda's future would be with the great family to which she belonged. She had prepared Miranda for that shining future by teaching her the manners and graces that were not those of the country folk among whom she lived, but those of the society she would one day join.

She had always said, "You must be prepared, Miranda, for one day you'll go to them."

"But when?" Miranda asked. "Tell me when."

"At the right time. Never fear, Miranda. I'll arrange it."

The dream had been the true sustenance of Miranda's life until six months before, when blue-lipped Martha rose one morning and fell near her bed. Her sturdy heart had begun to falter.

She had known what was to come, and gave Miranda a letter to post. It was addressed to John Haversham at

Haversham Square in Georgetown. She waited, day by day, weaker, and more fearful, for a reply.

None came, and it became quite clear that she had been a dreamer, too. The day before she took her last breath, she said, "Miranda, I'd hoped for better. I was sure that I could rely on John Haversham's family feeling and respect for his name. But it seems I was wrong. So you must go to your father in Georgetown."

"No," Miranda protested hotly. "No, I cannot. He doesn't want me, and never did. I'll go instead to John Haversham and speak to him myself."

She would have the courage, she knew. She would not be afraid. There was a lifetime of faith behind her. She had always known that her destiny was not the tiny cottage in Dealeyton. She had faithfully worn a sunbonnet to protect her smooth white skin when she walked out of doors, and heavy gloves when she gardened. She had practiced her walk and her curtsey before the long wardrobe looking glass in the nights when her grandmother dozed before the fire. She would not give up the future because of a letter that might have gone astray.

"You cannot do that," her grandmother said. "We do not beg. You must forget the Havershams and go to your father. I thought I had planned your future well, but it was not to be. Forgive me, child. Your father is weak, but he'll take you in. And when he does, remind him that I gave him my pearls. I gave them to him should he need money for food while he looked for work ten years ago. He has never returned them. Those pearls are yours, Miranda, and it's little enough I leave you. If he has them still, tell him I said they were a loan only. They belong to you, and you must have them."

Miranda thought she faintly remembered the pearls, but she wasn't sure until she saw them around the wrinkled neck of Susanah Kay. For her grandmother, looking into her young, resistant face, refused to rest until she heard Miranda's formal promise. She made Miranda say the words, "I promise you, Grandmother. I will go to Papa in Georgetown."

Then her grandmother lay back on her pillows, closed her fierce eyes, and smiled.

Two days after her grandmother's death, Miranda packed, tucked a small hoard of cash money into the neck of her mourning gown, and took the stage. She arrived in Georgetown in the bitter cold of an early February twilight.

She was exhausted and disheveled and half-frozen after calling at each building on two long narrow lanes to locate the Kayhome Arms.

She walked past the cast-iron gate and up the black, mud-spattered iron steps to the black, mud-spattered door, which was guarded by two urns of wilted ivy. The dinginess of the place made her dreams of Haversham Square all the more ridiculous. It was to this that her promise to her grandmother had brought her. She swallowed a lump of bitterness and sighed, and knocked at the door with a mittened hand that shook.

Susanah Kay herself opened it.

She was a very tall and thin woman, with straight hair unnaturally black. She wore it parted in the center and pulled tightly away from her face, wrapped in a severe bun. Her skin was dry, touched with yellow. Her eyes were dark and narrowed, as if perpetual suspicion crowded itself behind them. She wore a plain black dress, high in the neck and long in the sleeve, relieved only by small ruffles of Belgium lace.

Miranda knew her at once, and felt diminished under that suspicious gaze. She stammered, "I'm looking for my father. For Tom Jervis. I . . ."

Susanah Kay introduced herself. Then said, without warmth, "Come in. I'll call your father. We had your message on the telegraph, but there was no time to reply to it."

Miranda nodded and followed her into the vestibule, noticing then that Susanah Kay wore, just under the lace at her throat, a fine strand of milky-white pearls.

It was years since Miranda had seen her father, but he seemed unchanged to her. He was forty-two years old now, with a wrinkled face and faded blue eyes, and a blond, neatly trimmed beard. His body was thin, except for a small high round belly that jutted over his belt. He wore a white shirt and a black cravat, and a rusty black suit.

After the flurry of greetings in the vestibule, where the umbrella stand, clothes tree, and greasy spittoon took up most of the space, Miranda was shown her room, and she took her place in the Georgetown house which, in the three months since, never became home to her, and never would, she knew.

She had seen, within a day of her arrival, a dour look in Susanah Kay's eyes, and noticed that the older woman had the thin, pale, cold lips of a shrew. Miranda had known that she must not be a burden, and she offered her help, not saying that it would pay for her keep but privately thinking that. Susanah Kay made no demur, and Miranda was soon scullery maid and second cook.

She had managed to control her bitterness and, if not to forget her bright dreams, at least to know what they were, and to retain her equilibrium even in the face of Nan Cunningham's remarks, and Jake Rooker's advances, until that April night.

But now she shuddered, remembering the touch of his damp mouth at her throat, and his mention of the Havershams.

She had been abandoned three times in her young life. The first when her mother ran away and left her. The second when her father went to Georgetown and didn't send for her. The third when John Haversham ignored her grandmother's letter.

It seemed to her then that of the three the last was worst.

She threw herself on the feather bed and cried.

Downstairs the grandfather clock chimed half after midnight. The outer door opened and closed quietly.

But Nan, waiting in the parlor, heard it and was immediately on her feet. She waddled into the vestibule, her small eyes asking a wordless question.

"The news is the same," Susanah Kay said. "There's nothing more. The soldiers have closed all the exits from

Washington City. They say an actor named John Booth did it, and that he had a whole gang of others to help him."

"So I heard," Nan sighed. "A sorry night. And sorrier than you know," she added, with a heavy nod at Tom Jervis.

He cringed, not knowing what new challenge to expect but fearing it before it came. He nervously rubbed his damp blond beard, and asked, "What does that mean, Mrs. Cunningham?"

She drew the Jervises with her into the parlor, and closed the door carefully. "The others have gone to bed."

The room was dim, gaslights flickering from plain wall sconces, a tiny fire burning on the hearth.

Tom settled himself carefully in a chair and adjusted his belly under his coat, his faded blue eyes on Susanah Kay's dour face.

Nan was saying, ". . . that young fool Jake—he's had his eye on Miranda since she came. Surely you know that."

"And how is it your affair?" Susanah Kay asked dryly.

"It became my affair this evening," Nan retorted, the words ladled with her hoarse and suggestive chuckle. "I happen to know that he had more than his eyes on her this evening. I heard her scream, and went up. It was a real sight, I assure you. She can be a wildcat, your Miranda," she added as an aside to Tom, and then went on to describe in graphic detail, and with much relish, just what had occurred.

Tom listened silently. But he knew what he must do, although his soul trembled at the thought. At last he bestirred himself. "I'll . . . I'll . . ."

"Be quiet," Susanah Kay ordered. And to Nan, "And what else happened?"

"Why, not much. Just what I've said," Nan answered. "But that doesn't signify, does it? I won't always be about, you know. You must rid yourself of that bit of pestilence, that Jake. Or of the girl."

Susanah Kay was silent for a little while, her narrow

eyes studying the wilted aspidistra on the windowsill. Then
she said coldly, "Miranda may have led him to it."

"No," Tom disagreed. And added quickly, "I think not,
Susanah Kay."

She rose to her feet and announced, "I will talk to
her."

Tom followed her from the room and up the dark
steps. He knew that she was angry by the set of her shoulders. He sighed to himself. He could do nicely without a
long bitter harangue that night. The awful news . . . and
now Miranda . . . But harangue there would be. He saw
how Susanah Kay's thin fingers reached up to touch the
pearls at her throat, and he knew she would be remembering the day Miranda had spoken of them. It had been
Martha Appleton's fault, of course. Not Miranda's. And
certainly not Susanah Kay's either. These two had been
innocents, mere pawns in the hands of a woman who had
directed them from beyond the grave. Martha . . . She had
always blamed him. For Bess' desertion, and death. She
would turn Miranda against him and Susanah Kay. What
were silly pearls to a woman?

Why had Miranda so foolishly mentioned it hardly two
days after her arrival? "Papa, one thing that Grandma
told me to say to you. The pearls that Susanah Kay wears
were a loan only. Grandma said that they must belong to
me."

Why had Susanah Kay gone rigid with hate? She had
cried, "These are mine! Mine! Your father gave them to
me, you ungrateful girl. They are all he ever gave to me."
Which was true, of course. But what did that matter?

Miranda's eyes had flashed a strange cold fire. "My
grandmother left them to me."

"You'll not have them," Susanah Key retorted.

"Very well," Miranda answered. "You may wear them,
but they still belong to me."

It had been an awful scene. He closed his mind against
it as Susanah Kay knocked at Miranda's door.

There was a brief silence, and then Miranda asked,
"Yes? Who is it?" and at Susanah Kay's answer, unbolted
the door.

She was very pale, her eyes huge and glowing. "Is there more news?" she asked quickly.

Susanah Kay shook her head, brushed by her.

Tom followed at her heels, closing the door gently.

"Nan tells me that Jake Rooker tried to . . . to attack you," Susanah Kay began.

Miranda answered, "Somehow it seems nothing to me now." There was no sign of the tears she had shed, no mark of the bitterness that had overwhelmed her for a little while.

"You say it seems nothing?" Tom shrilled. "I'll—I'll—"

"Tom, if you please . . ." Susanah Kay did not look at him. She went on to Miranda. "It was regrettable, and I am sorry. How it came about I cannot imagine. Nor do I wish to. But it shall not happen again."

"No," Miranda agreed calmly. "It shall not, I assure you." She drew a deep breath. It was clear, as it had never been before to her, that death lingered to strike evilly out of the night. Time was short, and fate uncertain. Her life awaited her, and she must go out and seek it. She looked straight into Susanah Kay's dark suspicious eyes. "I shall leave here in the morning. You'll need no longer trouble yourself with me."

"But where will you go?" Tom asked hurriedly. "You are so young . . . and a girl alone . . . And you know that we're delighted to have you here. A father's love for his daughter . . ."

"Tom, if you please," Susanah Kay said again. And to Miranda, "I'd like to know your plans. If you have any, that is."

"You've no right to know them," Miranda retorted. "But since you ask, I'll tell you. I shall go to the Havershams and speak to them."

"*You'll* speak to them?" Susanah Kay demanded. "That's hardly fitting. It should be the task of your father to do that. If you feel you no longer wish to grace us with your presence, then he'll go to Haversham Square first thing in the morning."

"No," Miranda said coolly. "I mean to do it myself. My father has nothing to do with the Havershams."

"Nothing to do with them?" Susanah Kay repeated.

"Nothing," Miranda answered. "And I don't want him to try to have either."

"You are an ungrateful girl," Susanah Kay cried shrilly. "I mean only to help you. You should allow us to arrange—"

"But I don't intend that it be arranged that way," Miranda told her. "And I want you to remember that I have nothing to be grateful for. You wish only to ingratiate yourself with the Haveshams. Do you think I don't understand that?"

"Why, Miranda," Tom said sorrowfully, "I've always done my best for you . . . I . . ."

"It was nothing," she said. "Your best was nothing. I saw you twice in my growing-up years. Only twice in those years after you left me with Grandma. Then, when she died and I had to come here, I was your scullery maid and whatever else. Tell me, what do I owe you?"

"The roof over your head," Susanah Kay told her in a voice cold with open dislike. "And the food in your belly."

"I thank you for that then. But I'll owe it to you no longer."

"And what if your fine kin refuse to take you in?" Susanah Kay demanded. "Then will you come back, pleading for help?"

"Never," Miranda said coldly. Then, suddenly, she put out her hand. "And I'll have my pearls before I leave you."

Susanah Kay's stony face grew dark. "They are mine, I told you."

Miranda answered, "My grandmother gave them to me, and I told you when I came that they belonged to me." She suddenly curled her fingers around the gleaming strand and pulled it from Susanah Kay's throat.

Susanah Kay gasped, "Get out of my house," and fled from the room.

TWO

The garret room in which Miranda settled the next day was not very different from the room she had left behind at the Kayhome Arms. It was small and dark, lit only by a single smoldering lamp.

A narrow bed of laced hemp covered by a skimpy mattress filled one wall. A tiny chest, sagging on a broken leg, occupied a corner. A straight-backed chair stood behind the door.

But she was untroubled by her surroundings. She planned to make her small hoard of cash money last her as long as it must, and the rent here was cheap. Besides, she knew that she would not remain long.

It was an ominous day, one of shadows and whispers and slanting looks.

She unpacked her few belongings to the sound of tolling bells.

They had begun to ring just after seven-thirty that morning, wordlessly announcing the President's death. The deep bass notes echoed across the silent city, and soon the buildings were draped in black, and flags hung at half mast, and the cannon from the surrounding forts began to boom at thirty-minute intervals. The streets were gray with wind-driven rain and swirling mist, and the budding trees dripped steady drops that seemed like silver tears. In Kirkwood House, at ten-thirty, Andrew Johnson put a trembling hand on a Bible and took the oath that made him the new President.

When Miranda had finished hanging her frocks away, hoping to keep them fresh and uncrushed, she went to the window. Below, in the street, there were still crowds of people, heads bent against the rain and shoulders hunched against the cold. Beyond, only a few blocks to the north, there was Haversham Square.

A small smile curled her lips thinking of it. She would not go there today, wearing the completely unadorned black dress that she had worn for her grandmother and now wore again. She would not arrive breathless and bedraggled and soaked through with rain. Not when the bells tolled and the cannon boomed. She would force herself to be patient and wait.

A week later, the sun was bright and golden, carrying with it a hint of spring warmth, as Miranda picked a careful path over the uneven brick sidewalk.

She wore a dress of green broadcloth that was trimmed with matching braid. Small black jet buttons fastened the tight bodice and the narrow cuffs of its long sleeves. She remembered the painstaking care with which her grandmother had sewn these buttons on. The skirt swung over a medium-sized hoop, and with every step she took her crinoline seemed to whisper to her.

She went slowly past the now open shops that were still decorated with black bunting. She hardly noticed the bustle around her, she was that concentrated on marshaling her thoughts and forces for the interview ahead.

A small black-haired man came out of a barbering place and emptied a huge bucket of slops just beyond her skirts. That brought her back to her surroundings quickly enough, and with a frown of displeasure she danced aside.

From somewhere behind her a large uniformed policeman appeared. He gave her a hint of a wink and put his hands on his hips, and bellowed at the barber, "You there! It's a five-dollar fine under the code for throwing night waste in the road! And you know it, or you should. What do you think this is? Some uncivilized spot where you can dump your dirt as you please?"

The barber thrust the empty bucket under the policeman's nose, and grinned. "It's not night waste. It's shaving water and soap, the same as what you used this morning yourself."

"I'll kick your butt all the way back to Old Blighty," the policeman retorted. "That's where you belong if you're going to throw night waste into the road."

Smiling to herself, Miranda went on. Soon she left the shop area behind her. The road narrowed, and at each side of it there were tall lilac bushes and fragrant weigela and forsythia still sprinkled with fragments of golden blossoms. The trees—oaks and maples and elms—grew older and taller and thicker as she drew closer to her destination.

Haversham Square. The small rectangular brass name plate was so brightly polished that it gleamed, and the two words etched into it stood out in bold relief.

That was as it should be, she thought, peering through the tall iron gates. It was impossible to see beyond the tree-lined curving driveway to the house itself, a small disappointment. Soon she would be inside.

With her heart beating quickly, a flush of excitement on her cheeks and her eyes aglow, she tugged at the gate pull. When no one appeared to answer her summons, she tugged it again. Still no one came. At last, with a sigh, she turned away.

She returned later that same afternoon, and there was still no response when she rang. This time her hopeful spirits sagged a little, and as she returned to her garret room past the black-draped row houses, she began to wonder how long she could make her money last.

The following morning she made her way north again. She found the iron gates locked, the ivy-covered brick wall as impregnable as a fortress. A small thrill of fear touched her. Suppose the Havershams were gone? What if they had made a visit across the sea to the English branch of the family about which her grandmother had once told her? She shrugged the fear away. She told herself that these were not times when people traveled abroad.

The next morning when she tugged at the bell pull, once more aglow with hope, a tall slender Negro dressed in black livery came from the gatehouse and looked at her through the iron bars.

She said, "Good day. I would like to see Mr. John Haversham."

"I'm sorry," the man answered. "Mr. Haversham is not receiving."

"If you were to take my name in," she suggested, smiling.

"He has just returned from a trip and has left orders that he'll not be disturbed," she was told.

"It's very important," she replied. "If only you were to tell him that . . ."

The man looked at her briefly, then looked past her. After a hesitation, he said, "Perhaps if you were to write him a letter, miss . . ."

But she knew that she would not write John Haversham a letter. There had already been one of those. She must see him face to face, speak to him.

There was nothing to do but thank the man and leave. She did so, but her mind was already considering.

Plainly it was not the wisest thing to try to breech directly the defenses such men as John Haversham throw up around themselves.

There must be some other way. She was busily plotting and planning when she returned to her garret room.

It was the next day. She wore a white frock sashed with a length of lavender. It hung smoothly over her crinoline and belled out gracefully over her hoop. The long sleeves fit snugly to her narrow wrists, and the neck fit closely to her throat. As she regarded her faint reflection in the dirt-smeared windowpane, she frowned. It was wrong: too high, too prim. Frowning still, she undid the five top button loops and turned the two sides of the bodice in. Now the white of her skin showed, and the curve of her breasts. Yet it was not quite right. Finally she took the strand of pearls and draped them around her neck. She smiled at her pale reflection. That was much better.

When she went out into the brilliant sunshine, she carried a white ruffled parasol and a dainty reticule that matched it. A profusion of lilacs bloomed in the tiny yard that fronted the house, and as she passed them she saw that their lavender blossoms were the same shade as the trim on her gown. Impulse led her to gather a handful of them, to tuck them under the pearls at her bodice. Breathing the heady scent, she made her way along the sidewalk past the shops and taverns.

She was aware of, and pleased by, the many admiring glances that followed her. But her concentration lay on what was ahead of her. She had very little of her cash hoard left. If she was to do as she planned, it must be accomplished quickly.

She had just crossed the busy road, dodging drays and gigs, when she saw drawn up before the big bank at the corner an open carriage, and on its front seat a familiar figure in black livery.

It was an omen, and she took it as such, knowing immediately what she must do. She went to the slender Negro driver and asked, "Is Mr. Haversham inside?"

"He is," the driver replied.

"I would very much like to speak with him," she said.

The slender Negro said nothing, but he climbed down from his seat and stood beside the carriage.

She fished in her reticule and took out a coin. She put it into his hand. "I would prefer to wait for him in the carriage."

"Yes, miss," the driver said, with the barest hint of a smile, and helped her up.

She seated herself, arranging the wide skirt of the gown around her, and then opened the parasol. She leaned back to wait at ease, knowing then that she was where she was destined to be. From this place of plush and brass, looking down over the high wheels, the street was different. There was less dust and dirt, and fewer mongrels, and though it hardly seemed possible, the sun was brighter.

The dinginess of the Kayhome Arms no longer existed. The dark garret room was lost in the exotic scent of the lilacs tucked into her breast.

She was very nearly giddy with excitement when John Haversham let the bank doors close behind him, and stood there staring at her across the space between them.

Though she had never seen him before, nor even heard him described, she knew him instantly.

He was six feet five inches tall, a great bull-like man with massive shoulders that bespoke arrogance and assurance. He had dark brown curly hair and long full side-burns, and a heavy square jaw. He wore tightly fitting fawn-colored trousers and a long fitted black jacket, and carried an ebony cane with a gold-topped head.

As he strode toward her, she tipped the parasol back and smiled down at him.

He stood beside the carriage, looking at her, and she saw that his eyes were colored like wet granite, and just as cold. Her heart began to beat very quickly then.

But his chill appraising glance softened. He asked, "And to what do I owe this very pleasant intrusion?"

She laughed teasingly, and said, "If you dared to join me, I would explain."

He hesitated for a moment, wondering what sort of trick this was. He knew men who might employ any means to accomplish their ends. He was, after all, such a man himself. But he hadn't lived forty-two years, and come the distance he had, without learning how to protect his flank. And in this child's lovely face he saw mischief, but not guile. He swung up beside her and set the black cane between his knees.

"You must smile," she told him. "People are looking at us, you know."

"At you, I believe," he answered, breathing deeply of the lilac scent that wafted at him, and eyeing the exposed white of her bosom above the strand of pearls.

"How kind you are to say so. But still you do not smile. Do you want everyone to suppose that you are ungallant to your kin?"

"My kin?" His mouth hardened, and his big hands grasped the golden head of his cane. "Now I think you must explain that."

She slid an amber glance at the driver, who had climbed up and taken the reins.

John said, "All right, Timoshen. Drive on." Then, turning to Miranda, "That would be better, wouldn't it? Since you are concerned with appearances?"

"Not for myself," she said, laughing softly. "But only for you."

"And I concern myself with them not at all, and never have," he told her.

"That hardly seems possible," she retorted. "We must each one of us expect to be judged, mustn't we?"

He crossed his long legs, having set his cane aside, and took a gold timepiece from his waistcoat pocket. It was just after two, and he had an appointment at three. He had no intention of being late for it, but the girl had a quality that intrigued him. He said, "You've gone to some trouble, I'm quite sure, to arrange this meeting. Would you like to tell me why?"

"It is you who created the trouble for me," she answered, smiling mischievously from under the parasol. "You, and you alone. I called very properly at Haversham Square two or three times, and found no one there. Then, when at last I spoke to Timoshen, he said that you were not receiving and suggested that I write to you instead of attempting a personal interview."

"But you didn't," John said.

She shook her head. Her golden eyes were shielded under a fringe of black lashes. There was no smile now on the sweetness of her mouth.

"And why not? Since that was the sensible thing to do."

She did not reply at once. The carriage wheels clattered over a loose stone, and a drayman shouted oaths, and a dog barked. He was very still, watching her. At last she said softly, "Letters can be ignored, you know."

"So they can. As I have learned sometimes to do. As anyone in my position must learn to do. However, that explains nothing. Would you like to tell me what this is about?"

"You wish to end this opportune meeting," she said, with a quick smile. "And it is such a lovely day for a drive in the country."

He thought of his appointment. Josiah Hurley would be waiting at the Barclay Hotel. He would be annoyed to be kept there to no purpose. But what did that matter? The girl had made him curious now. He said, "Timoshen, drive out to the Canal Road."

Timoshen nodded. The carriage swung about in a wide arc, and Miranda fell against John.

She drew herself quickly away from him. "And now I shall explain," she said softly. "I'm Miranda Jervis. Does that name mean anything to you?"

His gray eyes met hers, then dropped to the flowers at her breast. The scent of the lilacs seemed stronger. "I know the name, of course," he said. "We're related through Martha Appleton, are we not?"

"Yes," Miranda answered. She was still smiling, but her full lower lip suddenly quivered, and her gold eyes grew even brighter with tears held back. "Before she died, she wrote to you, Cousin John. She asked your help for me. Not for herself. Only for me."

"I fear that I don't quite understand," he said gently. "I didn't know that Martha had died, nor did I dream that you were in need of help. We have had no contact in all these years, you see." It was easy enough for him to dissemble, a talent he had been born with. He saw no reason to explain to her that he had received Martha's letter speaking of Miranda, and had tossed it aside with not even a second thought. He had seen no cause then to assume responsibility for some distant relation.

"Oh," Miranda cried. "Then you really didn't know. You didn't simply ignore her."

"Of course not," he said. "I can only assume that the letter was lost. Wartime conditions interfere with all services. This isn't the first I've heard of such an occurrence." He paused. Then, "And what have you done since Martha died? Where have you been, and how have you lived?"

She told him quickly and briefly of the past three months. Her hatred of that time was implicit in the recital of the bare facts.

When she paused for breath, he nodded encouragingly. "I see," he said.

"It is an imposition," she told him, "and believe me, I know that, to ask it. But surely there is some way in which I could be of service to you. I am bright, as you will soon learn, though I must be so immodest as to tell you that myself now, and I am not badly educated for a woman. Perhaps you require an assistant. I have a very good hand with a pen." She stopped abruptly. She realized that she had come very close to pleading with him, though she had not meant it so. She was a Haversham, and a Haversham would never plead for help. She lowered her head and smiled up at him through the thick fringe of her lashes. "But we both know, Cousin John, you are under no obligation to me. I mean only to—"

He was a man who could afford to give way to a whim when he wanted to. He had no need to consider it. She was no longer some faceless distant relation to him. She was a young woman of great beauty and force, and her manner intrigued him. A plot began to form in his mind.

He cut in, "My dear child, you must not say another word. If I had had that letter from Martha which you've mentioned to me, you'd never have gone to your father in the first place. It's a most unsatisfactory situation for you. You will join my family at Haversham Square, of course."

Jake Rooker and Nan Cunningham stood together in front of the Union Hotel.

She thrust a fat elbow into his ribs, and her black eyes gleamed at his as he squinted after the passing carriage. "You saw that, I suppose?" she demanded.

"I'm not blind," he retorted, and turned to scowl at her.

"You sometimes act as if you must be." She drew her black shawl more tightly around her shoulders. "Little Miranda has accomplished what she set out to do. And now what has your foolishness got you?"

He ducked his wispy red head. "It's lost me nothing."

"Oh, and are you so certain of that?" Nan chuckled. "If I hadn't come up and stopped you when I did, it might have lost you a great deal. If Miranda once sees you at Haversham Square, she'll surely tell her dear cousin about that night. And when she does, then where are you?"

He didn't answer her.

She went on, "Old Tom will be relieved to hear the

news. And Susanah Kay as well. I've heard them speculating about the girl, and where she went and what she did."

Jake nodded.

"Not, of course, that they feared for her well-being or safety," Nan said slyly.

"It's the Havershams," Jake said. "And you know it as well as I do. They're dreaming of gold pieces in their heads."

"So are we all. But you, you're such a good friend," Nan said softly.

Jake's scowl faded, and he grinned. "Oh, yes, that I am. To the both of them."

"There could be something in the situation for you," Nan went on thoughtfully. "If you were clever enough to use it."

"Don't you worry your head about me," Jake told her. But the bright image of Miranda, smiling up at John Haversham from under the white parasol, lingered before his eyes and played havoc with his thoughts.

Nan chuckled hoarsely. "It's possible that there's something in it for the both of us, you know."

"May be," he agreed.

"You could, for instance, go to see him. Why not? You've worked for him for years, you said."

Jake gave her a narrow look. "Suppose you leave it to me, Nan."

"But if I do, you may go astray, as you know. You did that night. Great lout, seizing her as if she were a barmaid. What a sight that was . . ." Nan laughed. "And your face when I came up the stairs to keep you from making a bigger fool of yourself than you already had."

He looked her up and down. "Your face, too. Purple and sweating," he jeered.

She ignored that. She nudged him in the ribs again. "It's a warm day, and I'm dry. We might have a pint or two of ale and consider."

"Will you pay?" he demanded.

"I will. But only because I think it a good investment, I assure you." She turned and started down the street.

He fell into step beside her. She considered only what

she could get between her palms. He had other ideas in mind as well.

A hog came trotting along the gutter to wallow in a puddle. She quickly swung her black skirt aside. But the hog rose up and rolled hard along Jake's leg. He kicked out at it, and cried, "Be damned to John Haversham."

THREE

The next day Timoshen came to take Miranda to Haversham Square. She left the garret room without regret. Now the familiar ivy-covered brick walls of Haversham Square spread away as far as the eye could see. Now there were the gateposts, and the gleaming brass plate.

The carriage stopped, and she sat forward.

The tall gates swung open. She had a glimpse of a small Negro man in a black uniform as the carriage rolled through, and then rolled on, while behind her the gates clanged shut.

The sound gave her a breathless feeling. She had been wrapped in a glow of anticipation, about to embark on what she had always known must be her life. Suddenly, she was frightened. It had been the same when her mother died. The same when her father went away. She had been beset by a similar sensation when she approached the Kayhome Arms three months before.

She thrust her fear aside. This was what she wanted. It was here that she belonged.

Twilight had deepened into a dense purple-blue, and it was hard to see. She looked ahead, watching for her first glimpse of the house, but the driveway was a long curving tunnel through arching trees that cast heavy shadows.

It was as if she had come to some enchanted land from the teeming town, having left it behind forever. Here there was a silence so deep that she imagined she could pick out the individual whisper of a single leaf brushing against another.

Then, out of the dim tunnel of oaks, there was a blossoming of pale yellow light, and Haversham Mansion rose up before her.

It had been built in 1825 on a knoll which rose at the rim of the fifty acres that surrounded it.

The mansion was three stories high, made of red brick brought in by cart from terra cotta flats some ten miles away. It was long, and wide as well, with a glassed-in conservatory newly added at its east end, after John had seen the Botanic Gardens close by the Capitol. At its west end it had a big square two-floor ballroom. The high windows were trimmed in white, and each of them was capped with an elaborately carved cornice. The white double doors were flanked by huge brass lamps, within which burned, day and night, small gas flames. Over the door there was a circular balcony, enclosed in a railing formed of wreaths and flowers and vines cast in iron. The top-floor windows were tiny dormers, and on the flat roof over them were four huge chimneys and two open terraces enclosed in stone balustrades. From them the oval dome of the Capitol in Washington City was visible, and the white stump of the incompleted monument to George Washington.

Miranda stared, awe-struck, at the magnificence of the building. It was like nothing she had ever seen before. She could not imagine that men lived there, bred there. She could not imagine that anyone of her blood, however distant, belonged there.

The carriage stopped at the foot of wide circular stone steps that led to the big white double doors.

Timoshen got down and then looked at her. "We're here, miss."

He had, when he came for her, formally told her his name, and asked if she were ready. Those were the only words he had spoken to her until now. She had been intrigued by his careful pronunciation, and determined to know more about him, but now she answered through suddenly dry lips, "Thank you. I see."

He helped her down into the dusk and guided her to the first of the steps. Then he reached back and brought her portmanteau and followed her up.

When she hesitated at the door, he gave her the faintest of smiles and pulled the doorbell.

The door opened instantly, pale light spilling out to lay a path for her.

He said to the maid who stood there, "It's Miss Miranda Jervis, Lena. She's expected. Tell Mister John right away."

Lena was Timoshen's younger sister. She was sixteen years old, and had been born at Haversham Square before it was called by that name. She was very slim and small, with a head full of tight black curls held by a white band. Her eyes were brown and wide in her brown face. She wore a long black dress covered by a long white apron with a bib and a bowed sash.

She bobbed a curtsy to Miranda, and said, "Wait here, miss," then scurried off down the long reception hall to disappear behind an arched doorway.

Timoshen put down the portmanteau, nodded, smiled faintly again, and went outside.

Miranda shifted her weight from one foot to another, smoothed her plain blue dress, and adjusted her bonnet. Her eyes glowed golden under the light of the huge Waterford crystal chandelier that hung on a long brass chain from the ceiling above her.

The floor covering was a pale brown and very soft underfoot. It reminded her of the way long meadow grass felt to the step. The dark wood of the reception table, with its silver bowl for visiting cards, was as polished as a looking glass, and over it, a long, ornately framed mirror reflected tall brass candelabra and Miranda's own expectant face.

A little while passed. Then a tall but somewhat slouched Negro, with white hair and a thin ascetic face, came from a side door. "I'm Jefferson," he said. "I'll take you up to Mister John's study, if you please."

She knew, without knowing how she knew it, that this man was the father of Timoshen and Lena. She wondered if they had always been free men, or if they had been slaves before the proclamation. She wondered when they had had their schooling.

She thanked Jefferson, but as she followed him up the curving stairs she began to feel like a piece of not very important baggage, passed from coachman to downstairs maid to butler. She wondered who would actually greet her now.

Jefferson opened a door, stood aside, and announced her in a low, careful voice. "Miss Miranda Jervis."

She hesitated, then moved across the threshold.

The room was a magnificent study. There was a big mahogany desk, its top waxed to the brightness of glass. Hanging lamps scattered pools of light on silken floor coverings. The walls were lined with bookcases, rows on rows of leather-bound gold-embossed volumes. The two windows were draped in dark green silk, and the chairs, deep and wide and comfortable-looking, were covered in the same material.

All this Miranda took in with a single darting glance. She walked across the room feeling much like a lowly subject about to be presented to his sovereign, and heartily resenting the emotion. She reminded herself that she belonged here, and that this was merely a man awaiting her. The room, with all its beauty, was merely a collection of worldly and material goods. Both were, her grandmother would say, to be enjoyed but never revered.

John Haversham rose to greet her, a welcoming smile on his heavy face. He wore now an embroidered waistcoat of dark red, and narrow black trousers. His white shirt was trimmed with ruffles of lace at throat and wrist.

He said, "I'm glad you're here, Miranda. Take off your cloak and bonnet, and come and sit down. We must talk for a few moments. Then you'll meet the rest of the household."

It amused him to see that she was serious now, perhaps a bit frightened. The teasing glint had gone from her golden eyes. He supposed that she was awed by what she had seen thus far. She would soon get over that, he was certain.

She took the chair he indicated, and settled her skirts and smiled at him. "I'm happy to be here. As you know." But as he sat there, staring at her out of cold gray eyes, she began to feel uncomfortable. She could not read his thoughts, nor judge them. Was he already regretting his invitation? Was he preparing to tell her kindly that he had changed his mind?

At last he said, "It's a favor that I want to ask of you. No more than that. A matter of understanding . . ." He let the words trail off, watching her amber eyes. He saw wonder in them, and joy, and felt suddenly the impact of her charm.

She said softly, "Anything that you ask of me . . ."

"Anything?" His dark heavy brows went up. His smile became broad and suggestive. He was pleased when she responded by blushing. He was, and he had always been, a man who enjoyed seeing the effect of his power over others. Then he went on, "As I said . . . it's a matter of understanding only. You see, my wife Caroline is not a well woman. She suffers from ills you and I can't imagine, and intense pain, and this leads to spells of brooding and unhappiness for her. I would like you to know this so that you'll not be troubled if her manner should occasionally seem unusual to you."

"I thank you for telling me. And if there is anything that I can do, Cousin John—"

"Cousin John?" he cut in. "I think that much too formal. Please call me by my Christian name. And I shall do the same to you." He picked up a small bell on his desk, shook it twice.

Jefferson opened the door.

"Is Mister Reed around?"

"Yes. He is," Jefferson answered.

"Then get him for me, will you?"

The butler disappeared into the hallway.

There were muffled footsteps, the sounds of doors opening and closing.

John said, "I want you to meet my brother first. Then the others."

She nodded, turned expectantly, and yet, when Reed Haversham came into the room, she found herself suddenly breathless with surprise.

He was nothing like what she had thought he would be when John spoke his name. She had supposed he would be like his brother, and older. But no, it was not so. They were so dissimilar they might not have been blood relations.

Reed was twenty-six years old. He was just over six feet tall, but very lean. His hair was very dark and wavy, worn to his collar. His clean-shaven face was hollowed at cheek and temple, and an unhealthy pallor tinged the thin tan of his skin. His left arm was in a black silk sling. His eyes were a pale gray, almost silver in color, and he seemed enclosed in some invisible cocoon through which he regarded her, the world around him, with little interest.

John made the introductions.

Reed smiled at her distantly. "I'm glad to meet you, Miranda."

She controlled her breathlessness to say, "Thank you. And I'm glad to meet you." But she could hardly draw her gaze away from his face. It was, she thought, the one she had dreamed of through a thousand nights. Here, in Haversham Square, she had found that man she had always imagined who would claim her for his own. She was filled with a deep and quivering wonderment. Was this how love came? Did it strike suddenly when a man walked into a room? Were fate and love so strangely entwined that the one had brought her the other?

Reed was saying, in a very deep quiet voice, "I hope you'll be happy here."

She thought that she was already as happy as anyone dared to be. She had come to that life for which she had been born, and she had found the man with whom she would live that life. What did it matter that he hardly looked at her now? There was time.

John rose. "And now I'll introduce you to my wife."

He drew Miranda with him, drew her unwillingly out of Reed's presence.

She looked back once and saw that he was watching her, and took heart from that small symbol.

The hallway down which John led her was a great wide place. The chandeliers threw rainbows on the white walls, touching the gold-framed portraits that hung there with odd designs. The long narrow table along the one wall was set with bowls of fruit made cleverly in clay, and with small ornaments in colored glass.

John said, seeing her look at them, "Little mementos of my travels. The glass is from Venice, the rest from a town in England. Not very far from where our family resides."

"You know them then?" she asked eagerly. "The English Havershams?"

"Very well," he said in a dry tone.

He could have added that a goodly portion of the fortune he had managed to amass in the past few years was a result of his kinship with the English Havershams, and most particularly, with the son, Ian. They, too, were in textiles, and they had needed Southern cotton. It would have been greatly to their advantage had the Confederacy won the war. They had had good contacts in the gun trade. It had been easy for John to make his arrangements. There had been guns for Southern soldiers, and cotton for English mills. He had made the crossing three times, each one profitable for all concerned. He would have gone a fourth, but was discouraged from it when Northern ships began to stop English vessels in search of American commission men on journeys such as his. He had not cared to be returned to the port of New York in chains. And meanwhile, there had been no more cotton to trade for English guns. Which hadn't troubled him. He had other fields to till.

Now he tapped lightly at a door.

From within a petulant voice called, "Yes, yes, what is it? I'm resting."

Miranda felt a quiver of foreboding, but did not know whence it came.

John gave her a faintly conspiratorial smile, which also troubled her.

He said, speaking more loudly than he had before, "Caroline, I've brought you our cousin, Miranda Jervis. One look at her and you'll feel greatly improved, I do assure you."

He did not wait for a reply but thrust the door open forcefully and thrust Miranda through it, an insistent hand at her back.

It was a gesture that startled her. She felt suddenly that she had been swept up in something far beyond her own control. She was compelled now to go on with it. There was no turning away. John was behind her, and he would not permit her to escape.

Caroline Layton Haversham lay on a rich pink divan, a light coverlet of silk thrown over her thin body. She raised her blonde head, her green eyes narrow and intent.

She studied Miranda up and down, and something within her chest grew constricted and painful.

She was thirty-two now, but she could remember when she, too, had had that bright young expectant look. She had had it when she acted as her father's hostess, and there were parties every night, and great formal dinners, and she had waltzed with the Vice-President, and laughed with the Speaker of the House. She had had it when she was first introduced to John. But that had been eleven years before.

The constriction in her chest became even more painful. She could hardly breathe. The pink feathers at the high neck of her silk peignoir were suffocating her. She knew that John's cold eyes regarded her with impatience, and she braced herself for some cutting remark.

Instead he looked away from her to where another woman reclined in a big pink chair, and said, "Stacy, this is Miranda." And, "Stacy Gordon is a friend of Caroline's from New York."

Stacy straightened, offering Miranda a bright welcoming smile.

At last, gathering herself, Caroline said, "So you're Miranda, are you?"

Miranda dropped a curtsy. "Thank you for having me, Cousin Caroline."

"Don't thank me," Caroline retorted. "I've nothing to do with it. You are my husband's cousin, and this is my husband's house." Her narrowed eyes surveyed Miranda up and down. She sensed John's look again, and slid a sideways glance at him. "But I'm glad to have you with us all the same," she added coldly. "We two are, after all, related through marriage, I suppose."

Stacy's laugh tinkled. "There now. That's a bit better, Caroline. Do stop pretending to be an ogre, and be yourself instead."

Stacy was quite tall, willowy. She had a tiny waist and a high, round bosom. Her gown, cut low to expose the gleaming white of her breasts, was pale pink velvet and trimmed with small velvet flowers of a darker pink. Her hair was a deep chestnut brown with highlights of red, and worn drawn back from her oval face, accenting the clear line of her widow's peak, falling into a cascade of ringlets pinned to her head with another dark pink velvet flower. Her mouth was long and full and sensual, and her eyes were the fiery black of glowing coals.

Miranda didn't speak. There seemed nothing for her to say. But she wished the bright, laughter-filled voice had been Caroline's, and that the petulant one had been Stacy's.

Stacy, who appeared never to be at a loss for words, asked, "Where are you from, Miranda?"

"A town in western Maryland," Miranda told her.

"A town in western Maryland?" Caroline echoed coldly. "That's not what John told me. She's the child of some awful boarding house owner, and has lived in a low place near the canal. A terrible background. I hope she knows how fortunate she is to have escaped it."

Heat burned in Miranda's cheeks.

But Stacy smiled. "It sounds interesting to me."

Caroline went on as if she hadn't spoken. "But, of course, we shall do all that we can for her." Then, "John, dear, I do think Miranda would like a bit of a rest. Perhaps to unpack and settle in, and to change before dinner. If she has a change of clothes, that is. I know Stacy would be delighted to—"

"Of course I would," Stacy agreed. She rose in a swirl of swinging skirts.

"Please don't concern yourself," Miranda said quickly. "I'll manage quite well alone."

Caroline let her head sink back against the pink cushions. "I must have a nap before the evening. I'll see you then. And if there's anything you require . . ."

John said, "I'll attend to it, Caroline."

She turned her blonde head and sighed, and did not answer him.

Miranda backed from the room, Stacy and John with her.

When he had closed the door behind them, he said, "Stacy, I'll have a word with Miranda. Perhaps later on . . ."

"Later," she agreed with a smile, and glided away down the brightly lit corridor.

When they were alone, John bent his gray eyes on Miranda. "I should have perhaps explained more fully. My wife had several miscarriages many years ago. Those, and certain of her habits, seem to have greatly exhausted her strength and her fund of good manners as well."

Miranda didn't reply. Once again she had heard an odd note in his voice. She considered it improper that he should speak in that jeering tone, and in those words, about Caroline. She was herself, Miranda thought, still no more than a stranger to him. Such confidences were hardly becoming. And would not be so in any case.

It was as if he could see into her mind. He smiled down at her. "You must forgive me, Miranda. I somehow feel that I have known you for a long time."

He paused before a door at the end of the hall. "This will be your chamber. Within easy call of my wife, as you can see. I'm certain that you'll end up by winning her."

Now he opened the door for her, but stood barring the way, his big body blocking hers, his head bent, so that he seemed to hang over her. He said, "You must be sure to ask for whatever you should need, my dear."

Beyond him, down the hall, the door that he had just

closed so firmly moved. Miranda saw the small crack grow larger. She knew that Caroline had slipped from the divan and stood there watching.

She said, "Thank you again, Cousin John."

He prolonged the moment, not speaking. Then, at last, he moved aside. She saw the door beyond his shoulder close quickly but silently.

She nodded and stepped into her room, shutting her own door gently. She heard John walk away.

Finally releasing her shoulders from the rigid position in which she had held them since she entered the house, she let them slump. She allowed the careful, respectful, and admiring expression to slip from her face, and permitted the open expression of gratitude to fall away. She looked very much like a rueful and tired child in that moment. A tall, slender girl, enwrapped in her mother's blue gown, with her hair done up in her mother's fashion.

Then, with a proud lift of her head, she looked around her. She saw that the picture of Lincoln that had been beside her bed in the Kayhome Arms was now beside her bed here.

Someone had unpacked for her, had seen how meager her belongings were. Well, let them, she told herself. It did not matter.

She turned to survey the room.

The floor covering was a deep dark blue with great blossoms of white woven across it at random. The furniture—dressing table, wardrobe, and bed—was white, too, and intricately carved and trimmed with gilt that sparkled. The canopy and dust ruffles of the bed were white trimmed with dark blue.

She thought of the garret room she had left behind, the contrast nearly too much to take in. Aloud she said in a proprietary voice, "Oh, yes, it's certainly very fine."

There was, from near the draped window, a sound which might have been a cough or a laugh. She turned quickly.

She realized now that she was not alone. Her shoulders braced and then relaxed.

The woman who regarded her was of some fifty years, although she looked much older. She was black-skinned and small, with a thin wiry frame. She had a long white scar along her jaw, and very bright black eyes, and more white scars on her hands.

Her name was Abigail Ramsey. She was Jefferson's wife, the mother of Timoshen and Lena, and she tried to be mother, too, to the small Negro gatekeeper, whose name was Benjy, and whom she had found two years before timidly begging pennies in front of Lansburgh's General Store.

Until the age of fourteen, Abigail had been a slave. But after she rescued her master's young son from a fire, she had been given her freedom and sent to Washington to school, where she had learned to read and write. There she had met Jefferson, and they had come to work at Haversham Square.

"I'm sorry if I scared you, Miss Miranda. I'm Abigail."

Miranda answered, smiling, too. "I thought I was alone."

"So I saw. I ought to have spoken up right away. But you looked as if you were thinking." She went on, "Anyway, I got your things unpacked for you. Is there anything else you need?"

"I don't think so, Aunt Abigail," Miranda answered, using the term of respect for age that she had been taught by her grandmother.

Abigail's face quivered in recognition, then went impassive again. She felt concern as she left Miranda alone.

Caroline had listened to the sound of John's receding footsteps, then pushed herself with shaking hands away from the door.

She took a few wavering steps toward the window, and stopped, her hands small fists at her temples. With a gasp that was almost a sob, she went back to the pink divan. She lay there, rigid, trying to breathe slowly and calmly. Then, with a moan, she thrust a thin hand into the drawer of the bedside table. She withdrew a small silver snuff box and clenched it in her trembling fingers. With another moan, she took out a small purple pill. She studied it with burning eyes before she held it to her lips and rolled it onto her tongue, savoring its bitterness and then swallowing it.

When she had done that, she lay back, waiting.

She remembered the first time she had seen John.

He towered over all the others in the big flower-filled room. She had sensed in him the arrogance which others took for strength, and recognized at once the potentiality for power that he held. It was awful to contemplate that arrogance and power turned against her as it had been.

She remembered that she had looked at him, and in the way of Washington City, a place of transients, had asked, "Where are you from, Mr. Haversham?" When he told her, smiling down into her face so that she felt infinitely feminine, she said, "Oh, yes, I do know Lowell. It's a nice little town."

And he answered with the bold look that had touched her even then. "It's a grubby little town, as you well know, Miss Layton. But I am here now, and I don't plan to go back."

She had been considered something of a beauty in those days, well-loved and courted by many, and even though she was twenty-one, she was in no great hurry for marriage. That changed soon after she met John. Her father, who had first invited him to their home, liked him well enough but seemed to have certain reservations. He had urged a fashionably long engagement, but had permitted an early marriage at her insistence. She was intensely in love with John, and shocked at the brutality of his lovemaking. She was shocked again and again until, gradually, he taught her to yearn for the very brutality which left her bruised and shaken.

She became pregnant in the second year of their marriage, but the child, greatly longed for by both of them, was stillborn in her eighth month after long agonizing hours of labor. The following year she became pregnant again, and once again she was brought to bed prematurely. She screamed through two terrible days while her body was ripped and torn from within, and her hot blood gushed out. That time the doctor gave her opium pills, which helped her to survive the anguish of losing her second child, and to bear the knowledge that she would have no other. She considered for months that the pills had saved her sanity, but then she discovered that she was sane only when she took them. The doctor remonstrated with her, but made sure that she had them when she insisted that she could give them up only gradually.

John said nothing, but she knew that he saw the flesh drain from her body, leaving her thin and pale, with awkward collar bones and clawlike hands. She knew that he saw the lassitude that so often struck her, and the dizzy void in which she sometimes spun. When she locked the pills away from herself, she sank in a daze of pain, remembering the two small bodies lost to her forever. She unlocked the pills to save herself, and John ordered the servants to make up for him a separate bedroom. She was deeply hurt and frightened by that.

Then, one night, just as she had finished dressing for dinner, he had come to her and said, "I think I will tell our guests that you are indisposed, Caroline."

She stared at him nervously. She had dressed with particular care and used cheek rouge to hide her pallor. "But why?" she asked. "I'm not at all indisposed. I'm fine, and looking forward to seeing our friends."

He answered coldly, "I don't want to see you downstairs. You are feverish and flushed. In a little while your hands will begin to tremble. Your voice will be shrill. They'll all look at you and wonder. I cannot and will not bear that, Caroline."

He left her weeping in her chair. She did not go down, of course. She did not dare. Instead she took a small purple pill.

He might do anything to humiliate her if she did not obey him. That knowledge hurt and frightened. But worst of all was that he deprived her of the lovemaking that he had taught her to need, that he found her barren body disgusting.

Even now, with the sweetness of relief upon her at last, she felt her hunger for him. She looked into the shadows of the pink room, wishing he were there with her, and seeing instead in the cheval glass the pale reflection of her haggard face and crumpled body. She heard herself say aloud, but to no one, "Today he brought Miranda Jervis into the house."

FOUR

The great wave of emotion that had arisen in mid-April after Lincoln's assassination had slowly subsided. By the end of the month it was clear that the government had not fallen, nor would Washington City be forever destroyed. Though the flags still hung at half-mast, an everyday, workaday mood prevailed. Men plied their wares in the small shops and markets. The hotels were full, the saloons noisy. Drays and carts and hansoms clogged the streets. Small ships cut their furrows in the river, and barges moved from lock to lock on the canal. The long casualty lists had disappeared from the *National Intelligencer* and Washington *Star,* and the space was filled with descriptions of the capture of Jefferson Davis and his imprisonment at Fort Monroe. It had been impossible to survive at so high a pitch of terror, so a path back to stability had been beaten down through the passing weeks.

To Miranda, accommodating to her new life in Haversham Square, everything before her arrival had begun to seem a distant dream. The cottage in Dealeyton . . . the Kayhome Arms . . . the shouts in the lane that had signaled the President's death . . . Reality was only the present and what lay within the ivy-covered walls.

She stood now in the sewing room, the seamstress at her feet. She felt the silken warmth of blue peau de soie against her skin and thought of Reed, and wondered if his silver eyes would brighten if he were to see her in this gown.

"No," Caroline said. "I don't think that that is quite . . . It's too . . . too revealing." She leaned back in her rocking chair and gazed fretfully at Miranda.

Stacy, standing near the chair, gave it a single hard rock and then laughed. "My dear Caroline, that will do you no good at all, believe me."

Miranda remained silent, but the white-haired seamstress at her feet reared backward to look up and mutter around a mouthful of pins, "Is it the neckline you're talking about now? You can easily see that I'm just doing the length."

"Never mind, Mrs. Bannion, about the length for the time being," Caroline retorted. "That drape at the throat must be lifted."

Stacy tucked a small chestnut curl into her elaborate hairdo and grinned. "Don't worry, Miranda. No matter what Caroline insists, the dress will continue to become you mightily."

"Of course it will," Caroline snapped, her green eyes alight with annoyance. "Do you think I want to be ashamed of my kinswoman when we go out into society?"

"If we ever do go out again." Stacy sighed. "I vow this period of mourning for the President seems so long to me." She turned her back on the other women and wandered away to the small dormer window and peered out into the briliant sunshine, ignoring Caroline's strident directions to Mrs. Bannion and humming softly to herself.

She liked neither mourning nor trouble nor tragedy, and denied its existence by concentrating on laughter and music and men. She was twenty-five years old, and had grown up in the quiet and respectable home of two maiden aunts. They had been grateful, and relieved, when at seventeen she became engaged to a young West Point graduate, since they had come upon her one evening in the garden, when she and the young man had struggled together in the shade of the persimmon trees. Stacy was not unnerved by the experience for she passionately loved the young man. He was so unnerved, however, that he gave her a huge diamond ring the day he set out for duty with his regiment. He died of an arrow through the throat in a place called

Ute Canyon. She had wept for him, but soon there had been other men. She considered none of them seriously, having discovered that she preferred play to love. Two months before, she had left her home in New York to stay with Caroline at Haversham Square, when her aunts had made their dispositions plain. The affair she had been conducting with a man already married had become the talk of their acquaintances. They would not allow the Gordon name to be so dishonored. Stacy was relieved to leave them, and her married lover, behind. She had attempted a mild flirtation with Reed, who seemed not to notice, and another with John, who was plainly amused. It was he who had introduced her to several senators and a number of other men, so that she had plenty of beaux to squire her about. Though she saw very soon that John had his own purposes in this, she did not mind. She was enjoying herself.

She had turned away from the lavish view beyond the window to have a look at Miranda, when Caroline said, "Well, Miranda, what do you think?"

Miranda's heart-shaped face was pink. She wished that she had never allowed Caroline to order her into the sewing room for the fitting of a new wardrobe. She knew by now that whatever she received she would pay for in humiliation. Caroline would see to that. There had been, since the first moment of their meeting, this strange and terrible tension between them. Miranda did not understand it, nor its cause. But she was determined to ignore it, to win Caroline if only she could.

But when she had protested politely, and falsely, too, that she needed no additions to her wardrobe, Caroline had laughed thinly. "My dear girl, I do believe that you'll be quite presentable when you're properly dressed. If you're to be here in Haversham Square, then you must seem to belong here. We can't have it said in Georgetown that our relations aren't properly handled, you know."

Now Miranda replied, "Whatever you think, Caroline. I depend completely on your judgment." And then, before she could stop herself, she added truthfully, "However, I believe Mrs. Bannion has the neckline just right."

"I told you, Mrs. Bannion." Caroline spoke as if Miranda were deaf, dumb, blind, and insensible. "Lift the drape."

Mrs. Bannion rose stiffly. Her gnarled hands gathered folds of peau de soie at Miranda's breasts. Her mouth turned down around the bunched pins. "Like this?" she muttered dispiritedly.

"Higher."

"I would suggest a Chinese collar," Mrs. Bannion announced dryly, while Stacy laughed again.

"And I did not ask for your suggestions," Caroline retorted. She pressed her long thin veined hands to her temples. "I don't know why I allow myself to become involved in these difficult situations. If I trusted your judgment, Stacy, I might ask you to oversee the proper dressing of Miranda. But somehow I know that you'll be less than exacting. And—"

Stacy smiled down at her. "Caroline, I promise you that I will be exacting. It will all be just as you wish. So do take your poor head and put it down on a pillow if it ails you. Or else have a walk to the lily pond and rest. It's a gorgeous day. The sun will do you more good than all your medications, and when you return, you—"

But Caroline's hands dropped to her lap, fingers wrapped hard together in a single fist. "No," she said. "No, I think not." She had just heard a familiar heavy step in the hallway. Her fretfulness disappeared. She said briskly, "Move back, Mrs. Bannion, and let me see how it is now. We want the gown to be just right, you know."

Mrs. Bannion drew back, faintly bewildered by the sudden cordiality in Caroline's tone.

Miranda turned slowly, her golden eyes lowered.

John stood in the doorway, a smile on his lips. "Yes, it's very nice. Very pretty indeed. And you're pretty, too, Miranda." Caroline's eyes flashed to his face as he gave her a small bow, went on, "I knew that I could rely on your taste."

"Why not?" she asked coolly.

His smile widened. "Why not indeed?" His hand dipped into his waistcoat pocket. "I have a small gift for you,

Caroline." Two great amber eardrops dangled from between his fingers.

"Amber," she said. "How beautiful." But her narrow green look went to Miranda. Amber, the same clear amber as this girl's eyes. Something sickened within Caroline, but she asked lightly enough, "Where do they come from, John?"

"Why, by one route and another, I think they came all the vast distance from Russia."

"And what have you brought for me, and for Miranda?" Stacy demanded with a mock pout.

"Be sure I won't neglect either of you," he answered. "But you must wait and see. Your time will come."

There was nothing in his hard face to show that he was seeing Miranda with new eyes. Quite suddenly now she was more than a beautiful and endearing child. He was shocked by the intensity of what he felt. The crinolines and hoop and train could not conceal the strong shapely lines of her young body. The high draped neck, no doubt Caroline's suggestion, could not hide the thrust of her full breasts. The demure expression on her face could not mask from him the fire he knew was in her. She was a woman born to be consort to a king. To be consort of John Haversham. What had been nothing more than a whim to please her had suddenly become a need to possess her.

Caroline's hands trembled, enclosing the eardrops. She knew that she would wear them once or twice because she had to. John would expect it, and if she did not, he would ask her about them. But then she would put them away. The very thought of them shook her. It was years since he had actually bought her a gift. That he had done so now seemed ominous to her. Aloud she said, "John, dear, this is woman's business, you know. You ought not to be here."

He ignored her, smiling at Miranda. "There's important news this morning. Have you yet heard that John Booth has been captured in a barn in Virginia along with at least one of his henchmen?"

"I didn't know," she said. "What of Booth? Will they bring him back to Washington City?"

He shrugged his massive shoulders. "He's dead. Either he shot himself, or was shot. Though that was against the orders the soldiers had. A dead Booth can tell nothing of the conspiracy. I think some people will breathe more freely after this day."

"But what of the others?" Stacy asked.

"They have eight of them in the federal prison at Greenleaf Point. The trial will be very soon, I should think," he answered.

"I hope they hang them all," Caroline said thinly.

"I believe they will," John said.

But he was thinking it a shame that he could not have given the amber drops to Miranda. How well they would have complemented her eyes. Had he, deep in his mind and without knowing it, been thinking of that when he bought them for Caroline?

Mrs. Bannion asked tiredly, "Well, shall I go on, Mrs. Haversham?" and Caroline raised her pale brows at John.

He bowed, said, "Please do," and went in search of Reed, only to learn from Jefferson that Reed, as he did so often these days, had taken a horse from the stables and was out riding the estate alone.

John had intended that Reed go with him to the Barclay Hotel near Capitol Hill. It was time for his younger brother to display some interest in the Haversham affairs.

John mounted the carriage, instructed Timoshen, and sat back, his ebony cane between his knees, thinking of Reed with deep concern. He was not the same man who had joined the Army of the Potomac three years before.

John had not wanted him to go, had argued and fought, and even tried to threaten. It would have been easy to purchase a substitute. It was frequently done for a man of Reed's station. But he had been obdurate, speaking of duty, the draft riots in New York, the Union which belonged to all and not to some and therefore must be defended by all and not by some. Unlike John, Reed had something of a romantic and idealistic nature. It had been impossible to keep him from going. And he had come home a different man. It wasn't just the wound in his arm, nor the fever that periodically assailed him. Something more than a wound in the flesh, more than fevers, had affected him.

John ground his teeth and squeezed the cane. When a man built an empire, he needed an heir to receive it. Since Caroline had so grievously disappointed him, Reed must be the heir. But he showed no disposition to learn to accept the responsibilities that awaited him.

The carriage jolted past the bank owned by Caroline's cousin, Tad Layton.

It was just here, John thought, that he had first seen Miranda.

A cold kernel of anger expanded inside of him. It was Miranda who should be his wife. Not puny Caroline who had failed to give him sons. Not half-mad Caroline.

The bank was left behind. Timoshen guided the carriage east toward Washington Circle and Pennsylvania Avenue.

John surveyed the area carefully, an eye open for whatever might appear to be prime real estate. He was certain that with the war over the city would soon begin to grow. But at the same time, his thoughts went back to Reed.

Since John was so much the elder, he very often felt more like father than brother to Reed. Their mother had died at Reed's birth, their father when Reed was eight. John had put him into a preparatory school and set about making of his life, and Reed's, too, what he intended it should be. He had been left the cotton mills in Lowell, and he came down to Washington City, determined that government contracts would be the basis of expanding them. What he had learned in that small bustling city convinced him that he and his future belonged there rather than in tiny Lowell.

He met Caroline's father, Senator Morris Layton, through one of the older man's assistants. The Senator had been impressed by him, and invited him for an evening. His twenty-one-year-old daughter had presided as hostess. She was pretty, surrounded by eager swains. John set himself to cut them out, one after the other, and soon did. He became her constant escort, bought the big house in Georgetown, and married her. Instead of the children he had desired, she had given him, through her favored position as a senator's daughter, the associations he needed. He had leased the Lowell mills and received a royalty on every yard of cotton sold. He made certain that many were. Senator Layton had put him onto the possibilities in railroad stocks. He saw them quickly, investing the proceeds from the mills in rights of way, at small fees, through government lands. His railroad stocks prospered in peace. The company he called the Haversham Lines prospered in war. So did the cotton mills. He saw for himself what there was to be made in the gun and cotton trade, and handled that with circumspection. Now he was thinking about Washington City, which could, if he were successful, become part of his empire, too. But Reed must be drawn in, interested, made a part of it.

Timoshen swerved the carriage as a small black child jumped a big puddle and fell toward the heavy wheels. The child's mother shrilled imprecations and snatched him up and slapped him and kissed him.

They drove past Willard's Hotel, and then Grover's Theater.

John speculated briefly on what would be the fate of Ford's Treater. It had been closed down by the government since the night of the assassination. It seemed improbable that it would ever be reopened.

Straight ahead there was the shining dome of the Capitol.

A packed omnibus charged by, kicking up clods of horse dung, and a cloud of dust. Timoshen pulled out a large white handkerchief and wiped his face.

Soon he pulled up before the Barclay.

It was there that John, and a group of his business associates, maintained a suite for meetings, card-playing, and drinking. While John conducted most of his affairs from the second-floor study in Haversham Square, he came here when he wanted something special.

The desk clerk, a one-armed veteran with bitter eyes, told him that Senator Hurley and a few others were already upstairs.

John left a coin at the desk, crossed the quiet, plant-filled lobby past dark horsehair sofas, and went slowly up the steps.

There were voices and the rattle of chips from a back room, and the tinkle of glasses, too. John smiled to himself. The card-players had gathered here, rather than in the building across the way. That was not unusual.

Josiah Hurley sat in a chair near the open window, his boots up on the sill. He was a man of about forty years of age. He had curly black hair, a spade-shaped black beard with a few threads of gray in it, and a narrow moustache over a sensual mouth. His eyes were blue and sharp, his face thin. He wore a severe white shirt, a long fitted black jacket, and narrow white trousers. He was married and had three children, but his wife had found, in her first year in Washington, that she could bear neither the climate nor the company. She had retreated, with her family to her home in the state capital, and had remained there ever since. Josiah hardly noticed her absence, and since John had introduced him to Stacy, he had completely forgotten her.

He greeted John. Then, although there was a brass spittoon at his side, he shot a stream of brown tobacco juice through the window.

John set aside his cane, took off his hat, and sat opposite him, observing with a grin, "One of these days you'll hit the Capitol dome dead center."

"I intend to keep trying anyway," Josiah answered.

"Is there more news about those under arrest at Greenleaf Point?"

"The same rumors as before. Except it looks like somebody's going to collect the twenty-thousand-dollar reward the City Council voted."

"Can it be proved those half-wits were involved?"

"It depends on what you mean by prove."

John shrugged his massive shoulders. "I guess there's no use speculating."

"None," Josiah agreed.

John took out a cigar, lit it carefully. Through Josiah, for whose services he paid, he maintained a web of information-gatherers that reached into nearly every business and government bureau. He was referring to that when he asked, "Do you have anything for me?"

Josiah shook his head. "Nothing worth repeating."

John nodded. Then, "Do you expect any of the others in?"

"I made no plans. Just ordered up some terrapin and ale for us. And that'll be along soon. Why? Do you have something on your mind?"

"I do. But it can wait. You're the man I wanted to see. I have an idea. I've been thinking about it for quite a while. And this is a good time to bring it up. Washington City has a crying need for a new railroad bridge. That old trestle isn't enough to carry the freight that will soon be coming in. And very soon now it *will* be. We have to look ahead. This is the hub of the nation. There's going to be heavy growth within the new few years."

"If you want a new railroad bridge, then I think you're going to have to build it, John."

John smiled faintly. "I wouldn't have to if you took the matter up before your committee. All you need to do is get a bill passed building that new bridge, and I'll bring the lines in."

Josiah shot another stream of brown juice through the window. Then he swung his feet off the sill, and sat up straight. "I tell you," he said thoughtfully, "that's not going to be as easy as you seem to consider. This city is going to need a lot more than a railroad bridge. And I get the feeling that Congress is not going to be interested in supplying what it needs, much less anything extra for you." He leaned back, squinting through blue eyes at the ceiling. "Congress paid out one million dollars as compensation to Washington City slave owners. You've got forty thousand former slaves here, or maybe a lot more. They need whatever human beings need, John. Food, work, schools. It will take really big money to deal with. Congress is not going to interest itself in a puny railroad bridge. Besides, I think you're dreaming anyhow. The minute we adjourn, the town goes dead."

"Now, you know better than that," John retorted. He

released an expansive plume of blue smoke before he went on. "You don't head for home the minute the gavel falls, though some of the members do. So you're perfectly aware that business goes on and on and on." He grinned at Josiah suddenly. "And that business takes transportation in and out. You can justify it if you try."

"I doubt it," Josiah answered. But there was a certain question in the words.

"I happen," John said, "to have some extra shares of railroad stock. It pays, Josiah. It pays very nicely indeed."

"Oh?" Josiah swung his feet up to the sill again and looked out into the street. "Well, maybe. I can try anyhow. But it might take some time. You know what the order of business is these days. Now that the war's over . . ."

"I have plenty of time." John laughed.

Josiah nodded, then said thoughtfully, "Do you know, John, I think you're right about one thing at least. There's going to be some building soon. The federal government is going to grow. It'll have to. And it will need room." He swung his feet to the floor again, and turned and squinted at John. "If I were you, I'd get ahead of anybody else that's considering it and lay hands on some of that land along the avenue. South, let's say, near Tiber Creek, and where those shantytowns are." Once again there was a questioning inflection in his words.

"You would?" John asked. "Now that's a thought." He didn't tell Josiah that he already owned a fair number of acres in just that area. Rather, to be precise, Caroline owned them. She had inherited them in her own name from her father, a fact that never failed to irritate John, but also never succeeded in keeping him from believing that that land actually belonged to him.

"I would, and I would also reserve a piece of it for a useful friend," Josiah observed, with a grin that split his black beard.

"I don't see why that couldn't be arranged," John said. He saw no reason to tell Josiah that he had already decided, in terms of the city's probable growth, where the prime land was, and what would be the most likely use for it. He considered that a man who believes he has done you a favor, and will profit by it, is prone to do you another.

"And how is your family?" Josiah asked. "Caroline well? Stacy?"

"You must come and visit soon," John told him. "Stacy mentioned just this morning that she had begun to wonder if you were offended with her. I assured her that you were not." He smiled faintly. "Women will never understand, you know, Josiah, that men have concerns that go beyond the fair sex itself."

A servant brought trays of lunch then. Both men had bourbon first, and then ale with terrapin and boiled potatoes.

Soon after, Timoshen drove John home through the sun-bright streets.

He found Caroline sleeping. Her pale lashes made small shadows on her thin cheeks. Her mouth drooped. He stood over her for a moment, and suddenly she awakened.

Her green eyes opened and then widened. She gave a barely concealed start of alarm.

"John? John, is that you?"

"Yes," he said. "Of course it is. Do I disturb you?"

"Is it late? I think I was sleeping, dreaming."

"Perhaps you were, Caroline."

She sat up slowly, her thin hands trembling at her throat. "What is it, John? Why are you staring at me that way?"

She found it impossible to read the cold gray of his eyes, his stony face. Her heart began to beat very quickly. She felt a sheen of dampness on her flesh. Without conscious volition she reached into the drawer beside her bed and drew from it the silver snuff box. As she did, she remembered what her dream had been. A small still body . . . a tiny white shroud . . .

He allowed her to open the snuff box, even to go as far as to have the small pill between her fingers. Then he said,

"No, Caroline, my dear. Not now, if you please." His big hand closed tightly around her wrist and forced it down to the divan. "I should like you to have your wits about you, whatever wits you have left, at least, for just a few moments."

She lay very still until he released her, and then, dragging her white peignoir closely around her thin body, she sat up.

The room was very dim.

Somewhere outside a mockingbird suddenly sang out.

He gave her a smile. "That's so much better, Caroline."

"What do you want, John?" she asked anxiously. She was certain that he had some purpose in this visit. He so rarely came here, to her room. She wished that she had been up, dressed. She wished she had been wearing the amber eardrops he had given her.

"You mustn't be alarmed," he told her. "It's just a small matter of business."

"What business, though? And how does it concern me?"

"Do you remember those few acres your father left you, Caroline? In your name, that land was, wasn't it? I considered it a very peculiar thing that he did."

A stillness seemed to settle in her chest. A heaviness like that of stone. She said cautiously, "He wanted me to have it, you know."

"I wonder why."

She made no answer.

He said, "The land belongs to both of us, of course. Since you are my wife. And I have been thinking for some time that it doesn't produce the revenue it should. Those few shacks and warehouses are nothing, but the land beneath them will indeed soon be something." A glow came into his eyes. "Just think of it, Caroline. A long avenue of buildings south of Pennsylvania Avenue, reaching from the White House to the Capitol. Just imagine, if you can, what it would be, and how it would make your father proud."

She said quietly, "I'm not much interested in visions these days, John. What do you want of me?" Though the

words were calm enough, her voice trembled. Her eyes
slid sideways to the snuff box in her hand.

"I want the deeds to that land, Caroline. Your lack of
interest in visions notwithstanding. That is what I want.
It's not an unreasonable request for your husband to
make, is it?"

The weight was unbearable now. She could not breathe.
But somehow she found strength to say. "You'll not have
them, John. Those deeds are mine, and I shall keep them."

He lowered his head between his shoulders, and though
he sat at ease, some menace emanated from him. "I think
I *will* have them," he told her quietly.

She shook her head from side to side. "No, no. And
you must not even ask me again. My father left that land
to me, and in my own name. It's mine, and it remains
mine. It's all I have, really." She gave him a pleading
look. "You do understand that, don't you? That land
is all I have."

"It'll make you a fortune, and then you'll have that."

"You'll have it," she said simply.

"My dear," he said. "This is a fruitless discussion. I
want those deeds, and I shall have them. Where do you
keep them? Tell me that, and we'll have an end of this
and you can go to sleep, or whatever you wish."

"They . . . they are not here . . . they are . . ." She was
breathless, struggling to control herself. The room seemed
to spin around her as she tried to think, to plan. "They . . .
they're in Tad's vaults, John. I gave them to him immediately after the transfer was made, and there they have
remained."

"How foresighted of you," he said gently. "Unaccountably so." Then, with his voice hardening. "You must go
to Tad and get them for me, Caroline."

"No," she gasped. "No. I shall not."

"But you shall. You cannot oppose me, Caroline. You
will never be able to do so."

"No, no," she shrilled. "You cannot have them, I tell
you. You shall not." And she threw herself at him, small
fists beating against the broadness of his chest, her eyes
wild and streaming with tears, and her lips trembling.

He thrust her away from him carelessly, and she fell in a quivering heap on the divan. He picked up the snuff box, and said, "Get the deeds for me, Caroline. I want them at once," and strode from the room.

FIVE

The flags were no longer at half-mast. They rode proudly at the tops of their poles, gleaming red and white and blue in the bright sunshine of late May. The black crepe was gone from the windows and doors of the buildings, replaced by bunting dyed the nation's colors. The cannon no longer boomed and the bells no longer tolled in mourning.

A sense of festival had taken over the city, and long high stands of braced, fresh lumber lined Pennsylvania Avenue from the Capitol to the White House, where joyful crowds gathered under brilliant streamers to welcome back the returning Army of the Potomac. The fratricidal war was over, and this was to be the formal celebration of its end. Eight conspirators waited in shackles and chains behind bars and brick walls and bayonets at Greenleaf Point, and it was nearly six weeks since Abraham Lincoln had made his last long journey home to Springfield.

Now everywhere there was laughter, smiles. Everywhere a sense of relief that somehow the worst was over and had been weathered. Life could go on.

But scattered in the crowds, as mute testimony to the reality of the occasion, there were women in widow's weeds. Here and there were children with black bands on their sleeves instead of the red, white, and blue badges that read *Welcome Heroes of the Republic* and *Honor to the Brave*.

The President sat in his flag-draped box with General Grant, the two men surrounded by members of the Cabinet, and foreign emissaries in the full-dress uniform and gold braid of their various countries.

Through the night before, anxious people had been gathering. They had slept on benches, on the damp grounds of the quiet parks. They had scrambled to save a small inch on which to stand, and crowded on the roofs of the public buildings like determined ants.

They waited, breath held, and then, from a distance, they heard the tramp of feet, the slow thud of hooves, the rattle of caisson wheels.

A gasp went up, and then a great screaming joyful cheer, as the first of the returning two hundred thousand appeared at the end of Pennsylvania Avenue and began the march onward to the White House reviewing stand.

In the bank of rows just next to it, Miranda sat with Reed on one side of her and Stacy on the other. Her amber eyes were wide, gleaming with excitement. John and Caroline and Josiah Hurley were just in front of them.

The gowns of the ladies glistened, all gaily colored, and the brilliant parasols they held were like great open-petaled flowers. The men wore white ruffled shirts and embroidered waistcoats under dark jackets, and narrow trousers.

Miranda's breath was quick with happiness. It was here that she belonged, she thought. It was for this that she had been born. To be alive at this moment, to be in this place, with this company.

The first of the ranks came on. Cavalry on great horses, harnesses a-gleam with brasses. Sabers and sidearms and muskets. And then came the foot soldiers.

As they approached, the President got to his feet, with General Grant, to accept the salute. All rose with him. In a great surge, those in the adjoining stands followed suit. The air was suddenly filled with flowers. Great bouquets of roses, iris, and daffodil spun over the heads of the crowd, pelting the companies as they presented arms and then passed on.

Behind them came carts heaped with bedding and tents and various armaments, reluctant mules pulling them onward, and bands with drummers, buglers, and fifes playing, and standards from which the different regimental colors waved.

Miranda slid a look at Reed. He was rigid-faced, his silver eyes thoughtful and far away, and yet there was a softness in his mouth that she had never seen before.

She wondered if he wished that he had put his garments aside, worn the blue uniform which had once been his, and joined the ranks of men who marched before him. She wondered what his memories were.

She yearned to reach out and touch him. A sweet hunger she couldn't name possessed her. She had never known it before. Never until the first time she saw Reed.

But he seemed now as remote as when she had first seen him in the doorway of John's study. A tall, gaunt man with an unhealthy pallor on his face and his arm in a black sling.

Even though they lived in the same house, she saw him only at occasional mealtimes, and briefly even then. He held himself aloof always and went his own way, speaking very little and that simply what courtesy required. Still, she had a sense that he did not miss much of what went on around him, though she could not say why she thought so. She had caught a glimpse of him several times as he paced the roof terrace, a lonely silhouette against the sky. She had seen him standing on the front steps of the house, staring abstractedly at the wide swath of sculptured lawn and the neat array of formal plantings. Early on many mornings she had watched from the window as he rode off into the trees on a black stallion, the sun shining in his dark hair, and she had wished that she could have gone with him. When they did meet over the sumptuous dinners served by Lena and Jefferson, Reed was silent, ignoring Stacy's conversation and her own only partly concealed curiosity.

Rank after rank of foot soldiers passed, and the flowers fell in waves upon them, and the cheers rang out again and again as they presented arms and received the President's salute, and went on, the place where they had been standing to be taken by their brothers.

There was more cavalry then, and Stacy, squealing, sent

a wreath of woven daffodils into the air. A rider, his long blond curls blowing on his shoulders, reached out to snag it as it sailed by his musket. He hooked it to happy cheers, but his restless horse gave a leap and a start and broke stride to lunge ahead, until his rider fought him under sedate control again.

"George Custer," Reed said softly. Then he adjusted his aching arm and sat back, closing his eyes momentarily, shielding himself from the bright gaiety of the moment.

It seemed to him that he could not bear it. The deep pain of that gaiety, with his memories crowding him, was not to be withstood. He felt himself sinking in the quagmire of the past. He remembered the long months of struggle, of ambush in dark lanes and hand-to-hand fighting. He still saw the crushed limbs and cut throats, and the long-drawn ropes of entrails caught in bayonets which he had first seen in those days. He had seen lice and maggots attack living flesh, and gangrene swell trembling bodies, and lungs burst, and hearts break.

He remembered another sunlit day, one much like this one, it had been, with a warmth in the fields and fleecy white clouds hanging gently in the sky. He and his friend Jim Boardman had ridden through a quiet wood, and Jim had pressed ahead, disappearing into a shadowed clearing. When Reed caught up, he found Jim frozen in the saddle and staring down at a small bright-eyed girl of perhaps fifteen years, who crouched at a stream edge with a bucket at her knees and her pale hands full of blackberries.

Jim threw a leg over the saddle and began to lower himself to the ground.

"No, Jim," Reed said. "No, don't. She's hardly more than a child. Let her be and ride on with me."

But the boy seemed not to hear. He reached the ground and began to move slowly toward where the girl sat, still as a cornered rabbit but with her small hands opening, the berries falling away, and the bucket, too, falling away soundlessly.

"Run, girl!" Reed told her harshly. "Run home right now."

She flashed him a look, and rose and sped into the shadows.

Jim lurched forward as if to follow.

"No," Reed said, and saw that the boy would not stop. He could not. He was the victim of some awful spell.

Reed crowded close to him, leaned from the saddle, and brought his gauntleted hand down in a hard, chopping blow. Jim fell as if axed, and lay senseless, his boy's face turned up to the blue sky.

Later they pretended nothing had happened, but where they had been friends before, riding side by side, they were friends no longer. A constraint had fallen upon them. A week after, in a discussion too trivial to be remembered, Jim had suddenly drawn his pistol and fired at Reed, who defended himself with what he had at hand. The rock had split Jim's skull, and gray brain and red blood had washed the hate from Jim's face. Reed helped bury him where he lay.

After that, Reed rode alone. He found it difficult to remember now why he had killed. Jim and the enemy were the same. He had thought it his duty, and could not turn his back on the righteousness of the cause. But he no longer knew what duty was, nor even the cause. He had been everywhere and done everything, and seemed to have forgotten why. He looked at the men who marched before him and wondered if they somehow managed to remember better than he.

A slender white hand touched his sleeve, then moved down to rest on his fingers.

Miranda whispered, "Reed, don't! Don't torment yourself. Come away with me if it troubles you to be here. Come away. We need not remain, you know. You need not watch if it hurts you."

He looked into her eyes and saw tenderness, and accepted it. "Thank you, Miranda," he told her. "But no. No. It's all right. It's over now, you see. It's all over. I must accept that."

"And you must forget it as well," she said gently.

"You're very kind and very discerning, Miranda."

A hot flush burned her cheeks, and her throat seemed

to tighten. She said, "But we are . . . we are kin. I couldn't help noticing . . . I hope you don't . . ."

"Hush," he told her softly. "You must never apologize for a kindness."

He saw her now as if he had never seen her before. The smooth curve of her white cheek, pink fading. The high tilt of her chin, the glossy black of her hair, and the gold of her remarkable amber eyes.

He moved his hand so that it was his fingers that held hers, and at that moment they were again immersed in a wave of music from a passing band, and then great showers of daffodils fell upon them from the stands that rose behind them.

He turned back to the passing men, John's big dark head within his range of vision. Reed was fully aware of the deviousness of his brother's nature, and accepted it as he accepted his brother's stature and coloring. It was a part of the man, the part of him that had been instrumental in building the Haversham fortune and the Haversham name. Who but John would have foreseen the need ten years ago for soldiers' uniforms? Who would have thought to lease the mills and come to Washington City? Who would have known every possible means to accumulate those rights of way on which the railroad fortune was built? That was all part of what John was. Without it, the Havershams would still be obscure owners of a small mill in a small New England town. With it, there seemed to be no limit to what John could do. But now Reed wondered, knowing there was in John's nature nothing of the humanitarian, just what it was that had made him bring Miranda to the house. Having finally seen her clearly, Reed thought that he understood. John had been captivated by her beauty and spirit. It could only be that. Reed bent an uneasy look at the back of his brother's head. When had John allowed himself to be captivated to no purpose?

His fingers tightened around Miranda's, and he smiled at her as she sat forward to wave at the crowd below. In the row in front, Caroline moved restlessly. Reed heard her say, "Oh, John, I'm so tired. So very tired. How long must we stay here? Haven't we seen enough? It's all just the same."

Her blonde hair, so carefully piled and stacked and combed earlier in the day, had begun to wisp about her face. A sheen glistened on her forehead and pale cheeks. She felt that there was no air to breathe. The heat of the sun, the laughter, the scent of the flying flowers seemed to stifle her.

John said, "Why, this will go on for two days, my dear. That much is sure. But I think we shall not stay all that time. There's the reception at the Van Ewards' this evening. We will, of course, go home and rest, and then dress for that. But still . . ." he looked around at the others, "we are enjoying ourselves. Surely you'll not ask that we depart now."

"I find there's no air," she said. "I'm tired. I wish I hadn't come."

He smiled at her, but his gray eyes were cold with disgust. "It's not air that you need, my Caroline."

She turned her face away from his, her lips trembling, and cried, "I'm ill, I tell you, John. I'm ill and I must go home."

"To a certain small silver snuff box?" he asked.

She gasped, "John, please . . ."

"Look at me," he said. "Look at me, Caroline."

She turned slowly.

He smiled at her, then took her hand and put into it a single pill.

Shuddering, she swallowed it, and then closed her eyes against the brightness of the day and waited for her own brightness to overtake and finally free her.

Stacy leaned close to Josiah Hurley, her shoulder pressing tightly against his. "It's lovely, isn't it?"

His blue eyes regarded her hungrily. "It is. You are, Stacy, my sweet."

"I see now why your constituents adore you," she laughed. "You have such a way with words."

He stroked his black beard. "But the words they hear from me are not the same ones that you hear, Stacy."

She pouted prettily. "Well, I should hope not, Senator.

If that were so, you'd surely be spreading your interest, and your charm, rather thinly."

"Be assured, Stacy. That doesn't happen. A successful politician quickly learns to avoid that. Or he stops being a successful politician."

"You will join us at the Van Ewards', won't you?" she demanded.

"Of course. I've already arranged it with John."

Miranda listened, and wondered if Reed, too, would go to the Van Ewards'. She hoped he would. A shiver touched her as she heard within her head the sound of a waltz, and she imagined him taking her hand, taking it as he held it now, but for joy rather than for comfort. She imagined his good arm at her waist, and his face close to hers.

Finally she turned to him, asking, "Reed? Are you coming with us later? You will, won't you?"

A bright yellow rose dropped to his knees from behind them. A cheer went up from the crowd. The footsteps of the marchers thudded hard and rhythmically in the dust. The caissons creaked and rattled by. He took the yellow rose and slipped it into her hair. He smiled at her, and said, "Be certain to save me the first and last waltz."

Carleton Van Eward was a wily sixty-year-old bachelor, well cared for by his grim-faced older sister. Her name was Mary, and she was tall, gaunt, with shadowed dark eyes. He was short, round, and jolly, with pink dimpled cheeks and plump hands and feet. His thin hair was white and swirled into two neat wings at each side of his head. His moustache was white and full.

He and Mary greeted their guests in the reception hall of their Massachusetts Avenue mansion, a five-story building which one day would become a home for unwanted children. Now it was brilliantly lit with gas lamps, elaborate wall sconces, and tall tapers.

He and John had first met through Senator Layton, and he had known Caroline for many years. He smiled at her, pinched her cheek in welcome, and said, "Caroline, my dear child, you grow more lovely every day. How happy I am to see you."

"You're so kind, Senator Van Eward," she answered. "Why don't you visit us more often?"

"My dear, I'm a man of affairs," he laughed. "But I shall come, I assure you, if you ask me." His eyes were on Stacy's decolletage, Caroline saw.

"I shall invite you very soon, never fear," she promised him.

While he was speaking to the others, she saw her cousin Tad Layton standing near the punch bowl. She signaled him with a quick lift of her head and watched as he began to make his way toward her.

It would be impossible to speak to him then, but if he were to remain close by, there would come a moment.

"Miranda Jervis," Senator Van Eward was saying. "Charming. I'm happy to meet you," and though he sounded as if he meant it, his eyes were still on Stacy's high white bosom.

She cried, "Carleton, how truly lovely you are to have us," and beside her, Josiah Hurley stiffened and grew dour.

They moved as a group into the ballroom, and as they did, the musicians began to play.

Miranda smiled up at Reed. "There is the first waltz," she said.

But he did not smile back at her. Instead he stared at her as if he had never seen her before. His pallor had deepened so that his skin was very nearly the same shade as his embroidered yellow waistcoat. He pressed his aching arm to his side, and said finally, "It was a mistake, Miranda. I'm sorry. I can't possibly dance with you."

"Are you ill?" she asked quickly. "Shall I call John? How can I help?"

He answered none of her questions. "Forgive me," he said, made a small bow, and left the crowded room.

She was stunned with disappointment. She didn't understand what had happened, what she had done. Only moments before they had shared the warmth of the afternoon, the exchange of a continuing closeness. And now, quite suddenly, he had withdrawn from her. He had gone away in spirit and in flesh.

It seemed to her that the brightness of the room dimmed, the laughter faded. Where there had been joy there was now emptiness.

Then Stacy leaned close to her, whispering. "Don't mind, Miranda. He can't help himself. These moods do strike him so suddenly, and the fevers as well. He has gone home to ride in the dark, or to go to bed and brood. He'll be sorry tomorrow, I assure you."

Miranda nodded, lifted her small strong chin. It would be a beautiful party. She would enjoy it to the full. Then, in the morning, she would see Reed again.

"I must talk to you, Tad," Caroline said softly. "It's terribly important."

"Whenever you say," he answered. "Shall I stop by the house tomorrow? Say, in the afternoon?"

He was in his mid-thirties, unmarried. His style, as befitted a banker, was conservative. He wore a black frock coat, narrow black trousers. His blond hair was full, brushed carefully from his face. His sideburns were well trimmed. He had a real fondness for Caroline, and was concerned at the glitter in her eyes.

"No," she said quickly. "No, no. Not the house. Not there." She drew a deep breath. "I'll come in to the bank when I can, Tad. I want this to be between us, only us. Do you understand?"

"Of course, Caroline. But what is it? What's troubling you?"

She smiled suddenly, offering him a bright emptiness. "I'll be there," she told him, as John loomed over the two of them.

John shook Tad's hand, said, "We must get together. I spoke to Josiah Hurley about a project I have in mind. I think you'd like very much to have a part in it, too."

"I expect I would," Tad agreed. "What does it concern?"

While John explained briefly his proposed new railroad trestle to Tad, he watched Miranda talking to Carleton

Van Eward. Nothing but respect for decorum, to which he was rarely prone, kept him from going to her. She belonged at his side. Not Caroline. She should be his wife. Not Caroline. He lowered his head between his thick shoulders and described to Tad what he had done, and what he expected Josiah to do.

Listening, Caroline felt a sudden chill. The room began to spin slowly around her. A gray haze drifted in from the corners.

Then Tad took her cold hand, and said softly, "Come Caroline, I'm sorry. You surely don't wish to hear the two of us discuss business matters. The second waltz is about to begin."

SIX

Miranda went slowly up the steps, her arms full of dew-touched roses. Their heady scent surrounded her with a cloud of the most exotic perfume, and their colors made even more intense the brightness of the June afternoon. It was a combination that filled her spirit with longing.

She wore a gown of white, its tight bodice outlining her slimness, its skirts swinging around her over petticoats and crinoline. The high round collar was rolled back to frame her face, and the wide sash, edged with fringes, made her waist even more narrow. It had been part of her dream to be dressed thus, and to walk with her arms full of roses, but with that become real, she had discovered it was not quite enough.

When she reached the back terrace, she turned to look at the great shadowed lawns that rolled away into distant trees. Reed was nowhere to be seen. All was emptiness. If one didn't know, she thought, one would believe that the house stood alone in a vast and desolated countryside, with no ear to respond to a shout, none to see a struggle.

It was an unpleasant fancy. She tried to shrug it away. But that was not easy. Fancy was made impressively strong in such a place. But did fancy explain the strange currents and hidden qualities that she had begun to sense in those around her?

She saw that light glistened on the conservatory windows below, but within all was dark. The huge fronds of tropical plants leaned against the glass and scratched there softly, and the panes were tracked with silvery beads of moisture.

Beyond the great lawns, shielded away in a small copse of trees, were the tiny houses, rebuilt slave quarters, where Abigail and her family lived, and beyond them, both completely hidden from the big house, were the stables and carriage house that she had herself never seen. Perhaps Reed lingered there now. Was it the strange undercurrents that she had sensed herself which kept him away? Or was it the memory of war, working as a poison in his blood, which drove him?

It was useless to wonder. They had had those brief moments of closeness the day the soldiers returned. Since then Reed had retreated beyond her reach again.

She turned, went into the silent house, and then to the cooking quarters to see about vases for the flowers.

Abigail's domain was a huge square room. A large stone fireplace covered one wall and a big wood stove was set against another. There were cupboards and pantries and shelves lined with china and glassware. Gleaming brass pots and ladles and colanders hung from hooks on the ceiling. The brick floor was scrubbed and polished.

Abigail herself seemed polished, too. Her dark face shining, the white scars, standing out on her jaw and hands, seemed painted on. Her black dress hung crisply from her narrow shoulders, and her white apron rustled with starch when she moved.

"Would you want me to arrange the roses for you, Miss Miranda?" she asked.

"I'd like to do them myself," Miranda told her. "The scent is delicious. I need only be careful of the thorns."

Abigail brought out three heavy silver pitchers. She

thought, but didn't say, that many beautiful things have thorns, but Miranda herself didn't. At least none that Abigail had yet discovered. She asked, "Will these do?"

"They'll be prefect," Miranda told her, smiling with delight. It was a joy to handle the softly gleaming polished metal. It was warm to the touch, and seemed to breathe, to pulse with life. She hummed as she filled each of the pitchers to brimming, arranging, studying, and rearranging.

Abigail, pretending to be busy at the big stove, watched from the corners of her eyes, and thought that Miranda was a true lady. It was what she had told Jefferson the night Miranda arrived. "She's a born lady," Abigail had said. It was this young girl with her straight shoulders and heart-shaped face, with her warm glowing eyes, who should be mistress of Haversham Square.

Caroline appeared in the doorway, her white gown belling around her thin body. There was a high frantic flush on her sharp cheekbones. "I sent for you just one hour ago, Miranda. Why are you here, playing with flowers, when I want you?"

"You sent for me?" Miranda echoed. "But I don't understand."

"I told Lena to tell you that I needed you. I find it hard, and very unpleasant, to believe that you would ignore my request, for that is what it was, and go out to gather roses instead."

Listening, Abigail's heart sank. Once again she felt a pity for Miranda.

But Miranda swallowed the automatic protest that came to her lips. Lena had not told her of any such message. And hardly an hour before, Caroline had retired to her room, saying that she would have a late afternoon nap. Now Miranda gave the roses a last lingering touch, and said gently, "I'm very sorry, Caroline."

"What good is that to me? You are flighty and unreliable and even unkind. And I—"

"I can only apologize," Miranda cut in. "If there is anything I can do for you, please tell me."

"Come with me," Caroline retorted, and swept from the room.

Upstairs, in her lavender-scented bedroom, she said without sincerity, "I'm sorry, Miranda. You see, I changed my mind. I decided against a nap. I was lonely, and I thought we might take an outing together. Perhaps a drive to see my cousin Tad. So I sent for you and waited. And truly, I still don't understand why you didn't come."

Inwardly, though, Caroline shuddered. She was suddenly not certain. Had she sent Lena for Miranda? Or had she dreamed that?

Miranda didn't answer. She didn't know what to say. She felt in the wrong, yet in the right at the same time. She waited.

"You've no explanation, no excuse?" Caroline persisted, despite her own doubts.

At last Miranda said, "Lena did not tell me that you wanted me, Caroline. I could not do what I did not know."

Tears suddenly trembled on Caroline's lashes. She sank onto the pink divan. "I should think you would try to consider me," she whispered. "It's only through John's kindness that you're here. If you care nothing for me, surely you must respect his generosity."

Miranda took Caroline's thin white hand between her own. She said, "It was somehow a misunderstanding. You know that I'm grateful to you both for what you have done for me. Come, if you like, I'll have Timoshen bring the carriage around right now. It is a lovely afternoon for a drive."

"No," Caroline answered. "No. Not today. It's late now and I must rest."

"Tomorrow then?"

"Yes," Caroline said. "Perhaps tomorrow, Miranda." She lay back, her eyes closing.

Miranda stayed with her, sitting in the big chair beside the divan until the older woman had drifted off into fitful sleep.

Then, carefully, Miranda tiptoed from the room and went in search of Lena.

Abigail had already instructed her daughter, so there was no surprise on the young Negro girl's face when Miranda asked if Caroline had sent for her.

Instead, she hung her head and mumbled, "I forgot. I'm sorry, Miss Miranda."

"Never mind then. As long as you don't get into trouble over it," Miranda answered thoughtfully.

That was too much for Lena. She burst out, "Only I didn't really forget. That's what my mother told me to say. The truth is, Miss Caroline never sent me for you at all."

Miranda stared at her for a moment, then said, "Let's just forget it, Lena."

She knew that Lena was telling her the absolute truth. Caroline had claimed that she had sent Lena to find Miranda. But Caroline had not done that. Caroline had either imagined that she had, or she had deliberately lied. To Miranda, the implications of this were suddenly frightening.

•

The sun was brilliant, but a layer of thick black clouds lay across the western horizon, and the air was hot and heavy, a smothering blanket that made breathing difficult and movement slow.

The carriage jolted over the rough street, and Caroline winced.

She was discreetly rouged and powdered. Her blonde hair was done up in a high crown of waves and ringlets under a saucy yellow hat. The plume that curled from its brim dropped enticingly over the curve of her cheek. Her dress was yellow, too, and its full drape accentuated the smallness of her waist and billowed out to conceal the narrow line of her hips. She carried a yellow parasol and a reticule of lace, into which she repeatedly slipped her hand to finger the crumpled documents she had hidden there.

"I'm glad we're going," she said nervously. "And I do thank you both for joining me."

Stacy laughed happily. "Why, Caroline, I see no reason

for your apologetic tone. Miranda and I are only too happy to join you, as you well know."

Miranda nodded. She wondered why Caroline was so uneasy. She looked elegant and lovely, and yet a thin edge of uncertainty seemed to thrust itself through the cover of clothing and the mask of manners.

Caroline's green eyes narrowed. "Miranda, did you perhaps have other plans for today?"

"No, of course not," Miranda answered quickly, reassuringly.

"Well, you might have," Caroline retorted. "Or you might simply have preferred to stay at home."

"Caroline," Stacy cut in, "will you have done with your silly questions? We will, all three of us, enjoy the ride. Then I suggest we drive to Mr. Galt's to see what new jewels he has. Or, if that does not please you, we could go to the Palace of Sweets, and after that—"

Caroline said, "Perhaps we'll do both. But first I have told Timoshen to stop at the bank. You'll not mind waiting outside, will you? I just want a word or two with Tad. It will take only moments."

"Moments or longer," Stacy said. "We'll wait for you, never fear."

Caroline tipped her parasol and nodded at a huge brown house set back from the street in a grove of mimosa covered with the pink and white blossoms that looked like powder puffs when they hung on their boughs, and like gossamer feathers when they drifted away to ride the summer wind. "It's there that the Barrington sisters live," she said. "They are friends of ours, Miranda, and you'll no doubt meet them soon."

"I'm glad that the mourning period is all over now and we can begin to live again," Stacy said. "I did think it would drive me mad. The waiting. The thinking." She giggled suddenly. "But you know, Caroline, I'd rather that we left our cards at the Van Ewards' than at the Barringtons'."

Caroline smiled indulgently. "We'll do both, of course. Though I'm surprised that you should find the Senator's sister better company than Erna and Dorothea Barrington. I think Mary Van Eward rather grim."

"I'm not thinking of Mary Van Eward." Stacy laughed. "As you know perfectly well."

"And what of Josiah Hurley?" Caroline teased.

"I confess that I begin to find him a bore, and a boor," Stacy said. And then, thinking of John, she added hastily, "But don't imagine that I intend to drop him. Oh, no. I shall not do that."

"In your shoes I would," Caroline answered.

She turned back to Miranda and nodded to a small house half-hidden by bushes of ligustrum. "And that is Prospect Cottage. Mrs. Southworth, the novelist, lives there. I have her works, should you want to read them." She ignored Miranda's expression of interest to point at a vacant lot, where two black and white cows nudged each other, struggling for a spot of shade. "The bane of Georgetown. We live in the midst of city and farmland at the same time. Horse, cow, mule, and chicken vie for the very space we stand on."

Miranda listened, marveling. This was a new Caroline, an intriguing one, a woman in whom one could have interest and not only pity.

"John has visions of what Washington City and Georgetown will be one day, and not too long in the future at that," Caroline was saying. She smiled faintly, and her hand slipped into her reticule. "In those visions, at least, I do agree with him."

The carriage rolled downhill past a church built on a narrow triangle, its stained-glass windows ablaze with sun.

"A beautiful place," Caroline said, and after a moment, tipping her parasol again, she went on, "But even more impressive, though in a different way, is the Corcoran house just there. It's closed now, but I once visited it often. William moved away to England at the beginning of the war. I wonder if now he'll decide to return."

With those words, a sadness appeared in her face. She sank back and was silent, her fingers once more reaching into the reticule on her lap.

Then the shops and small row houses began to appear, and the stables and smithies and warehouses, and seeing them, Miranda thought briefly of the Kayhome Arms, and her father and Susanah Kay, but soon forgot them.

There was so much to look at. A one-legged man wearing a tattered uniform leaned on a crutch and looked in all directions, appearing not to know where he wanted to go.

A lonely chicken pecked its way across the road from one pile of horse leavings to another.

Two drunken men squared off with curses and fists raised, and then fell into each other's arms in a parody of a lovers' dance.

When Timoshen pulled up before the bank on the corner, the whole of the building seemed to shimmer in the heat, and Miranda thought of that bright April day when she had climbed into this very carriage, her heart beating with hope, to wait for John.

"Only a little while," Caroline said. "If you'll excuse me."

She leaned heavily on Timoshen's arm as he helped her down. She thanked him and smiled tremulously into his impassive face, and then, in a swirl of yellow hooped skirts, she glided into the bank.

The clerk rose instantly to greet her. He bent his head so sharply against his high starched collar that she thought it must surely cut his throat. "Mrs. Haversham. Good day. What can I do for you?"

"Is Mr. Layton in?" she asked. "And would he have time to see me?"

"Why, yes, of course. Allow me to conduct you to him."

She was led through the dim place, past polished mahogany and shining bars and counters, her own perfume trailing behind her in waves, through a swinging gate and into a small and simple office.

Tad dropped a copy of the *New York Times* on his littered desk and rose to greet her, taking both of her hands in his. "Caroline, it's good to have you here. Sit down and tell me how you are."

She sank gratefully into the cane chair he held for her.

Her knees had suddenly begun to tremble. She felt a sheen of dampness start through the powder on her cheeks. She folded her hands over her reticule. "Tad, it's . . . this is a private matter. You do understand that? You'll not give me away? Not to anyone? Not for any reason whatsoever?"

He grinned at her. "To whom would I give you away, Caroline? And why on earth would I?"

She studied his face anxiously. Then, reassured by the steadiness of his eyes and the openness of his grin, she said simply, "To John. It might be that John will speak to you about this. I'm almost certain that he will. I plead for your discretion and for your loyalty to me."

"You have my promise, Caroline." But a worried frown creased his forehead. "Now. Hadn't you better tell me what this is about?"

"It's the land that my father left me, Tad. John has always resented that I own it. Now he wants it for one of his schemes. I—"

"If so, it would only be of benefit to you, Caroline. You receive little from it."

"It would be of benefit to him," she said, her voice shaking. "Not to me. The land is mine. And I want to keep it."

"Then you shall, of course," Tad answered promptly.

"To make certain of that I want you to hold the deeds for me, Tad."

Again he frowned, but he said, "I will, and I'll be glad to."

She forced herself to go on. "I lied to him, you see. He asked me for them, and I . . . well, I told him that you had them already. I'm not certain he believed me. For though he hasn't brought up the subject again, I believe that he searched my room. I found . . ." A flush burned on her cheekbones. "Tad, it is not easy to talk like this. I hope you understand. John is my husband. But I fear . . . well, I think I mustn't keep the deeds near me. For if I did, in some way or other once he had them, I fear he would be able to persuade me to sign them over to him. I fear I might weaken and regret it later. So . . ."

She stopped as an ominous growl of thunder shook the room. She raised her head, listening. A pulse beat in her throat, and she put her hand up to still it.

He saw her fingers tremble, and wondered. He asked gently, "Caroline, is there anything more you want to tell me? You know that we can speak freely to each other. We're more than merely cousins. We're friends, too, aren't we?"

"Of course we are. And that's why I dare ask this of you. But if John should come—"

"Believe me, he'll not have the deeds. Never. Except from your own hand."

"He'll not have them from my hand," she said simply. "They're all that's left to me of my father, of my old life." Then, withdrawing the crumpled sheaf from her reticule, she leaned forward and put it on the desk. "You'll see that there's an added sheet of paper. It's . . . should anything happen to me . . . My will to dispose of the property." She smiled as she said those words, thinking grimly that she was entitled to her own small pleasures.

"Caroline," Tad said anxiously, "you must force yourself to overcome this morbid style of thinking. It's not good for you. Surely you know that. For some time now—"

"Tad, don't," she cut in.

"But have you seen Doctor Porter? Have you made any attempt at all to—"

"Please," she begged.

He forced himself to smile at her. "All right, Caroline."

She rose, he with her. He bent to kiss her cheek and saw that her eyes were filmed with tears, but she went to the door. There, she turned back. "Put those papers away, Tad."

"You'd like to see me do it?"

She nodded.

He went to the vault behind him and, producing three keys from his waistcoat pocket, he used them each in sequence. He pulled the heavy door out, then a long narrow paper-crammed drawer. He put the sheaf into a brown folder, wrote her name on it, and inserted it between red leather covers. He thrust the drawer in, slammed the vault door, and once again used the keys in sequence. Then he turned to her. "It's done, Caroline."

"Thank you," she said, and smiled at him.

She thought, as she walked through the bank, It's done. It's done. This time he'll not have his way. She was thinking it with such concentration and relief that she did not hear the "Good day, Mrs. Haversham," the "Come again, Mrs. Haversham," which trailed after her.

Miranda asked, as Timoshen helped Caroline into the carriage, "Are you well?"

She nodded, but Miranda continued to cye her anxiously. She saw the thin trembling hands clutch the reticule as thunder crashed in the distance. She saw Caroline's pale face grow even more pale as a great fork of white lightning split the lowering sky.

If this had been the casual visit that Caroline had pretended, then why, Miranda wondered, was Caroline so disturbed now?

Stacy seemed to sense nothing. She resettled her skirts with an annoyed flounce. "Really, Caroline, I didn't know you would take so long a time. We must forget Mr. Galt's now, and the Palace of Sweets. The weather is completely changed. If we're not to be drowned then we must return home at once."

"Home," Caroline repeated. Then, dully, "Yes, we'd better, hadn't we?" She nodded at Timoshen, and just as he set the carriage rolling, the horse stepping out briskly, three black crows rose from the roof of the bank, and with cawing shrieks flew in great swoops overhead.

"Miranda's well enough," Jake said, smiling across the table at Tom Jervis. "You can believe that. Thriving, you might say she is. Prospering even. She wears beautiful gowns made by a seamstress named Bannion. And rides about in the Haversham carriages whenever she pleases. She—"

Nan interrupted to say, "Oh, what a pity and a shame that you've had no word from her. Such a sweet child she was. Who'd believe . . ." Her small black eyes gleamed with malice. "But, of course, you did have words when she left, didn't you? And it appears she hasn't forgotten them. Or refuses to allow herself to forget them, either one."

Tom stared into his platter, eyeing the greasy food without appetite. He suffered these days, he thought morosely, and it wasn't fair. No, it just wasn't fair that he should suffer. At last he answered. "As long as she's well . . ."

Susanah Kay gave an unladylike grunt. As she pushed back her chair to rise, her hand went to her throat where she had once worn a strand of fine pearls beneath a ruffle of lace. Anger squared her shoulders, and she stalked from the room.

He would hear from her later, Tom thought tiredly. He would hear from her again and again.

"Still," Nan said. "Miranda might have come by . . ."

"I wanted only to do the right thing," Tom mumbled, a hand fumbling at his blond beard. "No more than that, no less. But she somehow didn't see it that way."

"Why, we know you did," Nan answered, in a voice full of false sympathy. "The child is ungrateful, I think."

"And it's not as I haven't tried to see her," Tom went on. "Believe me, I have."

Jake's shallow blue eyes narrowed. "You have, have you? I didn't know that, Tom. And did she refuse you?"

"She? Oh, no. She didn't. My own daughter, my Miranda, would never do that. But you don't know what the place is like. They've got this small black nigger at the gate. He says nobody's home. He says Mr. Haversham's not receiving. He says—"

"Not to me, he doesn't." Jake laughed. "You just don't know the right words."

"And *you* do, I suppose?" Tom demanded sourly.

"I do," Jake answered. "I've told you that I worked off and on for John Haversham. And, as a matter of fact, I'm going there to see him today. I've had word this morning that he wants me. I'm off as soon as I finish this meal."

Tom looked thoughtful but said no more then. Later he

found Jake in the back bedroom. "You're really going to Haversham Square?" he asked.

Jake grinned, flexing his long muscular arms.

"Would you take a message to Miranda for me?"

"Why not? If she'll have it, that is. I can't promise you that, can I?"

"She will. She's my own good daughter, no matter what you think. You can be sure she'll have the message. Just ask her to visit me. Better yet, ask her when I may visit her. Tell her I long to see her. Tell her—"

"I'll tell her that you long to see a bit of Haversham gold, that's what I'll tell her," Jake laughed.

"It's not so," Tom protested. "I merely want to be certain that she's happy, and well. That all is as she hoped. I merely—"

"Yes, yes, and yes," Jake agreed with a grin.

"Never mind that. Will you take the message?" Tom asked coldly.

It would, he hoped, at least silence Susanah Kay for a little while. She was after him, night and day, to turn to advantage the Haversham connection. He wished with all his heart that he had never told her of it. But he hadn't known then that Miranda would come to him here, then go to Haversham Square to live. He hadn't known then what Miranda herself would be. And most of all, he hadn't known how his bragging words would eventually be turned against him.

"I'll tell her," Jake was saying, "exactly what you told me." Then, with a sly grin, "Is there a message to John Haversham as well?"

"No," Tom said hastily. "At least not yet."

They went downstairs together, Tom with his high round belly preceding him, and Jake following.

Jake went outside alone and found Nan waiting for him there. She nudged him with a thick elbow. "Well, Jake, what do you think?"

"That's plain enough. Tom Jervis is a small-minded, slimy little fool."

"And that's all you think?"

"That's all," Jake said shortly.

"But at least he's not such a fool as to be blind to what advantages lie open to him," she suggested.

"That's so," Jake agreed.

"Even though he may not know yet how to use those advantages."

"He's not the only one," Jake snorted.

"But you've an advantage, too," she said. "And soon you'll see how to use it."

"I will," he told her, and grinned. "Believe me, my good fat Nan. I will."

She nudged him again as he turned away. "Be certain that you give sweet Miranda my love."

SEVEN

Jake smoothed his reddish hair, and pulled the doorbell. He scuffed his boots carefully, lest Jefferson, whom he knew disliked him, would pointedly overlook any marks he made on the fine floor covering. Waiting to be admitted, Jake wished he were any place but here. It was his usual feeling before he saw John Haversham. He had known it for a long time.

When he was finally shown into the second floor study, he wished it even more.

Without acknowledging his presence in any way, John said, "They are dragging out the trial, Reed. It's beginning to be no more than show. Too many witnesses, too much idle talk. The real issues are being obscured."

Reed gave Jake an amused glance, but answered John. "I think, perhaps, they're trying to discover what the truth is."

"The truth is that Mrs. Surrat and her son are clearly guilty. At least of some sort of conspiracy. Louis Payne, too. Poor Herold is some kind of defective, I suspect."

"There are a great many ambiguities. I'm substantially

less convinced about Mrs. Surrat, for instance, than you are."

John retorted firmly, "All this talk only creates more ambiguities."

With another amused glance at the silent Jake, Reed asked, "What would you want then? That no trial be held?"

"Yank them and be done with it," John answered. "That's what will happen anyway." He turned stony gray eyes on Jake at last. "It took you long enough to get here, didn't it?"

"I came as soon as I got the message," Jake told him.

Jake was somehow shrunken in this room. His lanky muscular body seemed smaller, more flaccid. His shallow blue eyes were hangdog. He lowered his head, and shuffled his feet in a parody of humility he was completely unaware of, although it was plain to the others.

"Come here," John said. "I want to show you this map." He moved aside a mahogany box trimmed with silver that held his dueling pistols and spread out a large sheet of paper.

Jake sidled close, leaned at his shoulder, and looked down. He saw a plat of the area just north of where the half-built monument to George Washington stuck up like a jagged thumb from the shanties and markets and railroad sheds that surrounded it.

John brushed a big hand across the thick black lines. "Now you go down there, Jake, and do a head count. I want to know how many people live there. Black and white. I want it exact, a true figure. And don't try to fake it for me, because if you do, I'll know. And I want you to make a count of the houses, too, or anything that is, or can be, used as a house. That means sheds, shacks, cribs, whatever."

Jake nodded and chewed his lip but didn't speak, though there were questions in his eyes, John saw.

They had met in the train depot in New York when Jake was a skeletal-looking fourteen-year-old. The boy had made the foolish mistake of attempting to pick John's pocket. He was as clumsy then as now, and was easily caught. John had given him a beating that left him bloody and bruised, but instead of sending him on his way, had followed a whim and bought him a meal. The boy gobbled his food as if fearful that it would be taken from him, while John sat and stared, caressing the black ebony cane he had just used as a flail. Afterward, John took the boy on to Lowell, his destination then, and back to Washington City with him later. There had always been small chores for Jake to do, so John had kept him on, though Jake had been less than willing. He was seventeen when he killed a man in what he insisted was self-defense in a fight over a woman, but what, to the authorities, might have seemed cold-blooded murder. John had witnessed it and covered for him, and had owned him ever since.

Now Jake said nervously, in response to the question he had not dared ask, "Never mind what it's for. Right? I just count up how many folks live there."

John nodded. "What are you waiting for? Get yourself started, why don't you?"

Jake hesitated briefly. Then, "See, I just happened to mention, over the breakfast table in the Kayhome Arms, that I was coming here. And Mr. Jervis, he asked me to say a few words to Miranda. So if you'd just send Jefferson to say—"

"What few words?" John demanded, his face darkening.

The thought of this guttersnipe even speaking Miranda's name enraged John. The idea that they had ever had words together disgusted him.

She belonged to him, to John Haversham. He had begun to believe that she always had. He was determined that she always would. Soon . . . very soon it would be arranged.

He got to his feet, his head lowered between his shoulders, his bull-like body tense. "Well, what are you talking about?"

Meanwhile Reed drew his long legs under him and straightened in his chair. He hugged his arm against his chest, a frown on his face.

"It's nothing," Jake stammered. "Just to ask if she's well."

"And what do you have to do with her?" John rasped.

"To do with?" Jake edged a step toward the door. "Why, nothing. How could I?" But then a faint smile curled his mouth. "Except we lived in the same house for three months."

"Then is the message from you? Or her father?"

"From her father, of course," Jake said quickly. "Certainly from him. To ask if she's well."

"You may tell him that she is."

"And to ask," Jake added hurriedly, "that she visit him when she has a mind to. A personal message, you see."

"If she felt any desire to see him, she would do so," John told him.

Jake didn't answer. He took another sideways step.

Reed cleared his throat and asked suddenly, "What is he like, Miranda's father?"

"A poor man. He has nothing. It's his wife that owns the boarding house, and that from her first husband."

John cut in, "We've no interest in the Jervises. None." Then, "What are you waiting for? You have a job to do, haven't you? Or do you find it beyond you?"

"But what about Miranda?"

John said, "Don't come back here until the job is completely done. Do you understand me?"

Jake nodded and went out into the hall, peering this way and that, hoping that chance would provide him the opportunity that John refused.

He dawdled near the table, examining the silver bowl for calling cards and the silver vases of roses, and when he heard the rustle of silks, he looked up the wide curving staircase.

He saw Miranda freeze in midstep and hold to the banister.

She wore a dress of yellow with tiny buttons that caught the light. They went from her throat to her waist in a gleaming parade. Her glossy black hair was piled high and caught in a loosely woven snood. He could see the neat slippers that peeped from beneath the hoop of her skirt. It was hard to believe that she was Tom Jervis' wench, the girl he had coveted for months, and he knew now by the dryness of his mouth that he still did. Hard to believe, yes. For she belonged here, he thought. Surely she belonged here.

She stared at him, not speaking. She felt his eyes undress her, strip away the soft silk to peer at the flesh beneath. She felt them touch her, as his rude hands had once touched her.

He banished his awe, and said, a sneer in his voice, "Why, you've come far, haven't you, Miranda?"

"What do you want?" she asked coolly.

"Me?" he sputtered. "Me? I don't want anything. What makes you think I should? It's your father. He's been worried about you. All this time gone, and not a word from you. You might as well have disappeared from the town and the face of the earth."

"I saw no reason to send him my greetings."

"He feels otherwise," Jake said slyly. "He's hurt, deeply hurt. He doesn't understand you, nor why you should have turned against him."

"Oh, I think he does, at least if his memory still serves him, and it should."

Jake put on a wondering look. "Who'd have thought you heartless, Miranda?"

"Who, indeed?" she snapped. "Who ever thought of my heart at all?"

He agreed with her completely, but he would have argued that she was wrong. He saw some faint benefit to him were she to establish a connection with her father again. He didn't quite know yet how it could be worked, but he was sure that he, with Nan, would find a way.

There was no time for further discussion.

John came out from his study to stand at the top of the steps. He divided a look between Miranda and Jake, and then said coldly, "Jake, I told you to go. Why are you hanging around here still?"

"I just happened to see . . ." Jake began in a whine. "I was just on my way when Miranda . . ."

John took one step down, then another, moving slowly

and heavily, his massive shoulders hunched and his broad face thrust forward.

Jake, all menace gone from him now, choked back his excuses and explanations, and made for the door.

When he was gone, John smiled thinly at Miranda, "Sometimes the man's a fool, but he has his uses."

She found herself moving back from John, from the heavy shadow he cast over her. There was something oddly possessive, and oddly intimate, too, in the way he looked at her.

But aloud she said only, "I don't like Jake Rooker, and never will. But I doubt he's the fool you consider him."

She watched as Reed walked down the steps and then disappeared into the shadows.

He wore boots and habit, so she guessed that he would be going to the stables, and soon he would ride alone through the hot twilight, thinking she didn't know what thoughts, but wished she did.

She waited for one more moment at the window, and then, seized by determination, she turned away. She went to the looking glass. She touched her curls. She moistened her lips and pinched her cheeks to give them added color.

Surely it was time that she had a walk in the park. If he would not come to her, then she would go to him.

She heard the murmur of voices from Caroline's room as she passed by, Caroline saying, "I cannot, I cannot," and John's indistinct grating rumble.

She hurried away down the staircase and then outside.

The walk was covered with crushed stones that slipped and sang underfoot as she made her way. A family of mockingbirds, disturbed by the sound, took wing, black against the dimming sky, and reminded her of the angry crows that had swooped from the bank roof over the carriage as it pulled away from the bank with Caroline trembling in her corner, and crying out at every lance of lightning across the heavens.

"I cannot, I cannot," she had been saying. What was it that she could not do? What had John been telling her?

It was difficult to know what troubled her so, though it

was evident that something did. Just as it was evident that something troubled Reed.

Miranda's eyes sought anxiously for a glimpse of him on the lawns. But she saw no one.

She followed a narrow path beyond a thick clump of rhododendrons starred with heavy white blossoms.

At the other side of it, in a dark and sheltered place, there was the lily pond. It spread out still and wide. Great clumps of lily leaves hugging thick unopened flowers dotted the glass-like surface. Two marble benches flanked the pool, and the white graceful figure of a startled fawn seemed about to leap away into the shadows.

There was an odd quietness here, Miranda thought. A breathless quality. A sense of waiting and expectation.

This was, she had heard Stacy say, Caroline's favorite place. Miranda found herself wondering why. What did the pond, and the stillness, mean to her? What did she think as she sat here alone?

Even as Miranda wondered, and herself absorbed the magical quality of the silence, the expectation of the drifting blossom buds on the pond, the stillness of the fawn frozen forever in its leap, she listened for the sound of horse hooves in the falling dusk.

Then there was a whisper of movement in the trees. A horse nickered. A dark silhouette appeared.

Miranda caught her breath as Reed looked at her across the space between them, his face in the shadows.

It was for this that she had hoped, sought, yet she was for the moment unable to move, to smile and acknowledge him. Would he simply nod at her and turn the horse away?

He slid from the saddle with a single lithe movement. He tethered his horse to a tree's low limb and came toward her.

She rose instantly, went to meet him, saying, "I wondered if it could be you when I heard the horse."

He looked down at her, grinned. "It's usually me, isn't it? I seem to ride often these days."

"Yes," she said. "I've noticed. But is it good for your arm?"

"If not for my arm, at least it's good for my soul."

"I wondered," she told him softly. "You see, it seemed to me that lately . . . since last month even more than before . . . you've seemed so . . . so . . ." She drew a deep breath. Then, "Reed, if I offended you that day—"

He said, "You mustn't think that, Miranda. It wasn't you. You helped me. But seeing the soldiers made me remember . . . there is too much . . ."

She answered with sweet reproach in her voice and in her amber eyes. "To speak so to me must mean that you think of me as a child. But I am not a child, Reed. I can understand, perhaps even help you, really help you, if you'd let me." She yearned to touch him, to feel his lean warmth. She clasped her hands tightly together to prevent the wish from becoming an act that would embarrass both of them.

But he laughed. "No, Miranda, you're not a child, that much I know." He paused. Then, "I'm sorry I left the Van Ewards' reception that night. I should have liked to dance with you. And I will dance with you, believe me. But then, that evening it was impossible."

"Why?" she demanded. "Were your memories plaguing you then, too?"

He laughed down at her, shook his dark head, delighting in her forthrightness. "It was a touch of an old fever returning. I went to bed and nursed it away."

"But you ought to have explained," she said. "If I'd known, I—"

"I have a distaste for parading my weaknesses unnecessarily, Miranda." He moved his arm in its sling against his chest. "This is enough of a disability."

"But you are better. You'll soon be completely recovered."

"Soon," he said, and took her arm and guided her around the clump of rhododendrons back to the crushed shell path. "Come. I'll walk you to the house. Timoshen will see to my horse for me."

When his hand dropped away from her arm, she felt such a sense of loss that she nearly cried out in protest.

She looked at him quickly and saw that his eyes were veiled and his face suddenly remote, and she knew that whatever small closeness there had been between them before was now gone. He was remembering again.

She would stop him from remembering, she vowed to herself. She would not allow the past to enchain him. There must be a way to set him free, and she would find it.

Just as they reached the terrace, they heard a faint far-away cry.

Some dark thing—call it shadow, call it raven wings, call it fear—touched Miranda. The warm dark was suddenly cool.

"It was only a bird, or some small animal in the woods," Reed assured her, and motioned her toward the door, and then followed her in.

But the faint cry had been Lena's.

She had gone to the conservatory thinking that Miranda might be there, to say that Caroline had asked to see Miranda immediately. Lena was determined not to go back without her, having seen the danger signals in Caroline's flushed cheeks and blazing green eyes.

But the hot airless room had been deserted. Darkness thrust at the glass windows from outside, and shadows from the big exotic plants in which John Haversham took such pride, and which Timoshen cultivated so carefully, loomed within. In that thick damp air, Lena felt that she could hardly breathe.

She was frightened when she heard the heavy step behind her. She knew it well. She started immediately for the door.

But he was before her. John, bulking tall and ominous. Lena had always been careful that they not be alone. She had always been able to read his stony eyes. She said quickly, "Miss Caroline wants me, Mister John. And Miss Miranda, too. She's very upset. She's waiting for us because she wants—"

"Miss Caroline can wait," he said.

Only a little while before, Stacy had smiled up at him

through her lashes and moistened her lips, giving him her most provocative look. He had thought of Miranda then, and had been amused by Stacy's flirtatiousness. He knew that she was only slightly disappointed when he left her to go into the conservatory. She had hoped only to persuade him that Carleton Van Eward was more important to him than Josiah Hurley. Her pretty pouts had not convinced him, and he had told her so.

He had not known that Lena would be in this steamy, sensual place. But she was. She was slim and small, with a high, hard round rump and shapely legs. He went toward her.

She saw the stony arrogant exultant look on his face and started slowly to back away.

He said softly, "I shouldn't, Lena. I should be very still and silent, and very anxious indeed to please, if I were you. There's your whole family, you see. Not just you. And you could all go. You're free, as you well know." He smiled at her, repeating in a jeering voice, "Yes, you're free," and stood over her so that his shadow completely covered her and there was no light.

She thought of Abigail and Jefferson and Timoshen, and her mother's terrible hunger that the family remain one and together. She thought of leaving their little house and going into the lanes of Georgetown, and begging at doors for work, and begging for garbage to eat, as so many others were doing then.

She dropped her head and closed her eyes, and let his hard hands force her down to the marble bench.

She was limp, unresisting, as her black gown was thrust aside, and the ruffled apron, too, so that she felt the heat of the moist air on her revealed breasts and belly and cringing thighs. She knew that he stared at her, for she felt the long cold examining look, and then her breasts were enclosed in his hands, crushed within them, mauled and mangled so painfully that she cried out once before she could help herself.

After that, she was still. She was still, though he squeezed the tender nipples between his fingers, and then,

panting, forced her shivering legs apart, and lunged between them, holding her hips firmly as he came down
against them again and again, until she felt that she must
be torn in two, split and rent and never to be whole again.

EIGHT

Caroline stood midway down the stairs, her billowing
gown an impossible barrier to breech, with the advantage
of being above Miranda and Reed, and thus able to look
down upon them. Her blonde head was high, her green
eyes flashing and frantic. Her face was dead white, but not
dusted with rice powder, and a mottled red was on her
cheeks. She said thinly, "I sent Lena for you, Miranda. I
meant for you to come. I meant for you to come, I say!"

In some subtle way, Reed seemed to change, to harden.
He moved so that his body was interposed between the
two women, shielding Miranda. But he said in a low gentle
voice, "Caroline, we have been walking in the park. We
have not seen Lena. Miranda could not possibly have
known that you required her."

Caroline gasped audibly, and her throat worked. Her
lips writhed as she turned on him. "You! I was not speaking to you! I do not ask for your explanations, nor your
opinions. What are you, Reed? A boy. No more than a
boy. Yes, yes. That's right. A boy again, for all that
you're twenty-six years old and been to the war and come
home again. You had a wounded arm, and you make us
think it was more than an arm that was wounded. Lying
about, dreaming, brooding. John could have bought you
out of it easily for five hundred dollars, but no. You
would go. You would risk yourself for some silly idea you
had. All right. It's done. You are what you are. But don't
interfere between Miranda and me."

His face was carved alabaster. Then slowly it changed

color, blood creeping up from his collar to his hairline, suffusing his cheeks with a dull red that still left a white line rimming his tight mouth.

His voice was deeper but remained gentle, as he said, "Caroline, all this is not necessary. You're unwell. You should go and lie down. When you're yourself you'll have completely forgotten what drives you now. So—"

"Don't use John's words to me. You're not John. You're hardly a pale imitation of him. He did so much for you. So much . . . everything! What have you done for him?"

Reed answered, quietly still, "That's between my brother and me, Caroline."

"And this is between Miranda and me," she flared. "And I'll speak to her whether you give me your permission or not. Or whether you leave us or not."

"I'll not leave you," he said steadily. "So say whatever it is that you think you must say."

Miranda, listening, was enveloped in the warm glow of joy that Reed should trouble himself to defend, yes, even more than defend her. But slowly it disappeared and a bud of fear began to expand within her.

For Caroline went on shrilly, "Very well, Reed. I tell you to leave us alone. If you insist not, then listen. You may be witness to this. It's your choice. Kindly remember that." She brought her hand up, and from it dangled the amber eardrops that John had given her. "I saw you look at these, Miranda. I saw the angry avarice in your eyes when my husband presented me with these. It was not enough that we took you in, gave you clothes, food, everything you could want. It was not enough. No. There was avarice in your eyes."

Miranda's gaze widened. She suddenly began to tremble. She didn't understand. She didn't know what Caroline meant. But she knew that something terrible was about to happen.

"Yes, I saw it," Caroline went on triumphantly. "And so, when I couldn't find these today, I thought of you. Which you ought to have considered, you know. Of course I thought of you. I'm not blind. Though you may think me so." She lowered her voice then, but its shrillness remained painfully cutting. "I questioned Lena and Abigail closely first. Believe me, I did. Neither of them had seen the eardrops. And I believe them. I've known them years longer than I've known you, Miranda. And besides, they wouldn't dare to lie to me. Be sure they wouldn't. And I know of your family, too. Who are you but the cheap little offspring of a cheap little handyman? No family at all. No breeding. Nothing. A nothing, but pretending to be someone. Pretending to be kin of the Havershams. And what you really are is a common thief!"

The chandelier lights seemed to flicker and fade and brighten again, and black shadows rippled along the high white walls and the embroidered hangings and the golden framed portraits. Miranda saw and felt herself a prisoner in some evil dream. But anger freed her. Hot raging anger swept her. She drew her breath in sharply, cried, "No. No, Caroline. You must not say that. It's not true!"

She had been expecting anything but this raw and ugly assault. An assault that struck at her pride, her very being and soul. She had known from the beginning that Caroline did not like her, and probably never would. But she could not understand the anger and the irrationality that drove the older woman now. She could only fear and despise it.

"And I do say that," Caroline retorted. She waved the eardrops in Miranda's suddenly drawn, white face. "I found them, as you must know. I found them where you had hidden them in your wardrobe. Amber to match your eyes, Miranda. Do you think I didn't notice? Did you think I wouldn't understand? Hidden away in the pocket of the blue gown that I had made for you. That's where they were. So how can you pretend? You must own up to what you did, miss. You must beg for my forgiveness."

Miranda shook her head slowly from side to side in wordless denial. A lock of her hair loosened and fell against her cheek.

Reed said with pity, but with an edge in his voice, "Caroline, you must be wrong. You must try to think, to control your disordered thoughts. We're not your enemies, you know. We're your friends. You and I . . . we have known each other for a long time . . . I don't mind what you say to me. I understand. But let me take you upstairs now."

"I'm not wrong. They were there. In that pocket, just as I say. What do you answer to that?" she shrilled.

"There's some mistake." Miranda's tall slender body swayed, as if windswept. Her amber eyes sparkled with unshed tears. Tears of humiliation as well as rage. "I assure you, Caroline, I never . . . I could not . . ."

"And your assurance is nothing to me."

"But it must be," Miranda cried proudly. "I'm a Haversham, too. In spite of what you said earlier, you know that I am. You know that my word is good."

John stood listening in the small parlor. At those words a faint smile crossed his lips and then faded. How clear and certain Miranda's young voice was. How truly regal. She might be Mary Queen of Scots denying treason. He had the same pride in her that he had in all he possessed. The railroads, track and trestle, bridge and abutments, cars and engines and the men who ran them. The land, meadow and mountain. Haversham Square itself. They belonged to him, as she would belong to him. He raised a hand slowly and smoothed his disarrayed curly hair and then his sideburns. He adjusted his waistcoat. Then he moved slowly away from the closed conservatory door, through the parlor, and down the hall. He held a huge, fragrant gardenia in one hand.

"A thief," Caroline was screaming now, while Miranda and Reed stood stiffly below her.

"No," Miranda said steadily. "No. It's not true. You shall not say that to me."

John said, "Now, what's this, Caroline? I could hear your shrilling clearly outside the house itself. It sounded as if a fishwife had wandered in and was peddling her wares in Haversham Square. Or as if a pig were being slaughtered in our fine hall. Could you not moderate your tone just a little? How can Senator Morris Layton's daughter behave this way?"

She swung on him, the whole of her face flaming now,

her eyes fired with wildness, her fists clenched into the folds of her gown. "I think you should know that you've brought home to me a thief. Yes, a thief. And perhaps even worse. Though I wouldn't mention that. I wouldn't dare."

"Hadn't you better explain that ridiculous accusation?" he asked silkily. "It's quite a remarkable thing for you to say. Even for *you* to say, Caroline, much as you are prone to remarkable comments on certain occasions."

"Here it is. The proof." She waved the amber drops at him. "And Abigail will bear me out. I found them in Miranda's wardrobe. The first place I looked. Your gift to me that she coveted and took and hid."

He sensed, rather than saw, that Miranda winced. He mounted the steps in measured strides that were heavily emphatic. He took Caroline by the shoulders, his fingers biting into her flesh. But he said coolly, "I think you must try to control yourself. If not, you'll be more ill. You're sure to have, at the least, another one of your awful headaches, aren't you? Or perhaps a different kind of collapse. And what will that accomplish? I insist that you come with me to your room at once and draw a calm breath, and then we'll hear the rest of this."

He glanced down at Miranda's anguished eyes and felt a pang of regret that she must suffer. He would, he promised himself, make it up to her in every way. He said nothing more, but under the force of his hands, Caroline began to retreat slowly up the stairs, mumbling, "She did take them."

"Be still," he ordered. And then to Miranda, "If you'll come with us, I'll settle it quickly, believe me."

"There's nothing to settle," Reed told him. "Caroline is ill. She doesn't mean a word of this. Allow her to rest, and—"

John didn't look at Reed, but ordered, "Allow me to decide."

He moved Caroline slowly to the top of the staircase, and then into her room. When he let go of her shoulders, she shuddered and sank onto the pink divan.

He moved from one carved wall sconce to the other,

lighting the gas, and slowly the room was suffused with a pale pink light.

A summer wind billowed against the drapes and they swirled around the windows and then fell limp and still once more, as limp and still as Caroline herself.

"If you'll excuse me," Miranda said from the doorway, "I think perhaps—"

"Wait," he said. He looked down at Caroline. "Now, my dear, I am sure you wish to apologize."

"Please," Miranda whispered. "There is no need."

Without looking at her, John asked, "Then tell me, Miranda. Did you take the eardrops?"

She drew herself up, clenching her hands into fists. Her cheeks burned, and her eyes, too. "No," she answered. "No. You heard me say so before. No. I did not. And you must believe me. I swear. I swear—"

Caroline raised her drooping head to shrill, "They were in your—"

John said, "Caroline, please. There's been some ridiculous mistake made obviously. You just heard Miranda's answer."

"But I know that—"

"Please," he repeated gently. "Must you prolong this scene? Must you embarrass me so in this way? Must you make so very clear to our young kinswoman that you . . . that you . . ."

Caroline's eyes flashed with sudden tears. She knew now that she had made a grave error. She saw how foolish it had been to accuse Miranda openly. It had only provoked John's anger and disbelief. These would be turned against her. And yet she was certain. She began, "John, you mustn't—"

He went on, as if she hadn't spoken. ". . . that you sometimes do make these awful mistakes? That you're not always aware of what you do? Now, we are all family here. We must be candid with each other. You know, Caroline, and Reed will bear me out, that this isn't the first time you've made such a . . . such a . . . mistake. Is it?"

"This is different," she said, all ire gone from her face and voice. She was sulky now, retreating. She had a sudden sense that she had twice gone into the blue and white room that was Miranda's. She remembered faintly moving through a midafternoon stillness, as Abigail had clumped down the servants' steps, and opening a wardrobe door. But she saw the granite gray of John's eyes. She roused herself. "I don't see how I could make such a mistake. I know what I found. I know where I found them."

"One never does see how one makes the mistakes that occur. But still, it will happen."

Miranda, bewildered, stared first at the one, then at the other. She could not understand these half-completed sentences. She did not know to what John referred, and to what Caroline responded. Did Caroline often mislay her property and then accuse others of theft? But if that were so, how had the eardrops come to be in Miranda's wardrobe? They could not possibly have come there by mischance. They would have had to be deliberately left there. But who could have done such a thing? Who except Caroline herself? And why?

Caroline said faintly, "Perhaps, somehow, I was in error after all," and lowered her eyes.

"You must apologize," John told her. "It is quite a terrible thing to accuse Miranda unjustly in such a way."

Caroline looked up. It was because of the deeds, she thought, the deeds to her land, and because of Miranda, too, that he was willing to humiliate her in this way, that he so enjoyed humiliating her in this way. Aloud, she said, "Miranda, forgive me." But there was no apology in her thin voice.

Miranda realized with an inner shock that when she looked into Caroline's eyes, she saw hate, and when Caroline returned her gaze to John, Miranda saw in her eyes not only hate but fear as well.

"Then we're all friends again," he said comfortably. "And we'll forget our foolish words." His even voice altered. He smiled at Miranda. "Here you are, my dear. I brought this in for you," and he held out to her the gardenia he had carried upstairs with him, the one he had plucked from its nest of leaves over Lena's bowed head and trembling body.

Miranda turned scarlet. It was as if flame itself swept up the smooth column of her throat and flickered on the curves of her cheeks. She lifted her hand in a protesting gesture.

Reed felt a coldness settle on him. He knew that John never acted without purpose. To offer Miranda that flower before Caroline, and after what had just happened, was only to anger his wife.

Miranda said unwillingly. "Oh, no. I can't take it. It's much too beautiful. It must float in a silver bowl in the morning room where we'll all enjoy it." Her eyes flashed anxiously toward Caroline. She saw the stony mask freeze on the older woman's haggard face. "I can't, John."

He smiled at her. "But, my dear, I promised you a gift. Don't you remember? You must take it. I insist."

Two days later, Reed suggested to Miranda that she accompany him on a canoe trip down the river.

It was the first time he had invited her to go out with him alone, and as she flew happily to prepare herself, she felt her heart lighten and heard herself humming. She put on a yellow dress, one fringed and flounced at throat and hem, but she left off the hoop that would make entry into the boat less than graceful. She slipped her pearls around her throat, and thought of her grandmother and smiled. Martha Appleton would approve. Her hat was trimmed with a yellow drape of veil and tiny bows, and her parasol matched it perfectly by grace of Mrs. Bannion's magical talents.

She and Reed rode across Georgetown, then along the Canal Road to Jacob's Landing. There they left the gig with a small Negro boy from a nearby shack to mind it, and crossed over the canal on the narrow wooden planks of the lock.

Reed hired the boat, helping Miranda settle herself safely with cushions at her back and her parasol overhead. Then, favoring his bad arm still in its sling, he pushed off and swung himself in, in one motion.

"Is it all right?" she asked, suddenly worried. "Are you sure that your arm won't trouble you, Reed?"

He balanced the paddle with one hand and slipped the sling off his arm. "I think exercise will be good for it, and for me."

The sun was very clear and hot, the air very still. A bluish haze lay along the Virginia shore, and the river was like a wide curved brown velvet ribbon stretched between the two banks furred with trees.

Small busy steamships passed, sending out ripples that made the canoe dance, and made tooting signals at each other. Barges laden with coal and great stacks of stripped lumber moved by so slowly that they hardly seemed to make their way.

The ferry from Georgetown to Alexandria carried a load of marketers and businessmen from one shore to the other, and a fleet of small fishing boats drifted at anchor.

Miranda lay back on her cushions, watching as he stroked the paddle slowly and carefully. She saw the muscles tighten and loosen in his arms, and she had to look away from him, from the intentness in his face and his set mouth.

He said, smiling at her then, "We very nearly had company, Miranda."

She raised her dark brows in question.

"Stacy," he explained. "I hope you don't mind that I discouraged her. I said that the canoe would not hold three, and that I doubted I could manage anything else. She decided that she would be content to stay at home with Caroline when I lied and said I could not swim."

Miranda laughed. "Perhaps she would have changed her mind if she knew that I can swim. There was a stream near our cottage in Dealeyton. I spent much time there."

"Be careful," he grinned. "I may try you."

"And welcome. It's a warm day."

"Anyway, I think it better that Caroline not be alone so much," Reed went on.

Miranda averted her face as the chill of remembering touched her.

"We must speak of it, Miranda. It's important that you understand. Caroline can't help herself. She's ill, truly ill, though it's a sickness that has no name. I've seen others like her. In the Army, it was. Men who took laudanum for strength so that they could keep going when all their inner resources were gone. Physicians who would have collapsed in their surgical tents but for it, and they and their patients died. And then, something happens to them . . . What laudanum gives in its brown liquid, and opium in its small pills, what they give, for they are the same, they gradually take away. That strength, that confidence and ease ebb, and a terrible weakness of mind and heart and body prevail."

Miranda shuddered. "But how could it happen to Caroline? Why does she allow it?"

"I think that perhaps she can't help herself, as I told you. If there is a cure, I don't know it. Though perhaps someday there will be one." He stroked silently for a moment, and the canoe moved smoothly. Then he said, "I was just a boy when she and John married, and away at school. So I didn't grow to know her very well in the beginning. But she was good to me then, and later, too, when I came down to Washington City. I'm troubled about her, but I don't know what I can do."

A small worm of jealousy moved within Miranda. She noted it wryly and asked herself if this was what Caroline had felt when John offered the gardenia to her? If it was, then Caroline had her sympathy again.

Reed went on, "I think their childlessness has embittered both of them."

She murmured an agreement, admiring the way his silver-gray eyes were set under his brow and the crisp waves of his well-brushed hair. In these moments, neither John nor Caroline seemed to matter. She wished there were some way to tell Reed so.

But now he fell silent, handling the paddle gracefully. The canoe drifted past warehouses and docks, and a foundry that poured black smoke into the still air.

He glanced at her, wishing he remembered how to make conversation. He had once had the reputation of being gallant enough. But he surely deserved it no longer. However she seemed comfortable enough in the quietness between them.

At last he said, "I had thought we might go as far as Washington's house at Mount Vernon, but perhaps, if you don't mind, we might stop and have the banquet Abigail prepared for us somewhat sooner."

"Your arm, Reed?" she asked, suddenly anxious.

"My stomach." He grinned. "I'm hungry, and we're hard by a good place to feed it."

"Then let's stop by all means," she agreed.

He guided the boat slowly to an island bank and rose carefully, making the canoe fast to an overhanging bush. Then he stepped out and offered her his hand.

She saw that his face had become drawn, and knew that his arm pained him. She didn't mention it, however. She gathered her yellow skirts and moved forward cautiously, catching his outstretched hand. The canoe shifted under her, throwing her off balance.

She might have fallen into the river, but he pulled her to his chest and lifted her to firm ground, and she stood close to him within the circle of his arm, breathless and with her heart pounding.

She raised her face slowly and looked into his eyes for a long moment.

Then he bent his head and pressed his lips to hers. Her arms went around him, clinging fiercely.

It was this that she had wanted since she had first seen him, this that she had waited for. She let her mouth, her body, tell him what she felt for a long suspension of time.

Then, very gently, he took her arms from around his neck. He smiled down at her and patted her cheek.

"Come along," he said, his voice deeper than ever. "You must be starved. Let's have at our feast."

He took the napkin-covered basket from the canoe and led her up and around three tall rocks to a spot that he said had been his favorite since he first discovered it soon after coming to Washington City to live.

She spread a linen cloth, and they settled side by side with a bottle of white wine between them, and thinly sliced chicken sandwiches on salt-risen bread, and a huge bunch of purple grapes.

He was touched and disquieted by her presence, and the feelings it stirred in him. He had asked her to come out with him in the hope that such a diversion would wipe away the bitterness of Caroline's behavior. But he knew now that the gesture had become more than that, at least to him.

He sought to distract himself by saying, "The pressures on the president are building up to fever pitch. It's a sad thing to observe. There are so many men in the Congress who intend to exploit the fallen South as if it were not our own. The accounts in *Harper's Weekly* are worrying."

She nodded gravely, watching the way his lips moved and the way his head went back when he tipped the glass to swallow wine.

"They'll destroy everything we paid so heavily to win, if they're allowed to succeed," Reed went on.

Again she nodded gravely.

"If only Lincoln hadn't been murdered. He was truly a man with no malice, Miranda. A man who would have brought the Union together again."

She listened, wishing that he would not talk with such forced interest of what hardly mattered to him, or to her, at that moment.

She drew off her bonnet and set it aside, and smoothed her gown over her knees.

Watching her, he fell silent.

She said, "You must have been lonely, Reed. Always away at school. With no family of your own. And then the Army . . ."

Instead or replying, he said, "And you, Miranda, do you miss your family?"

"I have no family," she said fiercely. She told him, in a quick rush of words, of her mother, then her father. Her voice softened and her words slowed as she spoke of her grandmother.

"Then you are happy with us?" he asked finally.

"Of course," she said. "How could I not be? You are kind, and John, and—"

Reed said, "You mustn't suddenly say to me that Caroline has been kind to you."

"No. But as you told me," Miranda countered, "she does not mean it."

But Caroline *did* mean her cruelties, Miranda knew. And that was what troubled her. Ill Caroline might be, and probably was, yet her distraught state was revealing of her true feelings.

"And what of Dealeyton? Do you think of it sometimes?" Reed was asking.

"Dealeyton?" She laughed softly. "Why, Reed, that town and our cottage there were strange places to me. It was as if I had blundered at my birth into the wrong life. I never belonged there. Never."

He was silent now. She looked up at him.

He watched her as he set his glass aside.

Then, with a smile, he took her into his arms again.

NINE

The landau was open because the day was fine, and decorated with red, white, and blue bunting as John had ordered, in honor of the first Independence Day celebration since the end of the war.

Timoshen perched on his front seat, in livery and black silk hat, and drove proudly past the flag-decked buildings on Pennsylvania Avenue.

"Do you know," Caroline said thoughtfully, "I believe this is a year, almost to the day, when we took the carriage out to Fort Stevens, to see the fighting up close. General Early had encamped near Rockville, and the rumors were terrible."

She went on, describing that day. The city had crouched in fear, expecting a Southern strike into its very heart. The sky had been blue, cloudless, but a wreath of smoke hung at the horizon, as if cannon had already been fired. The militia, the police, soldiers wounded and whole, on leave and on duty, had been rushed out Thirteenth Street. The lanes and roadways were clogged with gigs and carts and carriages, and snorting horses and sweating men.

John had determined that he would learn at first hand what was happening, and had, at her insistence, allowed her to accompany him.

The dusty drive was hot, frustratingly slow. But at last they reached the fort and climbed down behind the embankments. The President was there, too, studying the situation. There was a flurry of excitement when musket shots came flying over the barricades, and a young lieutenant yanked at the President's sleeve, and cried, "Get yourself down, you fool!" and the President had grinned and obeyed.

Listening to Caroline's smooth controlled voice, Miranda wondered at the change in the older woman.

She looked slim and elegant in her pink dress. The color became her fair skin and the gleaming coils and curls of her piled-high blonde hair. Both the high collar and the sleeve cuffs of the gown were trimmed with Belgium lace, and she carried a pink parasol.

Ever since the invitation to tea at the White House arrived, she had been as excited as Miranda herself, though she had made it quite plain that she had visited that august place before.

Now Timoshen turned the landau into the tree-lined driveway.

Miranda leaned forward and caught her breath. Though she had passed it several times before, the building had never looked as lovely as it did in the clear light of that July afternoon.

The slim lovely columns of the portico . . .

The long, balanced windows . . .

The simple stateliness of form . . .

It was like a dream to her. The landau came to a stop. John stepped down, offered his hand to Caroline, then to Stacy. Reed stepped down and offered his hand to Miranda.

She smiled her thanks but couldn't speak for the excitement that crowded her throat.

She moved with the others through a laughing throng, and then, quite suddenly, she heard John asking, "Mr. President, may I present my wife Caroline?"

Andrew Johnson was short and sturdily built. He had deep-set stubborn eyes, hair swept back from a high square forehead to curl on his collar, and a hard mouth. But now he was smiling as he said, "It is a pleasure, ma'am. I've known your husband for some time. He used to visit me often at Kirkwood House when I was Vice-President. And now I have the honor to see you at last."

"It is my honor, sir," she said.

"You are Senator Layton's daughter, are you not?" President Johnson went on, and at her smiling assent, "Yes, I thought I remembered that. A great loss to all of us when he died."

"And the rest of my party," John said smoothly, seeing that others were bearing down upon them and would soon begin adroit maneuvers to draw the President away. "My cousin, Miranda Jervis . . ."

He continued, naming Stacy and then Reed.

They each acknowledged the introduction, and the President spoke a few words to each. But Miranda heard nothing of what he said. She had curtsied and smiled automatically. She was so caught up in the wonder of the meeting, of being in the White House garden, that she could hardly take it in.

Her heart-shaped face was incandescent with delight, and her amber eyes glowed as she watched the President disappear into a new group of well-wishers.

She, Miranda Jervis, was in the White House. She had just exchanged greetings with the man who was President of the United States.

And, oddly, in spite of her wonder, she knew that it was right. She belonged here, among these people. She was, within her very soul, one of them. Some gentle finger of fate had touched her at her birth and made it so.

"He is really quite handsome," Stacy said, and then,

lowering her voice, "though they do say that he's a most fearful drunkard."

"It was a mere accident," John told her. "The man has no head for drink, and he was very nervous the day of the inauguration. Gossips made of it what it was not."

"As gossips always do," Caroline said.

Reed found it impossible to take his eyes from Miranda's excited face. There was about her such a compelling quality. She was like a rose among daisies, diminishing the glow of the other women present, and there were among them some of the great acknowledged beauties in society. He saw, as John shepherded them to the long trestle tables where refreshments had been laid out, that his brother, too, glanced often at Miranda. It was a recognition that disturbed Reed.

He said, as she glided along beside him, the tall slimness of her body rising gracefully from the profuse fullness of her white skirt, "You're very happy today, Miranda."

"Yes," she breathed. "It's a wonderful day. I am here, in this place, and I can hardly believe it."

She did not know where first to look, what first to absorb. Everywhere there were the famous, the wealthy, the powerful. Everywhere people of consequence. And, as she had always known, she was one of them.

With a silver-trimmed crystal punch cup in her gloved hand, she turned away from the table.

The military band beneath the pink canopy of the pavilion struck up a tune, and the blare of the trumpets seemed to announce to Miranda her triumph.

"This is the way it used to be," Caroline said softly. "When I was my father's hostess, just as Martha Patterson is *her* father's hostess." At Miranda's blank look, Caroline went on, plainly proud of her knowledge. "You see, Mrs. Johnson is an invalid. And . . ." Her voice trailed away. She spun her parasol gently. Then she said, "We knew everyone, and everyone knew us. We—"

"Why, Caroline," Stacy laughed. "You still do. I think it's so silly to dwell upon those days which are, after all, hardly different from now."

"Not to you, perhaps. For you were not here. But to me, yes. And besides, I am different," Caroline answered.

John and Josiah Hurley stood just a few feet away.

"Charming," Josiah murmured, stroking his black beard. "Completely charming, John." He did not need to say that he was referring to Miranda.

John knew that. He agreed shortly. It had begun to annoy him that other men might look at Miranda and see what he saw. He said, "Have you discussed the trestle bridge with your committee, Josiah?"

"In no detail, John. There has been no time. It's difficult, you see, with Congress in adjournment. So many members have returned to give their fiery speeches before their constituencies, and—"

"I didn't believe that it was a matter to be handled swiftly, Josiah."

"—and then" Josiah went on, his blue eyes suddenly hooded, "I fear that it'll take a bit of . . . of . . . spreading around, John."

"That can probably be arranged, when and if it becomes necessary," John said smoothly. He didn't think it important to tell Josiah that he had offered the two hundred and fifty shares of stock as bait only. There was another two hundred and fifty already earmarked for the purpose. They would be proffered when the situation demanded it, as John was certain that it would.

"Then, perhaps, and if you don't feel the pressure of time—"

"I have the rights of way," John answered, lowering his head between his thick shoulders. "When the bridge is built, the rails will be laid. But it's a long-term project."

"The creation of a city from a village must be a long-term project," Josiah retorted. "If it's possible at all."

John saw that Tad Layton and Senator Van Eward had joined the ladies, and unobtrusively he edged Josiah toward them.

Stacy immediately seized him by the arm, crying, "Josiah, there you are! I have been waiting all this time for you to turn your head just this way."

"I've been looking at none other," he responded, preening.

"Then come, you must show me the flowers." Her black eyes burned like embers in her oval face, and her voluptuous mouth was pursed sweetly.

"You will put them all to shame," he told her, and with apologies to the others, he led her away.

"You look well," Tad said, smiling at Caroline.

"Thank you," she answered. "You remain my favorite cousin."

"And you," he went on to Miranda.

She smiled at him, and then at Senator Van Eward, whose wistful gaze had followed Stacy as she walked away with Josiah.

His dour sister tugged his arm. "Carleton, let us find some shade. The sun is hot. Your head will be burned."

"Yes," he agreed. When he led her away, it was to follow directly in the footsteps of Stacy and Josiah.

There was a swirl and shift of groups. The ladies in hoops and crinolines seemed to float through some formal and patterned dance, bowing and smiling as they changed positions, took new partners, and then moved on to meet old ones again.

John, once more watching Miranda, knew again his need to possess her. She must be his. His wife. She was young and healthy and beautiful. She would give him the sons that Caroline denied him. She would be everything to him that Caroline was not. She was a Haversham from the top of her head to the tips of her toes. A Haversham . . .

Beside him, Tad said quietly, "Caroline appears much better today, John."

He nodded but did not answer.

"It's a relief to me. I had become very concerned about her."

John turned his head slowly, his stony gray eyes boring into Tad's more mild blue eyes. "I take it that you're concerned about her health."

"Yes, of course. What else?"

John grinned, but there was no mirth in that twist of sensual lips. "The deeds," he suggested. "You might have become concerned about those. Concerned enough, in fact, to speak to me of them before this."

Tad hesitated, then said, "John, you must try to understand this. Caroline has a sentimental attachment to the land that has been in her family for so many years, and to what her father left to her."

"Old Morris was a fool. What did that land bring him, and what is it bringing Caroline now?"

"It's not in the realm of profit," Tad replied. "It's in her feelings. A woman's feelings."

John laughed shortly. "Feelings! It's a madness."

Tad lowered his voice to say, "You're not suggesting that you are . . . that you are in some sort of a bind, John? If that were so, then it would be quite different. I could try to persuade her . . ."

John grinned again. "It's not a question of need, Tad. It's a question of wanting. Of big plans. I won't allow Caroline, or you either, to stand in my way. I shall have those deeds."

"I will not turn them over to you, John. Not without Caroline's express and written permission. I am sorry to have to say that. But it's my duty to her as a cousin, as well as my duty to her as her banker."

"I've not asked for them yet," John retorted. "You needn't begin to be so defensive so soon. When the time comes, she'll give you her permission. Both written and oral."

"In that case," Tad said uneasily, "it will be all right."

"Of course," John agreed. "Why would it not be?"

"Do you suppose that there will be fireworks this evening?" Miranda was asking.

The British ambassador smiled at her eager face, and drawled, "My dear, there must be fireworks, and bonfires at every corner, and general rejoicing. You are celebrating the success of a revolution against my country."

He was a very tall man with dark hair and a dark curled moustache. His uniform had gold epaulets and great loops of braid, and he wore three orders on his chest.

She said, smiling back to him, "But we are enemies no longer. How could we be? We have so much in common."

"I am pleased, and relieved to hear you say so," the ambassador told her. "Since I arrived in your city I have heard a great many anguished comments about certain of my compatriots."

"But you yourself? You do like Washington City, do you not?" she demanded.

"I? Of course I do, my dear. Regrettably, there have been, before me, a long string of Englishmen who came to carp. There was Dickens, you know. And Mrs. Frances Trollope. Thackeray alone was kind. But the others made my mission no easier, I assure you."

"It doesn't matter what some few have said. We remain brothers and sisters," she told him.

"I would be gratified to claim that honor," he said with a bow.

She smiled to acknowledge the compliment, and then went on, "In fact, we Havershams have family still in England. Perhaps you know some of them."

"Havershams. Why, yes, of course. They have holdings in an adjoining county to mine. Very profitable cotton mills, though Ian Haversham, I'm told, is looking for other interests."

"Then you must come and meet my cousin, John Haversham, for he knows them, too, though I myself do not."

"I shall be delighted, my dear."

John was plainly pleased with Miranda's conquest.

He and the British ambassador fell into immediate conversation, while Miranda, drawn away into a group composed of Stacy and Josiah and Carleton Van Eward, listened to their bright chatter and searched in the milling crowd of ladies and gentlemen for Reed's tall form.

She saw him finally, standing with Caroline and Mary Van Eward. His dark head was bent, his face intent on the two women's conversation, but at the same time he appeared to be faintly uncomfortable.

Miranda excused herself and went directly to him,

though she was careful to make it appear that she had come that way by chance.

Caroline acknowledged her arrival with a jerk of her head. A wisp of blonde hair had fallen from her elaborate coiffure, and her pink hat seemed to have slid sideways on the coils and curls. There was a sudden high color in her cheeks, and her green eyes glittered.

"It is a ridiculous position to take, Mary," she was saying. "Nothing more can be said of it but that it is ridiculous."

"Why, I don't think so," Mary retorted sourly. "A man must have his choice. If he wishes to remain a bachelor, then I see no reason for him to marry."

"But of course men must marry," Caroline snapped. "It is immoral. Totally and completely and finally immoral. The Bible says to wed and be fruitful. Yes, yes." Her voice was suddenly shrill. "That's what it says. Be fruitful." Her glazed green eyes were full of tears. They gathered and spilled over to run down her hollow cheeks. She didn't seem to notice them. She went on, "You must not pretend otherwise. It is wicked, evil."

Mary, frowning, said harshly, "That's your opinion only. A bachelor is as moral as any married man."

"And how can he be?" Caroline jeered. "Men being what they are."

"And what of women? What of a spinster such as myself?" Mary demanded. "Are you saying that the same applies to me?"

"You?" Caroline's eyes narrowed. "You cannot help yourself, I suppose. Women cannot help being spinsters, can they? And besides, they are not the same as men. They are not driven . . ."

Her words faded away as she saw John towering over a group of men and ladies just a few feet off. She saw him throw back his head and laugh, and a hot hunger swept through her. The bright sun faded. The drums and bugles and flutes were gone. The White House—chandelier and portico and gleaming columns—began to shimmer in a dark mist. A trembling shook her thin body. But women are driven, too, she thought. I am driven.

Reed said softly, "Caroline?"

She shook her head violently. She shrilled, "I detest self-righteous women." She glared at Mary Van Eward and turned on her heel.

"Forgive us," Reed said, and hurried after her.

"That woman is mad," Mary muttered. "Completely and irrevocably mad. How fortunate that her poor father is no longer alive to suffer the sight of it."

"I'm so sorry," Miranda told Mary. "You mustn't be offended. Caroline is ill, you see. No more than that."

"You're a kind child," Mary answered. She looked sideways toward where her brother and Stacy were laughing, chestnut head and white head close together. "Unlike certain other rather obvious flirts," she added, as she sailed away to join them.

Miranda caught up with Reed and Caroline under the poplar trees.

Caroline leaned trembling against the trunk of one, her haggard face shadowed by dancing leaves. "I'm all right," she was saying. "It's nothing, Reed. Please leave me alone."

"Perhaps there's something I can do," he said anxiously. "Caroline, won't you let me help you? You cannot collapse here."

"I'll not collapse," she cried. "You aren't able to make me. I will not shame myself. I never have. Not in all the years I was my father's hostess. I will not now."

Reed hesitated, not knowing what to say, knowing that with Caroline in this state, nothing he tried would be right.

The world was swimming before her very eyes. A pale shimmering nearly blinded her.

But she knew when John's shadow fell over her. She felt the chill of his presence touch her. She made herself reach out to him. Her fingers curled around his hand, sought in its palm for the pill she hoped to find.

It was not there, but she clung to him and raised her eyes beseechingly.

He released himself, taking her firmly by the elbow. "Come," he said coldly. "I'll take you home at once."

TEN

On July 7th, John and Josiah Hurley, together with Jake Rooker, were driven by Timoshen from Haversham Square through Georgetown and across Washington City to the federal penitentiary at Greenleaf Point to observe the executions.

That day Timoshen was uneasy. He did not sit up straight and proud on the driver's seat but hunched down, gripping the reins tightly in sweating hands and shooting nervous glances from side to side.

He winced visibly as they passed the Octagon House on 18th Street, when Josiah said, "It looks as if the ghosts still walk in that place, doesn't it?"

There had been rumors of the haunting of the great mansion for some forty years. But it was now being used as a federal hospital, and the ghosts to which Josiah referred were the walking wounded, who gathered in the sun below the Palladian window and leaned on their crutches, whispering about the day's events.

All along the route between Pennsylvania Avenue and the Arsenal Gate, there were ranks of uniformed troops. They stood at attention under the scorching sun, armed and ready to quell any disorder that might arise.

They rolled past the Old Capitol Building, used for Congressional sessions while the Capitol itself was being rebuilt after destruction by the British in the War of 1812, but now another prison.

From one of its boarded-up windows came a shouted and unmelodic rendition of a Confederate song.

Timoshen winced again, but the other men laughed.

Both John and Josiah were dressed soberly for the occasion in well-brushed broadcloth and crisp plain white linen. Jake Rooker wore black broadcloth, too. But his was rusty with age and wear, and both jacket and trousers

116

were too large for him, though they had been altered from John's hand-me-downs.

The sourly sung Confederate song faded away as the carriage jolted on.

A heavy silence hung over the street as Timoshen drew up before the sentry-guarded gate in the high red brick wall.

The three men stepped down into the quiet staring crowd, and the carriage rolled quickly away.

Josiah presented his credentials, introduced John and Jake, and received an impressive salute before being passed inside.

The courtyard within was full of people, huddled and whispering.

High on the walls, soldiers made long black silhouettes against the blue of the sky.

A full detachment of more soldiers, armed with muskets, clubs at their belts, waited opposite the ugly scaffolding. It was made of fresh wood, white, clean, and soft enough to splinter at the edges. In some places the sap still ran, its scent reminiscent of shady forests and the sweetness of growing things.

Near that menacing structure, umbrella-carrying civilians, there to bear witness, discussed the imprisonment of Captain Harry Wirz, the commanding officer of the prison camp at Andersonville, and speculated upon what his sentence would be.

There was a strange stillness in the place. It had settled there the day before, when at eleven in the morning, Major-General John F. Hartranft, governor and commandant of the military prison, had the prisoners brought out, and read to them, in a deep slow impressive voice, the findings and sentences determined after a seven-week trial. There were four who were condemned to death by hanging.

A hushed murmur went through the courtyard as these four were now led, blinking and staggering, into the sunlight, each accompanied by a guard and a churchman.

They walked slowly, in shackles and chains, to chairs

beneath the scaffold, and when they were seated, its dark shadow fell over them.

John, watching, felt nothing. It was an unreal spectacle to him. But then, as had begun to happen to him often, there crept into his mind's eye the image of Miranda. Her long slender throat, the tilt of her head. She was life. Here was the stench of impending death. He felt his gorge rise, and sweat broke out on his big face.

The chaplain came forward to offer a short prayer. He asked for forgiveness for the souls of the condemned. John found himself thinking that the prayer might better ask for forgiveness for the souls of those here to witness the thing to come.

Beside him, Josiah Hurley was still stroking his black beard, his blue eyes alight with some internal excitement. Jake shuffled his feet and looked grim.

The commandant ordered the prisoners to rise to their feet, and now the shadows were gone from their faces and sunlight exposed them.

One of the guards held an umbrella over the head of Mary Surrat, while another tied a white rope around her full black skirt.

Pale hoods were then thrown over each of the bowed heads. The faceless bodies remained on their feet, trembling, wavering. But some awful thing had happened. They seemed, while still in life, to have lost their humanity. They were mere effigies, straw-stuffed symbols wearing hoods, not a flesh-and-blood woman, not three young men.

There was a signal from somewhere beyond John's range of vision. At one-thirty the trap fell.

Jake gasped, "Oh, dear God," and shut his eyes, his angular face suddenly as gray as the dust beneath his boots.

Josiah murmured wordlessly.

John stood stiff and still, staring at the limp hanging bodies.

A thick hot breeze came up and touched Mary Surrat's skirt, and for a moment, as it fluttered around her, confined by the white rope that held it, she seemed alive again.

There was an audible whisper from the group of observers. John wiped the new sweat from his face.

The board of surgeons moved slowly from body to body, and then, at one-fifty, a second signal was given.

The commandant announced, "These prisoners are dead."

"Let's go," Jake said. "I don't know why you wanted to come see this anyhow."

But he did know. There was an awesome power to be tapped in seeing death formalized by soldiers and prayer, rope and trap. Such death made the witness believe that he would live forever. And Jake knew why he had been told to join the group. It meant that John was angry with him, reminding him that he was not, no matter what he liked to pretend to himself, a free man.

Now John confirmed this by putting a big hand on the back of Jake's neck, and asking, "What's wrong? Do you have a pain here?" and grinning.

It was a not very oblique reference to the thing John had held over Jake all these years, the thing that allowed John to own him.

But Jake shrugged the big hand away and slanted his mouth down. "It's my neck. I'll worry for it."

"You'd better," John told him.

"It's over," Josiah said, with a sigh in his voice, and led the way through the crowd and past the four bodies, now cut down and laid in a row for removal.

Outside the grim gates, the soldiers stood in tense groups, watching the silent crowds.

Timoshen pulled up at John's signal, and they drove swiftly across the quiet city.

When they reached Haversham Square, John poured each of them a stiff shot of whiskey. They downed it together. Then Josiah excused himself, saying that he had promised to take Stacy driving.

When they were alone in the study, John asked, "Now tell me, Jake, what about that job I gave you to do?"

"It's not finished yet. It takes a while. You start a count, and somebody comes and somebody goes." He added quickly as John's dark brows drew together in a frown, "You said you wanted it right, and I'm trying to do it right."

"I see," John said. He regarded Jake coldly. "You seem much affected by what you saw this morning."

"A man would be," Jake returned heatedly, "if he had a heart, that is."

John smiled. "For once we agree."

Jake edged toward the door. "Anything else you want of me?"

"Not at the moment."

Jake's mouth turned down. "Miranda's father was asking about her again. I told him I hadn't seen her. She's here, isn't she?"

"What's that to you, or her father either?"

Jake shrugged. "Nothing to me. Don't get me wrong. But her father . . . well, that's different. The girl *is* under age. He has the right to be—"

Jake stopped with a squeal as John caught him, bunching his shirt in a big hand, and threw him against the wall.

"You don't talk about her," John snarled. He caught Jake, shook him, and once more slammed him into the wall. The shirt tore in his hand, and he threw the shreds of it to the floor.

Jake, gasping, whined, "It wasn't me, I tell you. It was what old Tom Jervis said, and I thought you ought to know."

"Get out of here," John said coldly. "Do your job, and come back when you're through."

Miranda was in her bedroom when Lena came to say that Caroline wished to be read to.

Miranda immediately went to Caroline's room.

Tad Layton was on the threshold, taking leave of his cousin. He said firmly, "It'll be all right, Caroline. Don't worry. But remember, you must make the effort, too." He turned and bowed to Miranda, giving her a curiously searching look, she thought, before he nodded and passed on.

"He's a good man," Caroline said when Miranda seated

herself near the pink divan. "We're close, almost brother and sister. There are times when one needs such closeness."

"Yes," Miranda agreed, looking into Caroline's thin face. She knew the emotion to which the older woman referred. She had, it seemed to her now, lived with that need all of her life. There had been only her grandmother to turn to for solace, support, or advice. And now there was no one. She told herself quickly that she must not allow herself to contract Caroline's own weakness. She, Miranda, needed no one. She was strong in herself. She must be.

Caroline was saying, "Will you have a sweet? Tad had them brought up to me from Richmond. Velatis makes them. And now, perhaps soon, Tad says, they will move to Washington City."

Miranda accepted a chocolate from the gaily trimmed box and nodded her appreciation for its exceptional flavor.

"I think," Caroline went on, "that Tad would do anything for me. And I for him."

"You're fortunate then, and so is he."

Caroline turned her head, giving a sudden bitter laugh. "Oh, yes, I am certainly fortunate." Then, "Go on, Miranda. Read something."

"What would you like?"

"I don't know. I don't care."

Miranda rummaged through the stack of materials on the bedside table. There was an old issue of *Harper's Weekly,* folded open to a Thomas Nast cartoon. There was a worn copy of *David Copperfield,* another of the tales of Washington Irving. She shuddered at a tattered playbill advertising the appearance of John Wilkes Booth in a play called *The Apostate* at Ford's Theater, and smiled at a pamphlet of poems by a man named Walt Whitman, who had been pointed out to her by Stacy as they rode one day on 19th Street.

"Can't you find anything?" Caroline asked. "Then read from Mrs. Southworth's novel."

Miranda took up the copy of *Ishmael.* She opened it and began to read. The words rolled smoothly and with expression from between her lips. Independent of them, the thoughts rolled smoothly through her head. She had heard Josiah describing to Stacy the grisly scene witnessed that morning at Greenleaf Point. It had seemed indelicate of him to go into such sickening detail, but Stacy, listening with her eyes wide, had not seemed to mind the macabre discourse.

The big pink room was very warm, shadowed, though a streak of fading sunlight lay across the floor covering like a bit of fabric dropped there and forgotten.

The drapes were still at the window, and beyond it, in the high shade of the oak trees, the mourning doves cooed. There was a fragrance in the air, scent of lavender and lemon oil and dying roses.

At last Caroline said drowsily, "I think that's quite enough. For all the trouble taken to print it, you'd think the lady would have troubled herself not to be so long-winded. I say that even though she's a neighbor."

"Perhaps she's paid by the word," Miranda suggested, smiling. She closed the novel and put it back on the pile of reading materials. It slipped sideways, and everything toppled with a thud. Caroline winced visibly. Miranda hurried to neaten the stack and set it more securely.

"But," Caroline went on, "I suppose her very long-windedness is relaxing. You may draw the drapes and light the lamp."

The ribbon of pale sunlight was gone from the floor covering, and when Miranda drew the drapes and lit the lamp, black shadows seemed to leap at her from the corners of the room. She waited, but Caroline said nothing, only moved her head restlessly.

"Would you like me to brush your hair?" Miranda asked.

"No," Caroline said. "No. It will not help."

But Miranda laughed and took up the silver-backed brush with its big engraved H. "Perhaps it will. Come sit before the cheval glass."

She drew an acquiescent Caroline up, and seated her, and slowly removed the lace chignon that covered the blonde hair. She let the long full tresses fall to Caroline's shoulders, and then, slowly and carefully, began to draw the brush through them.

It was impossible to believe then that Caroline had ever stood on the steps, and shrilled terrible words at her, Miranda thought. Impossible that she had ever had such thoughts in her mind. For slowly, the stiffness went out of her. Her rigid shoulders eased, and her hands lay loose upon her lap. A new young face seemed to grow on her. Her haggard and hollow cheeks filled out. Her green eyes softened. A look of expectancy and joy was shining there, and Miranda knew that she was seeing the Caroline that had once been but was no more. That Caroline had been gay and hopeful, and loving. She had been then what Miranda was now. They were sisters in spirit. Miranda accepted the current of warmth and closeness she felt flow between them.

And then this Caroline asked in a soft voice, "Miranda, what is it that you think you want out of life?"

Miranda laughed quietly. "Why, Caroline, I don't know. I haven't thought of it."

"Not yet? And you already seventeen and past that? When will you think of it, if not now?"

Miranda didn't answer. She knew that she could hardly explain to Caroline what Caroline could not possibly have learned. She, in her protected situation, would never understand what Miranda had learned as a child. That all strength and soul must be concentrated on finding that place in life in which one belonged. With that ensured, there might be room for the consideration of other needs.

"When I was your age," Caroline said dreamily, "I knew what I wanted. I knew." She sighed, turned her blonde head, and looked at Miranda's face in the glass. "I wanted only to be loved."

Again Miranda didn't answer. She wondered that Caroline should consider that unusual. Surely every woman wanted to be loved.

"Don't you, Miranda?"

The younger girl thought of Reed. The brush stilled momentarily on Caroline's hair and then moved on, stroking, smoothing. She thought of Reed. Her throat tightened.

She pictured his lean dark face and his bottomless silver eyes. It was a useless exercise to consider him, to feel what she felt, to dream her dreams. One kiss, no matter how sweet, wasn't a symbol or a promise. He had become, since that day, as remote as he had been before.

"I knew," Caroline was saying, "at seventeen, but I was twenty-one before I found love. That was when John came. When I was twenty-one, and we married a year later."

Slowly Miranda drew the brush down and through the shining hair, and set it aside. She did not want to hear Caroline's confidences. Not such confidences as these would be. The closeness and warmth had suddenly gone. Even the sound of the drowsy but insistent voice frightened her.

But Caroline said, "Wait, Miranda, don't stop. You must hear how it was. I was my father's hostess then. Yes, I know. I've told you that before. But it is important to remember. It was so beautiful. Oh, you can't imagine what a place Washington City was ten years ago. Quiet, a small town. The balls we had . . . the men in their uniforms . . . how dashing those Southern boys were . . . Dead now, most of them, or dishonored, in spite of the amnesty. How we danced through the nights . . . and laughed through the days . . . the gossip we exchanged . . . such strange love affairs . . . Oh, it's all different now, of course. There's a grimness in the very air."

"Perhaps it will soon be again the way it was before," Miranda suggested.

"No, Miranda. Never. It cannot be. It's ten years later, you see. And ten years take their toll in every way. We have lost a certain innocence. The bloom is off the rose. Did you know, this morning I found a gray hair in my head. Another one. Which makes a great many."

"But how does it matter?" Miranda asked.

"You learn how it matters by and by," Caroline told her. "Now, when you look into the glass before you, you don't see what you *will* see. And even if you could imagine it, which you cannot, you are still unable to imagine what it will lead to."

Miranda drew a slow careful breath. There was a certain triumph in Caroline's voice, as if her grim prophecy brought her pleasure. Did she see Miranda's dark hair silvered and thin? Did she picture the curve of cheek hollowed and the pink lips pale and bloodless?

Miranda put the brush aside and drew Caroline to the divan. "Is there anything you'd like before I leave you to rest?"

"I'd like to be young again, Miranda. I'd like to have love again."

"You ask for what is beyond my power," Miranda answered, forcing herself to laugh.

"Oh, do I?" Now Caroline's voice was sharp, no longer drowsy. "Consider what you say to me, Miranda, as you go down to dine tonight with my husband."

Miranda didn't reply. It was useless, she knew, to protest, to deny, to remonstrate with Caroline. This was what the older woman believed, perhaps what she wanted to believe.

As Miranda lowered the lamp, then eased the door open, Caroline took the silver snuff box from the drawer nearby.

It seemed to Miranda that the air was suddenly full of the thick cloying scent of gardenias. Some might think it sweet, but to her it was a noxious thing. She remembered John holding out to her the huge blossom, and the glitter of Caroline's watching eyes.

It was a relief to be alone in her own room. It was still, lit only by a single light, flickering in its sconce against the wall.

Abigail had already been in to turn down the coverlet on the fourposter bed and to fluff the pillows. The white gown with its blue ribbons was laid out neatly.

Miranda took a few quick paces first in one direction, then in another, hugging herself at her slender waist. Caroline's jealousy and her accusations were insupportable. Yet there was no answer to them. They must be ignored. For they were the delusions of a sick mind. Could not Caroline somehow feel the cruelty of her false charges? Was she determined to drive Miranda away?

Now a sudden restlessness possessed the young girl. The room was too small. It held no air. The gardenia scent invaded even this private place. She did not want to dress and go down and join the others. She wanted the silent streets and the dark trees around her. She wanted, for just a little while, to escape into an anonymity of purpose and spirit.

She knew, even as she pulled her dark cloak and bonnet from the wardrobe, that she was being foolhardy. Yet she was driven. She dressed quickly, and, after listening at the door, she slipped into the hall.

The house was still. She crept down the steps, ashamed to be furtive but unwilling to risk being stopped.

Then, from somewhere at the back, there was the clinking of glassware and china. Lena and Abigail would be setting the table for dinner. A wave of soft teasing laughter drifted from the music room. That would be Stacy, still entertaining Josiah Hurley.

The chandelier in the reception hall had been turned low. It threw a soft light on Miranda as she drew open the big front door and let herself out.

Silently, and with held breath, she went down the circular steps and into the shadows of the big trees.

She moved quickly from one layer of darkness to another, past the rhododendron plantings and the banked azaleas, along the driveway to the tall gates. It seemed now, in the dark and on foot, a much longer way than she remembered it. But at last she was there, and the gates loomed above her, impregnable to any assault.

A light burned in the gatehouse, but though she waited a moment, Benjy did not come out to challenge her.

She set her hands busily to work at the fasteners. They were not easy to manage. The metal was hard, rough. Two of her fingers were rubbed raw. But finally she inched the gate open. She slipped through, pulled it nearly shut behind her, hoping the faint hot wet breeze would not undo her by blowing it shut and leaving her stranded outside the brick walls.

She wasted no time, though, in decision but set out hurriedly along the tree-lined lane.

There were people about, she soon realized. Men stood at the corners, heads bent in conversation, as they puffed on big cigars. She shuddered at the snatches of conversation that she heard.

"Took them down and buried them right away in limestone."

"Should have thrown them into the river."

"Still three left . . . and maybe more . . ."

"The daughter went to beg the President at the White House, did you hear? But he wouldn't see her. And then it was too late."

She hurried on. It was an evil dream from which the whole world must someday awaken. She could not listen to the tale of death and retribution.

Most of the shops were closed. Here and there, though, light spilled through a window, revealing stacks of magazines and great basins of tobacco, or, in another, the tall jars and mortars and pestles of the apothecary trade. In one place, chickens and rabbits hung limp on strings, giving her a horrible start. In another, there were ribbons and laces.

Carriages rolled by, and gigs and hacks for hire.

She heard the bray of mules and the bargemen's bugling signal, and knew that she was only blocks away from the canal and the Kayhome Arms. She slowed her step, for that was not her destination. She had no destination. She was simply out to walk alone in the night.

Tad Layton's bank, lit by gas lamps within and without, loomed at the corner. A crowd was gathered there. She sidled closer to see what had drawn it, and caught her breath in fascination and in pity.

A tiny dwarf of a man, dressed in a red shirt and blue trousers and holding a pewter cup, led on a chain a huge black bear.

"Dance!" the crowd yelled.

"Dance, darling," the dwarf whispered.

And the huge bear lifted first one foot and then the other. He rocked and shuffled in a wide circle, his big sleek head lowered, and his small beady black eyes filled with a sad intelligence.

She drew forth a coin from her reticule and dropped it into the dented pewter cup, and the dwarf whispered his thanks.

As she smiled at him and turned away, a tall officer in Army dress seized her hand, laughing, "Come along to the tavern with me, lassie, and we'll have some ale and tell each other lies."

She stared up at him in angry bewilderment and tried to get free, but felt crowded in and jostled at her back.

Then Jake Rooker pushed his way through the group. He draped a sinewy arm around her shoulder, and said, "Oh, there you are, sis. Come out to look for me, did you? Then we'd better go home, for Da will surely be wanting his supper."

She tried to release herself and couldn't. She tried to move and couldn't do that either.

He made a path for her, pressing with his shoulders and shouting imprecations. He led her as if she were a small child away from that busy corner and back to the tree-lined lane.

There she said through gritted teeth, "Let me go, Jake Rooker."

His arm fell away from her. He grinned, "And here's the boardinghouse keeper's stepdaughter pretending to be queen of the realm again."

"I am not," she said.

"Then why are you out at this hour, masquerading as a wench?"

"It's none of your affair," she retorted coldly.

Again he grinned, "Well, I didn't mean to offend you by calling you my sister. But if that handsome young stud had thought otherwise, I'd have had a fight on my hands, you know."

"I appreciate your cleverness, I assure you," she retorted.

"And does John Haversham know where you are? Did he give you permission to come on foot and alone through the night?"

"And that's none of your affair either. I wanted a walk, and I've had it. I need no permission for that."

His mouth turned down, and his shallow blue eyes swept her up and down.

She turned away from him and set out for home.

Jake followed along after her, no longer speaking, as far as the gate. He thrust it open and disappeared into the darkness without a word.

ELEVEN

John went slowly up the steps to Caroline's room. He knocked at the door with a clenched fist, then entered without awaiting a reply.

He found Caroline sitting in a chair before the open window, her head limp against a pink cushion, her hands loose in her lap.

"Caroline!" he rasped. "Caroline! Open your eyes! Look at me! Listen to me!" He leaned over her. "Are you in command of your senses or are you not?"

She was unresponsive for a moment, but then she did open her eyes, raise them to his face. "What do you want of me?"

He straightened, his bulk towering over her. "Why, my dear wife, you know very well."

She didn't answer him. She listened to the faint whisper of wind in the trees, and closer, to the sound of her heart's erratic beat.

"The deeds, Caroline. I know that Tad has them, as you told me. It was clever of you to leave them with him."

She made a small gesture of protest, her body rising in the chair, then falling back.

He ignored that and went on. "Yes, that was unusually clever of you. Though I could get them easily enough if it were actually necessary. The fact is that I prefer to have them directly from you. So you must retrieve them.

You must assure him it is your desire that they be signed over to me. And see that it's done."

"I will not," she said, and her voice shook.

"But you will," he answered softly, contemptuously.

He turned his back on her and walked the length of the room, walked it once, twice, allowing her to wait, wonder what he would do next. His heavy tread was a series of blows to her heart, and she felt her breath begin to come more quickly.

At last she said, in what she knew was a useless attempt at reason, "John, you *do* understand. That land is mine. I can't give it up to you."

He looked at her over his shoulder, then gave a short exclamation of hard and jeering laughter. He came and stood over her once again. "You waste my time, Caroline. You waste yours. I'll have what you refuse me, and you know it."

She set her pale mouth and moved her head from side to side.

"I could almost admire your stubbornness," he said softly, "if it weren't so useless."

"I'll not give in on this, John," she cried. "I'll not do it. Never. No matter what you say to me. No matter what you do."

"Such courage," he said coldly. "Such strength. Where can you have found it so suddenly?"

She struggled to her feet. "Leave me alone," she screamed. "Stop it! Stop it, John. Leave me alone, I tell you."

He put a big hand at her shoulder and thrust her back. She collapsed into the chair, shaking and sobbing, "I won't give you the lands, John. Never."

He did not answer. He went to the table near the divan and took the snuff box from it. He opened its fragile carved lid and poured a small stream of pills into his hand. He looked up and gave her a faint smile.

"No," she gasped. "You can't do that!"

"It's done," he told her.

"No!" she screamed. "John, please, please, I beg of you . . ."

"When you've changed your mind and are prepared to be reasonable and wifely, then come and tell me so," he answered. Without another look at her crumbling face, he left her alone.

She sat, trembling, while the hot tears ran down her cheeks. She had taken nothing that day, trying desperately to hold herself back, yet always knowing that relief lay within reach if her agony could not be borne. Now there was no relief.

She knew that she could send none of the servants to the apothecary shop for her. John would have told them this was one errand not to be performed for their mistress. One of them might be persuaded if she pleaded earnestly enough, but how awful of her to provoke John's anger that way. She didn't dare to ask Stacy, who would sigh and lecture her, and finally agree, but then smilingly confess day after day that she had simply forgotten, and would try to remember tomorrow. She couldn't permit herself to send Miranda . . . That left only Reed.

But she had heard him go out earlier. She must wait for him.

She remained in her chair. She drowsed in wicked dreams, and awakened to be swept by nausea and fits of shivering. She sank into dizziness and drifted away into the memory of childbirth, the searing pain which had brought forth from her resistant body only cold flesh. She came starting awake with a scream in her throat and found herself tearing open the lid of the snuff box before she remembered that it was empty. That John had taken away her pills.

Sobbing, she threw herself on the pink divan.

But later, when she heard Reed's footsteps in the hallway, she was up and on her feet. She flew like a hunted thing to the door and tore it open.

"Reed," she cried. "Help me!"

He stopped, took a single look at a tear-stained, supplicating face, and went into the room with her. He closed the door gently, breathing the still, suffocating air, and asked, "Caroline, what's the matter?"

She twisted her thin hands together. She said, "I am humiliated that I must ask you, but I am not able to bear it. I cannot, Reed. You must understand. It's not my choice. If it were only that, then I would have done with it long ago, but I—"

"Caroline, don't," he said gently. "Just tell me what's amiss, and how I can mend it for you."

"I've been cruel to you sometimes," she said. "Even though I am your sister-in-law, even your sister in my heart, I've been cruel to you. I never meant a word I said to you, though every one is engraved in my mind, and sometimes in the nights I think of them and weep. But you do know I never meant them, don't you?" she implored.

His silver eyes darkened, and color swept up into his face, then faded. He said quietly, "Caroline, I remember none of those words. And you must not either. Now. Tell me."

A hectic flush burned in her cheeks, and her eyes glittered, and he saw that she was near to collapse.

She said, "He has taken my pills. He's very angry with me, you see, and he punished me in that way. Reed, I can't go on another hour without them."

"All right," he said. "I'll get them from him."

"Please, no. You two must not quarrel. Never, Reed. Never. You're all that he has. And you don't know him as I do. Please, Reed. Only go to the apothecary for me. Say nothing to him."

"I've no reason to fear John," Reed told her.

"You've had no reason to fear him until now," she said softly. "But if you oppose him—"

"Even if I should—"

"Reed, for my sake. Do not tell him. If he knows he'll simply come in the night and remove the pills again."

"But it's for your own good, Caroline. You do know that surely. John intends you no harm. He's trying to help you overcome this curse."

"No. No, he's not. He is not," she answered. "I told you. He's angry with me. And this is how he thinks to punish me."

She sank slowly onto the divan, watching Reed's face with anxious eyes.

At last he said, "All right, Caroline."

"You will go at once?" she whispered.

"Yes. Of course I will."

"You won't tell John?"

Reed hesitated, and she very nearly screamed, but she held herself back, and finally he said, "I won't tell him this time, Caroline."

TWELVE

"Night doctor!"

"Night doctor!"

The cries came from somewhere in the shadows.

Jake walked more quickly down the muddy lane, feeling animosity in the eyes that followed his back. He was not an imaginative man nor a sensitive one, but now he could picture hate as a knife driving through his flesh into his bone, and the blood spurting forth while he screamed for help that did not come.

This was alien territory. Not his, not any white man's. It was Louse Alley, a shantytown inhabited by a mass of men who had been slaves. He had been through Cabbage Alley, and through Swampoodle. He suspected that his face and red hair were known and watched for. He suspected that if he did not finish the job John Haversham had given him soon, the job would be the finish of him. Not that anyone would ever know it, since the city policemen avoided these places as much as he would like to himself.

He had counted the number of shacks, holding his breath against the stench. He had calculated a rough average of the occupants in each one, and wondered what they ate. He was now doing a hasty recheck to be sure that he had missed no possible habitation.

Two small boys darted across his path and disappeared behind a pile of debris, shouting, "Night doctor! He's here! He's here! Night doctor!"

Jake stopped, looking after them in bewilderment. What in the bloody hell was the night doctor? Or who? And why did they call him that?

"Night doctor coming!" a young voice shrilled.

"Night doctor!" the cry went up.

Jake quickened his step. He didn't like the way the shouts were coming now from every direction, echoing back and forth through the twilight. He was dead center of Louse Alley, a long run to get out.

A tall black man with a bald scarred head, dressed in the tatters of the Union Cavalry, came out of a broken shed.

"Night doctor! Night doctor!" the cry continued.

The big black man ignored it. He looked directly into Jake's suddenly sweaty face. "What you want? What you doing here?"

"I got lost," Jake said. "Which way is the avenue?"

"You got lost how?"

"Taking a shortcut."

"Dumb," the black man told him.

"Looks like it," Jake agreed. "But I'm no night doctor, whatever that is the boys are yelling."

"No, you ain't, I don't think." The man lowered his voice. "They come after dark, by twos, and whoever they find out of doors, they steal away." A shudder moved his big frame. "They take them to the hospital and put them on stone tables and drain out the blood. They drain out the blood, and cut open the bodies and do their experiments on them."

"Is it true?" Jake asked, his stomach rising up into his throat. "You think they really do that?"

"Maybe," the man said. "Maybe they don't." He turned Jake north, gave him a push. "That's the way out. Start walking."

Jake walked, trailed by fading cries, "Night doctor coming . . . Night doctor . . ."

At Pennsylvania Avenue he hailed a hack. He would have liked to have gone to Cow Town for a little while. After the stress of the day and this twilight, he felt that a woman was the relief he required.

But Nan was waiting for him in a tavern in Georgetown, and business was business. So he decided to defer the more pleasurable expedition for evening.

She said, as soon as he joined her at the Five Feathers, "There was a message for you from John Haversham."

"What message?" Jake demanded.

"You're to go there," she grinned. "I tell you, Jake. It very nearly broke Tom Jervis' heart to hear that."

Jake, too, grinned. "I don't doubt your word."

"As for Susanah Kay . . . she's eating fire still. She goes around mumbling to herself, saying over what you told her about Miranda's dress, and the pearl beads you saw her wear."

Jake shrugged it away. "I'm not concerned with them, Nan. Only with myself."

"With ourselves, if you please," she said with a hoarse laugh.

He nodded, frowning. His shallow eyes were thoughtful. "Do you know what I'm doing for him now?"

"For the big man?"

"Yes. For Haversham." Jake explained the project on which he had been engaged, not telling her how he had felt in Swampoodle or in Louse Alley.

"A head count, Jake. Now you know, that's very interesting. What could he want to know how many people live there for? But that doesn't really make much sense. I expect they're all squatters."

"I'd expect that, too. Which means they could all be thrown off any time."

"Do you suppose that's what he's planning to do?"

"Anything's possible. But I'd think, a better thing, and a favor to the city, too, would be to set those towns to the torch and let them burn to the ground."

"Why, Jake, what a bloodthirsty thought." Nan laughed. "Think of the blood that would be spilled."

"It's just what I am thinking of."

She shook her head at him, her fat face lined with disapproval. "That's the trouble with you. You waste your time on the unimportant. Listen, Jake, you've no quarrel with the people there. What you should be thinking about is what John Haversham has in mind. Why is he curious about those shantytowns? What would he do with them if they were his? If we knew that . . ."

Jake grinned. "You're right, Nan. I'll see what I can do."

She reached across the table and put a fat hand on his big gnarled arm. "You do that, Jake," she said softly. "We'll be better than good partners one of these days. Just wait and see."

He pulled his shallow eyes away from her doughy face with the eyes like small black raisins. He pulled his arm away from her hand. He knew that she was proposing a partnership that covered more than business. He wasn't disposed to anger her, for he saw uses for her, though he didn't know just what they were at the moment. But he much preferred to take his chances in Cow Town, and promised himself that he would.

He winked at her and rose. "I'd better get up to Haversham Square, and find out what the big man wants."

THIRTEEN

A stillness enwrapped the house, but from somewhere far away, from beyond the high brick walls and the cast-iron gates, there came the slow, placid thud of hoofbeats and the creak of a rolling carriage.

It was a lonely sound, Miranda thought, leaning at the window, and listening.

She was ready for bed, dressed in her gown, with the drawstrings tight at her throat and wrists, and her dark hair caught up in a white lace snood.

A lonely sound, too, was the sweet song of the mockingbirds in the oaks along the shadowed driveway. She wondered if Reed heard that music, or if he slept. He had seemed troubled in these last few days, a faint frown gathered between his dark brows, his mouth set and his eyes remote again. She supposed he had given way once more to the malaise that had affected him since the end of his Army career, yet some subtle difference in him suggested to her that now his thoughts were drawn elsewhere. If only he would learn to trust her, to accept her love . . . She would help him. She would heal him and make him whole again.

The clear notes of the mockingbirds' song faded, and she sighed, turned to go to her bed.

Her breath caught. She gave a gasp of fear.

John stood in the open doorway, and she had not heard him knock, nor enter, nor known he was there.

He touched his fingers to his lips in warning, and then came across the dark room toward her.

The lamp he held bathed her in pale light, and his face, too.

She asked urgently, "Cousin, what is it? What's wrong? Why are you here in this way?"

"I must speak to you, Miranda."

His voice was grave, his expression, too. He loomed above her, his big head bent on the bull-like thickness of his neck, and his wide shoulders hunched. It seemed to him that he had thought of that moment forever, to know her in her night attire, her hair thus, her eyes wide and her lips trembling. The compulsion to make real what he had so often imagined had driven him here tonight.

She whispered, "Not here, Cousin John. Not like this. I'll come down at once. I'll dress more properly, and we can speak below." She felt the sudden rapid beat of her heart against her ribs. She did not know what he intended, but knew that his presence in her room would only add fuel to the flame of Caroline's jealousy.

But he set the lamp on the table near her bed. He said softly, "Do you fear me, Miranda? Do you not trust me after all? Surely you have come to know something of me in these past four months. Why do you look at me in this way?"

"Of course I trust you," she said desperately. "But this . . . now . . . it is unseemly. You must not be here in my room. You must go away at once. I'll attire myself immediately and join you downstairs. I'll—"

He smiled at her. "I am master here. This is my house and my land. Why am I barred from this particular room when I am barred from no other one?"

She said helplessly, "But you know why."

"I do not. Come. Tell me."

She made a small gesture. "Cousin John . . . please . . ."

He bent over her. His big hands cupped her cheeks, turning her face up to his. He saw the fear in her amber eyes, but said, "You're very lovely, Miranda. Do you know that? Do you realize what such loveliness can earn for you?"

She drew away, though it took effort to do so. It required a bruising effort, he held her that firmly. She drew away, feeling his strength. But she was free for only a moment. His hands found her cheeks again, and this time, too, his fingers were bruising.

She remembered Jake's hand at her wrist, and his arm at her waist. She remembered that night when she had struggled with him in the silent dark. And yet, remembering, instinct told her that there was something quite different here. John was not Jake Rooker. She could not deal with him in the same way.

John said, "So lovely," in a strange crooning voice. "It's no wonder at all that every man who sees you desires you. They're not for you. Only one is for you." He would not name the one. The way must be laid first. She must be willing and unashamed when the time came.

"I encourage no one," she cried.

"I doubt such men require encouragement, Miranda." His granite gaze was bright. "Men who aspire to such as you are not men who need much of that." He was thinking of himself more than any other. He was such a man. He had only to know what he wanted that he would reach out and take it.

She thought instantly of Reed. If John's words were true, then why must it be she that pursued Reed? It was she, always, who sought him out. She who studied him, trying to reach beyond the distance that he maintained between them. She who struggled to know and learn him, and still burned with the sweetness of his kiss. Had John seen her yearning?

The expression on her face intrigued John. He wished that he knew what she was thinking. The fear he had seen flash in her eyes was gone. Instead there was a sudden blind look of hunger. It was not for him, he knew. Not yet. Then who had touched her thoughts? Something hardened inside him. He told himself it did not matter. He would allow no one else to have her. No one. He tightened his hands on her cheeks and saw her wince. "Are you happy here, beautiful Miranda?"

She managed to whisper, "Yes, yes. But you must not—"

"Must not? What a poor choice of words to use to me," he answered. "They only act as a challenge. Surely you know me that well by now."

"Please," she said. "Do let me go. Tell me why you have come here."

He dismissed his earlier resolution to wait. He saw no reason to. She already belonged to him, and he would make the way clear. He said, "I'm here because I have dreamed of it for a long time."

"Oh, no!" she cried. "Cousin John . . ."

"Cousin John . . ." he mocked her. "That's no barrier between us."

She didn't answer but only stared at him.

"Am I so displeasing to you?" he asked. "Do you truly find me that repulsive?"

A painful blush stained her cheeks. The thought of Caroline burned in her. She had believed the older woman's accusations to be products of a sick and disordered mind. Now she realized that Caroline had seen more, sensed more, than Miranda herself had. It was she who had been wrong, at fault, though never willingly.

She whispered, "Cousin John, you mustn't speak so. Oh, please, you must not. You are my kinsman, and I have never considered you otherwise. I could never have done. You are married, and Caroline cares very deeply for you. I could never . . . truly . . . I cannot believe that you have said such words to me. I have not heard them, nor will I remember them."

"But you have heard them," he said, seeing then that his obsession with her had drawn him into error. It was not one that could not be mended. But it was a mistake all the same, and he had already learned from it. He must gracefully withdraw. He said softly, "Yes, you're right. It was a poor jest to have spoken so, and a poor test of you as well. We'll both forget it, Miranda. It means nothing."

She nodded at him, her eyes aglow with relief and gratitude.

But when she tried again to draw away, his fingers curled around her cheeks, held firm. It was difficult to speak, even to breathe as they tightened.

"A small question, Miranda . . . Has Caroline sent you out to buy pills for her?"

Miranda stared at him. Something dark and cold seemed to hang over her in the stillness that followed. Something invisible seemed to brush her with cold fingers.

Then there was the rustle of silk in the blackness beyond the open door.

John turned his head, his eyes agleam in the lamplight. A small smile touched his lips, and his hands at last slowly fell away from Miranda's cheeks.

She knew suddenly that he cared nothing for the opinion of others. He would do as he pleased always.

"Caroline?" he asked gently. "Is that you? Why are you wandering about alone in the night?"

Caroline was as pale as the loose lace gown of white that enwrapped her thin, trembling body. The blonde hair framed her hollowed face. She clung to the door and said, "I see. I see."

Miranda took an involuntary step toward her, then

stopped at the glare of hatred, red-eyed and raging, that Caroline gave her.

John said smoothly, "Oh, Caroline, what do you see now? What troubles you? Have you been having nightmares in your bed?"

"Real nightmares," she answered harshly. "And this is one of them. I am awake . . . I am not asleep. But I see. I see you, here in my house, and this . . . this . . ."

"You misunderstand," Miranda gasped. "Oh, please, you mustn't think—"

"I do," Caroline answered. She swayed against the door frame. "I understand. I've known from the first. I had only to look at you to know."

"Please . . ." Miranda said again. "It isn't true. John, you must explain."

John spoke softly, spacing each word with a breath between them, a breath denoting his forcibly held patience, as if he were speaking to a child or to an idiot. "I came here to ask Miranda if she had been so ill-advised and foolishly underhanded out of pity for you as to go out and buy that awful poison with which you destroy yourself. You seem to believe that you can conceal from me the fact that you have somehow gained a new supply. The servants have not brought it to you. You have not been out. I questioned Miranda."

"It was not she," Caroline said quietly. "Of that you must not accuse her. And you must not think that you mislead me. I doubt you came into this bedchamber to speak of me."

"You've no right to indulge your sick mind against Miranda," he said. "Nor me."

The words were right, and true, Miranda thought. Then why was there no ring of conviction here? Why did he deny this ugliness sounding as if he repeated by rote what he had planned before? Why did he sound so insincere when that quality alone would be a torment to Caroline?

Caroline's shoulders lifted, sagged. "I have no right," she answered, "except that right my own eyes give me." Her voice was loud, piercing, and it cut through the stillness of the upper hallway.

The door to Stacy's room opened a crack, but she did not come out. The door to Reed's room opened wide, and he stood there in plain view.

John said soothingly, "I believe you should return to your bed. Surely this kind of adventure can do your health no good, Caroline."

"Thank you for your consideration," she told him coldly. "And I believe that Miranda Jervis should begin to pack at once."

He shook his big head slowly. "Caroline, you do try my patience to its very limits."

"I'll try it further if I go to my cousin Tad Layton and tell him of this night."

John laughed. "Tell him what? That you found me in Miranda's bedchamber asking her about *your* health, and with the lamp lit and the door open? He is already concerned about your condition. He has spoken of it to me. He will think you quite mad if you make such a complaint about Miranda."

"It was not about me that you were here," she said. But she had begun to sound less certain. Her eyes flickered from John to Miranda and back again.

"I believe that you yourself heard a part of what I said," John retorted.

"Then you deny any impropriety?" she asked shakily.

"You know that I do." John took a deep loud breath. "What am I going to have to do with you, Caroline? Why are you forcing this on me? I fear I must speak to the doctor again in the morning. Perhaps he will be able, better than I, to make you see how you are destroying yourself."

Her trembling body shrank back against the door. "It is not me, John. You know that it isn't. I just saw you, you, with my own eyes, with your hands on her cheeks. You, bending to kiss her . . . I saw you . . ."

"You saw me comforting her, as I would any child that I had wrongfully accused and hurt by that accusation. And it is for that that you scream at me, and at her. All for no real reason, except for what exists in the strange chamber which we kindly call your mind."

She turned swiftly and fled to her room.

Reed, standing in his open doorway, saw her agonized face and wondered that she did not know, did not feel the truth of what had just happened.

He was certain that whatever reason John had for being in Miranda's room, John had seized the opportunity of Caroline's discovery to turn and rend her, to drive her deeper into the pain with which she lived.

John was saying, "I'm sorry, Miranda. I didn't mean to create such a scene. But you know Caroline. By tomorrow she'll be sorry. She'll weep hot tears for her ugly thoughts and ugly words."

Miranda murmured and shook her head.

"Just forget it, my dear. It has nothing to do with you, you know. The woman is sick, and we are all aware of it." John took the lamp with him, came out into the hall, and closed the door behind him.

Reed stepped into the corridor, blocking his brother's way. "What was that all about?"

"You heard," John said.

"You must realize that it was I who brought Caroline her pills. She must have them. You cannot torture her by withholding them. Not for any reason."

"Yes, yes, perhaps you're right," John answered, and Reed saw that his eyes were ablaze with triumph.

It was morning at last.

It seemed to Miranda that she had watched each star go out in the night, watched the moon sink inch by inch below the horizon. She had seen the long shadows shorten, the dark recede before day, and now there was sun at last on the trees and lawn.

It was day, but the nightmare of the night had not gone. She would have to dress, to go down. She would have to face Caroline, face the others, with the memory of John's whispered words and the compelling look of him and his hands holding her cheeks.

She had not realized that he had those feelings for her. She had in her inexperience never thought of him in such a way. She was certain that she had not deliberately encouraged him, and more certain that she had not meant to. But Caroline had seen more than she. Sick and half-mad, Caroline might be. But she had seen more.

Miranda sighed and took up her yellow frock. Her hands were clumsy on the long row of back buttons. She struggled with them for a long time. She had just barely finished settling the full skirt when there was a tap at the door.

She raised her head fearfully. "Who's there?" Her voice was uncertain and fearful.

"It's me, Miss Miranda," was the answer. Abigail's slow voice was steady, uninflected.

Miranda told her to come in, relieved that she would have at least a little more time before she had to go down to face the others.

Abigail pushed the door open. "I have these shifts and collars. I thought you might need them. They're all cleaned and pressed now." She put the things away in the wardrobe and stood with her scarred hands on her hips, regarding Miranda out of shuttered eyes.

Miranda said, "Thank you, Aunt Abigail. But you needn't have hurried. I doubt I'll need them immediately."

Abigail didn't answer for a moment. Then she said gently, "Sit down, Miss Miranda. I need to talk to you."

It was, Miranda thought, in the same tone of voice she would use to Lena. The voice she would use to help and comfort her.

She sank down on the bed and raised her eyes to Abigail's face, suddenly chilled. She saw pity in the older woman's eyes, pity and something that must be fear.

Abigail said, "Now listen to me, Miss Miranda. There's an evil in this house and always has been. You don't have a chance against it. You ought to get your folks to come for you. There's something brewing here that I don't like."

Miranda thought of her father then and quickly dismissed him. She would not ever return to the Kayhome Arms. She would never belong there.

"If you don't have folks to go to," Abigail continued,

"then find yourself a husband to marry right away. Find yourself a good man to carry you off and care for you." She drew a deep breath, twisted her hands before her. "Maybe I oughtn't to say it. Since it's none of my business. But somebody . . . somebody needs to look after you."

"But why?" Miranda cried. "Why? What is it?"

Abigail muttered, "That's all I know. I told you." She tightened her lips and avoided Miranda's pleading gaze as she hurried from the room.

It was well-meant advice, Miranda thought. But she had already found the man she wanted. He was here in Haversham Square. She could think of no other now that she had known him. If she were to flee now, she would leave him as well as the major part of herself behind.

She looked at the small gold clock on her dressing table. It was nine-thirty. She must go down.

But she dreaded what was to come. What would she see in Reed's eyes? What in Caroline's?

John had said that Caroline would be tearful and sorry, regretting the scene she had made, the accusations of the night. But Miranda wondered if she would see, deep in Caroline's eyes, the hatred and the certainty and the fear that she had seen in them before.

It was not Caroline, however, that she met in the morning room.

Stacy was there, working at a small wooden puzzle, her white hands flashing back and forth between each piece.

She wore a dark blue skirt that spread around her in a great swath, a long-sleeved blue jacket that buttoned at her waist. She looked composed, rested, and not at all censurious.

Miranda bent over to look at the puzzle, pretending an interest she didn't feel. She was very nearly weak with relief.

Nothing would be said. What had happened the night before was to be forgotten, or ignored, by all except herself.

She would be careful now of John. She would maintain that discreet distance between them which would protect herself, and protect him, too. She would make certain that she gave Caroline no cause for anger, no cause for pain. She would make certain that she was not forced to leave Haversham Square.

FOURTEEN

The great square ballroom was lined at one end with rows of small gilt chairs covered in red velvet.

The huge Steinway had been carried in and placed on a square of red velvet at the ballroom's center, with music stands grouped nearby.

At the far end, near the mirror walls, there were long tables covered by red damask cloths.

Jefferson had filled silver vases with tall sprays of red and yellow and pink roses that scented the air with their sweetness.

The entertainment, planned by Caroline and Stacy for three weeks, had become under John's instructions a musicale. He had thought to consult with Tad Layton about the program but finally decided to discuss it with his chosen ensemble instead. They had suggested an all-Mozart evening, with piano, cello, viola, and violin, and he had acquiesced.

He had checked and rechecked the guest list. He had twice rewritten the menus for supper, and had himself interviewed and hired the extra servants to be brought in.

Now, in the hush before the music was to begin, Miranda, sitting near the back and close to the door where John himself had placed her, surveyed the group that had been invited to Haversham Square.

The women were beautiful, each one of them different in age, form and gown, but each one of them alike in qualities of importance, of grace, of charm. Their frocks billowed around them over great wide hoops. Their powdered shoulders glistened. Jewels sparkled in their hair, on their wrists and hands. The men were of varied age and form, too, and though they were by no means all handsome, they were, she knew, men of substance and power. They were on the boards of directors of the Riggs Bank, or the Washington National Bank. They were the publishers of the Washington *Star* or the *National Intelligencer*. They dealt in the great tracts of land that surrounded Georgetown, and owned the ferries and steamships and barges that plied the Potomac River. Or, all else failing, but hardly less important, they were in the government.

She knew that John made it a practice to encourage only those for whom he had use. He plainly had use for the chief of police, a tall, dark man with a big black mole on his chin, and for pudgy, pink-cheeked Carleton Van Eward, and for Josiah Hurley, returned from his visit home.

A shiver swept over her in spite of the perfumed warmth of the room. She had believed that he had invited her to live at Haversham Square out of generosity. But since that night he had come to her room and had touched her, she had known to what use he had thought to put her. She reminded herself quickly that from then until now he had been entirely circumspect. There might have been no visit in the dark. No impassioned declaration made into jest at her protests. But she was still troubled to know what had been in his mind then.

Now he bent over her, whispering, "My dear, I'm sorry to disturb you. But Caroline doesn't seem too well. Would you go and sit with her? Would you make sure she is all right, and never out of your sight?"

He wore a ruffled white shirt and a black, gold-embossed waistcoat under his black, braid-trimmed coat. A large diamond winked from his cravat, another from his right hand.

The pianist struck a chord, the violinist responded. To a polite patter of applause, the music began.

Miranda rose quickly. She made her way to Caroline's side as quietly as she could and sat down next to her.

The older woman glanced at her, then looked around,

plainly searching for John, who stood near the conservatory doors. Then her narrow lips set firmly, and she faced the musicians, while her thin fingers did a small dance on her knees.

Miranda, observing that, was touched. There was something sweet and childlike in the gesture. It seemed, in spite of what John had said, that Caroline was looking particularly well that night. She wore a blue silk dress over a great billowing of crinoline and petticoats. It had a deep square neck fringed extravagantly with tiny pearls, and that motif was repeated in wide bands around the skirt. The sleeves were long and loose but fit tightly at her bony wrists. Her hair was bound in a high round chignon covered by a net of woven pearls.

The musicians played for some three-quarters of an hour. When, to enthusiastic applause, they rose and bowed, the listeners were led by Caroline to the flower-decked buffet tables, where huge platters of cold fish and caviar, and chafing dishes of sliced meats, awaited them.

Caroline moved with grace among her guests, pausing to speak a few serious words to Tad Layton, to whisper, smiling, at Josiah Hurley, to kiss the cheeks of the Barrington sisters.

As unobtrusively as she could, Miranda followed her, though even now she didn't see that Caroline was either unwell or troubled. But she knew that she must do what John had suggested. He had, she noted now, disappeared with some of the men into the library. She supposed there would be a moment or two of private conversation before they rejoined the others. And those few moments, perhaps, were the reason for the musicale.

Reed was saying to Tad Layton, "Have you heard the talk about the horse bus between Georgetown and the Capitol?"

"Which talk do you mean? There's enough of it these days to confuse any man. And I own I can be confused as well as the next one."

Reed did not smile, though he knew that he was supposed to. He lowered his head and hardened his jaw. In that moment, something of John showed in him, a rare resemblance which threw Tad off balance. "I refer to the very foolish discussion on the subject of not allowing Negroes to be seated on the horse bus."

"Oh, that. Yes." Tad shrugged. "There has been some such talk. And it's entirely possible that it will come to something. I didn't know you interested yourself in such matters."

"It's of real interest to me. When I send Timoshen to the Capitol with a message for a friend, I don't intend that he spend a full day walking there and back. I want him to be able to use the horse car." Reed paused. Then, "The horse bus company is chartered, Tad. By Congress. You're on its board of directors, so you already surely know that. What was given can be taken back, and given to someone else. I think John may be interested in developing a transportation company for the city. It would be a reasonable adjunct to the railroad, you know. And he has friends among the aldermen, as well as in the Congress."

Tad said, "I understand you, Reed. Though I certainly don't pretend to know your motives."

As he nodded and passed on to speak with someone else, Reed thought he was as unsure of his own motives as Tad was. But one thing he knew. He was determined that if Tad was unsuccessful in preventing the proposed change, he would, as promised, discuss what could be done with John.

He found himself at Miranda's side, and smiled down at her. Her gown was amber, nearly the same color as her eyes. It hugged her tiny waist and fell in a wide graceful circle around her matching slippers. He felt the desire to take her in his arms, and his smile broadened. He had much to thank her for, he thought.

He saw that her eyes anxiously scanned the crowded ballroom, but said, "We have here a motley crew, if there ever was one. Would you believe that that stout gentleman is a Supreme Court justice? And the man behind him, the one with the greedy look, is the Senator from Maryland?"

Miranda nodded but didn't answer. Within these few

moments Caroline had gone to consult with Jefferson. Then she had spoken to Abigail. But now, quite suddenly, Miranda could no longer see her.

She frowned, turning her dark head back and forth in a quick search for a glimpse of Caroline's blue gown and thin form, but even then, in the midst of her uneasiness, she was totally aware of Reed's proximity.

"What is it?" he asked.

"Caroline. I don't see her anywhere, Reed."

"She's busy playing at hostess, a role which she adores."

"But John said she wasn't well."

"She seemed all right to me a little while ago when I spoke to her," Reed answered, frowning slightly.

He looked as if he would say more, but Stacy took his arm and smiled up at him. "Come along, my dear. Erna Barrington insists that you neglect her. You must prove otherwise." With a sweet smile at Miranda, she drew him away with her.

Miranda stood where she was near the door, gripped by a strange unrelenting fear, and watched for Caroline as the music drifted through the room, and Jefferson passed shining goblets of champagne to the laughing guests.

"It was a very good idea," Caroline said, "to have the musicians play during the buffet as well as at their own little performance, too. I'm glad you thought of it."

"Yes," John agreed. He raised his head. "And how good it sounds from out here." He held her firmly, an arm around her waist, as they walked down the shell path.

"But I do think we should go back. Our guests . . ."

"Never mind our guests," he told her.

"More easily said than done, John. And remember that it was all your own idea."

He smoothed his sideburns and sighed. "Caroline, must you always, always, always spoil my mood? Our guests can take care of each other very nicely indeed. They are being fed, watered, and entertained. They have no need of us." He drew a deep breath, and a small smile touched his mouth. "And you, you look lovely tonight. More like yourself than you have for months, perhaps for years. I want to be with you, my dear. Just a few moments alone at the lily pond."

Her body began to tremble. It was impossible. She knew that they must return to the house at once. But she could not refuse him. It was there, at the lily pond, that he had first made love to her. He had been showing her about the grounds on their wedding night. They had paused near the pond, and he had taken her in his arms and kissed her, and then forced her down to the cold marble, and kept her there nearly until dawn. He could not, she thought, be remembering that now. But it was impossible to refuse him.

She smiled up at him breathlessly, her body gone liquid with longing, and leaned her blonde head against his shoulder. Together they went slowly into the darkness of the rhododendron bushes.

He paused for a few moments in the heat of the silent conservatory, breathing deeply of the exotic scents that perfumed the moist air. He waited while his racing heart-beat slowed, and his quick breath became normal.

Then he smoothed his hair carefully and his sideburns. The sleeves of his coat were wet, and the ruffled cuffs of his white shirt hung limp and gray. He took another breath, and opened the door and stepped into the morning room. It was but two steps more into the servants' stairway. He moved quickly and met no one on the way to his room. He changed shirt and coat and met no one on his way down again.

The company in the ballroom, having finished its buffet, now grouped, and regrouped. He had chosen it well, with an eye to its perennial self-involvement. The ladies in their flowing gowns, with brilliants in their thick hairdos, were like flower pieces on a vast table, each posing for her own enjoyment. The men, in not such bright finery, seemed but to stress the gaiety of their partners, while studying their own reactions to them.

He thought of the stillness outside and listened to the

uneven chatter for a moment. Then his eyes began to
search carefully in the gathering for Miranda.

He saw her, finally, standing alone near the mirrored
wall. He moved toward her but paused where Stacy was
talking, with great animation, to Carleton Van Eward.
She glanced at John as he asked, "Stacy, have you see
Caroline? Forgive me for intruding on your conversation.
But I don't find her among the company."

Stacy answered, "She was with Miranda a little while
ago. You must ask her, I think."

He nodded and took two quick steps to Miranda's side.
He bent over her. "Miranda, my dear, where has Caroline gone?"

"I've just been wondering," she answered. "I don't
understand it, John. She was with me a few moments
ago, and then, quite suddenly, she was gone. I was certain
that she had stopped to speak to Jefferson, and after that
to Abigail, and they tell me that she did indeed, but
they've not seen her since."

Miranda felt troubled as she looked at John. She didn't
know why, but she had the feeling that something was
different about him, something wrong. It was no more
than a brief flicker in her mind, forgotten in her growing
concern over Caroline's absence.

He frowned, "But I did specifically ask that you stay
with her, beside her. She didn't seem well to me, not herself, and I felt that she oughtn't to be alone."

"Yes," Miranda whispered. "But you see, with so many
people here . . ."

He ignored her words, turning his big head in a surveying stare. Then he shrugged. "Perhaps she has gone up to
her room. Would you do me the favor of seeing, Miranda?
I don't like to leave my guests. If the hostess has actually
abandoned them, then surely the host must not."

"Of course," she said. "I'll go at once, John."

He watched as she made her way through the room.
He was filled with a burning impatience to hold her, to
make her his. It would be soon, he told himself. He
would, of course, make his small bow to the conventions.

But after that . . . He noted that Reed's eyes followed her tall slender figure . . .

It took her only a few moments to reach the huge pink room that was Caroline's. It was, she saw in a single glance, empty.

Miranda went in. She examined the room carefully, certain though she was.

The stack of books and magazines was undisturbed on the table near the pink divan. The candelabra were in their usual places on the mantel with the softly ticking ormulu clock between them. A small doll, some token of Caroline's childhood, hung at the corner of the dressing table mirror. The pots and creams there were undisturbed. An open box of Velatis' chocolates was nearby. Caroline had eaten only a portion of Tad's gift to her. The rest remained discolored and partly melted. The cheval glass was tipped as she must have left it after a final look at herself before going down to greet her guests.

There was something frightening in the room, Miranda thought. It was familiar enough to her, and it was in its usual order, yet it seemed, suddenly, a strange place. She even went so far as to peek into both dressing room and wardrobe, in neither of which did she find Caroline. And, from the decorous order of these places, too, Miranda was sure that she had not returned to them since she had earlier gone downstairs.

Miranda closed the door gently behind her. Where could Caroline have gone? Why should she have deserted her company and wandered off alone?

She looked anxiously up and down the long hall. She saw her own reflection in the mirror over the narrow table, and the sight of her pale troubled face startled her. She decided that Caroline might, for some reason, have become confused and gone into some other room. With embarrassment, but driven by uneasiness, Miranda made certain that Caroline was nowhere on the floor, and then went downstairs to where the music continued softly.

She saw John, his head bent attentively to Dorothea Barrington.

Miranda decided to look further for Caroline before confessing her failure to him.

But Caroline was in none of the many rooms on the lower floor of the house. With a growing uneasiness, Miranda made a search that became increasingly more hurried and less casual, including even the cooking quarters and the dim storerooms, and finally the servants' staircase.

The very last place that she could think of was the conservatory. She went into the big, glass-enclosed area, remembering the gardenia John had given her, the sickening sweetness of its scent.

It was there, as she looked thoughtfully at the white and pink oleander blossoms, at the flickering lantern that threw its slowly moving shadows on the damp brick of the floor, that she began to think of the lily pond.

Caroline, Miranda knew, had gone there often, to brood, to be alone. It was there that she went when one of her unhappy spells took her. She had once told Miranda that it was her private place, where she went to think her own thoughts and study her feelings, to remember the past and consider the future.

Miranda thought it not so likely that Caroline would have gone there when she had a houseful of guests. But who knows what mood had suddenly struck her? Who could imagine what chance word might have hurt her? Or what pain might have sent her fleeing into the night? And John had said that she felt unwell when he asked Miranda to look after her.

With sudden determination, Miranda slipped out of the back door of the conservatory and into the shadows of the parklands behind the house.

The terraces were lit with lanterns that glowed in the dark but threw their beams only a short distance. Beyond that range, there was only a heavy silent blackness, the blackness of an August night with no moon and few visible stars.

She gathered her skirts in both hands, lifting them with hoop and crinoline to avoid the heavy dew that soaked instantly into her thin slippers.

She moved cautiously until she found the shell path by stumbling upon it, and then she knew her way with certainty.

The clump of rhododendrons were like some huge squatting animal with a hundred flickering eyes. The white fawn was an enchanted thing, frozen now, but awaiting only the breaking of some mysterious spell before leaping gracefully into the night.

The two marble benches that flanked the dark and silent pond were empty.

Miranda's heart sank within her.

Caroline was not here either.

Then where could she be? Where had she gone?

Miranda knew that now she would have to return to the house to speak to John. She would have to draw him away from his guests to tell him. But to tell him what?

The lilies, once no more than thick buds, had opened into wide and heavy blossoms. They drifted on the black water surface. Their petals were white and smooth and firm, with small drops glistening on them and small shadows at their hearts.

She noticed as she was turning away that one was misformed. The whiteness of the petals did not spread outward ... the shadow at its heart ...

She swung back, no breath in her lungs. A thick cold knot of terror hardened within her.

She knelt at the edge of the pond, careless that a fold of her gown slipped into the slimy water. She leaned forward, straining to see clearly through the veiling dark.

And then she knew with absolute certainty what her mind had recognized but refused to accept.

Among the lily blossoms, and one with them, drifting with the dark surface of the still pond, there was a white face.

She rose to her feet, a muted cry on her lips. She cast an agonized glance back toward the house. Through the barrier of thick trees, she saw only a glimmer of yellow light. She heard only faintly the sound of music, the deep strong voice of the cello, the sweet reply of the violin.

There was no help at hand, and she knew that she must not waste a moment.

She stepped cautiously from the marble rim and into the chill water. It reached immediately to her knees, her soaked gown weighing her down. She managed, using all her strength, to move ahead.

It was only a few steps, but lily roots clutched at her, dark, slimy tentacles that tried to seize her. The warmth of the night was gone now into winter cold. The velvety petals of the flowers brushed her, but there was no gentleness in their touch nor pleasure in their caresses. She fought her way, sobbing, to that strange flower amid the others, and looked into Caroline's wide staring eyes.

In a daze of horror, Miranda wrapped her arms around Caroline's limp body. She hugged her close, as a mother hugs a child in hunger and tenderness. The thin wet arms hung like pale strings. The blonde hair, loosened from the pins that held it, net with pearls gone, trailed on the cold wet shoulders.

Unable to lift her awful burden, Miranda drew it with her along the pond surface to the marble edge.

It took the last ounce of her strength and the end of her courage to lift Caroline from the chill blackness to safety.

To safety. These were the words that Miranda thought in some still-refusing part of her. She knew then only that she must remove Caroline from the pond.

With that accomplished, she knelt beside her for a single look. Full acceptance forced itself upon her.

The marble ledge was no longer safety for Caroline. Caroline was dead.

Her green eyes were wide open now, and full of shadows. Her cheeks were sunken, the same dark blue as her soaking wet gown. Her lips were drawn back in a snarl of hate.

For the rest of her life, Miranda would remember crouching beside the still body in the dark, with her own gasping breath loud in her ears and the distant music drifting to her through the shadows. For the rest of her life, Miranda would remember rising to her feet with the wet frock clinging to her, weighing her down, and fighting against the burden it made, to flee through what seemed endless miles.

The white fawn was alive now, dodging into her path to obstruct her. The rhododendrons lunged at her. The shells shifted and swelled and sank under her.

At the steps to the terrace, she paused, hardly able to breathe, a stitch burning knifelike into her side.

What was she to do? How was she to gain John's attention?

It was then that Jake Rooker came lounging out of the shadows. "Hey, girl," he said, grinning at her, "how does it feel to be one with the gentle folk? Do you like that caterwauling they call music?"

"What are you doing here?" she cried.

But he didn't reply to her question. He would never admit to her that he had slipped in through the gates along with one of the arriving carriages to peep at the gay entertainment through the window, that he had been watching for an hour, eaten by envy and malice, before going into the cooking quarters to empty the half-full champagne goblets as Jefferson carried them in, and stayed there until, only moments before, he had come outside to watch again. Instead, he flung a crumpled cigarette into the night and came closer. His shallow eyes narrowed, staring her up and down. "What's this? What's wrong with you, Miranda?"

"You must get . . . must get Mr. Haversham for me," she gasped. "Now. At once. There's been a terrible accident. Go in, Jake, and speak to Jefferson."

"What kind of accident?" Jake demanded.

"Please . . ." she whispered. "You must . . . right away . . ."

"Not until I know what's going on," he told her.

"It's Caroline." Miranda's voice broke. She went on, sobbing now, "I don't know what happened. I can't think how it could be. But she's there. Near the lily pond where I found her. She's there, Jake, and she's dead."

Jake made an inarticulate sound deep in his throat. Then, "You wait here," he ordered, and disappeared inside.

The music stopped briefly. There were waves of applause, and trilling laughter. A violin began a sweetly woven tune.

The door opened. Light made a pale pathway across the terrace. Within it, John stood with Reed.

It was Reed who came down the steps most quickly, so that he reached her first. He smiled at her, a flash of even white teeth in the leanness of his face. "Don't be so troubled, Miranda." He frowned then, touching the tears on her cheeks. "Why, Miranda, you're crying."

She realized then that he didn't know yet what had happened.

By then, John had joined them, with Jake trailing after. John said, "What is it, Miranda? Jake says—"

She could not contain herself. She knew of no gentle way to say it. She burst out, "Oh, John, Caroline's at the lily pond," and thought he understood.

But he said, "Caroline is? And she refused to come back with you?" Then, with a glance at Reed and a shrug of heavy shoulders, "I'm really concerned that she should behave this way, tonight of all nights. This entertainment was all her own idea. I finally gave in to her because she wanted it so much, even though I feared it might be too arduous for her. I suppose I'd better go down, since she won't listen to Miranda."

He took a step.

Miranda sighed, clutched his arm.

He looked at her impatiently, dark brows drawn. "What is it, Miranda? You know that I must—"

She whispered, "John, I'm sorry. Jake should have warned you, told you. Caroline is drowned."

Reed's breath whistled through his teeth.

John said, "What madness is this?" in a disbelieving voice.

Then he, with Reed following swiftly, ran down the shell path and disappeared into the shadows.

Jake was beside Miranda again, peering into her face. "You, girl," he said. "You'd better get yourself indoors and change your clothes."

"Why didn't you tell him?" she whispered. "Why, Jake?"

"Too many people," he said. "And not enough time. That's why. And you'd better put on a dry gown. Listen to me. I know what I'm saying."

"I must wait until they return," she told him.

He bent closer to her, too close. She could feel his breath on her cheek. She could see the flash of his eyes. It was no physical familiarity that he attempted now. He didn't touch her. He said in a low, wheedling voice, "What happened, Miranda? You can tell me. You'd better tell me. I'm on your side, always on your side, you know. I'll help you, if I can."

"But I don't know what happened," she answered, giving him a wide-eyed look. "How could I know? John sent me to look for Caroline when we did not see her among the guests. And then . . . then . . ." Her voice broke. She took a deep breath, steadying herself. She was cold, the wet frock clinging to her body imparting its own chill. Another chill was growing within her. She saw an odd expression on Jake's face. One that she could not read, but one that frightened her. She had good reason to be frightened, though she did not realize it then.

He said dryly, "It's all very peculiar, I think."

At that moment, John and Reed appeared on the path below. They began slowly to climb the steps.

Before they reached the terrace, the door opened.

Stacy came outside. The brilliants in her chestnut hair seemed reflected in her dark eyes. Her oval face was lit by her warm smile. It slowly faded as John reached her. She said, "Why, John, whatever is wrong? You look as if the wrath of God had touched you."

He said heavily, "It has." Then, "Go in and get Doctor Porter, Stacy. Ask him to step out here. There has been an accident. I am sorry to tell you that Caroline is dead."

There was an instant of stillness. Stacy seemed to sway, and the color drained from her face, the brightness from her eyes. Then she gasped, "Oh, John, no. What's happened to her?"

He said evenly, "She's drowned herself, Stacy. Or," he added quickly, "she's fallen into the pond somehow."

"John!" But Stacy's eyes were on Miranda now. "Why? How could she? She was perfectly all right. Perhaps a bit nervous. I noticed that during the buffet. But I heard you tell Miranda . . ." Tears gathered in her eyes, and spilled down her cheeks. "I can hardly believe it, John."

Reed cut in, "Stacy, do control yourself. Go and get Doctor Porter. And dry your eyes. Not a word to anyone else. We must do this quietly, if we can. For Caroline's sake."

"Of course," she agreed. She stared hard at Miranda a moment longer, and then slipped inside.

She did not return with the doctor. He came alone, and frowning. He was a short man, very broad. His face was red, his beard a thick burly brown. His head, more than half bald, gleamed in the faint light of the lanterns. "What's this, John? Stacy says there's been some sort of accident . . ."

"Caroline," John said. "If you'd come with me . . ."

The two of them started immediately down the steps.

Reed made as if to follow them, then turned back to Miranda. "You must go in," he said gently. "Change to dry clothing, and go to bed. You can do nothing here now, and I know it has been a terrible shock for you."

She didn't speak, but looked into his eyes. She seached for accusation there, for anger, for disgust. She searched to see if he blamed her. She saw nothing but concern. Was it for her? For Caroline?

Jake said softly, "It may be that the doctor will ask questions."

Reed nodded abruptly, glancing at Jake with dislike. "The formalities . . ." Then, to Miranda, "But you must dry yourself and wait inside. Speak to no one about this." He turned away, adding. "Jake, come with me. We might need you."

When she was alone, she hesitated. Within, the music still played. Within there would be light and warmth and laughter. But down there, in the dark near the lily pond, lay Caroline.

John, the others, would be with her now. What would they be saying, thinking? What would they decide?

Jake's words came back to her. "It's all very peculiar, I think."

Suddenly she was terribly afraid.

The music stopped in mid-note. There was a rising crescendo of voices. It grew louder, came closer. The door opened again, and light spilled over her.

She shrank back as Stacy, surrounded by people, stepped outside.

Dorothea Barrington murmured, "A terrible thing."

"Yes," Tad Layton agreed grimly.

"But why? How? I cannot believe it," Josiah Hurley growled.

Eyes swept Miranda up and down. Brows rose in eager question.

Then Stacy said in her clear high voice, "Why, Miranda, you're absolutely soaked from head to toe."

With a murmured apology, her face flaming, and her eyes streaming tears, Miranda fled indoors.

"Mister John wants you, Miss Miranda," Abigail said tonelessly through the closed door. "Will you come down?"

Miranda opened the door. She had changed her frock and now wore the only black one that she owned. She had brushed and recombed her hair and put it up again, the curls subdued in a thick dark snood. Her hands were icy cold and her eyes were huge, rimmed with red. "Have they gone yet?" she asked.

Abigail regarded her from veiled eyes. "They've gone. Finally. Nobody's here now but the family. And the doctor."

"You know what's happened, don't you, Aunt Abigail? They've told you?"

"Yes. They told me. First Miss Stacy did. Then Mister Reed. And I'm not the only one that knows. So does half Georgetown by now, I guess. The other half was on the terrace when Reed and that Jake Rooker brought poor Miss Caroline in."

A shudder touched Miranda. "I'll come down with you," she said.

They were waiting for her in the library. It still showed signs of the earlier entertainment. There were glasses and dishes about, and ash trays full of cigar butts. There were great vases of roses. Yet it was hard to believe that only a little while before there had been laughter here, and music, and flirtatious smiles, and joy. It was all gone, wiped away in a single horrible moment.

Doctor Porter said to Miranda, "Now, miss, if you please. I would like you to tell me exactly what happened."

Before she could attempt to reply, Reed said, "Miranda, take a chair. This is a sad but necessary formality."

She nodded at him, grateful for his concern and kindness, and seated herself. She fixed her eyes firmly on the doctor's booted feet. She dared not look at John, nor at Stacy.

Then John said gently, "Yes, Miranda, just take your time and tell us exactly what happened."

She felt that they sat in judgment upon her. She was the prisoner in the dock, defenseless and alone. Not only defenseless and alone, but already condemned. She sensed the verdict in the waiting silence that hung, pall-like, in the room. She sensed it in John's question, though it had been gently spoken. But what her crime had been she did not know.

John awaited her answer.

She looked up.

Reed did not move.

Stacy sat straight and stiff within the froth of her gown, suddenly looking like a solemn child.

Doctor Porter cleared his throat and stroked his beard.

At last Miranda replied, "You told me, John, to stay with Caroline, and I did, though she did not much seem to want my company. When the buffet was served, we went there together. She spoke to several of her friends, and I tried to stay by her side. I don't know quite how it happened that she left me. It was difficult, so many people and all moving about. I caught a glimpse of her talking to

Jefferson and Abigail, and then she was gone . . . I can't remember any more of it."

The doctor asked, "Then how did you come upon Caroline at the lily pond?"

She spoke to John. "And then you came and asked me about her. And I told you . . . surely you recall that I told you what had happened?"

"Of course I do. You said she was gone. I sent you to look for her. I had guests. I didn't feel that I could desert them."

She was remembering now that flickering uneasiness she had felt when she spoke to him, the feeling she had that something was wrong. She forgot it once more as she told how she had searched the house, upstairs and down, and then, in the conservatory, had remembered the lily pond. "You know the rest," she said, and stopped.

"Forgive me," John said softly. "We all of us know how difficult this is for you, Miranda. But Doctor Porter must know the facts, you see, of how Caroline's death came about. Now. Why did you think to go to the pond?"

"We all knew," Miranda said, "that there were times when Caroline was angry, or unhappy, that she went and sat there and stared at the flowers for hours. I somehow recalled that, and—"

"And when you found her?" Doctor Porter asked, moving restlessly, as though these moments were more prolonged than he wished.

Miranda swallowed, her dry throat working painfully. She whispered, "I saw her face among the flowers. I didn't realize, at first, that . . . I climbed in and pulled her forth. I thought then, you see, that there might still be time. But then I realized that . . . that it was much too late."

"So your own gown became wet, and your hair disheveled," John said.

Doctor Porter cleared his throat, and asked, "You're certain that Caroline was already in the pond when you . . . when you found her? She spoke no words to you? She said nothing?"

"Caroline was dead," Miranda answered.

There was a brief silence.

Then John said softly, "Doctor, you know very well what my poor wife's problems have been in these past years. It seems obvious to me, as it must be to you, that she sank into a sad depression and went out to the pond. There she must have become dizzy and tumbled into the pond. And being alone, weighted by her gown, she was unable to save herself, even though there was little depth."

The doctor nodded, tugged his beard, then rose. "I will file the report, of course."

John saw the doctor out, then returned to the library, a faint smile hovering on his lips. Everything had gone exactly as planned. He was an unhappy widower now. But surely six months of circumspect mourning would serve when a man had a home that needed a good woman's attentions. He could wait that long. He would be busy dealing with the proper disposition of Caroline's lands. He composed his face as he sat down.

All had remained in utter silence while he was gone.

But now Miranda said, "John . . . Cousin John . . . I feel . . . I'm so sorry. What can I say to you? If only I had not lost sight of her . . ."

John raised his brows, studying her. At last he answered, "Miranda, my dear child, you could surely not help that. Not when Caroline was determined to evade you. It is very clear, since we know what Caroline was, that she slipped away and destroyed herself in some mad mood. The doctor will, of course, kindly call it an accident. And we shall not disagree."

FIFTEEN

For two days Caroline lay in the small downstairs sitting room that opened into the conservatory while her friends and a few surviving relations came to pay their final respects.

Tall white candles burned at her head and feet, and her casket was banked by great crests of flowers. She looked young again, at peace, and beautiful.

On the morning of the third day, the casket was closed and sealed. A long cortege formed in the driveway. Black funeral plumes rose over the heads of the horses, and black gauze was wound through their bridles and harnesses.

It had stormed in the night, but now the sun had risen, gleaming on the wet lawns and striking small sparks from the trees.

The hearse, piled high with wreaths, led the way along the few blocks to Oak Hill Cemetery, and past the tall black gates tipped with shining gilt that caught and held the sun. As the procession rode through, a covey of black crows took wing for the tall oaks, cawing defiance in the still air.

Listening, Miranda trembled. It seemed to her that nature itself was making an ominous comment on what had happened to Caroline.

It was a relief to escape into the silence of the small chapel, where the minister spoke a brief sermon and a good part of the society of Washington City and Georgetown bowed heads and prayed silently.

Senator Hurley sat on one side of Stacy, and Senator Van Eward, with his sister Mary in attendance, sat on the other. Tad Layton was near them. The British ambassador and his wife, and the Barrington sisters, sat not far away.

Miranda, leaning on Reed's arm, was heavily veiled as she followed the coffin to the graveside.

She had known death before, but this seemed so sense-less to her, so terrible. The numbed disbelief of the past two days had begun to fade, and now the shock of accep-tance gripped her, and with it, grief compounded of pity and regret.

All that Caroline had cried out to her in pain and anger and fear was expunged. What remained was the memory of a few moments of closeness in the pink room.

No one had spoken of Caroline's pills. But they, surely, were at fault, Miranda thought. It was her need for the drug which had failed her that had finally destroyed her. And Caroline had been entitled to more. Yet she seemed to have left so little behind. A half-finished embroidery in the morning room that Abigail had found and quickly put away. A wardrobe of silken gowns. A quietness. An empty place.

Miranda blinked back tears and felt Reed's hand tighten on her arm.

John stood alone, dressed in sober black, his uncovered head bent as the clods of dirt fell on the casket and hid it. A man never burdened by conscience, never troubled by tenderness, he felt nothing as he watched one part of his life being buried, and prepared to move on to another. When he turned away, Tad fell into step beside him, and they returned in the same carriage to Haversham Square.

Abigail and Jefferson had prepared a simple luncheon and served it in the morning room. The mourners ate and drank, and spoke in halting whispers.

"I can't believe it," Stacy kept saying, and allowed first Josiah to press her hand in sympathy, and then Carleton Van Eward.

The British ambassador made small talk with John about the English Havershams, while his wife discussed horses with Reed, who answered her absently.

Miranda was relieved when, at last, it was over. She felt oppressed by uneasiness. She kept hearing the music of the piano and violin, and seeing Caroline's fingers tap ner-vously on her knee. She kept remembering. The more she tried to turn her thoughts from that night, the more her memory insisted on it.

She went up to her room and remained there until the late afternoon, when Abigail came to her. "Miss Miranda, there's a man downstairs. He says he's your father and wants to see you. I told him that you were tired out and resting, but he's insisting, so I thought I'd better—"

"It's all right," Miranda told the anxious woman. "I'll see him. I'll come down."

It would be the first time they had met since mid-April, but she felt nothing but an angry impatience. Where had he been in those ten years when she needed him? What did he want of her now?

She was braced stiff when she entered the library.

Tom rose to his feet, his small high belly riding over his belt, his rusty black suit plainly freshly brushed. He gave her a compassionate smile. "I came as soon as I heard, Miranda. I knew you'd want me to."

She regarded him blankly. "I'd want you to?"

"Because of Mrs. Haversham's death, of course. It must be terrible. What an awful accident. What a pity. And she so young. And Jake Rooker says you found her. You, my poor girl."

She was filled with impatience at his hypocrisy, but asked in an even voice, "What has it to do with you?"

"Why, Miranda, when there's a death in the family, we must all rally round, mustn't we?"

She cut in, sighing, "Papa, what do you want?"

"Want?" he cried. "Nothing. Except to offer my condolences, and to tell you Susanah Kay sends hers as well."

"Thank you," Miranda answered, seeing how avidly his pale blue eyes examined all that which she had come to take for granted in her months at Haversham Square.

"It's a long time since I've seen you," he said reproachfully. "I did think you'd come to visit, in spite of our foolish quarrel."

"I told you how I felt, Papa."

"You were hurt and angry, poor child. Such words are meaningless. I forgive you. You're my only child."

She looked down at her hands. They were smooth now,

white and perfumed by rosewater. She remembered when they had been roughened by strong soap in Susanah Kay's kitchen. But she said only, with faint sarcasm, "Thank you."

He sighed gustily. Susanah Kay had insisted that Miranda would have forgotten by now. But he had known better. It was too bad that Susanah Kay had been so unkind to her when she lived at the Kayhome Arms. It was Susanah Kay's fault that it seemed impossible to develop a fine and natural relationship with the Havershams.

Miranda said, "Papa, forgive me. I'm tired. It has been a difficult day."

He got to his feet unwillingly, following her into the hall toward the big front doors.

It was then that John came out of the morning room. His rocky face was sober, his eyes expressionless. They gave Tom a single hard searching look, then dismissed him.

Miranda made hasty introductions, and Tom said gravely, "Mr. Haversham, I'm glad to have this opportunity to tell you that I'm sorry for your trouble. Life is that way. It brings sorrow. I remember when Miranda's mother—" He stopped because Miranda shook his arm firmly.

John acknowledged the words with an abrupt nod. So this was Tom Jervis, he thought. This was what Miranda had sprung from. It was some sort of miracle.

"As I told my dear daughter, if not for your tragedy," Tom went on, "I'd never have dreamed of intruding. Without invitation, of course."

Miranda made some restless movement of the feet under her hoop. Her black gown swayed around her. John saw and smiled to himself. She did not welcome this visit. She wanted nothing to do with this small, blond-bearded, ineffectual man. Why, John didn't know. But it certainly didn't matter. For he was in complete agreement with her. He saw, in those moments, down the corridor of the years to come. Miranda at his side, and Tom Jervis dancing behind them, his hand held out, his face wreathed in hopeful smiles. Plainly the man considered himself one of the gentry, of small means now perhaps, but of growing expectations. Well, he would learn to live with his coming disappointment.

John nodded his big head, and Jefferson, materializing as silently as always, pulled open the big doors.

Tom looked at them, then at Miranda. "You'll pay me a visit?"

"Perhaps," she answered. "One day."

"Goodbye, Mr. Jervis," John said coolly, and then, taking Miranda by the elbow, he guided her back into the library, leaving her father hesitating at the threshold of the big doors while Jefferson eyed him noncommittally.

She seemed relieved when she heard those doors close. John saw the play of expression across her face and the quick lift of her chin.

It was that, as much as his own feeling, that led to what followed.

SIXTEEN

The clerk slipped down from his high stool and made what was almost a bow. "Good afternoon," he said. "How are you, Mr. Haversham? And how may I help you?"

"I want to talk to Mr. Layton," John answered. He tucked his cane under his left arm, the one on which he wore a black mourning band, and stripped fawn-colored gloves from his hands.

"Of course," the clerk was saying. "Just let me see if Mr. Layton is occupied."

But John followed the man to the small office, brushed him aside, and strode in.

Tad looked up, rose, and put out his hand. "How are you, John?"

"Well enough, I suppose." John settled himself in the chair that Caroline had taken on her earlier visit.

Tad, remembering, winced inside. He recalled so vividly

her agitation then. He had been troubled by it and done
nothing. Of what use had his small reassurances been? His
gifts of chocolate? Poor Caroline was gone. He reached
quickly for the humidor and offered John a cigar.

John accepted it, nipped its end with a gold cutter. Then
he said, "I'm here on business, Tad. Do you know who
holds the paper on the Kayhome Arms, if there is any?
And I think there is." He gave the approximate address,
and briefly described the place.

"I can find out in a few minutes," Tad told him. The
blond man rose, went to the door, spoke a few quiet words
to the clerk, and then returned to his desk.

John regarded him silently, and waited.

Tad said, "I thought that you had come about the deeds
that Caroline held."

"The deeds?" John repeated. "Yes. Of course. In the
pressure of these last days that matter had slipped my
mind."

Tad made no remark on that unlikely statement. He
could recall no instance in twelve years of knowing John
when any matter of business had slipped the big man's
mind. He would not be where he was today had he been
that sort. Or had he not married Caroline.

"But, since I am here, Tad," John was saying.

Tad got to his feet and went to the big safe. He slowly
proceeded through the ritual required to open it. He slowly
slipped a red leather-covered folder out, and then brought
it to John.

John opened the folder, removed the crumpled envelope
that Caroline had clutched in her fingers, and the single
sheet attached to it.

He reads the words written in Caroline's hand. Then he
read them once more, rocked by wry amusement.

To my husband, John, whom I dearly love, she had written, *I convey these lands to be his.*

How like Caroline, he thought. What she had so foolishly refused him in life, she had proffered to him in death.

But it was no more, no less, than he had expected.
Though if she had surprised him by doing differently he

would have known how to deal with that, too. He considered that those lands were his, and had been since Caroline's father left them to her.

He put the paper, and the deeds, before Tad. "You knew of this, I suppose?"

Tad glanced at the paper and shook his head. "I didn't. Caroline never discussed it with me."

Tad hoped that his relief did not show. It had occurred to him that Caroline just might possibly have decided to thwart John, and Tad was her closest relation. He did not relish the thought of what could have happened had these lands become his. John Haversham would have destroyed him for them.

"No matter," John was saying. "Will you attend to the legalities for me?"

"Of course," Tad agreed, then looked up as the clerk hesitated on the threshold. "Yes? Did you find it?"

"I did." The clerk sidled in, placed a note before Tad, who glanced at it and then smiled.

"Yes?" John asked.

"It so happens that we ourselves hold the paper on this house, John. Now that you know that much, what about it?"

John waited until the clerk had gone, then said, "I want to buy that house, and I want the present holders out of it as quickly as possible."

Tad leaned back, protested, "But John, what do you need a broken-down boardinghouse for? We have a few really fine properties already available that—"

"That's the house I want," John said firmly. "What can you do?"

"I'll have to examine the situation before I tell you that."

"But there are ways," John told him. "It would be a favor to me if you were to find them."

Tad glanced at the note before him. "The house is now held by a woman called Susanah Kay Hardy Jervis." He paused, awaiting some comment from John, but none was forthcoming. He went on, "Jervis? Some relation of Miranda's perhaps?"

"Not the woman," John said indifferently. "But the Jervis is her father."

Within the week two large men wearing dark greatcoats and hard round hats appeared at the door of the Kayhome Arms.

Susanah Kay admitted them nervously when they had identified themselves as coming from the bank on an inspection tour.

Their booted feet tramped the house up and down and back and forth, inside and out, and their big plump hands busily made notes, and their gruff voices conferred for hours.

Listening, Susanah Kay's pallor deepened, and her thin hands rubbed anxiously together.

Within the month, a thick official-looking document was delivered to the house, informing Mrs. Susanah Kay Hardy Jervis that the bank was reclaiming the property on the grounds that its value was being depreciated by lack of adequate care and improvement. A long list of details was appended. A small cash settlement was offered by way of payment for the equity involved. The bank also offered the holders sixty days and no more in which to vacate.

Tom watched in horror as Susanah Kay's hard face broke and tears streamed from her eyes. He had never seen her weep before. It never occurred to him to connect what had happened with his visit six weeks earlier to Haversham Square.

He leaned against the brick gatepost under the brass sign, shivering and cursing Benjy who had, for the third time in a week, refused him entrance. He had to see Miranda. There was no other way. But how was he to do that? When it seemed that he would not be admitted to the house. How? When his own daughter was kept from him?

The red leaves of the maples drifted down with a sudden gust of misty wind and lay upon the wet road like great splotches of blood. He hastily averted his eyes to study the scattering of golden leaves, and be comforted to think how much they reminded him of gold pieces. It was small comfort though. He had no gold pieces, as desperately as he needed them, and he saw small prospect of obtaining them. If only he could see Miranda . . .

He straightened, still shivering, when the big carriage turned into the road and rolled up to the gate, and stopped there.

He saw, through the velvet-draped window, that Miranda was within, and with her, Reed Haversham, whom he had never met but recognized through Jake Rooker's description.

Miranda was laughing, her head back, her face rimmed by the band of white fur on her hood. She was beautiful and joyful, and for a moment, Tom's heart lurched within him, and he hesitated.

But then he bounded forward, jerked the door open, and cried, "Miranda, dear child, I must speak with you."

She looked down at him, the joy fading like the light of a snuffed candle, and asked with weary patience, "What it is now, Papa?"

Reed Haversham leaned forward to say, "Step up and in. Ride to the house with us. It's too chilly to talk out here."

Tom leaped into the carriage with more speed than Miranda had known his round-bellied body possessed.

He said breathlessly to Reed, "I'm Miranda's father. Tom Jervis. We've never been made acquainted before."

Reed glanced at Miranda and saw the reaction she had to her father's words. Resolution hardened her mouth. Her hands slipped into her muff and tightened. He wondered.

He wondered further when, indoors, Tom Jervis said, with an apologetic grin at Reed, "A few words alone, Miranda?"

She sighed, handed her fur-lined cloak to Jefferson, excused herself to Reed, then led Tom into the morning room. She remained standing, asking, "What is it, Papa?"

He had rehearsed carefully, and Susanah Kay had helped him. But now all preparation was gone from his head. He told her in a great gush of incoherent words what had happened.

She understood enough of it, however, to know that he had come to her for money. She felt a certain pity for him. She knew what it was to feel frightened, with everything gone. But she said, when he had paused for breath, "Papa, I have no money. I'm sorry, believe me. But you must realize that there's no way I can help you."

"But you must," he cried. "We shall end up beggars. Don't you see? You have to help me."

"I've nothing to give you, Papa," she said patiently. "Surely you understand that."

"But Cousin John . . . a loan . . . if you were to ask . . ."

Her small hands became fists, clenched into the thick velvet of her gown. She cried, "Papa, you mustn't expect me to ask nor must you ask for money from him. I won't have that. I will not, do you hear me? Have you no pride, no shame? He does so much for me as it is. Everything. Everything I have, he has given me. Because I'm a Haversham, and belong here. But you . . . you come for alms . . . I can't bear to think—"

She stopped suddenly, hearing the shrillness, the anger in her voice, as Jefferson opened the door and stood there, smiling apologetically.

"Miss Miranda," he said, his face expressionless, though she knew that he must have heard some of her tirade at least. "Miss Miranda, Mister John asks that your father step upstairs to his study for a few moments."

She gave a gusty sigh and nodded. "We'll be there immediately."

"Your father is to come alone," Jefferson said. "I'll show him the way."

Tom Jervis gave Miranda a beseeching look, straightened his coat, smoothed his beard, and then followed Jefferson upstairs, hardly seeing in his excitement the elaborate decor of the second floor about which he had spent so much time speculating and about which, he knew, Susanah Kay would question him.

John was waiting behind the big desk. Only moments

before Reed had mentioned the meeting at the gate, the agitation of the small man and Miranda's reaction. John had smiled grimly, and said, "I'll speak to him myself."

Now he stared at Tom Jervis coolly.

Tom shuffled his feet, edging closer. "I'm happy to see you, Mr. Haversham. I stopped by to talk to Miranda, and—"

"What about?" John demanded. His big head was lowered between his massive shoulders, and he exuded an air of menace.

Tom openly eyed the chair nearby and hovered closer to it, but did not dare seat himself without invitation. John did not suggest it. So Tom sighed heavily, answering, "I'm in trouble. I have no place to turn. If a man can't go to his relations—"

"Miranda has nothing," John said calmly.

"So she says . . . so she says. But you . . . you're also a relation."

"I am not," John said. "And I'll thank you to remember that in the future. I have nothing to do with you and yours." But he would have one day, he thought, hence his determination to be rid of this small encumbrance once and for all and forever.

"Miranda," Tom said. "My daughter . . ."

"She's another matter altogether."

Now some of the things that Susanah Kay had shouted returned to Tom's mind. He swallowed nervously before saying, "That's another thing we must speak of, you know. My daughter can hardly stay in your house under these circumstances."

John's granite eyes became hooded. He knew instantly which way Tom was headed. Aloud he demanded, "Under what circumstances?"

"Why, as young as she is, and unchaperoned, my goodness, man, you should realize—"

John leaned his bull shoulders against the back of his chair and smiled faintly. "I am Mr. Haversham to you, and I'll thank you to remember that, too. Miranda is here where she wants to be and belongs."

"Mr. Haversham, I know that you're a man of honor,"

Tom said hastily. "I didn't mean that the way you may have taken it. I'm only—"

"And you're not particularly a man of honor, but we need have no more of this," John said evenly. He moved the mahogany case of dueling pistols from one corner of the desk to the other, and then fingered the inlaid silver on top. "I had already heard of your problem. I'm willing to help you for Miranda's sake, in spite of your low attempt to blackmail me. But under certain conditions."

Color flooded Tom's face. He gasped in relief, but then demanded suspiciously, "What conditions?"

John smiled faintly. "*My* conditions," he answered. He opened a drawer, drew forth a bank draft, and passed it to Tom. "You'll agree, I think, that this covers a considerable sum. And it's yours, if you leave the vicinity."

"Leave the vicinity?" Tom echoed.

"Leave," John told him quickly. "Bag, baggage, and wife as well."

"But—"

John rose, towering over the much smaller man. He put out a big hand, and Tom ducked as if expecting a blow. But John's thick fingers merely touched the bank draft. "You must decide now," he said.

Tom drew himself up. He stuffed the draft into his pocket, and said, "Mr. Haversham, I'm truly grateful for your help."

SEVENTEEN

As the carriage swung into the curved driveway that led up to the Barrington mansion, John looked at Miranda.

The cold November wind had brought a flush to her cheeks, and it seemed to him that he saw flickers of the lemon-pale sun in her eyes.

Lovely, he thought. So lovely. And soon to be his. His.

He resisted the sudden urge to draw her into his arms, and folded his big gloved hands around the head of his cane. He had waited so long. He would wait a bit longer.

She settled the white-furred hood around her dark curls and drew the fur-lined cloak more closely around her.

"Do you feel the chill?" he asked quickly.

"Why, no, thank you," she said, smiling.

But he decided, in that instant, what he would do. Christmas was coming. He could already see her, in his mind's eye, wearing what he would buy for her.

Aloud he said, "The air does seem to do you good, my dear. I fear you've been out too little of late. We must remedy that. And I promise you that we shall. Meanwhile I'm glad that you're joining Stacy at Dorothea and Erna's."

"It will be pleasant, I think." Miranda answered. "I enjoy the sisters, you know. And there'll be others to visit also."

"And you're quite certain that you and Stacy will be escorted home? I could easily return for you after my meeting with Josiah."

"Oh, no," she replied. "That's surely not necessary. Though I thank you for the suggestion, John."

The carriage rolled through the grove of leafless mimosa trees and stopped before the big brown house.

Timoshen opened the door, but John waved him off and climbed down.

Then, as Miranda reached for the step, he put both his big hands at her waist and lifted her easily.

She felt the pressure of each of his fingers into her flesh. She felt his overwhelming power.

For just a moment, he held her thus, held her in midair, gently, carefully, and she knew herself to be completely at his mercy.

At last, with a small, satisfied laugh, he set her on her feet and released her, saying, "I'll see you soon at home, my dear."

She looked at him with a quick flash of startled golden eyes, and said breathlessly, "Yes, John. Thank you," and hurried to the door.

He waited, watching her until she had been admitted. Then he climbed back into the carriage and directed Timoshen to go to the Barclay Hotel.

He found Josiah in his usual chair near the window.

After an exchange of greetings, Josiah grumbled, "A French emperor on a throne in Mexico!" He sent a long stream of brown tobacco juice into a nearby spittoon. "If it hadn't been for the war, it would never have happened. They wouldn't have dared. But what good were Seward's protests when he made them?"

John was interested in affairs that lay much closer to home, but he smoothed his sideburns and smiled faintly. "The Monroe Doctrine still holds, Josiah."

"And how does it?" Josiah demanded irritably. "What can we do?"

"If President Johnson makes it plain . . ."

"You have to be prepared to back up what you make plain, and we're not prepared. Not at the moment."

John laughed outright. "You have only to be able to appear prepared, Josiah."

The Senator nodded thoughtfully, squinting at the small flame that danced behind the crystal balls on the chandelier. He let himself sink deeper into the black horsehair chair, and stretched his long legs toward the fire blazing on the hearth. "Be able to appear to be," he said finally. "Maybe you're right, John. But I would hazard a guess that the whole world knows what this war has cost us in blood and armament."

"The world *does* know. But what counts is will. Not blood, not armaments. If the President sends General Sheridan and his army to the Mexican border, Napoleon will understand. It's all he'll understand." John paused to puff on his cigar. He waited a moment, allowing an intermission to permit a graceful change of subject. He was reluctant to waste any more time on observing Josiah play elder statesman and foreign policy expect. At last he asked, "Have you considered further on the trestle bridge, Josiah?"

Josiah stroked his dark beard and then grinned. "It can be done, John. The subcommittee will recommend it for early next year, I think." He pursed his lips and spat again, and this time he hit the side of the spittoon and swore softly.

John laughed.

Josiah glanced at him sideways. "But, of course, it all costs money, John. You know that as well as I do. That's where the rub is."

"I'll see that the shares are properly ascribed and noted. You need only to give me the necessary names, Josiah."

"I'll attend to it," Josiah reared himself up. "Where's the boy? We need a drink. How about some oysters, John?"

"No oysters, thanks. A drink, yes."

Josiah bellowed, and a white-coated attendant appeared to take his order for two bourbons.

When the drinks were brought, he raised his glass. "To a profitable association, John. To a growing railroad system, and to a great nation!"

"Now and in the future," John answered.

They were joined by several other men, which ended their private discussion, but before John left the suite, he said, "Come over this evening, if you have time, Josiah. We are, as you know, much at home these days."

Josiah looked at the black band on John's sleeve, and pulled a sad face at this slight reference to John's mourning. "I'll probably do that," he said.

When John reached home, and was handing his hat and cane to Jefferson, he asked, "Is Miss Miranda returned yet?"

"No, no yet," Jefferson said softly.

A frown drew John's dark brows together. He ought to have arranged to stop for her. She had surely had enough time with those silly chattering women. He had been certain that she would have been home by now, and had come back expressly to be with her. She was the magnet that drew him. It was thus day after day. But, he told himself reasonably, she did not know that. Not yet.

He went up to his study. The house was still. The lemon-pale sun had faded, and now a cold rain had begun to fall, slanting against the big windows. He pulled shut the drapes. He found himself restlessly pacing the floor. He told himself that the waiting would soon be over. Another month and he could easily open his heart to Miranda. She would remember, of course, that night he had so foolishly declared himself, and then pretended he had been speaking in jest. But the obstacle that had been between them was gone now. She would accept him. Impatience was a hot pulse pounding through his body. He was taut with hunger. He had waited for so long. He pictured her heart-shaped face, the glossy black curls. He imagined her hair down on her bare shoulders, her breasts rising under the filmy French gown he would give her for their wedding night. She would be his, then and forever. He saw the two of them moving side by side, into the Blue Room at the White House, and later, coming back to share the same bed . . .

His hand was sweating when he took up the bell on his desk.

Jefferson appeared in a few moments.

He said, "I want you to send Lena up here at once. With a rag and some polish. She's ignored this desk for weeks. I won't have it. The fact that there is no longer a mistress in this house is no excuse."

"I'm sorry, Mister John," Jefferson answered. "I'll attend to it myself, and immediately."

"You will not. Lena must do it, to learn her lesson," John retorted. "Get her up here."

Jefferson soundlessly withdrew.

When Lena came, her eyes wide and her lips quivering with apprehension, John was examining one of the dueling pistols from the mahogany case on his desk. Without looking up, he said, "Lock that door."

She hesitated only briefly, then did as she was told.

He put the pistol aside and caught her by the shoulders, and without speaking, he forced her stiffened body down to the floor. He brushed her black gown and ruffled white apron aside, and stroked her dark satiny breasts, and buried his face in her throat, inhaling the sweet muskiness of her, and that scent which was a sign of her fear. Both were intoxicating to him. He held her high round rump in his big hands, squeezing hard and feeling her cringe away, and feeling her hatred in the heat of her unwilling flesh. He smiled down into her sullen face as he lay between her silken thighs and thrust deep and thrust again, and kept on until he was spent, while her white teeth bit hard into her lower lip and her wide brown eyes brimmed with tears held back.

Later, though, he found that he still carried the burden of hunger, and knew that only Miranda could satisfy his need.

"It's a summons," Nan said, smiling, her black eyes bright in her doughy face. "So he wants you, does he?"

"He must, if he's sent for me," Jake answered glumly.

"There now," she chuckled. "It's not so bad as all that, is it?"

He shot her a cold look. "What do you know about it?"

"I know you're afraid of him, though I don't know why."

"Afraid?" Jake sneered, his mouth slanting down.

"You do have the figures for him, don't you?" she asked.

"I do. Though it's taken me all this time to get them and make sure they're right. If they remain right."

"Then you needn't look like a sulky schoolboy being called to the master's office for a caning."

Jake shot her another cold look. "You read me wrong. I'm just thinking."

"A fat lot of good it'll do you," she grinned. "If you can't figure out what he wants those numbers for."

"But I have," Jake said.

"Only you haven't seen how you can turn it to your advantage."

"Yes, I have," he answered. "If I had the money to do it."

Her small black eyes widened with pretended disbelief. "Go on," she cried. "You can't tell me that, Jake Rooker."

"They're all squatters," he said coldly. "They don't belong on that land. Swampoodle and Louse Alley and Cabbage Alley . . . all those shantytowns are built on land that John Haversham owns."

"How do you know he owns it?"

Jake grinned at her and ran a hand through his wispy red hair. "I have my means of finding out. And it's true. It belonged to his wife, and went to him when she died."

"That's interesting," Nan purred. "But what does it mean to you?"

"There's a small tract left, just north. A piece of old Burney's land that nobody seems to have thought of. He'll want it when he finds out. I'd like to own it then."

"And that's what you need the money for?" Nan shook her head in disgust, and her two chins danced. "You're a fool. He'll know about that parcel and have it before you learn to spell your name right."

Jake jumped to his feet. "Damn you," he cried. "You don't know about it! Stop talking me down on everything I say."

Her small black eyes narrowed. "I'm not talking you down, Jake. I'm trying to make you think."

"I don't need your help for that."

"But perhaps you need it in another way," she suggested. "Now how much money for that parcel?"

"More than I've got, and more than you."

"There's Susanah Kay though. She has something now," Nan suggested artlessly.

Jake grinned. "That's right. There *is* Susanah Kay. And I'll bet that between you and me we could handle her."

Nan burst into boisterous laughter, falling back in her chair, her thick shoulders shaking, "Why, Jake, she'll not part with a penny of what she has. She's packed and moving within the week. She and Tom are going to Philadelphia. They've a new place all picked out."

Jake's face turned white. "More of your foolish talk," he snarled.

He bent over her and caught her arm, pinching the fat flesh cruelly while he whipped his open palm across her face. "You keep that tongue of yours in your head," he yelled. "I know what I'm doing. And I don't want you talking me down."

She muttered protestingly through swelling lips, "Stop, Jake. I won't. You needn't take on so. It's not—"

"Then quit," he yelled. He hit her one last time for good measure, and left.

When he arrived at Haversham Square, he learned that all his thought and time had been wasted. He was not the only one who knew about the tract. John did, too. Nan was right, damn her!

John accepted the soiled pieces of paper that Jake offered him and studied them in silence. At last he raised his head, and said, "Just north of these shanties there's a vacant spot."

Jake held his breath.

John went on, "A small plot, mostly given to corn-raising, I think. Part of the old Burney place itself. You know where I mean?"

Jake nodded unwillingly.

"Go and have a look at it for me sometime. See if it's really what I think, or if it's already built on."

"It's not," Jake said, without thinking.

"And how do you know that?"

"I already looked."

John regarded him thoughtfully. Then, "Have you considered something about it yourself perhaps?"

"How could I?" Jake demanded. "Land costs money." He could already hear Nan's sneering laughter. A fire built in his chest. If she so much as looked at him sideways, he would pummel her black and blue. Aloud he went on. "And besides, it won't do you any good. None of that land will. No matter what you're planning for it. Those people are there, and with no place to go. You'll never be able to move them out."

"That's not your problem," John answered. "Nor, when I'm ready, will it be mine." He tossed Jake a gold piece. "Where are you living now?"

Jake described the place, not knowing that it was the same rooming house from which Miranda had moved to Haversham Square. Then he asked, "What do you figure to do with that land anyway?"

John gave him a hard stare. He had taught Jake long

before that he must not ask questions. It did not matter that this wasn't an unreasonable one. He said, "That's no affair of yours."

Jake shrugged. "I only wondered."

"Don't," John retorted, with a gesture of dismissal.

Jake went downstairs slowly, his shallow blue eyes darting about him eagerly. Someday, he thought, he would have such a house as this. He would own the fine crystal candeliers and the wall hangings. He would walk as master on such deep, soft floor coverings. He would drink the wine stored in the cellars, and eat the meat hanging in the pantries. He would—

He heard soft laughter and recognized Miranda's voice. He stopped. The sound came from the morning room. He turned that way.

John's voice enveloped him from the top of the stairs. "You're supposed to be on your way out. I'll send for you when I want you. Don't come back until then."

Jake directed a quick look over his shoulder and hurried to the door.

EIGHTEEN

From window after window, Christmas candles twinkled through the lightly falling snow, and glistening holly wreaths tied with red satin bows hung from brass knockers at every door.

The close-pressing fleecy gray quilt of the sky spread a magical hush through the cobbled lanes and byways, and across the vacant fields and crystal-touched trees.

There was only the muffled clump of the horses' hooves, and the soft sound of church bells ringing in the distance, and the high sweet singing of unseen carollers.

Miranda listened and smiled to herself. She sat straight and tall against the cushions in the carriage, as regal as any princess in ermine. And that was how she felt in that moment. She was a princess, not of the royal purple but of the spirit and soul. She was Miranda, of the Haversham family. No longer an unwanted and abandoned waif in Dealeyton, nor her stepmother's scullery maid in the Kayhome Arms, but Miranda Jervis of Haversham Square.

"It was a fine service," Stacy said. "I love to go to church on Christmas Eve. And," she added with a giggle, "I also love to go home afterwards and unwrap the presents."

"As you shall in a little while," John told her with an indulgent smile. He went on, "We've always, as far as circumstances permitted, made a big thing of this holiday, haven't we, Reed?"

"We have indeed," Reed answered.

"It's what makes good memories," John continued, savoring ahead of time what he knew would come.

Miranda thought he was in fine fettle that evening. And she was glad to see it. In spite of the pleasurable excitement of these past few days of preparation for the holiday, the secret planning and shopping, the wrapping and tying, she had noted in John a subtle impatience with Reed on several occasions. He had asked that Reed accompany him to a meeting with Carleton Van Eward, and frowned when Reed made his excuses. He had asked that Reed go with him to examine certain properties he was considering, and muttered in annoyance when Reed refused.

For her part, Miranda did not understand why Reed seemed determined to try his older brother by rejecting any suggestion that Reed begin to participate in Haversham affairs. This was, she was determined, purely a temporary response. When he was completely recovered, he would enthusiastically become John's lieutenant. Meanwhile, though Reed surely showed signs of improvement when his eyes became intent and aware, there were still moments of deep withdrawal. She had studied him for so long with the concentration of love that she believed she knew his every mood. It could be more festive this evening because of the holiday, and she hoped to accomplish that change for him if she could.

The carriage jolted over the slippery cobblestones and flung her against John's heavy bulk.

He put out a big, gloved hand to steady her. She was so lovely, he thought. A prize well worth all his planning and his carefully enforced patience. He found it difficult to release her when what he wanted to do was crush her closer and closer to him.

But she drew away with a quick apology and was promptly flung against Reed. That time she felt a quick singing in her blood and drew away more slowly, giving him a rueful smile.

His lean serious face suddenly brightened with a grin. "You're having a rough ride, Miranda."

"But we're almost there," Stacy said, leaning forward to peer from the window as the tall iron gates came into view.

The carriage stopped. Benjy opened the undecorated gates, and the carriage rolled through and up the driveway under the snow-glistening oaks to the house.

John hurried the others inside, and as soon as they had given their wraps to Jefferson, he hurried them into the morning room.

The air was scented with the rich perfume of burning cedar and pine needles, and popping embers danced over the flames on the hearth. A tall display of poinsettia blazed in a corner.

Stacy had herself directed where the mistletoe must be hung. She stood beneath it now and gave it a pointed glance. John laughed and touched his lips to her forehead. Then he took Miranda by the shoulders and turned her face up, cupping her cheeks with his big hands, and brushed a light kiss on her curls.

She was, for that instant, speechless. She was suddenly transported back in time to the night he had come to her room and held her thus, with the lamplight flickering in the shadows. And there came into her mind, too, the memory of how he had held her, swung her down from the carriage, only a few weeks before.

Then, as his hands fell away, she said, mustering laughter, "Thank you, Cousin John. For everything." She looked past his massive shoulder to where Reed stood, watching with an expression she couldn't read.

But, though she stayed beneath the mistletoe for a long moment, he did not come to her.

A giant tree, shining with silver and tinsel and fragile blue ornaments stood in a corner, towering over a snowy white field in which miniature horses and cows leaned at tiny fences, and red barns and brown farmhouses nestled in make-believe valleys. The country scene was encircled by a wall of packages.

Miranda and Stacy had done these arrangements together late that same afternoon, but as Miranda looked at them, she saw something was different. She realized then that one large package had been added to the others.

Abigail had set a bowl of eggnog on the sideboard, and a tray of iced green cress, and tiny sandwiches of ham and chicken, and a platter of red and green cookies.

Reed brought Miranda a cup of eggnog and sat beside her. "On other Christmas Eves this house was crowded, Miranda. It wasn't just the family then, but all of our friends."

She had no need for others, she thought. He was here. She wondered that he did not know her feelings, and then she wondered if he did know them, but, for his own reasons, pretended not to.

But she answered aloud, "It's a good holiday for me, Reed. The best I've known."

"I hope so. Though it's not as gay as it might have been."

The oblique reference to Caroline's death touched Miranda with a brief sadness. No one had mentioned her for so long. It all seemed almost a bad dream now.

And yet something remained of that night, a trailing residue of the fear known then. Miranda wondered if Reed were aware of it, too.

He said hastily, "But we're together."

She breathed, "Oh, yes," and saw his warm smile

spread to his eyes, and promptly forgot the troubling thought.

She and Reed were together.

John stood before the fire, his head bent and thrust forward.

Was he thinking of Caroline? Reed wondered. Of Christmases long past? Of what might have been had Caroline not died?

Stacy swept up to perch on the arm of the sofa. "John behaves very mysteriously. I wonder why."

"You'll soon see," Reed answered.

John turned then, grinning. "Shall we begin?"

"If we don't, I'll die of the suspense," Stacy cried. "I was never one to stand and wait."

"Nor should you be. But please bear with me, Stacy. We have something of a ritual to perform." Then, "Reed, will you have the servants in?"

As Reed left the room, Stacy sighed and pouted. "Then shall I light the candles?"

"Miranda," John said. "Would you?"

Next year at this time, he thought, she would perform that duty as his wife. But there was no need to delay his pleasure at seeing her engaged in such activity. He could enjoy it now.

She made a quick business of lighting the tall red tapers on the mantel, the tall green ones on the sideboard. She was aware that he followed her every movement with his dark granite eyes, but the room had a rosy glow from candle and fire and chandelier, and the air was sweet with pine, and by the time she had finished, Reed had returned, the servants with him.

John took a big chair and leaned back, savoring the sight of Miranda acting as mistress of Haversham Square. He motioned to the gifts beneath the tree. "My dear, will you do me the favor?"

"Of course," she said. She knelt beside the display and began to distribute the packages.

There was a red one for Abigail, a blue one for Jefferson, a green one for Lena. Timoshen's was white and so was Benjy's. She presented to each of them her own small gifts, each wrapped the same but labeled.

The formal thanks and good wishes were entwined with giggles and grins, and then John, his patience at an end, said, "That will be all for tonight." When the servants had gone, he rose, his hard face softened by firelight. He said, "Thank you, Miranda. Shall I do the rest of them?"

She got to her feet. "If you like."

Stacy cried, "John, I can't bear it. Not another moment."

He bent a long look at Miranda, but then, leaning to the pile, he took from it a small box, saying, "Stacy, this is for you, I think."

She leaped to her feet in a swirl of cherry-red velvet and accepted the glittering package. She opened it excitedly and then held the gleaming golden bracelet out to Miranda. "Isn't it lovely? Oh, I do thank you, John."

The gift-giving continued. There were scarves and lace collars for Miranda and Stacy. There were cravats and woollen mufflers for the men. There were boxes of candy and bonbons imported from France. There were books and stationery.

Reed had given Miranda a pair of pearl eardrops.

"Oh, Reed," she had cried. "How I love these. They will match my pearl strand."

"I had hoped so," he told her.

She had given him six silk handkerchiefs embroidered with his initial and blue forget-me-nots. He had immediately tucked one into the sling that bound his left arm.

There was one package left under the tree. It seemed to grow larger in the firelight.

Stacy eyed it expectantly. "And that is . . . ?"

"For Miranda," John told her. He picked up the box, held it out. He had been planning this moment for weeks now. At last it was here.

Miranda hesitantly took the box into both hands, her cheeks pink with excitement. She opened it carefully, folding the silver ribbon aside neatly, and then the heavy blue paper. Within, the dark silken sealskin glistened. Her amber eyes widened in a disbelieving stare. She flashed a look at John.

He drew the fur from the box, shook it. It became a long cloak. "Come," he said gently. "Come, let me see if it is the proper length."

She said breathlessly, "Oh, it is, it is. I know it is. Oh, John, John, you are so kind, so generous to me!"

He carefully placed the cloak around her shoulders, and she felt his hands touch them, cup them, stroke them, in a slow but covert caress, and when he smiled down at her she saw that his granite eyes had melted into a new softness.

Her heart gave a hard thud against her ribs, and her breath suddenly crowded her throat. But she smiled at him and thanked him again. She carefully removed the cloak and put it aside, and returned to her place beside Reed.

Reed frowned into the fire, though he did not actually see it. He saw, instead, the pale outlines of Caroline's face.

John did nothing without purpose. There must be purpose in this, too. And there had been an open possessiveness in the way he had settled the sealskin cloak on Miranda's shoulders. Was that gesture a sign of love? What did he feel for Miranda?

A heaviness settled on Reed. His joy in the evening was gone.

"Magnificent," Stacy said, with a touch of envy. "It's a truly magnificent fur, John."

He smiled at her. "I'm pleased that you approve of my choice, Stacy."

"How could I help but approve?" she answered.

Miranda hardly listened. She was aware only of Reed's stillness beside her, aware only of the quick hard pounding of her heart.

She knew that Caroline had been right. John's declaration by lamplight in the bedroom had been no jest. He had wanted her then, as he wanted her now.

A small shiver touched her. John was a man who took

what he wanted. But that could not be. It was Reed she loved. Reed. There would be no one else for her.

She determined that she would show him, as gently and subtly as she knew how, that she was not for him. She determined that she would be careful, as careful as she had been in Caroline's lifetime, that he think of her only as a young kinswoman under his protection, as that and nothing more.

But when he came to her three nights later, saying, "Come, Miranda. Let us go out together. I am tired of the house and all that's in it," she did not know how to refuse him even though she wanted to.

Stacy was out with Carleton Van Eward, and Reed had retired to his room early in the afternoon. Neither of them could be expected to accompany her and John. And she did not want to go out with him alone.

He saw her brief hesitation. He said, "Surely you won't refuse me the favor of your company. I've a small dinner party planned. Perhaps I should have mentioned it before, but I'm sure you will enjoy it."

Her hesitation vanished then. She answered, "I'll be delighted to join you, John," and within the hour they were riding through the early dark.

Timoshen stopped the carriage before the Ashley Restaurant. Pale gaslight glowed from its windows, and snowflakes drifted down from its brown canopy.

Sweet perfumed warmth drifted out when the door was opened to admit the two of them.

"Mr. Haversham, how good it is to see you again," the owner cried, trotting up to meet John and bowing to Miranda.

"You have my room?" John asked.

"Of course. Of course. All as you wished. Let me show you the way. You will be delighted, I'm sure."

With John leading her, Miranda went through the rank of waiters and serving maids, the owner leading the party.

He thrust aside a silken drape and then stood back, beaming.

John handed Miranda across the threshold.

The small room was dimly lit and scented with huge

bouquets of flowers. There was a fire on the hearth, and before it a narrow banquet set for two.

"Now, it is what you wanted, Mr. Haversham?" the owner asked. "Is there something else?"

"The champagne," John said impatiently. "Have the champagne brought in."

The owner nodded, smiled, patted his hands together, and disappeared behind the silken curtain.

Miranda said quietly, "Is there no dinner party as you said? Are we to be alone?"

He looked at her gravely for a moment, then asked, "Why? Is that so terrible? Are you afraid to be alone with me?"

"Cousin John," she said. "Why, surely you know—"

"Cousin John . . ." he mocked her. He took the sealskin cloak from her shoulders. "Sit down, Miranda."

She sank into the chair he indicated.

The owner bustled in with the champagne and served it, looking as if he would like further conversation. But John waved him off, and as he departed, a sweet tune drifted through the room.

Startled, she looked up.

"We have our own musician," John told her, as he seated himself beside her.

She saw, then, back in the corner behind a screen of flowers, a small wizened man playing a violin.

John poured champagne for them both, and as she sipped at hers, she thought there was something heady about being with John Haversham. To be greeted like royalty and led into a private room. To have one's own musician. To breathe the scent of flowers in late December.

John leaned back, his big body relaxed. He felt a surge of intense satisfaction just in looking at her in that moment.

She wore a gown of white velvet. Her shoulders were smooth and very white, and her slender arms shapely. Her throat was a proud column under her tipped-back head. She was perfection. He found suddenly that he had to avert his eyes from her. His need to possess her had become so strong in these past months, his obsession so intense, that he had to exert an unusual control. The formal mourning period was a year, but he refused to countenance such a delay. He would wait only six months, and society would have to make do with that. He would allow himself two months in which to woo and win her, to offer her what she would not refuse.

He leaned forward to refill her glass, and his hand touched hers. A fire seemed to spin through him. He said in a low thick voice, "Miranda, this is good. To be here like this with you."

She set aside the champagne and looked at him, and answered gently. "It's always good to be with you, Cousin John. Do you know, you are kinder to me than anyone has ever been in my life. Kinder surely than my own father."

John gave an exclamation of hoarse laughter. "Than your father, Miranda! But I'm not your father. And you mustn't think that of me."

"Of course not," she said gravely. "But still . . . I do wish that you were . . ."

"I don't wish it," he answered evenly. "Not for a moment."

She pretended to misunderstand. She pouted, "Then you must think I am not worthy."

"You're worthy of more," he told her.

The food was brought in on silver trays. There were small filets and tiny pearl onions and a salad of fresh greens. There was more champagne, and then there were huge red strawberries heaped with cream.

Yes, she thought, as he smiled at her, there was a heady excitement in being with him, near him. But it came from his power. It was not love. It could never be love. She wished she were with Reed.

John said, "Your eyes turn golden in the firelight, Miranda."

She looked up at him.

"They will make my gift to you seem nothing, I fear." He smiled, and took from his pocket a small package wrapped in satin. He placed it on the table and opened it.

Diamonds on a golden chain blazed up at her like bits of flame.

She gasped, "Why, John, it's so beautiful, but I cannot . . . I cannot take it."

"Cannot?" he repeated. "You can and you shall."

He took up the diamond necklace and put it around her throat. She froze within the circle of his arms, feeling his fingers caress the back of her neck. His touch sent a chill through her. She moved away as gracefully as she could, and took up her champagne. "Thank you, Cousin John. I'm grateful for all you do for me, believe me." Her voice was steady, but her heart was pounding. And her mind whispered, *Reed, Reed . . .*

A small fat red candle guttered on the bare wooden table and cast a shadow on Jake's face as he thrust his plate away, saying, "Goose, eh? Well, it's not bad, Nan. I've heard of it, but I never had it before."

"A good treat," she told him, "for celebrating the holiday season. Though it wasn't easy to come by, I assure you. What I went through to get the landlady to prepare it as I suggested? She was, I think, though she wouldn't admit it, as much a stranger to goose until yesterday as you were until tonight."

"It's not a feed for the poor, I'll warrant." He leaned on his elbows and rubbed between his big gnarled hands a thick mug of rum. "Nor is this a drink for the poor."

She laughed comfortably, settling her black skirts around her. "Then we're not so poor, are we?"

"I don't feel that I am. Not at the moment." He grinned at her. "What with the new suit you bought me, and that embroidered waistcoat . . ."

"Small tokens," she answered.

"But tell me, Nan, how did you manage to pay for them?"

"I've been wondering how long it would take you to ask me that question," she retorted, her black eyes gleaming.

"I've asked it now."

"It's Mary Bennett," Nan said. "She has a neat little room in the Barclay now."

Jake stared at Nan over the rim of his mug. "And . . . ?"

"And she has a few friends in now and then."

"And . . . ?" Jake repeated.

Nan pursed her lips. "Mary Bennett is an extremely helpless and foolish woman, you know. She has need of someone to advise her and protect her, and she had desperate need of someone to assist in setting up her small nest."

"In return for which," Jake said, "you share in her profits."

Nan nodded, "And so do you." She went on quickly. "There would have been more of them, in fact. But poor Mary, like all whores, is so very sentimental. She was doing so well, all those lonely Congressmen about, you see. But then she takes it into her head that she must go off and see her Ma for Christmas. I could hardly hold her here, could I?"

"I could have," Jake said softly.

"Then next time perhaps you will." Nan smiled.

NINETEEN

In mid-January Reed learned that Jim Boardman's father had died.

The news struck Reed with the force of a blow and sent him spinning back in memory to the awful moment when Jim's face had burned with hate over the smoking barrel of his gun, to the moment when Jim's empty eyes were turned to the empty sky.

Jim had been an only son, and his mother would be left alone on the small Maryland farm that Reed had once visited.

He knew he would have to go there again.

He didn't want to. He didn't want to leave Miranda, nor Haversham Square.

He wanted to be here, to see her, to sense her presence close by. He wanted to hear her laughter.

But he had to go. He would have no rest until he saw Jim Boardman's mother, alone in her double bereavement, and did what he could to help her.

He packed a portmanteau quickly and went in search of Miranda.

She was in the morning room, working at her embroidery hoop. The pale gray light of the gloomy day was behind her, casting a shadow across her face, and the red light of the fire on the hearth made her burgundy-colored gown seem black.

Unease touched him at seeing her thus. She did not know she was being observed. Why did she look so troubled? But there was no time to question her. His train would be leaving within the hour. He made his voice matter-of-fact as he said, "Miranda, I must go away for a few days, perhaps for a week."

She started, dropped her embroidery hoop, and golden threads trailed across her lap. Her eyes flashed up to his face. The pallor appeared more pronounced in his lean cheeks than it had for some time. She had begun to think him much better, though he still wore the black sling and spent a good deal of his time alone. "You're going away?" she asked. "But Reed, why? What is it?"

He explained only about the funeral, Jim's mother, the obligation to a dead friend.

Miranda said, "I'm sorry." Then, "You're leaving now for the train?" At his nod she rose. "I'll ride to the depot with you."

They spoke little in the carriage, but Miranda was glad to have those few moments more with him. She dreaded being parted from him, even for a few days. All brightness would be gone with him.

And there was John, who continued to press his suit upon her. She had, thus far, managed to avoid an outright rejection of him. But she feared that soon, very soon, she would have to tell him that she would never have him.

Would he then send her away from Haversham Square? From Reed?

The carriage jolted to a stop and Reed helped her down, and he continued to hold her arm as they went into the crowded steamy depot together.

"Only a few minutes now," Reed said.

She nodded.

There was suddenly a lump in his throat. He said hoarsely, "Miranda, you will be all right, won't you?"

She raised her face. "Of course." But there was a quaver in the word. She hurried on, "Be careful of yourself, Reed. Watch out lest the fever overtake you again."

There were whistles, shouts. A cart rattled by.

He bent to her, took her into his arms. He held her close as he kissed her.

She clung to him, feeling as if he were going away forever, until he put her gently aside, and said, "I'll be back soon, Miranda."

That night John sat at the head of the table, his eyes gleaming with satisfaction.

The huge mirror centerpiece was a replica of one used in the White House for state dinners, where John had seen and admired it, and decided he would have one for Haversham Square.

He had, long before, come to take for granted the possessions he had amassed, but the centerpiece and the matching candelabra, both specially cast for him by master workmen in Paris, never failed to excite and please him.

There was more, too. Josiah sat across from him, his attention firmly centered on laughing Stacy. Which was what John wanted at the moment. And Miranda sat at his right. Which was what he also wanted at the moment . . . and forever.

Soon she would have the mistress' place at the foot of the table, and raise her golden eyes to him across the wine carafes. But now she was close to him. Close enough so that he could enjoy the scent of her perfume.

He took a deep savoring breath.

She gave him a faint smile, but a vague uneasiness stirred

in her when she looked at him. There was something about him this night, something particular that she could not quite identify, that troubled her. She tried to ignore it. She turned to Josiah, "Did you have a good sojourn at home?"

He nodded, and replied with no enthusiasm, "Very good indeed. But now I'm returned to the usual problems."

He went on, outlining in more detail than she wished to hear, the proposals that were being considered in Congress.

She nodded, a listening look on her face, but she allowed her attention to wander. Reed's chair was empty.

She wondered if he had yet reached his destination, and how he fared. She wished that he were already on his way back.

The need for him became even stronger when she glanced at John again, and felt once more a peculiar frisson. A tingling in her nerves. Something was wrong.

Jefferson poured more wine.

Stacy raised her glass, and cried, "And this is to John Haversham, our host." Then, smiling, "That's such a handsome outfit, John. I've not seen you wear it since the night Caroline . . ."

Stacy's voice trailed off.

But Miranda finished the sentence in her mind. "Since the night Caroline died . . . the night Caroline died . . ."

That was it!

The jacket! The jacket! John had changed his jacket that night!

Miranda sank back, holding the wine glass to her lips as if hiding her horror behind it.

John had murdered Caroline.

Miranda flashed a quick look at him.

He raised his big hands, smoothing his curly dark brown hair in a gesture that had suddenly become unspeakably familiar to her. That movement and the words just spoken by Stacy told Miranda the truth.

Josiah's grating voice went on, and Stacy's laughter tinkled, and John made some comments. These were all a muted background to Miranda.

For she lived in that terrible night again. She heard the

music of Mozart, the piano, the deep strong voice of the cello, the sweet reply of the violin. She heard laughter, applause, and the tinkling of champagne goblets. She saw John come into the room, pause at the door. She saw him raise his hands to smooth his hair. Then his hands dropped, and he settled his black jacket.

She remembered now the confusion she had felt then. The bewilderment which, in the events that followed, she had completely forgotten.

Now, though, she understood. Because of Stacy's teasing words.

He had changed his jacket. What he wore when he came to ask where Caroline was was not what he had worn earlier. At the beginning of the evening he wore the same black, braid-trimmed coat that he wore at this moment. The same gold-embroidered waistcoat showed under it, and the same large diamond winked from his cravat. But at the evening's awful end, his coat had been trimmed with velvet, and he no longer wore the diamond. Stacy was right. He had not worn that same outfit since the night that Caroline died.

Miranda's understanding was immediate and hideous. She could imagine the darkness of wet sleeves, and splash marks that signified a struggle. She could picture the hurried change of outer garments and the race down to the ballroom.

The big dining room was suddenly stifling. The candlelight seemed to fade.

But by an effort of will she continued to maintain her composure through the rest of the evening.

She smiled at John and laughed at Stacy's sallies. She listened attentively to Josiah's pronouncements.

At last the evening ended.

Josiah took his leave, holding overlong to Stacy's hand. She was giggling as she started up the steps.

John asked, "Miranda, will you have a last glass of wine with me?"

With horror crowding her throat, she smiled and answered, "No, John. I think not. I shall go to bed."

Her voice was steady, though within her breast her heart seemed to shake.

John had murdered Caroline. And now, in his freedom, he had turned to her, to Miranda, to court her, win her.

She went up the stairs just behind Stacy, feeling his gaze go with her all the way. She bade Stacy a calm good night and stepped into her own room. She closed the door softly behind her.

The very walls seemed to warn her to flee. The very silence seemed to whisper that she must escape.

Tears stung her eyes. Sobs choked her. But she would not give way. She fought both down, and at the same time fought down the warnings and the whispers.

She would not run away from John. To do so would be against her nature. She belonged here. She would not give up the place to which she had been born. Even now the Haversham name held a hint of magic. Yes. Even now.

And beyond that, she would not give up the hope of loving Reed, having Reed.

But he was not here now. It would be days before he returned.

She was alone with her terrible knowledge.

She pictured Caroline's face adrift among the lilies, and shuddered.

That night she dreamed. She saw John walking toward her, offering her in the one hand a huge gardenia, and in the other a pair of amber eardrops. His dark coat was trimmed with a velvet collar, and both his sleeves were soaked up to the elbows, and his gray eyes were cold as stone.

TWENTY

Dawn brightened the window. Later there was the thin pale yellow light of the winter sun, which was soon obscured by the chill gray winter mists.

Miranda watched the change as the hours went by and heard the faint tick of the clock on the mantel, and counted the passing moments with despair.

What was she to do?

How could she keep this terrible knowledge to herself? Yet how could she cry it aloud for all to hear?

When she did not go down to breakfast, Abigail came to inquire.

"I'm tired, Aunt Abigail. Perhaps I'm coming down with a cold. I'll stay abed today."

Abigail studied her, and said, "I'll bring you toast and tea."

Miranda protested that she wanted nothing. She wanted only to rest, sleep.

Abigail left her, but soon returned with a tray. "Mister John wants to know if he should send for Doctor Porter," she announced. "And he sent you these." She indicated the two huge gardenias in the silver bowl.

"No, Aunt Abigail," Miranda gasped. "No doctor," and turned her head on the pillow.

Much later, Stacy came in, crying, "What is this? Are you ill, Miranda?"

"No," Miranda answered, but added hastily, "Or perhaps I have a bit of a cold coming on. I shall keep to my room today and rest."

"Oh, what a pity. You mustn't have a cold. Remember there is Josiah's party the end of the week. I do believe he has gone to a great deal of trouble. And all to impress us."

Miranda wished that she would go, and soon Stacy did,

sighing that the house seemed too empty with Reed gone and Miranda taken to her bed.

Twice during the day she heard John's heavy step beyond her door, and heard his knock, but pretended to be sleeping.

Abigail brought her a meal she did not eat, and finally night came, but she did not sleep.

What was she to do?

When would Reed return?

She watched dawn come again, and heard the morning sounds of the house again.

When Abigail appeared with a tray, John was with her.

He stood silently by, observing while Abigail uncovered hot buttered bread and fruit, and poured the tea. Then he sent her away.

He stood over Miranda, smiling. "Come now, what is it? If you are ill, we must have a doctor." And he touched her forehead lightly. "I see that you have no fever."

She cringed inside at the touch of his hand, but concealed it. She retreated into feminine confusion, a blush rising in her face, and stammered, "John, really, I'm not ill."

He said, "Then forgive me for intruding. But I was concerned. It's not like you to take to your bed, you know."

She had dreaded this moment above all. The moment when she must see him. She had imagined that he must look into her eyes and see the horror there. He must see how what he had done sickened her soul.

But he saw nothing. He knew nothing.

To him, Stacy's words had been a mere compliment, not a revelation that had unmasked him forever.

Miranda said aloud, lightly, "It will pass, John."

"I hope it does. And soon. We are invited to Josiah's, you know. We can't disappoint him."

"I'm not certain I shall be able to go, John," she ventured.

His big hands tightened, and his head thrust forward. "But you shall be able, of course. You'll wear the necklace I gave you, and dress in all your finery, and discover that going out in society is the only medicine you require."

She laughed softly, though she quaked inside. "I hope so, John."

"You'll see," he answered.

She knew that under no circumstances would he permit her to remain at home.

She was trembling, though not from cold, when she closed the bedroom door behind her after their return.

It had been the effort to maintain her composure throughout the hours of Josiah's party that had so drained her. The gaiety and music had underscored her terror, and then, on the way home, John had taken her hand and held it so firmly that she could not draw away.

She began to take down her hair as she moved to the dressing table.

How still the house was . . .

John listened to that same stillness and paced the room.

A fire burned in him, burned as brightly as the fire on the hearth.

By now, he thought, Stacy would be asleep.

By now, Miranda would be in her bed.

How beautiful she had been that night, his necklace blazing at her throat.

He imagined her dark hair spread on the pillow, the slenderness of her white arms reaching out to him.

She was his.

He went to the door . . .

The light flickered, and shadows danced along the walls. Within the frame of the mirror before her, Miranda saw her door open, saw John's massive body moving through it.

Her hair was down on her shoulders, and her gown unhooked and dropped to reveal her breasts. She swiftly covered herself as she turned, saying, "John, what is it?" remembering as she did another time he had entered her room thus.

He didn't answer but came slowly toward her, a young yearning look in his eyes.

"John," she said. "You must not . . ."

"Let me help you," he said thickly. "Let me undo your gown."

"You must not," she whispered, backing away. "Please, Cousin John . . ."

But he reached out for her, and swept her into his arms. He held her against his big chest and buried his face in her throat, murmuring, "Miranda, you're mine. Mine. You belong to me. You'll always belong to me."

"No," she cried. "No, John, I cannot. Don't touch me, John."

"There's someone else," he said. "Someone who stands between us."

"No," she answered hotly. "It's not true!"

"There can be no one else for you, my darling. You belong to me," he told her. And he thought of Reed. Reed. She had given her heart to Reed. But he was only a boy. He could not oppose John. He could not matter.

"No," she said despairingly. "John, you must believe me. I cannot . . ."

He didn't seem to hear her. He said, "I'll give you the world, Miranda. The whole world. All of it. You'll be my wife, my darling. Soon, just a few months more, and we'll marry."

She struggled, turning her face away from his searching lips. The terror contained within her for the past three days rose up and overwhelmed her.

She cried, "Don't touch me, John. Don't touch me. I know the truth. I know, I know, I tell you. You murdered Caroline. And then you sent me out into the dark to find her drowned body."

The words were said, and hung in the still air, never to be recalled.

The young yearning look was gone from his eyes. They were stony wet granite again. But nothing else in his big face changed.

"You changed your jacket, John. I remember it well. And I know why. It was wet, wasn't it? You had to change after you drowned Caroline."

He only smiled faintly. He moved his hands caressingly along her arms as he released her. "My poor darling, you've been more ill than I thought these past few days, haven't you? But how can you allow yourself to entertain such awful imaginings?"

It was thus that he had often spoken to Caroline, Miranda remembered.

He went on, "We'll talk of my plans for us another time. When you are completely yourself again."

"No," she whispered. "I do not imagine. It's true, John. You know that it's true."

"You can't possibly think that I take such words seriously, Miranda." His smile broadened. "You are beset by some feminine trouble, and have confused yourself. Such accusations only prove so. You know as well as I do that Caroline committed suicide."

"No," she whispered again.

"But yes, my poor lovely darling. Everyone is aware of that. Even though it is listed as an accident in the official reports. Everyone is aware that Caroline was mad and died because of it."

She could only shake her head from side to side in wordless denial.

John said gently, "You must go to bed now, and to sleep. Surely you'll have forgotten this strange idea of yours by morning." He went to the door, opened it. When he looked back at her, his head was lowered between his hunched shoulders. "It's a pity," he said, and now there was no gentleness in his voice. "A pity, my dear Miranda, that you are so clever. It's a quality that could easily destroy you."

He paced the room, allowing the fury within him that full rein he had not allowed before.

His heavy footsteps beat a drum roll of rage, and his fists clenched and unclenched at his sides.

She knew.

She knew.

Everything he had planned, all his cherished resolutions must be abandoned. He was balked as he had never before been balked in his life. And all because of a slip of a girl with a slender white body and golden eyes.

But he would not allow her, not even lovely Miranda, to destroy him.

He found himself touched with brief surprise at how easily danger had freed him from the spell in which he had been bound.

A last quiver of longing touched him, of the hunger that had driven him. It burned in his heart, his loins. Then it died like a sinking fire, and he began to think.

He stood very still near the window, his motionless body a block of stone, and looked along the slope of the lawns toward the hidden lily pond beyond the rhododendron grove.

From somewhere far across the winter-bound town a train whistle sent out a long lonely wail. It might have been one of the Haversham engines, pulling into the yards on the other side of the river.

He tipped his head to listen until the sound had faded away.

She knew . . .

TWENTY-ONE

Miranda spent another sleepless night looking forward with dread to seeing John again.

What could she say to him?

What could he say to her?

What would he do?

What would he do to her?

But when they did meet over the breakfast table, he only nodded his big head, and said, "How nice you look today, Miranda. I hope you're fully recovered."

She answered in cold composure, "Thank you, John. I am."

It was as if nothing had happened.

And that frightened her even more.

She saw that he smiled faintly, as certain as always of his power, and enjoying it as always.

Her only protection against him would be proof. Evidence of what he had done. That was what she needed. Only that could save her.

When the meal was at last over, she went into the cooking quarters.

Abigail was rolling out dough. She glanced up at Miranda, her scarred face questioning, and then concentrated on what she was doing.

"Aunt Abigail," Miranda asked, her voice soft, choosing her words carefully. "Do you remember the night Miss Caroline died?"

Abigail's hands tightened around the rolling pin so that the veins stood out against the wrinkled skin. She slid a glance upward at Miranda. She jerked her head in what was plainly an unencouraging nod.

"She *did* stop and speak with you, didn't she?"

"It's no good dwelling on that night," Abigail answered brusquely, "And you oughtn't to."

"But she did?"

"She wanted more heated rolls on the buffet," Abigail said with a sigh.

"And then she talked to Jefferson, didn't she?"

"She said he should bring up two more bottles of champagne from the cellars."

"Then where did she go?"

Abigail answered, "I don't know. I was, we all were, too busy to be watching her. We had all we could do, what with directing those other people brought in to help. They were more trouble than they were worth, or paid for either."

Miranda cut in, "What about Mister John? Was he about? Did you see him with her? Did you see him on the servants' staircase?"

"I didn't see anything," Abigail said. "I don't know anything about Mister John. Nor where he went, nor what he did. I do my work. And so does my family. You oughtn't to ask questions I can't answer, Miss Miranda."

Miranda heard restrained fear in the irritable voice, and

sighed and turned away. Abigail could not help her, and it was unkind and wrong that she be expected to do what she plainly could not.

Still, Miranda told herself, somewhere there must be evidence of what John had done.

She was not mad. She knew. She knew.

At the end of that week, Reed finally returned home. He looked tired and drawn, and he moved his left arm awkwardly. In answer to her question, he said that Mrs. Boardman was bearing up as well as could be expected, and that her needs would be seen to.

Her heart sank when she saw the veiling of his silver eyes. He was not thinking of her, not really seeing her. She had waited for his return with such hunger, such despair. Now it meant nothing, she thought. Nothing. She had no one to turn to.

But later that day, he asked her to join him in a game of chess. They settled before the fire in the morning room.

They had been playing only a little while when the heavy front doors slammed with a great booming echo.

He saw how nervously Miranda started at that single commonplace sound.

Watching her, he asked in a quiet voice, "Miranda, what is it? Why are you so unlike yourself? Did something untoward happen while I was away?"

He saw very clearly that something was wrong. There were faint purple bruises beneath her eyes, as if she no longer slept well. Her long beautiful hands fidgeted anxiously with each other, trembled over the chess board between them.

His concern for her only proved what he had come to realize gradually. She was dear to him, and always would be. He could not be blind to the turmoil within her, though he saw the effort she made to conceal it.

"You must trust me," he said at last, in the face of her silence. "Can you not try to, Miranda?"

All that she had held within her in his absence welled up, became words that crowded her lips. But in that moment, she saw that she could not speak.

She trusted Reed. She loved him.

But she could not tell him that his brother John was a murderer. How could she say those terrible words with no evidence? And without saying those terrible words, she could not explain that she had given herself away, that John knew of what seemed to shriek in her mind like a long silent scream.

"Tell me what troubles you," Reed said. "I'll mend it, if I can."

She very nearly cried out. She saw quite clearly that Reed must not know the truth. She could not ever tell him. What would he do? How dare she turn him against his brother? Even though she knew what John was. Even though she knew what John could do.

Reed leaned forward, took the chess board, and set it aside. "Very well then. But I think that you can't concentrate today. We'll play another time."

She rose, unwilling to leave him, but knowing it would be better if she did. She found it difficult to withstand the gentle questioning look in his eyes. She found it hard to choke back words she dared not say.

If only she could prove that John . . .

Reed got to his feet, too. He smoothed a lock of hair from her cheek, and said softly, "I'm glad I'm home again, Miranda."

Nan's mouth turned down, and her black currant eyes narrowed in suspicion. "It's a pity," she said. "Here we've got our own little nest now, snug as we could be, and we do well enough. Why do you have to go up there?"

"Because he wants me to," Jake said.

"And I suppose that seems good reason to you?"

"If it wasn't, would I go?" Jake retorted.

She surveyed the small drab room, then grinned. "Well, it is snug enough, but I can't say that I blame you," she grinned. "Who'd refuse Haversham Square with this to leave behind?"

"I wouldn't," he sneered.

"You needn't be all that enthusiastic. I know a man must do what he must do. But you've had it pretty good here." She waited, but Jake didn't respond. So she went on, "And I doubt you crave John Haversham's company all that much."

Jake grinned slightly.

"Then there's some other reason for your enthusiasm," she suggested.

"Maybe it's the thought of getting away from you."

She laughed hoarsely. "Maybe. But I never noticed that you hurried to do that until Timoshen brought you the message a little while ago."

Jake didn't answer.

"What do you suppose it is?" she mused. "Some job for you?"

"Why, it has to be."

"Do you think it's more about that land along the avenue?"

"No, I shouldn't think so." His mouth slanted down. "Tell me, Nan, what makes you so nosy? You could get yourself into trouble that way, don't you know it?"

She continued to think about the land that John Haversham owned but had still not begun, as far as she could see, to make use of, and ignored Jake's two questions to say, "I still believe you handled that badly, Jake. If you'd gotten the Burney tract there—"

"Which John already had. And already knew what I was trying to do," Jake said harshly.

"Well," she said reasonably, "I didn't know that. You didn't say. But there'll be another time, and another tract. It's not all done."

Jake rose, shook back the wispy red hair from his forehead. "What have you got to give me before I go?"

"Give you?"

He looked down at her, his eyes narrowing. "You've got something from Mary Bennett, I know."

Nan sighed deeply. She thrust a fat hand into the neck of her dress, reaching between her melon breasts. "Well, it's not so much as it should be. She came back from visiting her Ma with a bad case of the weeps. I've just managed to get her over them." She brought out a few pieces of hard money and dropped them into Jake's outstretched palm.

He looked at them and frowned. "It *must* have been a bad case of the weeps. Well, hit her where it won't show, and put her to work."

"I needn't be told my business," she answered softly.

"Looks like you do. You might tell her to extend herself a little. Josiah Hurley hangs around the Barclay quite a lot. And so does John Haversham."

"I'll remember," she promised. "But you won't forget your poor old Nan, will you? Now that you've gone to join your fine employer in his fine home?"

Jake grinned. "Don't worry. I'll be down to collect my share from you, and maybe buy you a pint or two now and then. And when the job is done I'll be back."

"It'll be interesting to know what the job is," she told him thoughtfully.

He took up the canvas sack in which he had packed his few belongings, not answering her. He considered it not likely that she would ever learn what it was that had led John Haversham to send for him. He saw no reason to tell her that he wouldn't be back to the small room she called their nest, except in the most dire emergency.

It had been snug enough when he needed it, but he needed it no longer.

He left after a brief farewell, and walked up the road, his sack over his shoulder.

It was late afternoon and had been raining slightly. He cursed the gigs and carriages that spun by, splashing him with a muddy spray, and the two lean dogs that trotted behind him to snip and snap at his boots.

But he had begun to feel good. The sun was hidden now, but it had been bright enough that morning to remind him of spring. And more, much more than the promise of spring, was the promise that he might find, in this summons, the opportunity which he had long sought.

When he reached the gates of Haversham Square, he was admitted by Benjy without question or delay. He walked slowly up the long driveway under the still-bare trees, and mounted the white circular steps to the big double doors.

Jefferson greeted him without enthusiasm, and Miranda,

in the act of emerging from the music room, froze on the threshold.

"Well, girl," he greeted her, with a sly slanting smile. "Wouldn't you want some news of old Tom, if you could get it?"

"Have you heard of him lately?" she asked coldly, unwillingly.

"He and his Susanah Kay have moved themselves to Philadelphia. Didn't you know?"

"I did not." Nor, her tone said, did she much care. Which was certainly not dissembling. Ever since John had told her that he had given Tom Jervis a substantial sum of money in exchange for his promise to leave the city she had dismissed her father from her mind. He had acted in character as always. He had bartered her away, as men had once bartered their slaves. She had no use for him, and never would, and never wanted to. At the time it had been done, she had been grateful to John, believing that he sought to protect her from the embarrassment of her father's determination to profit by her life with the Havershams. But she was no longer sure of what John's motive had been. She was no longer sure of a great deal that she had once taken for granted.

Now she turned her back on Jake and withdrew into the music room.

Reed said, "That was Jake Rooker, wasn't it?"

She nodded.

"Come to see John?"

"I suppose so. I didn't ask him." She drew a slow breath. "I don't like him, Reed, and never have. I have the feeling that where Jake Rooker is, there's bound to be trouble."

"You may well be right. But it has nothing to do with you. Come and sit down, and allow John to deal with him."

She seated herself in the deep chair on the far side of the hearth, where small flames did a quiet dance among the half-burned logs. It was so still that she could hear the ticking of the ormulu clock on the mantel.

She thought suddenly that they were, the two of them, like a husband and wife, taking time out from daily affairs to spend a few moments together alone. It was a pleasant idea, but touched with wistfulness. She was quite sure the idea would never occur to Reed.

He pressed the arm in its sling against his chest, and watched the play of expression on her face, and wished that he knew what she was thinking, what had brought that sudden flush to her cheeks.

She said suddenly, "You're not at all interested in John's affairs, are you, Reed? You don't concern yourself with his business, even with the railroad or his other holdings, although I've noticed that he often does try to ... try to ..."

"To draw me in," Reed said in a dry tone. Then he grinned, and his lean face looked younger than his twenty-six years. "John was so determined that I join him that I fear I rebelled. Though I did study the law, which is what he wanted."

"But why should John have wished you to do that?"

Reed answered thoughtfully, "Most probably because he felt he could use my talents in the legal field to his advantage." He hesitated then, not quite knowing how to explain to her that John's interests were not his, and never would be. He did not see himself dedicated to the accumulation of power as John was. At last he said only, "Perhaps I don't really know."

"When you're ready," she answered, "it will all become quite clear to you. It's only now, when you're still recovering, that you're uncertain of what you want."

Her voice trailed away. She realized suddenly that in these few moments, speaking with Reed, she had forgotten her terror. She had forgotten what John knew of her inner mind. Reed had done that for her.

He saw the soft look of her golden eyes, and would have risen to take her into his arms, but at that moment Jefferson came in to announce that tea was being served in the morning room, and that John was waiting there with Stacy for Miranda and Reed to join him.

TWENTY-TWO

In the next two weeks, John continued his varied activities, but he spent an ever-increasing amount of time in Haversham Square.

He watched Miranda.

He watched her now from the cover of the oak trees as he rode with Stacy and Reed.

She walked slowly along the path. She wore a gown of heavy brown broadcloth, and a thick hand-woven shawl of the same color, with fringes that hung to the tiny heels of her slippers. She moved with that same proud grace that had never failed to move him. It did not touch him now.

Though the lawns were brown and dull, the February sun touched her face with faint warmth, and in its brightness there was a hint of spring to come.

She took no comfort in it. The fear that bloomed within her like an ugly flower gave her no rest. Always, always, she sensed a hostile gaze upon her. John's cold gaze.

And there was Jake Rooker, too.

If she walked on the back terrace, he was there, whittling at a stick. If she walked at the front, he was there, smiling at her around a bit of leaf between his teeth.

But she was alone now, and she still felt the hostile gaze upon her.

The heavy stillness, so much a part of the sense of unreality that had lately enveloped her, was suddenly torn by the thud of horses at the run.

Below, at the rim of the oak stand, and moving through the thick laurels, she saw Stacy, riding sidesaddle in a habit of black, with her chestnut hair flying from beneath her small plumed hat. She raced from the trees on a huge palomino, shouting exuberantly.

Reed, then John, galloped behind her.

Miranda stood still to watch, her eyes on Reed. He held the reins in his right hand, his left arm, still in its sling, pressed to his chest. He was smiling in a way that touched her heart. She felt a slight stir of jealousy. She, rather than Stacy, should be riding with Reed. It was her own fault that she was not. She could have been. But she had lately been withdrawn into her own macabre thoughts. Thoughts she dared share with no one. The weight of John's concentration had blinded her to all but the terror within her, and the necessity to conceal it. But that blindness had been an error. She was determined to rectify it. She loved Reed. She would have him. Why else had she stayed in Haversham Square, knowing the threat that hung over her.

The three horsemen were much closer now, within yards of where she stood.

She could see the horses' flashing eyes and flying manes and whipping tails. She could see even the small sparks strucks off their shoes on the stones.

Then John's black stallion rose skyward, forelegs knifing the air viciously. For an instant, John seemed to hang there, set firmly in the saddle, immense and immovable. Then he fell sideways and rolled, and the horse came down and hit hard and raced thundering wildly on.

Fright washed over her in a cold, freezing wave. She could not move. Oddly, there passed through her mind a series of quick blurred images. Reed's face when he bent to kiss her as he helped her from the canoe . . . The young look of Caroline when Miranda brushed her hair . . .

She heard Reed cry out, and Stacy's shrill horrified scream as the riderless horse plunged toward her, iron stirrups clanking.

Then Reed's roan leaped from behind, swung in, driving the maddened stallion off, while Reed himself, leaning low in the saddle, lifted her from her feet and carried her yards away to safety.

It seemed that the sky whirled around her, darkening with the pulse of blood behind her eyes, while Reed held her against the roan's sweaty, heaving side. Then the sun was bright again. He lowered her carefully to her feet and stepped down to hold her.

"You're all right?" he asked thickly. He was remembering the feel of her slim body in the tight circle of his good arm, and the tender closeness of her heartbeat in his own flesh. In those swift and terrifying moments he learned that he wanted her as he had wanted no other woman in his life. The gradually developing need had come to full flower. It made speech difficult, his voice heavy, his words unsure. "Miranda . . . you're not hurt?"

She only nodded, too shaky now to attempt words. But there was a whisper in her mind. John . . . ?

Stacy's palomino danced closer nervously. The girl called down, "Oh, what a fright that was! I could hardly believe it was happening! I am quite breathless. I even feel giddy. Miranda, my sweet, do you realize how terribly close the stallion was?"

Miranda still didn't speak. There was nothing to say. She knew.

John rose slowly to his feet. He took up his crop and dusted off his habit. Then, with his spurs jingling a sinister music, he came to Miranda to say gravely, with a faint smile on his lips, "I'm sorry, my dear. I don't quite know what hit that fool animal. He'll pay for doing that, I assure you."

She looked into his gray eyes, and answered evenly, "But nothing has happened, Cousin John," and felt, at the same time, a coldness settle around her heart.

The suspicion that had churned in her, infecting every moment with a species of poison that spoiled but did not kill, was no longer mere suspicion. John had planned this.

Reed's good arm slid from around her shoulder. He said with a sudden grin, "One good thing has come of it. Miranda," and pulled the black sling from his arm and over his head. "I see now that I need this no more."

"Have a care," John told him. Then, "And see to the horse for me, will you?" Without another word, he went into the house.

"He's very angry," Stacy said. "And it's fortunate that

he wasn't hurt. You, too, are fortunate, Miranda," she added with a sudden shudder of slim shoulders.

Reed tossed the reins of his horse to Stacy. "You take them back, will you?"

She nodded and rode off, and he took Miranda's hand. He felt as if some invisible bond that had held him had fallen away when he removed the black sling from his arm. "Come," he said. "Let's go inside. It's over now."

John had poured himself a glass of brandy. He looked at Miranda, then poured one for her.

He brought it to her, saying, "Miranda, my dear, I hope you weren't too frightened."

She accepted the glass, drew her hand away, hating the touch of his fingers. She said, "No, Cousin John, I wasn't. You see, it seemed to be over with so quickly." But she saw silent laughter in the depths of his eyes.

She knew that the incident just passed out of doors was not what it seemed. He had somehow goaded his horse out of control, let himself safely fall, and thought to rise after she had been trampled to death under those awful flailing hooves.

A shudder touched her. She could not repress it, nor could she hide the paleness of her heart-shaped face.

John said quietly, looking at her from his great height, "I fear that Miranda was much more frightened than she is willing to admit."

She didn't answer him. But she raised her eyes briefly to his face.

She stood straight and unmoving, yet the long fringes of her shawl trembled as if wind-touched though the air in the room was still.

Yes, Reed thought. She was frightened. Of John.

What had happened while he was away?

Had John pressed his suit and been refused? Was that why terror burned in Miranda's eyes?

She finished the brandy he had given her, and excused herself, and then went up to her room.

John poured another glass of brandy and went to stand before the small fire. He knew that Reed was watching him, but said nothing.

So that it was Reed himself who finally said, "What do you suppose got into that horse of yours?"

John shot a look at his brother's speculative face, then shrugged. "I've no idea. Perhaps something startled him, though I didn't notice anything at the time. As Miranda said, it happened so quickly."

Reed stretched his arm. "I think I've worn the sling too long."

John nodded.

"You're very preoccupied," Reed went on, uneasily aware of the stony look on his older brother's face.

A deep disquiet filled him as he reviewed those quick moments outside. He got to his feet, sweat suddenly gathering on his forehead. Miranda might so easily have died, crushed and bleeding under the slashing of the stallion's hooves. And if he had lost her, he would have lost all that he wanted.

John was apologizing, "I'm sorry to be abstracted, Reed. I have things on my mind."

"Yes. I see," Reed answered, and excused himself and went directly to the stables.

The three horses had been groomed and brushed, and were now in their stalls.

He examined the stallion carefully but found no mark on it.

He heard Jake Rooker moving about in the loft above but didn't call out to him. Instead he went back to the house, and found Timoshen, and asked, "Was Mister John's horse all right when Miss Stacy brought him in?"

"Lathered up and excited," Timoshen answered.

"You didn't see a bite, or a sting, or cut?"

"I didn't."

"Then perhaps he needs training still," Reed said. But there was a grimness about his mouth, a stoniness in his jaw that made him, for the moment, resemble John. John was, Reed thought, not an easy man for any horse to unseat.

"Perhaps he does need more training," Timoshen agreed. "But I never thought so until today."

There was sweat on Reed's forehead again, and a chill

in his flesh. He realized tiredly that an attack of fever was coming on him at the worst possible time. He moved his arm wryly, and thought that having survived that injury he would somehow survive this onslaught as well.

But when he left Timoshen, he found that the chill had become a raging fever. He took his medicine and managed to get to his bed before he collapsed.

It was days before he was fully himself again.

There had been brief moments of consciousness when he opened his eyes and saw Miranda leaning over him, and felt the touch of her hands on his forehead. There had been other brief moments when he heard John and Doctor Porter conversing.

Now, opening his eyes once more, he raised his head. Abigail moved quickly to his side. "What can I give you, Mister Reed?"

"Nothing," he whispered. "Is everything all right?"

She regarded him blankly. "All right? You've been mighty sick."

"I know that." He forced a smile. "I think I know it anyhow. I meant otherwise. Miranda . . ."

She answered, "Nothing's changed."

He let his head fall to the pillow as shadows seemed to grow in the corners of the room. "I think I'd better sleep, Abigail."

He didn't hear her leave the room.

He dozed, and when he awakened again, Miranda said, "How are you, Reed?"

"Better, I think."

"I'm so glad. You frightened us. It seemed to come on you so . . . so suddenly."

"Such fevers do that." He studied her carefully. Yes, the dark places were still under her eyes, and her face still showed signs of fear. He asked in a deep tired whisper, "Miranda, did you take care of me all this while?"

"Only some of it," she answered. "John wouldn't allow me to stay with you very long. Abigail was here mostly."

He leaned back and closed his eyes. "Has anything happened?"

"Happened, Reed?"

"You, you yourself have been all right?"

"Yes," she said. "I have been."

He allowed himself to fall asleep again.

When he awakened once more it was night. He sat up cautiously and found that the chill, the weakness, was gone. He fingered his days' growth of beard distastefully, and decided that he would allow himself the comfort of shaving the first thing in the morning. He thought of the fear in Miranda's face and decided he would not admit too quickly to his recovery.

That day Miranda wrapped her cloak around her and went down the circular steps to the waiting carriage.

Timoshen opened the door for her and helped her in. He was about to mount to the driver's seat when the doors opened again, and Jefferson signaled.

Timoshen took the steps at a run, spoke a few words with his father, and then, very slowly, returned to the carriage.

"Miss Miranda," he said, "I'm sorry. But Mister John says he'll be needing the carriage in a few minutes. He asks me to apologize to you. And says would you please go on your outing another day?"

"Why, of course." She stepped quickly down from the carriage, her cheeks flaming. She was embarrassed that she had ordered the carriage without first consulting John. But she had not thought. She had simply wanted to be away from the house for a little while.

She hesitated, then asked, "What about the gig, Timoshen?"

"It's . . . there's a . . ." Timoshen paused, then began again. "Jake's working on it. It has a broken axle, I think."

He was plainly lying, and plainly he had no reason to, unless he was repeating what John had told him to say.

A shiver went down her back. Her hands within her muff were suddenly cold.

She nodded, turned, and went slowly down the driveway. She heard him mumble something, but didn't turn back.

She found the tall iron gates locked. Benjy was not in the gatehouse. There was nothing to do but return to the house, though it was certainly not what she wanted to do at that moment.

She was midway on the drive when the carriage rolled to a stop beside her.

John leaned out, smiling. "I'm sorry, Miranda. I hope Timoshen explained."

"He did," she said briefly.

"I'd take you with me, but I have a special errand, and I'm in a bit of a hurry."

"Then I had better not delay you," she replied, thinking that he did not seem in a hurry.

"If there's something you would like to do . . ."

"It can wait," she answered.

She caught the quick satisfaction in his eyes, and in his faint smile. She wondered if she were imagining it. She added, "I only wanted some ribbons for a new hat and a supply of embroidery silk."

"I promise to arrange it for tomorrow," John assured her.

She thanked him, then added as an afterthought, "I was surprised to find the gates locked, Cousin John, and Benjy gone."

"Were you, my dear?" That time he smiled broadly. "I have a key." He tipped his tall hat to her, leaned back, and motioned to Timoshen. "Drive around to the stables and pick up Jake Rooker. He'll take me in to town."

TWENTY-THREE

John stood at the window, observing from behind the red damask drapes of the parlor as Miranda and Lena entered the carriage, and were driven away down the avenue through the tall, wind-swaying oaks.

Moments earlier he had told Miranda that her outing had been arranged and that Timoshen was waiting for her at the door.

She had thanked him gracefully and hurried to prepare herself.

Now, as the carriage rolled through the wide-open gates, she settled her skirts and drew a deep breath. She had been despairingly certain the day before when she found those gates locked, and Benjy gone, that she was not to be permitted ever again to leave Haversham Square.

But John had permitted it. That frightened her even more. Why did he allow her to leave today? What did it mean?

She was so preoccupied with her own thoughts that she did not notice Jake sitting on the stoop of a small saloon. He watched, his mouth slanted down, as the carriage swung by, then leaned inside and shouted to know the time. He nodded at the answer, and settled himself to wait.

The carriage drew up at the broken curbing.

"I have a small errand to do for Mister John, in town," Timoshen said, as he helped Miranda from the carriage. "I'll be back for you by the time you're done here."

Miranda thanked him and pushed open the door of the notions shop. It was small, dim. There were great bins of embroidery silks, and of laces, and racks of yard goods in every imaginable fabric and color, and shelves and shelves crowded with flowers and ribbons and feathers.

Miranda chose a packet of hairpins, which she could always use, and then chose the ribbons and silks she would have to display on her return home. She had needed no such things, but only wanted to be away from the house for a little while, out from under the shadow of danger which hung over her. In fact, she had lately been so unable to think of fashion that she had made no protest, though Stacy had, when John sent Mrs. Bannion away, telling her that Miranda was not in good enough health to trouble herself with fittings. That bit of information had been but another spur to her fear.

She noticed now that Lena peered interestedly at the

ribbons, watching as she chose a yard more of pink, then of green and red.

"Pretty," Lena said finally, with longing in her eyes. "They'll surely be nice colors for you."

Miranda smiled. "But they aren't for me, Lena. They're for you."

Lena's face lit up. Her hand reached out to stroke the ribbons. "Thank you, Miss Miranda. They'll be nice colors for me, too."

The two girls sorted flowers, and studied bows, and peered at veilings, and when Lena, with a small cry of pleasure, pulled from a bin a heavy skein of silver embroidery silk, Miranda thought instantly of the color of Reed's eyes. She would do a vest for him, embroidered in just that silver.

By the time she had signed the bill, and the purchases had been wrapped, and they had gone out into the street, it was near twilight.

A cold wind sent paper flying in all directions, and dead leaves and a gray biting dust swirled through the air.

There were people walking, riding. Carriages and carts and drays crowded each other between narrow footpaths.

A surge of idlers gathered at the distant corner, and seemed to spread outward, suddenly thickening, toward where Lena and Miranda stood together.

Lena muttered, "Now where's that brother of mine? He knows you're waiting for him right here where he said he'd be."

Miranda looked anxiously along the road. She had thought surely that Timoshen would be back by then. She couldn't imagine what might have delayed him, or where he had gone on his errand for John. She was suddenly as anxious to return to Haversham Square as she had been determined earlier to have her outing.

But now a cart piled high with barrels pulled into the small intersection and stopped suddenly, spilling its load. There were shouts and curses.

Scuffling sent dust swirling in a thick cloud into the deepening twilight.

Lena whispered, "I don't like what's going on there," and looked both ways along the street, too.

It seemed to Miranda unaccountably empty at the place where they stood. Behind them, the shopkeeper closed his doors, and the sound of bolts being thrown came clearly to her.

At the intersection, the crowd broke open. Men and boys and barking dogs burst in all directions.

"No," Lena said. "I don't like that," with a whimper in her voice.

The boys and dogs ran past, with some of the men following. But four hulking types in worn workingmen's clothes, caps pulled low over jowly faces, formed their own gang.

Miranda, with hardly a glimpse of them, was still certain that she had seen none of them before. But they hesitated around her. They were on each side of her and before her and behind her.

She cried, "What do you want?"

There was no answer.

Lena was knocked to her knees, and Miranda was sent spinning into the road just as the dray, still raining beer barrels, thundered past.

She believed that she was lost. She saw no way to save herself. She felt her bonnet fall away, and her frock rip, and tasted and swallowed foul-flavored dirt. Her packet of hairpins and ribbons and embroidery silks spun out of her hand, and lay unnoticed near a pile of horse dung.

The four men surged closer, bending to seize her. She smelled their sweat, even saw their gleaming eyes. But Lena screamed shrilly. She jumped up, and threw herself at the bunched shoulders, scattering them momentarily. She pulled Miranda to her feet and drew her bodily, toes barely touching the ground, into a dim lane.

There was no time to speak, or to question. And no breath for either. The sound of heavy, plodding boots followed them at a run, pounding like blows into the dirt, and muttered words became curses, and an angry hail of stones clattered against the brick wall behind them.

She and Lena went darting away down the lane and into a dimmer alley, where the odor of the canal was stronger, and a mule brayed steadily.

The pounding footsteps came on and on, and there was no longer any place to run.

Miranda held hard to Lena's hand and turned, crying out, "What is it? What do you want? Who are you?"

But there was no answer.

The men were close, closer, breathing hard and crouching to move in.

Each had a knife now, Miranda saw. A knife held at the ready.

"Oh, no," she whispered. "No. No."

But Lena was torn away, flung aside, screaming wildly.

There were hard callused bruising hands on Miranda's shoulders, her arms, and the wicked touch of cold metal at her throat. She cried out in terror, and struggled, and fell heavily.

There was a shrill ear-splitting whistle. A horse came pounding down the lane. A voice shouted, "What's going on? Hold there. Hold and stand where you are!"

As suddenly and unbelievably as they had been there, the four men were gone. They melted silently away into the falling dark.

The policeman leaned down from the saddle, cried, "I'll get them," and galloped away.

Lena helped her to her feet, and they leaned against the wall, fighting for breath and not even daring to whisper.

The policeman did not return, and it was only after a little while of clinging to Lena, of straining to hear more threatening footfalls, that Miranda suddenly knew the place she and Lena had come to. She recognized the back yard of the Kayhome Arms.

It was piled high with rubbish, the house vacant and dark, with windows and doors boarded over.

Miranda shivered and asked herself what strange fate had made Lena lead her here, to this very place from which she had once fled.

"Rowdies," Lena muttered in a deep sobbing breath. "A person's not safe on the streets these days."

"But what did they want?" Miranda asked, remembering the hard bruising hands at her shoulders, the cold bite of the blade at her throat. "Why would they behave so? If it was money they were after, then why didn't they demand it, take it? We could hardly have defended ourselves."

Lena didn't answer that. Her eyes were narrowed thoughtfully, and her head was cocked to listen. At last she said, "I don't hear anything, do you?"

Miranda heard only silence, and the painful whisper of Lena's breathing mingled with her own. She shook her head.

"Maybe Timoshen's at the shop," Lena suggested. "And wondering where we got to. There's no need to wait for the policeman. If he'd found them, he'd have brought them back by this time."

Miranda agreed. She asked, "Do you know the way?"

But now Lena's mouth puckered, and her eyes ran tears. She had used up all her courage when she dragged Miranda into hiding. She stood and waited for Miranda to do the rest.

So Miranda did. With Lena clinging to one sore wrist like a frightened child, she set out to find her way back.

The sky was black, unlit by stars or moon. Here and there candlelight flickered at a covered window, offering only a hint of human presence. The air was cold, and a noxious mist rose up from the canal. She was uncertain of the route and wandered into several blind and impassable alleys, and found herself forced to retrace her path, listening always for the sound of following footsteps, while Lena moaned softly, and shuffled beside her.

At last they found the street, the shop.

The place was empty. No one lingered in the dark. Even the yapping dogs had disappeared.

Miranda had the feeling that she was being watched, watched by eyes as stealthy as those of a hungry animal. She stared into the shadows but saw nothing.

At last the familiar carriage spun around a corner and jerked to a stop. Timoshen leaped down.

He cried, "Miss Miranda, I'm very sorry. I bought Mister John's tobacco the way he told me to, and I couldn't get right back. There was a cart over in the road three blocks away. It couldn't be moved. It took more than an hour to get by." And then, seeing the stains on her dress and her face, and Lena's tear-stained cheeks, "What happened to you?"

Miranda shook her head, climbed into the carriage, and settled herself with a relieved sigh.

She listened as Lena excitedly, and with new tears falling, described the event to her brother, but she was thinking of John. Now she knew why he had permitted her to go into town.

The carriage returned by the same route it had come, and when it passed the saloon where Jake still waited, he leaned forward from the shadows to peer past the pale light of its lamps. He saw first Timoshen's grim face, and then, within, he saw Miranda, and with her, Lena, still weeping.

Jake ducked back, shivering as the carriage raced by.

It wasn't the cold of the night air that chilled him. It was the cold in the marrow of his bones, the cold in the blood in his veins. It was fear.

He had been waiting here for word that his plan had been successful.

He need wait no longer. He knew it had not been.

For Miranda had just ridden by, and soon she would enter Haversham Square.

John would see her. John would know.

Jake shivered and squinted into the shadows as he hurried away, heading for his only refuge. Already, he heard in his mind John's following footsteps, and the rasp of John's angry voice.

When Jake reached the garret room, it was empty.

"Nan," he cried despairingly. "Nan, where are you? I need you, Nan."

He locked the door and crouched, trembling, by the fire, and listened for her footsteps on the stairs.

Footsteps finally came, but it was not Nan who made them.

John climbed down from the gig, tethered its horse to the fence.

He gave the house a grim look, then moved slowly, heavily, through the dimness, balancing his cane between his big hands.

He went in, then up the rickety stairs, and felt them shake under his weight.

His big head was lowered between his shoulders, his eyes cold with fury.

He touched the door of the garret room and found it locked, and smashed it open with one swift kick.

Jake cried, "I did the best I could! I did what you said!" and cringed against the hearth.

The room smelled of stale mutton, and old clothes, and Jake's terror.

John loomed over him. "Miranda came home," he grated. "She came home, you fool!"

"But I—"

"I told you to take care of it. I told you how and when. Did you do it?"

"I tried, I tell you. It was all set. I don't know what went wrong."

"You tried," John repeated. "You tried, did you? And when was that good enough for me? When did I give you leave to *try?*"

He reached down, dragged Jake to his feet, and hurled him against the wall. He caught him and shook him and threw him against the wall again.

"Now wait," Jake moaned. "Listen, listen . . ."

"I told you," John grated. "I gave you your orders. Why should I hear your excuses? What are your excuses to me? I told you what to do, and you failed. That's all that matters. You failed."

He brought the cane down hard on Jake's head, and bent over him when he fell, slamming it into his body over and over. "That's for failing, fool!"

The cane broke, its golden head rattling across the room to disappear into the shadows.

John flung the splintered flail aside.

Jake yelped and struggled as John dragged him up and shook him as if he were a broken doll. He slammed him twice into the door frame, and then hurled him into the hallway.

He followed, picked Jake up and held him, while his open hand lashed again and again into Jake's face. A cut split the flesh under both his eyes, and blood ran down his cheeks. His nose spread and swelled, and his teeth grew loose in his mouth.

But John's fury was not sated. He slashed hard backhand blows at Jake's jaw until the flesh was laid open to the bone.

"I'll do it for you," Jake whined. "I swear I will. I'll get rid of her for you. Just give me time."

"You'll do nothing," John grated. "Nothing for me. Not ever again. Forget the whole thing, do you hear me?"

He smashed Jake into the wall and caught his falling body and hurled it down the steps.

Jake lay where he fell, breath held, and swollen eyes squeezed shut.

John walked heavily down the stairs. He dragged Jake to his feet.

Jake whined through bleeding lips, "I tell you I'll never say . . . I swear I won't . . ."

John laughed softly, dangerously. "Of course not, Jake. I know that."

Then he opened the door and hurled Jake into the yard.

Jake sprawled heavily and did not move.

As John stepped over him, he said, "You're lucky I let you live."

TWENTY-FOUR

Jake lay on the narrow mattress, squinting at the cob-webbed ceiling through swollen eyes, while a stream of monotonous curses rolled from his broken mouth. Bleeding, hardly able to see, his body aching, he shivered when Nan touched him.

She patted his puffy cheeks with a damp cloth and sat back, chuckling. "You'll do, I suppose. You'll do nicely. But it'll be a while before you look yourself again."

Jake swiveled his eyes to glare at her. "Never mind it."

"Never mind it indeed," she returned. "You drag yourself in here, half dead, and that's where I find you, yelling for drink and help on my very own bed. How could I never mind it? If I had, I'd have left you alone to drown in your own blood."

"Then I'd have escaped listening to your talk at least."

"You could tell me what happened," she wheedled. "Were you hit by a dray? Run down by a carriage? Did a dead tree limb fall on you?" Her black eyes gleamed with malice. "Or was it just the sky itself that fell on you?" She saw knuckle marks in his flesh, and cane streakings, too, and had her own ideas of the explanation, but she wanted him to put it into words. It would gratify her to hear how he had come by this beating, and somehow ease the memory of the marks he had put on her.

It was quiet in the dim room. The small fire on the hearth popped and sputtered. The lamp hissed and smoked.

She eyed the smashed door but did not mention it. Instead she brought him a stiff tot of rum and watched while he drank it. Then she washed the cut under his eye that had begun to bleed again. She adjusted his pillow and covered him with a light blanket. She brought him a second tot of rum and settled herself close to him.

"Damn John Haversham to hell," Jake whispered finally. "Damn him!"

She rose and went to the table and blew out the lamp. The room was in darkness but for the pale glow of the fire. She opened the bodice of her gown and lay down beside him, and enfolding him in her thick arms, she took his face to her breasts.

"Should you be down?" John asked. "You're still very pale, Reed."

"Perhaps it'll do me some good. It has been a long siege," Reed answered.

He found it difficult to look directly into John's face. He had found that he could not remain in his room that night, pretending at a fever that was quite cured, or wandering out for only a few moments at a time to see how Miranda fared. It was difficult to hold his silence when accusations crowded against his tongue.

He had been there when she returned earlier. He had seen her torn gown, the bruises on her arms, the terror in her eyes when she looked upward at the door of John's study. But why? What had he done? Reed knew only that silence and dissembling were required if he were to force John to reveal himself.

A sickness welled in Reed, and as he crumbled bread between his fingers, they trembled slightly.

John saw, and said, "You're not at all steady yet. Perhaps Doctor Porter . . ."

Reed shook his head and glanced at Miranda.

She sat with her eyes downcast, picking at the food on her plate without appetite, the wine in her crystal goblet untouched.

He said, "I'm sorry your trip to town was spoiled for you, Miranda," and was rewarded when her golden eyes flashed up to meet his. He went on to John, "They say some fool loosed a few pigs and dumped a cart, and then there was a near riot. And then a street gang took advantage of the confusion to assault Miranda. Timoshen described it to me quite graphically as he heard it from Lena."

John's hooded look gave away nothing, nor did his deep, "What's this about, Miranda?"

Fear crowded her throat and set the pulses beating there, and burned along her skin in quick stinging waves. She drew a hard steadying breath and answered, "Why, I don't know what it was about, John. It happened so fast and was so very unpleasant. And poor Lena was half-frightened out of her wits, just as I was, too. She dragged me away and those men followed." She paused for another breath and went on. "And then the policeman came. But were it not for Lena I truly believe I'd not have had the good sense to find my way safely home again."

Reed's pallor-touched face tightened. "Then what Timoshen claimed was true? Though you tried to withdraw from the area of the melee you were actually followed some distance and assaulted again?"

"It seemed so. I'm quite certain of it." Her voice quavered. "We were cornered finally. And . . . and they had knives . . . If the policeman hadn't come . . ."

John reached for his wine, sipped it, and murmured, "We have a rare backward lot in our town these days," and concealed his amusement at his own double meaning. A backward lot indeed. It was hardly a large chore to deal with Miranda, and yet, she had not been dealt with. He went on, "You must forget all about it, Miranda. But I shall insist that you no longer leave the grounds without a man to protect you."

She nodded a wordless acceptance of his decree, recognizing the terror in it.

A week later she stood before the full-length mirror on her wardrobe door.

Abigail gave her skirt a final twitch, and then stepped back. "There you are, Miss Miranda. You're ready now, and you look good, too."

Abigail's eyes met hers in the looking glass. It was as if, without words, the older woman was trying to say something encouraging to her, but Miranda did not speak. She felt that she knew neither her own body nor her own mind within it.

"Are you sure I didn't lace you too tight?" Abigail asked. "You're suddenly so pale."

There was no time to answer.

The door burst open.

Stacy stood there, smiling. She was in her usual high spirits, and now her dark eyes shone with excitement. "Are you ready to go down? John will be waiting, and I heard some of the carriages a little while ago."

She wore white, with glowing red roses at her waist. There was a sparkling of jewels in her chestnut hair, and at her bare throat, too.

"Yes, I'm just coming," Miranda replied. "But what of Reed?"

"He's with John," Stacy answered, and swept ahead to the top of the curving stairway.

Following, Miranda knew that Abigail's dark watching eyes went with her. She told herself that she must not be afraid, and paused to look down at the reception hall below.

John and Reed were greeting their guests under the huge chandelier.

This late supper would formally mark the end of the mourning period for Caroline, which had been John's decision and had been arranged at his suggestion and under his careful direction.

Stacy, all smiles and grace, began to descend, her white gown flowing around her.

Miranda followed more slowly. She had told herself that she must not be afraid, but now dread filled her.

Tad Layton greeted Stacy with lavish courtesy and extended the same warm greeting to Miranda. He made some small talk about the fine weather, and then, as if he couldn't help himself, he said, "Do you know, whenever I come here, I must remember Caroline. I miss her. What a terrible loss, and a terrible death. She confided in me, you know. I knew her heart, and her trouble. It's a shame that it ended in such a way."

Miranda breathed some few words of agreement, a chill on her lips, in her fingertips, seeing that John, bulking large nearby, was listening.

She was relieved when she was cornered by Erna Barrington, who wore gray silk that did nothing for her coloring, which was also gray, and diamonds, it was said, passed down by relatives who had escaped the guillotine in France.

Erna twitted, "My dear girl, were you about when they had that street riot in town? My goodness, Dorothea and I sat in our carriage for hours. It was disgraceful. Absolutely disgraceful. And not a policeman to be seen. No one to help. We might well have been killed."

John came and joined the two women, his big face blank, his wide shoulders rigid. "But you were not killed," he said gently. "No one was."

"And no thanks to anybody for that. Just thanks to chance," she retorted. "You must take it up with the council of aldermen, John. Something must be done to protect ladies who desire to visit, shop, and do errands."

"I agree," he said. "But I don't know that I, or anyone else, knows what must be done."

"Surely the clever gentlemen will think of something," she purred.

"We will try," he assured her.

Across the room, Reed was standing with Josiah Hurley, but he did not listen to the Senator's invective-filled comments about Thaddeus Stevens. He was looking at the smooth curve of Miranda's pale cheeks, and the way the champagne goblet trembled in her hand. He saw the dark fringe of long lashes making shadowy crescents when she concealed her eyes. He saw her eyes move to John, and recognized the fear in her look.

He remembered how she had been, defenseless, vulnerable, when John's runaway horse bore down on her, and how she had felt in the circle of his arm as he swept her away and out of danger. He remembered, too, now, how she had been the evening she returned from town.

He nodded absently at Josiah and excused himself, and went to her.

"Are you well enough, do you think, for this?" she asked anxiously.

"Just for a little while," he told her. "I still tire easily, I'm afraid."

It was increasingly difficult to maintain the fiction of his ill-health. How could he be with her, watch over her, when he was in his bedroom? Yet so far he had succeeded, by listening, by ascertaining her whereabouts in the grounds, and by knowing who went with her.

She suddenly asked, "Reed, would you refill my glass?"

After he returned to her side, chatted with her for a little while, always feeling John's penetrating gaze on him, he excused himself, saying that he felt he had better rest.

It was essential that he continue to seem unattending. How else could he protect her from John?

"Have you become feverish again?" she asked quickly. "Is there anything I can do? Shall I go with you?"

"No, no, Miranda. Stay and enjoy the party."

She watched him leave the room, his tall body straight and strong-looking, then, when John put a big hand on her shoulder, she started.

But he smiled down at her. "Come, Miranda. Your champagne has gone quite flat. You must allow me to give you a fresh one."

"Oh, no, thank you," she answered. "This is fine, John."

"Indeed it's not," he insisted, rolling the two small pills in his palm, as he took her glass from her and substituted another. "I cannot allow you to drink spoiled champagne, can I?"

"Thank you," she said unwillingly.

"But you must drink it, my dear. I insist that you drink it for me. Wine is known to bring color to pale cheeks."

She held the goblet to her lips and tasted the champagne, and he said, an insistent hand on her arm, "It's very good, isn't it, Miranda?"

She nodded, drank a bit more, and was relieved when Carleton Van Eward drew John away.

She gave her half-empty glass to Jefferson, and spoke a few words to Stacy, a few more to Josiah. As she moved away from the Senator, she felt a wave of dizziness, a sudden closing in of the walls around her.

She went to the open window, thinking that the air might help. But it did not. The dizziness grew until she thought that she might lose consciousness and drop to the floor. She waited until it receded slightly, and then, very carefully, she made her way through the guests, across the crowded room, and up the steps.

Laughter and loud voices followed her. She leaned against the closed door of her room, breathing deeply, while she listened. She thought that the faint aura of her own scent would surely choke her.

The dim light wavered, brightening and darkening before her eyes, and her breath came in pants and then in long shallow sighs. She felt beads of perspiration on her face and went to look at herself in the looking glass.

Her golden eyes seemed to burn like yellow fire. There was a hectic flush on her cheeks. She saw a pulse beat in her throat. As she stared at herself, her vision seemed to blur. She saw another face form before her terror-stricken eyes. She saw a proudly lifted blonde head and narrow green eyes that shone with strange lights. She saw hollow and pale cheeks. Caroline . . .

Then, as she watched, the vision disappeared.

She saw herself again.

But the room began a slow spin, and the laughter and talk from below became a distant blur, and the walls crowded in on her.

She crumpled to the bed.

When, not long after, she opened her eyes, she saw Abigail's face and heard her say softly, "Let me be, Lena. I know what to do. I've done it often enough for Miss Caroline, haven't I?"

As she caught Abigail's hand and clung to it, Miranda at last understood what had happened to her.

TWENTY-FIVE

Spring had arrived, and with it memories of another spring when the news of the shooting on 10th Street sped through the misty dark to spread terror through the city. But now the despair of that night was muted, and once again the willows were veiled in early green, and the lilacs spilled purple blossoms along walls and gates and wooden trellises. Now mule teams plodded the towpath, drawing their loaded barges from lock to lock, and carts and hansoms crowded the muddy streets. Vendors sold fresh-killed rabbits, squirrels, and chickens, and great sides of pork. The shops were open, the presses rolled, the business of life continued.

But it seemed to Miranda that everything beyond the ivy-covered walls of Haversham Square had become no more than a dream, a dim recollection of place and time past.

Reality was the nightmare of fear that dogged her, shadowing her days and claiming her nights.

Since the evening of the supper three weeks before, she had been careful to accept no food or drink from John's hands. She was determined that he would have no second opportunity to dispense to her Caroline's terrible pills. She was determined that he have no opportunity to destroy her as he had destroyed Caroline.

She knew that he must try again. There was nothing to do but watch and wait.

She had made up her mind that she would not, no matter what the risk, be driven away from Haversham Square, from Reed. It was far too late to alter that resolve, far too late to flee. John would not permit it.

The iron gates remained locked, and Benjy remained absent on unknown chores.

John had made certain that she did not go beyond the

environs of the house. He had, in these past three weeks, seemed to withdraw from all his affairs. He was ever-present, studying her with threatening eyes.

Now she sat in the morning room, a book in her hand, with the print blurring before her so that she was unable to make real sense of the lines of the poem.

The room was so quiet that she heard the faint tick of the clock on the mantel, and imagined that it was whispering to her.

She remembered very clearly how Abigail had tended her until the effects of the pills had at last been dissipated.

John . . .

She recalled that she had once thought, before she even met him, that she would like and admire him. Her grandmother had celebrated his name. Now Miranda saw him as evil incarnate.

She shuddered, and the book slipped from her knees to the floor. She let it stay where it was.

From the hallway beyond, she heard the tinkle of Stacy's laughter, and then the deep rasp of Josiah's voice. John was having his way in that, too, Miranda thought.

Stacy came in, smiling, her face flushed. "We're going out for tea, Miranda. To Reeves. Would you like to join us?"

Josiah stroked his black beard and seconded the invitation with somewhat less enthusiasm.

Miranda did not need to consider. She agreed on the instant and jumped to her feet, saying she would just get her wrap. Surely, with Stacy and Josiah accompanying her, John could not object.

But, when he appeared on the staircase, she knew at once that he would not allow her to go.

He gave her a faint smile, asking, "Where are you bound?"

"Out to have tea with Stacy and Josiah," she said coolly.

"I am so sorry," he answered. "I shall have to ask that you join them some other time. Surely that would do just as well, wouldn't it?"

She waited, but he gave no explanation. He simply

stood there, looking down at her, with the faint smile still on his lips.

At last, she asked, "But why not, John?"

"It's Reed, you see," he explained. "He's in bed again. Though he is asleep now, I should like it if you were here when he awakened. Perhaps you can do with him what I cannot. Perhaps you can persuade him to have the doctor come by. I don't know what I shall do with the boy if he doesn't soon collect himself."

She was immediately concerned about Reed, but at the same time, she knew John had used his brother as an excuse to prevent her once again from leaving the grounds.

Still, she returned to the morning room and explained matters to Stacy and Josiah.

The Senator only partly concealed his relief that he would be alone with Stacy.

After they left, the house seemed hushed, almost breathless. The ticking of the clock on the mantel seemed to grow louder.

Miranda went up to the second floor, thinking to look in on Reed. But John immediately called to her from his study that Reed was not to be disturbed. She would be summoned when she was needed.

She pretended not to have heard. She began, gently, to turn the doorknob.

John came into the hall. "No, Miranda."

She said quietly, believing that Reed slept, "I'll not trouble him."

But John drew her away to the head of the stairs. "You must learn to obey me, Miranda."

She stood very still. She had no proof of what he had done, and she must, at any cost, protect Reed from John's wrath. But somewhere there would be the evidence to convict him. If she couldn't find it, another must. Tad Layton. Tad would believe her. Tad had been close to Caroline.

"You say I must learn to obey you?" Miranda whispered angrily. "When I know what you are?"

He only smiled, openly enjoying the effect of his power over her.

He would not have that power much longer, she vowed silently.

She said, "You stopped me a little while ago from going with Josiah and Stacy, but you can't keep me here a prisoner forever, you know. One day, perhaps tomorrow, perhaps the day after, I'll escape you, John. And then I'll tell the whole world what you've done."

"My poor girl," John said quietly.

"The truth can always be found," she cried. "Those men who attacked me . . ." And then, striking from the depths of intuition, "Jake Rooker . . . who I've not seen since that day . . ."

"How terrible to think of what has befallen you," John said. "I wonder what I can do."

She turned and went downstairs, anger still drumming in her blood. It was true. All that she had told him. She would do it. Somehow . . . somehow . . .

She walked out onto the back terrace, drawing her pink stole around her. This much, at least, she would be allowed.

She could walk across the lawns and breathe the sweet air and watch the silver stars come out.

It was late twilight now. Purple shadows fell thickly on the grounds and rimmed the windows of the house.

A silhouette appeared briefly between the open drapes of one of them, and then disappeared.

She did not notice.

A mockingbird sang in a holly bush.

A squirrel chattered in a laurel tree.

The door behind her slowly and soundlessly opened.

She did not notice that either.

Lena glanced past the kitchen curtains, then frowned, muttering to herself, "Where's she going, I wonder? It's going to dark soon."

"Instead of talking to yourself," Abigail retorted, "you can get to those dishes."

But Lena remained at the window, staring into the deepening twilight. At last she said, "Mama, look," in a nervous whisper.

Abigail made an irritated sound but went to stand beside Lena, peering out. Then she gasped and leaned forward, clasping the sill in her scarred hands.

She saw Miranda walking on the shell path where it wound past the conservatory, her gown floating around her and her head tipped back so that she could see the fading sky.

John—big, dark, menacing—stood midway on the terrace steps, and as Abigail and Lena watched, he went down them slowly. His shadow fell before him, black, ugly, like an animal preparing to leap into the night.

Lena made a soft, choking sound, and buried her face in her mother's breast.

Abigail held her, shivering, and watched with terror as the two outside moved slowly from her sight.

Reed saw Miranda's slender form, blurred by falling darkness, disappear into the black mass of the distant trees.

He saw John's tall form stealthily follow but remain some distance behind.

Fireflies rose up and scattered warning signals against the sky.

The mockingbird's song was suddenly gone.

Reed left the window and hurried downstairs.

The evening hush enfolded Miranda.

She paused, listening to the breathless stillness.

Then a mourning dove sang out of the darkness, and another answered.

Somewhere there was a rustling in the trees, and a cloud of fireflies danced like sparks in the shadows.

She turned to look back at the house. There were a few pale lights blooming against the purple darkness. She thought she saw a figure at the kitchen window. She thought she saw a drapery move at the second floor.

She turned and went on. Some time, between one step and another, she thought she heard a sound behind her. She paused to listen but heard nothing. Slowly, with the first dew silvering her slippers, she followed the shell path beyond the massed blackness of the rhododendrons, pausing to finger a shiny leaf.

It was then that she had the sense of eyes upon her, eyes that peered at her through the dark. She strained to listen. Again she heard nothing. Yet she knew John was there. He was watching her. He waited, unseen, somewhere between where she stood and the safety of the house.

An arrow of fear knifed through her.

She stepped off the shell path and went swiftly across the empty black lake of the meadow toward the tall silhouette of the laurels.

But he was behind her, a predatory shadow leaping before him, reaching out to seize her.

Her breath came quickly now. She heard the hard pulse of terror in her ears and felt it drumming in her throat.

She flung herself into the grove and turned, and suddenly, a big warm hand settled on the nape of her neck.

John said softly, "Why, Miranda, what is it? Why have you been running?"

"Oh," she gasped. "Cousin John . . . I thought . . . I heard someone following . . ."

"You did hear someone. Me. But why should you run from me, my dear?"

She looked up into his shadowed face, his stony eyes, and saw the fury there, and tried to step back from him, back and away, preparing to flee again.

But his hand tightened, held her, bruising and pitiless, and he said, "Miranda, tell me why you have turned against me? When I first brought you here I was certain that we would be friends as well as kin. And that was important to me. I looked forward, you must know, to long years of association." He had looked forward to more than that. He had imagined her in his arms and felt her flesh melt to his. He had dreamed of cherishing her as the finest possession he owned. But he said nothing of that now for he hardly remembered that. He went on in the face of her stubborn silence, "I don't know . . . it seems that we're in opposition to each other. We've nothing between us any longer. I wonder how this came about. I wonder why."

She knew that he enjoyed this taunting of her. She

supposed it was this sort of pleasure that had once led him to treat Caroline as he had. But she answered evenly, "We never had anything between us, Cousin John, except for the gratitude you earned by taking me in when I had nowhere else to go."

"Then what can have happened? Where is that same gratitude now?"

She did not answer him.

He sighed and took his hands from the back of her neck. His arm settled firmly, heavily, across her shoulder, holding her close to his side.

"Come," he said. "We'll go back."

She flashed an angry look at his grim face. Her body stiffened with resistance. She knew that he did not intend that she return to the house with him.

But he laughed, drew her closer, and forced her to walk with him.

Slowly, slowly, they moved from the grove of laurels where she had sought escape back into the black lake of the meadow.

Anyone looking at them would have thought that they were going for a casual stroll, would have thought that he was kindly guiding her lest she take a misstep in the dark and fall.

Anyone looking at them might have thought that. But she knew better. This was no aimless after-dinner stroll, when all other forms of entertainment had failed. John had his purpose.

It was with a numbed fatality that she continued to walk beside him. She knew, even if she should try, that she would not be able to break away from his deadly, bruising grasp.

A cloud of white moths suddenly rose up at their feet, fluttered briefly before them, and then sailed away. The velvety grass whispered underfoot. The scent of spring, renewal and growth, perfumed the breathless night.

His arm, holding her, turned her toward the heavy clump of rhododendrons. She saw the thick shadow it cast, and its opening blossoms. Just beyond, in starlight, she saw the slender marble fawn. It seemed even to breathe, to gather itself for a long leap into the dark.

She felt the same tension in her own muscles, the waves of terror. She, too, must gather herself. But how? She was powerless.

He said, "You're so quiet, Miranda."

She did not answer.

His fingers tightened even more, fastened viselike into the flesh of her arm. "We're very nearly there, my dear." He led her past the slender fawn and then to the edge of the lily pond.

The fragrant lilies drifted, white and glowing, against the smooth velvet black of the shallow water.

There Caroline had slept. There, too, Miranda herself would sleep, she knew.

She gathered the folds of her gown closer, and held tight to her shawl. She said softly, "You cannot do this, John."

He seemed not to have heard her. He said, "Poor Caroline . . . she had so much to live for until . . ." His sigh was a new mockery. "I was her whole life, you know. And she was mine. And then you came, Miranda."

"I came?" she asked numbly.

"You, with your youth and beauty, and your terrible determination to have what was Caroline's own. I suppose it was the Jervis blood in you. Surely not the small amount of Haversham blood that you have. If, indeed, you really *do* have it. Who knows that you are truly Martha Appleton's granddaughter?"

"You *know* that I am," she cried.

"Then, even so, you're like your father. Yes. Yes. That must be it. You're cast in his own mold. Determined to have your way at any cost. Too weak to have it by direction, thus turning to indirection."

"You must be mad," she said hotly. "There's no other explanation." Her fingers crept up to touch the pearls she wore, her grandmother's pearls, as if they were a talisman. When she tried to draw away from him, she found it impossible.

He held her firmly in what would appear to an onlooker

an affectionate embrace. Yet it was not that. There was no affection nor kindness nor pity either in those iron fingers at her arm, her waist.

The stars were gone now. The sky had become a great black bowl overhead with no glimmer of light to leaven the dark. The trees loomed like towering sentinels. The pool was bottomless. An ominous hush hung like a great net across the lawns.

"You say that I'm mad," he said quietly. "Yes, I suppose you would like to think so. Caroline destroyed herself, and you know why. It has weighed desperately on your mind for so long. You've come here, to this place, many times to brood on it, just as Caroline so often came here herself. And then, tonight, knowing that you could live no longer with the pain of your guilt, you've come here again."

"No," Miranda breathed.

She was briefly free as he released her. Free so that she flung herself back and away from the pool even as her gown spilled over the edge and floated there.

But then his hands were at her throat. The fingers did not press hard, but they held her immobilized, just as that cool fury in his gray eyes held her immobilized.

"What a pity," he said. "What a pity that you knew, my dear. I would have made you a queen."

She could not answer him.

His face darkened. His fingers clawed into her flesh. She saw the murder grow within him. She knew that she saw the same face that Caroline had seen in the last moments of her life.

In the morning, Timoshen, passing by, would see the new body drifting among the lilies, and set up a great shout of horror. And that would be the end.

The great thick bowl of the black sky suddenly burst into a brilliant glow, its light blazing across the empty heavens. And somewhere in the white fire there were trees, shadowed and swaying.

She crumpled within the imprisoning circle of John's arms as his big thumbs pressed in, closing away all breath and consciousness.

But he felt the faint pulse fluttering against his fingers, and held them there, sweating now, and hearing over the roaring in his ears, sounds that were close but seemed to him a long way off.

Reed came swiftly out of the shadows, a dark avenging angel.

John knew him, saw his approach, and felt the last faint flutter of pulse against his thumbs.

She was dead. Now he would deal with Reed. He threw her slender limp body aside as Reed leaped at him.

Reed saw the whiteness of her arm trailing in the black water of the pond, and a part of her gown slowly darkening, and an end of her pink shawl floating.

He made a wordless sound of anguish as he hurled himself at John, whose massive body was braced and ready for him.

They fought in bitter silence, the only sound their panting breaths, and from somewhere nearby, the anxious chittering of disturbed mockingbirds.

Twice Reed went down under the big battering fists, and twice he leaped up, blood pounding in his ears, and pain cramping him, but ignored in his rage.

"Reed . . ." Miranda's whisper was weak. "Reed . . ." Then she was silent.

John held him, shook him, saying, "Listen! Listen to me!"

Reed gave the stony face a single look. This man had been brother to him and more. The very cornerstone on which his own life had been built. He broke away and made those few steps to where Miranda lay, and took her into his arms, murmuring words John did not understand, or even try to.

The big man stood, head bent, thick shoulders hunched. He considered briefly what he might say, but there was nothing.

He turned and went slowly past the marble fawn, beyond the rhododendron clump, and up the shell path to the silent house. The house that he had made his own and called Haversham Square. It would be a part of that dark legacy bequeathed to those that followed him.

He did not notice when he passed Abigail and Lena, who clung to each other and wept.

He went slowly into his study and took a seat behind his big desk. He sat back in his chair and opened the mahogany pistol case, and thought about the avenue of buildings he had planned, and the web of railroads he had begun. And then he thought of Miranda's golden eyes.

Below, near the lily pond, Reed bent his face close to Miranda's and pressed his lips to hers, forcing his breath between them, believing that she was already dead, and his name her last word, and his life lost without her, but determined, even then, to bring her back from wherever she had gone.

He breathed, then once again, his mouth pressed to hers. Now the sweetness of her lips was suddenly warm under his, and the softness of her camellia skin was part of him. He felt the touch of butterfly wings as her lashes brushed his cheek, and her eyes opened, stared so closely into his that he saw his own gaze there, as if his and hers were one.

Cautiously, he took his lips from her mouth and saw the beginnings of her smile.

And in that moment, they heard the clear sharp report of the gunshot from the house.

Part Two

ONE

"Dearly Beloved, we are assembled here in the presence of God to join this man and this woman in holy matrimony . . ."

The minister paused, but his words seemed to float, lingering in a soft after-sound over the solemn scene.

A ray of August sun burned a path that pierced the interior dimness of the church, so that Miranda and Reed, their heads bent before the flower-banked altar, stood within a mantle of blending blues and golds and red, an arched rainbow blazing around them.

There was a faint rustle, the whisper of silks, the sibilance of in-drawn breaths while Miranda silently repeated the minister's words in her mind. "Dearly Beloved . . ." She glanced sideways at Reed. "Dearly Beloved . . ." Oh, yes. Yes.

Now the minister was saying, ". . . If any man can show just cause why they may not lawfully be joined together, let him speak now, or forever after hold his peace."

A sudden hot wind stirred Miranda's veil, billowing her skirt, so that the rainbow arc around her broke for a moment. Then the air was once more still, and the arc made whole.

There is no cause, Miranda cried within her mind. None. None. And again she looked sideways at Reed. This time her gaze met his, and she read the clear and confident message in his silver eyes.

The minister asked, "Wilt thou, Reed, have this woman to be thy wife, and wilt thou pledge thy troth to her, in all love and honor, in all duty and service, in all faith and tenderness, according to the ordinance of God, in the holy bond of marriage?"

"I will," Reed said firmly. He restrained the urge to reach out, to touch Miranda, to assure himself that the moment was real.

Now the minister turned to Miranda and slowly, softly, repeated the question. "Wilt thou, Miranda, have this man . . ."

Once again, she said his words silently with him, and then, when he paused, she turned her head and looked fully into Reed's face, and whispered, "Oh, yes, yes, I will," and all her love and hope was in her reply.

Tad Layton, listening, felt a smile touch his lips. He was glad to be a part of this, proud that Miranda had asked that he give her away. She would never know what mixed feelings that honor had aroused in him, nor how deep the wish that he might have stood in Reed's place.

"Who giveth this woman to be married to this man?" the minister asked now.

"I do," Tad answered quickly in a choked voice. He took Miranda's hand in his and placed it within the minister's, and then stepped back.

The minister joined her hand with Reed's, and holding them together, he began to intone the vows they offered to each other.

"I, Reed, take thee, Miranda, to be my wedded wife, and I do promise and covenant, before God and these witnesses, to be thy loving and faithful husband, in plenty and in want, in joy and in sorrow, in sickness and in health, as long as we both shall live."

Reed said the words slowly and carefully, his voice low and certain.

Giving the words a sweet, singing eagerness, Miranda whispered, "I, Miranda, take thee Reed . . ."

And Stacy, gowned in blue silk and veiled in blue lace, with hot embers in her eyes, listened and looked at Carleton Van Eward, and made a certain vow to herself before the words of the ritual caught her attention again.

"This ring I give thee in token and pledge of our constant faith and abiding love," Reed was saying, and he placed the wide golden band on Miranda's finger and smiled down at her.

The minister rejoined Reed's hand to Miranda's, clasping them together in his own, and said, "By the authority vested unto me as a member of the Church of Christ, I declare that Reed and Miranda are now husband and wife according to the ordinance of God and the law of this territory." He drew a deep breath, waited for a still moment. Then, "Whom God has joined together, let no man put asunder."

There was another still moment.

He took a step away from the altar.

Miranda threw back her veil and smiled radiantly at Reed.

He forgot the minister standing by, forgot the others. He took her into his arms and bent his head and kissed her with passion and promise, the sweetness of her mouth a wine that set his pulses beating even more quickly.

He released her only when Tad made some small throat-clearing sound, and Erna Barrington sighed loudly, and Dorothea snifled, and Mary Van Eward cried, "Beautiful, beautiful . . ."

But, through the round of hand-shaking and congratulations and good wishes that followed, he still held onto her hand, even when Tad and Carleton claimed the privilege of kissing the bride.

Then he hurried her up the church aisle, the others following behind them.

As they stepped out into the hot sunshine, a shower of white rose petals fell upon them.

This was Stacy's planning, he knew, and Timoshen's execution. Those two confirmed the thought by exchanging swift conspiratorial smiles.

Brushing the fragrant drift from his hair, Reed said, grinning now, "I wish we were going directly to the train, Miranda."

Her eyes glowed with golden promise as she answered, "I, too, Reed. But it shall not be long."

"Long enough to make me believe we ought to have simply slipped away and—"

He had spoken in an undertone to Miranda, but Stacy overheard.

She cried indignantly, "You do not. How could you? This is a joyous occasion for all of us. And we've waited a long four months for it. My arrangements are made, as you know very well. There's to be no sudden change in them at this time."

"You must allow me to tease you a little," Reed retorted. "Since, after all, it's my wedding day."

"Tease indeed," she grumbled. "And tease all you like. But go into the carriage and return to Haversham Square. You and Miranda shall have these few moments alone. Tad and Carleton and I will follow." She shot a hot look at Mary Van Eward, adding, "The others, too, of course. But mind you don't attempt to evade us. For we shall all be watching you closely."

Miranda laughed and allowed Reed to help her into the open carriage. He settled himself next to her.

Timoshen closed the door. "I wish you happiness," he said solemnly, and then with a quick shy grin, he hurried to climb up and set the horses on their way.

The two carriages behind fell into line, forming a small procession, and over the quick steady thud of the hoof-beats, Reed heard the sound of Stacy's laughter.

"It's done," he said softly, and reached for Miranda's hand.

"The beginning. Oh, Reed, I'm so happy now. It's as if it were a wonderful dream."

A ruffle of white veiling blew against his cheek. He

touched it, held it there on his flesh for a moment, then drew her close to him. "May we never awaken, Miranda."

She sat within the tight circle of his arm, her white gown billowing around them both, soft as a fleecy cloud, as they rode along Pennsylvania Avenue under the fluttering poplar trees through the brilliance of summer sunlight.

Here and there, at quiet corners, passers-by turned to look up, to smile and wave. A cart loaded high with brown potatoes pulled over to allow the three-carriage procession to pass, and its driver raised his blue cap. A pair of horsemen reined in and waited, with approving grins.

Very soon, it seemed to Miranda, Timoshen stopped the carriage at the tall iron gates, and Benjy swung them open.

The black crepe had been removed from them. There was no sign now that John had died on a still April night at Haversham Square.

There was only brightness, and the warm sun filtering through the tall oaks that lined the driveway.

As the carriage rolled on, Miranda sat up straight and drew a deep breath. She had been Miranda Jervis when she left this morning. Now, returning, she was Miranda Haversham. Miranda Haversham, coming home. The magic of the name, promised to her all her life, was here at last. She would, she told herself, be worthy of both promise and magic.

Slowly she and Reed mounted the broad white circular steps.

Jefferson, Abigail, and Lena waited at the big double doors. They were dressed in their very best for this occasion, the women in black silk that gleamed in the sunlight, with ruffled white aprons and small caps of lace and ribbons on their heads, and Jefferson in black broadcloth and a white tucked shirt.

Abigail curtsied and said in a soft, solemn voice, "May I speak for all my family to wish you happiness, Miss Miranda? And congratulations to you, Mister Reed?"

"Oh, thank you, Aunt Abigail," Miranda cried. "Thank you for everything. And you, too, Lena, and Jefferson."

Lena made her own small curtsy.

Jefferson bowed.

A knot formed in Miranda's throat, and tears suddenly veiled her eyes. But she smiled as Reed drew her into the house.

She was Miranda Haversham now, and she was home.

As if in response to the thought, Reed took her into his arms, held her close, and kissed her.

They were standing thus, rapt and lost in each other, when Stacy and Erna and Dorothea surrounded them, and released new clouds of fragrant white rose petals.

Laughing, but unembarrassed, Miranda and Reed separated and led the way into the dining room.

The long table was set with silver and china. Bowls of yellow and white roses bedecked with sheaves of ferns stood on white lace centerpieces.

It was Abigail who had chosen the menu, a group of sumptuous courses, the recipes of which she had learned from Caroline. But Abigail did not think of that as she busied herself in the cooking quarters, her practiced eye scanning the big platters. There would be time for champagne before the meal was to be served. She adjusted tomato roses and listened to the laughter.

Miranda listened to it, too, and smiled at Erna, answering Erna's questions. "No, we did not cater anything. Abigail determined that she would allow no strangers' cooking for this event." Her golden eyes fell upon the four-tiered wedding cake on a small table in the corner. "Except for that."

Erna answered, "I know the cake, of course. It's from Reeves. And, if you don't mind, I'll have a piece for under my pillow, as well as one to eat."

Dorothea trilled disapprovingly, "Erna, you don't ask for double portions. It's not done."

"It is," Erna retorted. "By me." She gave the cake a hungry look, then majestically turned her back.

Jefferson brought in the champagne and passed it around quickly.

Tad stroked his blond beard, considering a proper toast,

and raised his glass, but paused when Miranda caught his eye.

She turned to Jefferson and said, "Won't you and Aunt Abigail and the others join us for some champagne, Jefferson?"

The mask of his thin ascetic face broke apart, showing surprise and cautious pleasure. He looked slowly at the other guests.

Reed said, "Do call the others in."

Jefferson answered nothing but gave a quick nod. He loped awkwardly into the cooking quarters, preparing himself to argue with Abigail. It was one more shock that there was no need to argue. She gave a sigh, and smiled, and gathered Lena and Timoshen to her, and then pushed them into the dining room, where they stood in a group, holding the champagne Jefferson served them.

Tad raised his glass and said softly, "Miranda, Reed, may all of us here who love you wish you a long and happy and fruitful life together, and love between you to sustain you always."

There was a moment of silence.

The drapes at the big windows suddenly billowed inward on a hot afternoon wind. The sweet high notes of a mockingbird trilled through the quietness.

Stacy flung back her head, and said, "I shall drink to that. We all shall!"

There were quick seconds and thirds, and Abigail hurried her family back to their chores.

Stacy caught Carleton's plump hand and smiled happily into Mary's disapproving face. "Carleton, you and I shall lead the parade into the music room. For we shall have dancing before luncheon. And I will allow no one to hang back."

She drew the grinning Senator with her, and Erna seized Tad by the hand, and so they all swept down the long hallway and into the music room.

Stacy seated herself at the Steinway, made a great show of warming and flexing her hands, and then, with a soft laugh, she began with one finger to pick out a waltz.

Reed smiled down at Miranda, held out his arms to

her. She moved close as his hands settled on her shoulder and at her waist. She caught her breath as a warmth spread from where he touched her through the whole of her body in swift physical awareness. She tipped back her head so that she could look up into his face. His eyes were silver now, gleaming like polished coins. She knew that she would remember him that way for the rest of her life. The look of pride, joy, and love she saw would be engraved forever on her mind.

Stacy's sweet notes drifted around them, and it seemed to Miranda that she and Reed floated into the dance on a cloud of enchantment. They moved together, moved looking into each other's eyes, both seeing the long path of a wonderful future.

The single notes of the waltz trailed away.

Miranda and Reed danced on, their bodies attuned to a sweet silent music until the spell was broken when the clock on the mantel chimed, and Mary cried, "Play again, Stacy, for I shall have a dance with my brother."

Stacy obeyed, laughing silently to see Mary grip and lead an unwilling Carleton, while Erna seemed to envelope a forebearing Tad.

The two couples, with Miranda and Reed, slowly circled the room until the clock chimed again.

Then, Stacy, managing still her part of the arrangements, rose and said, "It's time now . . ."

Jefferson, hovering anxiously at the dining room door, looked relieved when Miranda and Reed, followed by the others, took their places at the table.

There was more drink, more laughter, as the meal was brought in.

Carleton was determined to discuss with Reed the itinerary of the wedding trip. He had himself been abroad three or four times. He strongly, and at length, recommended Siena for the marvelous cathedral, and Venice for its canals.

Stacy, listening, wished that he would think to consider instead the itinerary for his own wedding trip. But then, with a small inward chuckle and a glance at Mary, she decided that the project would best be kept within her own hands.

Tad asked about the English Havershams, and Erna about English china, and Stacy peered at the clock on the mantel just as it chimed once more.

Miranda whispered to Reed, "I must change now," and slipped from the room with Stacy hurrying after her.

She chattered briskly as she helped Miranda undo the buttons of the white lace gown and lay away the glistening veils.

Miranda would have preferred Abigail's help. But Abigail herself would have to change to traveling clothes, and make her farewells. For Reed had determined that Miranda must not make such a trip without an extra pair of hands to see to her wardrobe. Stacy chattered on. But Miranda did not listen.

This beautiful day, so long dreamed of, was proceeding just as she had decided it must.

Reed had said, "Miranda, it shall be as you wish. Tell me, and I will make it so."

She had considered, but only briefly. She would not allow the long shadow of the memory of John to touch her, to touch Reed. She would wear white in St. John's. She would have as her attendants only her friends. She had permitted Stacy to plan the wedding luncheon.

Within weeks after the terrible April day that Miranda was determined to forget, Mrs. Bannion had been on her knees, fitting this very gown. This gown, and the trousseau she would need for the wedding trip that Reed planned with the help of a Baedeker guidebook. Meanwhile Stacy rocked gently in the chair once Caroline's and wholeheartedly approved of Miranda's choices in color and style.

Now she slipped on a traveling outfit of yellow silk, adjusted a plumed hat on her curls, and took up a yellow beruffled parasol and a yellow beaded reticule. "I'm ready, I think."

"And you look like a bride," Stacy chirped. "Beautiful and poised. Shall we see if Reed is waiting for you at the stairs?"

Miranda paused on the threshold, looking back at the room. She was leaving it and her girlhood behind. She smiled to herself.

Reed stood below the sun-touched chandelier, looking up for a first glimpse of her.

She started down toward him, stately and careful, and then it was too much. Halfway down, she broke stride and gathered up her gown in both hands so that it floated around her like sunlight, and ran to meet him.

He swept her up into his arms and spun her to the big doors before he set her on her feet.

There was a quick flurry of goodbyes and good wishes, and then they were riding away, clattering down the long drive under the tall oaks, rolling and jolting past the open gates and out into the quiet lane.

She turned for a quick look behind her. The big house seemed to float above the trees in the early twilight.

It was home. It was where she belonged. When she came back she would be mistress here. The whole of her life would be lived here.

Reed said gently, "Never fear, Miranda. Haversham Square will be waiting for our return."

"Oh, yes," she agreed, and turned to look ahead.

There was a brilliance in the very air. The small cottages along the lane seemed to burn with a special light. The dust of the road rose up to twinkle like fairy motes. There was a shimmering magic thrown like a veil over the once familiar streets.

Even the shoddy depot was touched with beauty now, its grime suddenly invisible, the warped wood straight and smooth, the sagging building merely made interestingly askew.

Reed handed her down.

Timoshen brought the few small cases to the private car and gave them over to the steward, who disappeared inside with them.

Timoshen hesitated, his thin face solemn and his eyes squinting. Then he made his farewells and turned quickly to lose himself in the crowds.

Reed drew her up the two steps and into the car, and

closed the door. He stood there, leaning his wide shoulders against it.

"At last," he said, smiling. "What a long day it has been. And what a long time it has been, Miranda."

"Yes," she answered. "Oh, yes, my Reed," and went into his arms in happy and eager breathlessness.

The train hissed, spreading steam on the velvet-draped windows, and rattled and jolted. There were shouts outside, and red lanterns swinging, and then they were rolling, clattering through the yards and on the way to New York.

He released her, but kept her within the circle of his arms while he unpinned her hat and set it aside.

The private car, she saw, was well-appointed. It had a dark green floor covering to match the velvet at the windows. It had several comfortable-looking green plush chairs and, at its far end, a low wide divan.

There was a bottle of champagne chilling in a silver bucket, a huge bouquet of white roses on the small mahogany table nearby.

Reed drew out a single flower and tucked it into her curls, and she knew that he was remembering the brilliantly sunny day when he had done the same with a yellow rose, while George Custer fought his plunging stallion before the White House reviewing stands.

Now Reed asked, "Will you have some champagne?"

She shook her head, suddenly at a loss for words.

She walked the length of the car slowly, sank down at the edge of the wide divan, struggling with a wave of shyness.

He came and stood over her, bending to take her face gently in his hands and to tip it up. "Miranda, you're not afraid of me, are you?"

"No," she whispered, and felt a blush rise in her cheeks. "Not afraid of you, Reed. Only . . . only fearful that I'm so . . . so unknowing."

"And that troubles you?" He was amused to think that she would be concerned over what was pleasing to him.

"Fearful that I might not be what you wish," she answered.

"No chance of that, my darling," he told her in a low, very gentle tone.

He sat beside her and she instantly shifted away. There was a sudden mischievous glint in her golden eyes.

"Do you know, Reed, I think I must see to Aunt Abigail, now that we are under way."

"Oh, do you? Well, I think Aunt Abigail can see to herself this night. She's no doubt well settled in her own little compartment, and wouldn't care to be disturbed."

"Perhaps," Miranda agreed. "But then . . . there's this gown . . . my hair . . ."

He took her into his arms, and lay back, cradling her body against his, while his mouth claimed the softness of her lips.

She felt the quickening beat of his heart against her own, and a deep quivering at the center of her body, as, murmuring her name, he moved his lips to her throat. His hands cupped her breasts, held them lightly, and hot arrows of excitement streaked through her so that she found herself pressing to him, straining to him to know the hardness of his body and tensing muscles. He put his mouth to hers once more, holding the kiss, so that they shared a single breath between them, and now his hand moved, stroking her back, curving slowly around her hip, caressing the shape of her thighs. She forgot all shyness in the deep hunger that swept over her.

Soon he drew the rose from her hair, and then the pins. He ran his fingertips gently through the long silken hair and buried his face in it.

When he unbuttoned her gown, she helped him draw it away, so that the whiteness of her breasts was exposed. He caressed them gently while she laid ardent kisses on his mouth.

"More barricade than adornment," he muttered, drawing the folds of her gown away from her completely, and then the layers of undergarments, so that, finally, she felt the warmth of the air against her bare flesh. She closed her eyes and felt him leave her.

When he returned, he drew her to him again, and held her for a long time, and she felt his skin, silken but male, against her. Again she felt the quickening of his heartbeat echoing in her own breast.

The train rocked and jolted through the night, its rhythm slowly taking their clinging bodies. New sensation seized her, held her, and once she cried out, "Oh, Reed," in a gasp of pain, and then, later, she cried out again, in joyful pleasure, "Oh, yes, Reed," and her body arched up to meet his.

She awakened to muted sunlight, to the slow rocking of the car and the scent of roses. She smiled at the pale green ceiling edged with gilt flowers, and stretched voluptuously against the pillows.

Reed came from the end of the car. He was wearing only trousers. His bare chest was brown and smooth. The scar on his left arm was hardly visible. He bent over her and drew her face to his shoulder, and buried his in her hair.

"We'll be arriving in New York in a little while, Miranda, and then we must go directly to the docks."

She hugged him to her, whispering, "Soon? Very soon?"

He laughed softly, lay down beside her, and took her into his arms. "No, my darling, not all that soon."

TWO

Less than two weeks later a thin trail of dark smoke hung briefly against the endless sky, and pale light glimmered through uncovered portholes and danced away in broken reflections on the heavy seas, and an urgent expectancy touched crew and passengers alike, for by dawn the lookout would be crying, "Landfall!" and by midday the gangplank would be lowered at the Southampton docks.

But Miranda, though she listened politely to Captain

Harry Ruggles, did not look ahead with him, nor share his open anticipation, as he described how quickly the loading would be accomplished, and how soon he would himself set out for the town called Rye in which he made his home when not on the bridge of his ship. She thought, rather, that she would be content if she could remain forever in this small world, with Reed's lean body pressed to her by night, and his constant presence given her by day. These were, she reminded herself, the feelings of a happy bride, and she repressed the joyful laugh that rose within her.

The lamplight pouring from high round globes made a brilliance of her eyes as she looked across the table at him.

He raised his wine glass to her and spoke without sound.

She was easily able to read the words as they left his lips.

"I love you, Mrs. Haversham," was what he said.

She smiled, and the brilliance of her eyes became golden fire.

Captain Ruggles, observing, faltered in his description of the small fishing village from which he had run away to sea at the age of fourteen. He was now a hard-bitten man of fifty, frosty blue eyes set in a permanent squint from staring at the horizons. But he was soft-hearted in the face of love. He had looked from the bridge often during this quiet sailing and watched these two, the tall, slender girl with the heart-shaped face so elegantly molded, and the tall, dark-haired man, walking on the promenade deck, her wide skirts blowing around her, and his coat making swallows' wings at his back. He had seen them lean together at the railing and stare off across the silver waves, plainly bound in a shared dream. He knew little about them beyond what the purser had told him as they went over the passenger list the day before sailing.

In his quick dry voice, the purser had said, "Yes, now let's see. The Blacks. He's taking up his post for the first time, some sort of lower attaché in the legation in London. His wife . . . well, I'd guess her to be presentable

enough. Then there's a James. H. James, that is. Traveling
alone. A journalist or some such, I believe, though I'm
not certain of that. And oh, yes, the bridal suite has a
Mr. and Mrs. Haversham, of Washington City, and
Georgetown. He owns railroads, I understand. In any
event, the main office requests all possible consideration
for them. Extra stewards, though she has her own maid
with her. Flowers every day . . ."

The captain had been delighted to find them excellent
dining companions, amused by his stories, contributing a
few of their own. But the journey was nearly over. He
said, "Is there any possibility that you'll go down to the
southeast coast while you're visiting London? The trip to
Rye is not overlong. And it's quite a charming place. One
of the famous five ports, you know. I could recommend
a delightful hotel, and smugglers' walks, and old hideouts
and caves that you'd enjoy."

She withdrew her lingering glance from her husband,
and answered, "We plan to see only London, and an area
just outside it, I believe. Then we shall go on to the Continent."

"A pity," the captain said, "once you've made the
crossing, to see so little of England itself."

"Perhaps," she agreed. "But we have family. Cousins
we've never met before."

Captain Ruggles sighed and abandoned his small and
plainly hopeless plot to ensure that they meet again by
persuading her to stop for a weekend in Rye. With that,
he turned his attention to Mrs. Black on his right.

Miranda saw that Reed was smiling at her again, amusement silvering the pale gray of his glance. It was as if he
could read her mind and know that she wished only for
the very fine but interminable meal to come to an end so
that they could be alone. Then she would wrap her arms
around him and bury her face in his neck and whisper
against the sweetness of his warm flesh all that she felt
for him.

There had been, in these past two weeks, a deepening
in their relationship. Though they had lived in the same
house for a year, and seen each other every day, the

physical passion between them now had opened the path-
ways to a new closeness, an intimacy that was as much
of the mind as of the body.

To Miranda, who had felt alone all her life, alone and
abandoned and born into the wrong world, this new closeness was both dependency and strength. She recognized
and cherished it, and was determined to see it flower.

While conversation and laughter flowed around her, she
sat back, listening to the ensemble's airy tune while she
took a last sip of wine.

The thick blue velvet drapes were closed at the portholes, shutting out the hugeness of the night. The thick
blue floor covering muffled the footsteps of the liveried
stewards hurrying at their duties. The great cluster of pink
carnations at the center of the big table scented the air
with fragrant promise, and the crystal and fine china
gleamed softly in the lamplight.

There were, here, all the luxuries of home. It was the
same in her suite, too. The bridal suite. The furnishings
were fine, with silken sheets and soft thick towels. Fresh
flowers appeared every day, still icy from the storage
rooms. She enjoyed it all, remembering those days when
she had been scullery maid and second cook in Susanah
Kay's kitchen. Her hands showed no signs of her labors
then, and on the left one she wore the wide gold band
intricately carved with tiny orange blossoms that Reed had
put there. On the right one she wore a huge blue sapphire,
Reed's engagement gift to her.

She sat very straight in the high-backed chair, and her
narrow waist was emphasized by the ruffles and folds of
pale lace below. The bodice was of lace, too, but lined
with peau de soie, and buttoned with tiny seed pearls, and
a sprinkle of more seed pearls clung to the net that bound
her black hair in a high chignon.

"It's been a fine trip," Mr. Black was saying.

"Indeed it has," she agreed politely.

Neither she nor Reed had felt the desire for any com-
panionship beyond each other, and there had been virtually
no exchanges except those required by courtesy. She was
sure that she, for one, would scarcely remember past the

next day at noon the names of the Blacks, nor even of quiet and pleasant Mr. Henry James, who had such a penetrating gaze and knew the city of Washington so well. She suspected it would be the same for Reed.

Now he rose with a murmured apology and came to her side. She was instantly on her feet in a swirl of whispering lace skirts, and made her good-nights quickly while Reed settled the lace cape at her shoulders.

As she left the dining room on his arm, she felt the glances of the others go with her. But no one could see the quickening of her breath at Reed's touch, nor the tremor in her knees. No one could measure the depth of the look he gave her as they stepped across the high threshold and out into the faint warm breeze of the sheltered deck.

"Shall we walk a little?" she asked.

He bent his dark head and smiled at her. "I thought you'd become restless."

"The meal was too long, I think. And I don't enjoy being seated so far from you."

They paused to lean at the railing, arms linked and shoulders touching. The breeze took a single black curl of Miranda's and blew it along her cheek. He stroked it and then tucked it neatly into its place to nest with the others.

The sky was like jewelers' black velvet, and strewn over with a king's ransom of countless diamonds, each one unflawed and perfect. There was no moon to detract from their brilliance. There was only that thick darkness which was endless and unknowable space.

But Miranda supposed that the moon must be somewhere, watching the two of them, looking down from an invisible spot approvingly.

"Go in now, my darling," Reed said. "It's too cool for you, and that bit of lace is no more than a frippery, offering no protection from the night air. I'll have a last cigar and join you in a little while."

She brushed a kiss along his lean jaw as she turned away.

In the suite, she found that Abigail had already turned down the heavily embroidered coverlet, and laid out the peignoir of white lace with silver fringes, and the long-sleeved gown that matched it.

Now she delicately rearranged the heavy, silved-backed brushes with their big engraved H's, and the twin mirror and comb, and then looked at Miranda to nod approvingly.

"You're earlier than I thought you'd be, and it's good you are. There's sure to be a world of confusion tomorrow. I'll finish the last of the packing as early as I can. The big trunks are ready to go."

There was some small and unaccustomed tremor in her voice that made Miranda ask, "Are you scared, Aunt Abigail? Will it be so different for you, do you think?"

The black woman shook her dark head, a sudden softness in her eyes. She would never forget how Miranda had concerned herself with where Abigail would sleep, where she would take her meals and with whom, and not leave such affairs to strangers but insist on making sure herself that Abigail was comfortably disposed.

Aloud she said only, "It doesn't matter to me where I am, Miss Miranda. It's all the same." She reached out with her scarred hands. "Let me help you with the gown."

Miranda undid the seed pearl buttons of her bodice, then turned to allow the dark fingers to undo the hooks and ties at the back, and then bent at the waist to permit the frock to be drawn over her head. She stepped out of hoop and petticoats, and Abigail unlaced her. She moved behind the tall Japan screen, scrolled with dragons and flowers in gilt and red, and drew off her chemise and the rest of her undergarments, and passed them out to Abigail, to receive in return her night clothing.

Having donned robe and peignoir, she went to sit at the dressing table. In a little while, Reed would undo the fragile bows, and count the buttons as he slid them through their loops, and tease that the ladies who fashioned such impediments must know not a whit about love.

She recalled now, with some amusement, how she had been at the first a prisoner of her innocence and shyness. He had so gently freed her of both, and her own feelings had helped. Now, though she sometimes still blushed when he looked at her disrobed, sometimes even mischievously pretended to modesty, she knew that she enjoyed it, and enjoyed equally his reaction.

She drew off the net with its clusters of pearls, and took the horn pins from her hair, and allowed the glossy black curls to fall in a shining stream to her white shoulders.

Abigail reached for the brush, but Miranda said, "I'll do it myself tonight," and added, as if in explanation, "Mister Reed will be in very soon."

Abigail nodded. She thought that it was now as she had always known it must be. Miranda and Reed. The two of them together. Master and Mistress of Haversham Square. She went to the door. "Good night, Miss Miranda."

"Good night, Aunt Abigail, and thank you," Miranda answered.

When she was alone, she slowly picked up the hairbrush, drew it through the thick waves that framed the smoothness of her cheeks, readying herself for Reed, and waiting for the sound of his footsteps at the cabin door.

By the time they came, she lay high on the silken pillows, the golden lamps turned low, a faint smile on her lips.

Reed hesitated on the threshold, thinking her already asleep, and for the moment held immobilized by her beauty.

It hardly seemed possible that she was his.

He moved quietly, preparing himself for bed.

At last, in a deep quiet voice, he asked, "Miranda? Miranda, my dear?"

She opened her golden eyes. Her faint smile widened and warmed. "I've been waiting for you, my husband."

He crossed the room and lay down beside her, burying his face in the perfumed warmth of her breasts, and then, rising up, he took her fully into his arms.

THREE

"Heads up below!"

"Mind the hawsers!"

"The gangplank's coming down!"

The winches screeched and squealed.

Barrels clattered, and whistles shrilled.

A thick yellow mist lay over the Southampton docks, and from it, cranes and derricks and loaders loomed like mysterious phantom figures.

The ship, once proud-riding and free, had been captured by small tugs hours before, and now it was imprisoned, bound to the docks by great hawsers.

High above, where white-breasted terns spread black wings to swoop and soar, the Union Jack fluttered from the crow's nest, and below it, the guy wires were brightened by multi-colored dancing pennants.

Shouts, cries, greetings and warnings and imprecations filled the air.

Reed watched Miranda tilt her head for a last long look. Her cheeks were flushed with excitement.

"I'd thought it would be hard to leave the ship behind me. But I find it isn't so." And it was true. Her pulse beat quickly with anticipation. There were, beyond the yellow mists, whole new worlds to conquer, and she was eager for whatever might come.

Close by, the band, now dressed in uniforms of brilliant red with frogs and loops and ribbons of gold, began to play.

Captain Ruggles appeared for a last goodbye. Then the Blacks, and a few of the other shipboard acquaintances, too. Though Mr. James passed by with only the briefest of nods and a final penetrating glance.

Miranda made her farewells politely, her mind and heart already leaping ahead. Here, below her, at the foot of the gangplank was England! It was from this place that her family had sprung. How joyful Martha Appleton would be to see the moment when Miranda's slipper set its mark upon the ancestral soil.

Reed led the way down, warning her to have a care on the slatted boards, and Abigail followed after, carrying jewel case and carriage blanket.

"Will Ian Haversham be here, do you think?" Miranda asked.

"He *is* here," Reed told her, gesturing with a gloved hand.

She understood at once. It was impossible to mistake the man who moved toward them for anyone but a Haversham.

He came across the distance between them with a quick, almost lunging stride, the thud of his boots clearly audible through the clatter and chatter of arrival. His shoulders were wide, carried square and robustly. His body was lean, with a horseman's narrow, muscular flanks. He had the Haversham head, but his hair was a reddish bronze, cropped long. It was a color well-suited to the high flush of his craggy face. From beneath reddish brows his blue eyes blazed with an extraordinary warmth and color.

There was, Miranda thought, something of John in him, and something of Reed, too. Yet he was so plainly his own man. Even his clothes expressed that. Many of the men on the docks wore conservative black, some less conservative small checks, but each and every one of them wore some sort of head covering. There were tall silk hats, high bowlers and low ones, curled brimmed ones and flat-brimmed ones, and even some of straw. Ian Haversham was defiantly hatless. She was to learn, though she didn't know it then, that he never wore a head covering, no matter what the weather or the circumstances, and that it never troubled him that to be hatless was considered, in English society, to be somewhat plebeian. Now he had on a gray single-button coat, long and flared, a plain gray waistcoat, and trousers of the same variety. His black boots were narrow, untrimmed, and polished to a sheen.

Behind him, trotting on short legs to keep up, was a

small, dark-haired man in a neat royal blue uniform, burdened by a great armful of flowers.

Ian Haversham came to such a quick stop before them that he rocked on his heels. He grinned widely. "You are here at last! Let us dispense with the formalities at once, if you please. We're cousins by blood. I am Ian, Miranda, my dear. Reed, welcome." His voice was very deep but very smooth. When he became silent, nodding at the small man beside him, it seemed still to echo in the air.

It was his vibrant quality, more than his voice, that set up such a clamor around them, Miranda thought. He seemed overbursting with health, warmth, and power. It was shown even in his stance, legs wide apart, rocking slightly on his heels, as if eager to be up and away. His gestures were strong: his hands, lightly touched with bronze hair on their backs, chopped at the misty air.

The small, dark-haired man beside him panted and nodded and bowed. Then he offered the flowers to Miranda, revealing, finally, a narrow face, gleaming black eyes, and a smiling mouth.

She accepted the bouquet with thanks, and then thanked Ian. But the excitement within her was too much for decorum. She threw back her head and drew a deep breath of the bitter yellow mist mixed with the heady scent of the bouquet, and cried, "Oh, it's all so beautiful! I'm so happy!"

The two men looked at each other, and in that moment was born a sympathy and understanding and friendship that was to last them as long as they lived.

Ian knew very little of Reed, and that little had been through John's eyes. He had last seen John nearly three and a half years before, when the last of their business dealings had been concluded. The few offhand remarks John had made about Reed had led Ian to imagine him a much younger man, so that he was surprised to see that Reed and he were of roughly the same age, with he himself perhaps a year older.

As he led the couple through the quickly concluded formalities, he decided that he would speak later, privately, to Reed about his older brother so recently dead. Ian would say nothing now that might mar the happiness he saw in Miranda's face.

Her eyes were like great lanterns, he thought, watching her settle herself in the compartment and turn quickly to the window with the train under way.

The yellow mist broke, and the sun shone on small cottages with thatched roofs smothered with purple clematis, and long narrow lanes whose high, wall-like hedges burned with yellow blossoms.

Harvesters working in the shining fields lifted their hands in salute as the train sped by, and horses danced at the road crossings, and everywhere there was some new sight to see and treasure, some new thrill to savor.

The whole of the honeymoon journey was to be that way.

They arrived in the great city of London just at twilight, and as they jolted through the narrow roads in Ian's carriage, the mellow tones of Big Ben chimed from its bell tower across misty buildings.

The gaslit lanes were crowded with men pushing barrows, hawking oysters and winkles, offering buns and fruit, flowers, scarves, caps and veils. Beggars struggled with each other at the corners and darted between the carriages, grinning while they tempted the drivers' skills. Conveyances of every description skimmed past each other. Gigs competing for space with drays, and great coaches drawn by prancing horses, and two-wheel carts hitched to shaggy ponies. Even the bustle of New York seemed mild by comparison to this old metropolis. And Miranda decided then that the London Mr. Charles Dickens wrote about, was real, and familiar to her through his words.

All was overwhelming and beautiful; even the soot, the spoiled garbage in the street, had its exotic charm, and that, too, was to be the way of the rest of the journey.

The place to which Ian brought them was a four-story city dwelling, white stucco with big windows, in an area called Belgravia. It was, he said with a grin, newly acquired.

He went on, as he led them up the steps, "You'll be surely wondering about my wife Grace, and why she's not here with me to welcome you. I've had so much to say, I've just not come to that yet. It's because of my young son Rory. He's just past seven, and off to boarding school in two weeks. But now he's down with a bronchial attack, and my Grace is nursing him through it in hopes he'll be able to go in time. It's a fearful thing to start late, you know."

All this he spoke of, and meanwhile directed his man-servant, called Dudlun, to show Abigail the basement quarters, and to serve up tea for Miranda and brandy and soda for Reed and himself.

The pale gaslight illumined large and well-proportioned rooms, with carved lintels at the doors and decorated chimney pieces, and an Adam fireplace of pale green marble.

The newly acquired house had a newly acquired name, Ian said, with another of his broad grins. It was called Haversham Gate.

While the men had their brandies, and she had her tea, Miranda wondered what sort of woman Ian had married. He spoke of his Rory again, and she asked, "You have only the one son, Ian?"

"Only the one," he told her. "And not much expectation of another, I regret to say." And then, "Ah, well, a man can't in this life have all that he wants, can he?"

"It wouldn't be this life if that were so," Reed answered. He thought then of John, who had believed always that he could attain any desire. John, who would use any means to achieve such an end. Now John lay in his coffin, and what were his desires to him?

Miranda's mind drifted away from the conversation. Poor Ian and Grace . . . to have only one son. Her own children would be many. Her body was young and strong, and so was Reed's, and between them they would produce tall handsome boys with their father's dark wavy hair and his slow smile . . .

She saw that smile when she said, as they prepared themselves for bed, "I'm sorry to see this day end, Reed. I feel like a greedy child who wants more and more and more."

"And you shall have it," he told her.

She watched him dispose of his collar button into the compartment of the jewel case in which it belonged, his studs into their own. She saw him remove paper money and hard coin from his trouser pockets, and lay both aside. She saw him hang his cravat and his shirt.

His hands were lean and brown and quick, and learning these neat habits of his gave an added fillip to her days.

In the morning, having breakfasted on thick slices of bacon and country eggs and broiled tomatoes, and warmed themselves on innumerable cups of tea with milk, Miranda and Reed set out to learn London, for she had expressed the desire to see more of it before they proceeded to Haversham Manor.

Ian had business affairs to attend to, so they went alone. They drove to the Tower of London, that great prison in which queens, and soldiers of fortune, statesmen, and traitors, had died.

They visited the Houses of Parliament at Westminster, rebuilt within the past ten years after a devastating fire. They saw Whitehall Palace, and Buckingham, and stolled in the lavish gardens across the road.

They paused in Fleet Street to admire the newspaper plant that Ian had recently purchased. After luncheon at Wheeler's in Old Compton Street, they shopped for a little while on Regent Street.

That night they went to Covent Garden, and early the next day they left for Haversham Manor, and the tiny village north of London in which the early Havershams had been weavers and then manufacturers, and from which they had spread.

Haversham Manor was built of raw gray stone, its central section some two hundred years old, its wings much newer dating from the beginning of the century. It was set in a small valley, and was surrounded by a ring of shallow blue hills. From its upper windows, the church spire could be seen beckoning at the village center.

It was here that they finally met Ian's wife. She was a

small, smiling woman, with pale brown hair and light brown eyes, a woman who seemed shadowed by Ian's rugged force. She wore a brown moiré dress with a scarf of cherry red, and her hair was dressed in a neat braided coronet over her small ears.

She said, as she showed Miranda and Reed to their apartment, "Our Rory is much improved, but I must keep him in bed another few days. Perhaps then you'd like to meet with him?"

"Of course we would," Reed assured her. "We look forward to it."

"He's very impatient," she said, "to see his American cousins." A shadow touched her face. "When I say those words, I always remember that foolish play, and what happened that night in Washington . . . I feel so . . ." She stopped herself, giving Miranda a timid and shamefaced look.

She need have been neither. Nothing could have more quickly gained Miranda's interest. That Grace should know, or care, or be reminded that Lincoln had been assassinated while seeing this particular play, formed a bond with Miranda herself. They could never be strangers after that.

Miranda deliberately set out to ensure that they would not be. When the men went to explore the vast manor property on horseback, she made certain that she found Grace alone and settled down with her near the open window for conversation.

"I enjoyed seeing your house in London," she began. "Ian tells me that you've not had it long. Have you thought much yet of what you propose to do with it?"

Grace folded small, birdlike hands in her lap, and smiled faintly. "It's a good question. I've asked myself the same many times recently. But you see, I've no fondness for London. Nor for the society one finds there. But Ian *would* have the house, though I doubt I shall ever live in it. He feels it important to him regardless."

"Important? In what way do you mean?"

Grace shrugged. "Men of his position must have a London house, he thinks. He's no doubt correct. I must suppose that. For I know nothing about it, nor do I want to know. I care very little for such things. I can't imagine myself a shining hostess. I don't see myself holding small intimate dinners for statesmen, nor entertaining members of the court."

Listening, Miranda felt a great swell of excitement. It was just so that she saw herself. It was just such a life to which she had been born. She didn't understand Grace's objections.

"Ian has the season in mind," Grace went on. "I would prefer there be no season, and no Haversham Gate. I like the Manor by far the best, and the country, too, and my books and garden, and I shall never be happy in London."

"But it's such an exciting place," Miranda protested.

"In your eyes," Grace answered, smiling.

"And if Ian's business takes him there, as surely it does . . ."

"Then he must go, of course," Grace said. "And, of course, should it prove absolutely necessary, I'll go with him."

Now Miranda smiled. "But only if it's absolutely necessary?"

Grace said quietly, "My dear, we've been married eight years. And we have our Rory. And Ian's interests . . . it's so difficult to explain . . . I just don't understand them. Nor do I want to. He buys newspapers, one after the other, and makes them successes, and then buys more." She shifted her pale brown eyes to look at the blue hills beyond the window. "My life is here."

Miranda suddenly thought that she understood. Ian's vitality and quickness had somehow closed Grace out of his life. She did not like the idea of London because she did not understand his goals and hungers.

Miranda did not know then that Grace was the youngest and most homely daughter of a titled family. Her parents had been relieved to marry her off with a small settlement to Ian, even though his background was hardly suitable. He was the son of factory owners, and though the factories had been sold, and he now owned several newspapers instead, he remained in the eyes of society, what he had been bred. That is, the son of merchants, descended from artisans who had once been serfs on her own ancestors' lands. It troubled her not at all. Nor did it trouble him. Theirs had been a love match from the beginning, though none of her friends believed it. They insisted that she had married out of desperation; she was twenty-five then, and he was twenty, and already known to be ambitious. What these two so different beings had between them was unknowable to an observer, Grace supposed. It was compounded of peace in each other, relief from strain, of respect freely given, and the answering of complementary needs. It was, Grace told herself often, love.

That evening, as she and Reed dressed for dinner, Miranda thought of her conversation with Grace, and pondered its meaning, "There is one small thing I ask that you promise me," she said finally.

"Anything," he answered, frowning over his cravat.

"Please don't be so quick to commit yourself. You may find that you regret it."

"Never," he told her. "I promise you freely whatever you ask for."

She fastened a small sapphire drop to each of her ears, and then turned to look at him seriously. "I've been thinking about something Grace told me. She knows nothing of Ian's business, and cares nothing about it for that reason. I'd say it builds a wall between them, one that might someday prove insurmountable, even though they love each other dearly."

Reed threw back his dark head, laughed softly. "Miranda, my love, is this what comes of spending our honeymoon with old married folk? Have you been led to examine and find fault with marriage already?"

"Not with marriage. No. I can no longer imagine any other way to live but to be married. But only with this sort of relationship."

He gave her a quizzical look. "It's that way between men and women, Miranda, and has always been so. Why not? Why should a pretty woman trouble herself with what must be only problems? Why wouldn't her husband desire to protect her from them?"

He remembered how John had used Caroline's feeling for him, her feelings, her money, her friends. That was linked forever in his mind with what Miranda was saying now.

She sank down on the edge of the bed, her body rising from the fullness of her spread skirts like a tall and strong young tree from the brush that surrounded it. She said, "I don't care what is the usual way, and I'm not concerned to be protected. I love you. I want to share everything with you, and I want you to promise me that you'll share everything with me. We are either one in all things, or we are not. I can be no other way, Reed."

He forced himself to swallow his distaste. He made his lean face expressionless. "Why, Miranda, you're quite serious, aren't you?"

"I am indeed."

He saw no reason to discuss now what could more profitably be discussed at some time in the future, some very long time in the future. He loved her, and wanted to please her, and so, with a hidden reservation, he said, "We shall be one in all affairs, Miranda."

"In your work as well as in our lives together?" she demanded.

"In all affairs," he repeated, hugging her to him.

The next day they found Rory well and out of bed. He was slight and very pale, with his mother's brown hair and light eyes. He had remarkable manners and a serious voice. He was as delighted with Miranda and Reed as they were with him. But they saw little of him, for he was kept busy with preparations related to his departure for school.

That afternoon, riding alone with Reed, Ian spoke finally of John, saying, "It was a shock to hear the news of your brother's death. He was so young a man, and one of such great strength. It's hard to accept the thought that such an accident could befall him." He saw Reed's features tighten and a pallor touch his cheeks, and his eyes hood themselves. "I owed much to John, you know," he went on quickly. "Perhaps he told you."

"He spoke hardly at all of his affairs, Ian."

"It was through our arrangements together that I was able to buy the newspaper in Fleet Street. The heart of the business, and the seat of its power. Within three years' time I shall own another. Then I will be someone to contend with, believe me."

"We Havershams are intent on our empires," Reed said quietly. "It must be a trait in the blood."

"And you?" Ian asked.

"The same, I suppose," Reed answered. But he had not, in Ian's judgment, sounded particularly interested.

Ian supposed that Reed could at the moment consider nothing but his joy in Miranda.

When Reed looked at him sideways, suggesting, "Shall we return to the manor?" Ian understood, and agreed.

It was only later that he realized that Reed had told him nothing of John's death, and the accident that had brought it about.

There were teas, dinners, balls. There was a hunt and several picnics. The days were full to overflowing, the nights heady. The time went quickly, and then Miranda and Reed set out for Paris.

They stood at the rail of the small packet, as the white cliffs receded into a silvery mist.

"Our cousins are lovely," Miranda said. "Do you think that they liked us as much as we liked them?"

"I'm sure of it," Reed answered. "But I'll tell you now that I'm relieved to be alone with you again."

"And I with you," she said contentedly. She reached to hold his hand. "I'd like to think that we could maintain a certain closeness with Ian and Grace," she went on, looking back toward where the white cliffs had now disappeared. "Even though we'll be separated by the sea." She turned, looked into Reed's face. "I've always been alone, Reed. Always. Until now. I'd not want our children to know what that means."

His arm settled around her shoulder. "You're no longer alone, Miranda."

She smiled up at him and lay her head into the curve of his shoulder. "No," she said. "No. Now I have you."

Paris gleamed white and beautiful in mid-September. Small girls sold anemones on the street corners, and Reed bought Miranda baskets of them, and pinned some to her cloak and some to her hat and piled the rest into her arms. They hired a fiacre and rode through the Bois de Boulogne, nibbling horse chestnuts that had been roasted over open braziers on the wide boulevards. They rode grandly down the Champs Elysées, wheel to wheel with other splendid equipages. Though they carried letters of introduction from home, and more from Ian, they made no attempt to use them. They preferred to be by themselves.

They spent hours in Notre Dame, and more hours wandering through the Left Bank. They attended the theater, saw the opera, and climbed rickety steps to dingy garrets to study the works of artists as yet unknown.

One morning, walking in the clear sunlight of the Place du Tertre, they paused to observe a young man working at his easel, and were soon in conversation with him. Reed's French, and her own, though small, sufficed. His name was Claude. He was plainly poor, and not very well fed. When they left him, they took away with them a painting of an island in the river. It was signed Monet.

That purchase was the first of many. The baggage they carried grew heavier as they bought more paintings.

"The Grand Tour," Miranda teased, "is not only a fine education but also a shopping trip as well."

"We buy nothing that we don't require," Reed assured her.

"I require nothing," she whispered. "As long as I have you."

Florence was crowded, gay.

Music seemed to fill the crooked streets.

The Arno ran slow under brilliant sunshine, and the sprawling brown palaces gleamed. By morning, they wandered through the lanes, the gardens, through the churches. Everywhere there was a feast for the eye, the glory of curved line or of color.

Here, too, Ian's connections and their own might have brought them into society. But they preferred not.

They were tourists by morning. One day Reed rented a small flat-bottomed boat and sat beside her while a slim young man guided it downriver, and she remembered the day Reed had taken her for a picnic on the Potomac. They were tourists by morning. But they were lovers through the long golden afternoons. Then they closed the heavy wooden shutters and lay in each other's arms.

She would kiss the scarred place on his left arm, as if that would wipe away the memory of pain, and press close to his body, no longer shy with him but knowing his flesh as well as her own, and glorying in both.

"We'll have a big family," she said one day. "I've been thinking of it. Four, or perhaps even five sons."

"And a daughter or two," he smiled.

"A daughter or two," she agreed.

He drew down the sheet and spread his big hands at her waist, and then spread them wider, his fingers moving in quick butterfly strokes against her flesh, leaving small trails of heat where they passed.

She kissed him lingeringly and drew him close, giving herself up to the hard warm strength of his body.

Later, when they were still and at peace again, she said, wonder in her voice, "We're so fortunate, Reed."

"To have found each other. That was our good fortune."

"Oh, yes," she whispered. "And now we will go home."

FOUR

Miranda's heart beat quickly as the horses trotted along the sun-filled lane toward Haversham Square.

Home. Home. Soon she would be home.

She reached for Reed's hand as the tall iron gates appeared. "Oh, it's good," she breathed.

They rode under the October bare oaks, and then the house was before them.

The carriage jolted to a stop.

Timoshen opened the door, and Reed stepped out, and then swung her down.

Lena and Jefferson were waiting, wreathed in smiles.

The big double doors stood open.

Reed grinned, took Miranda into his arms, and carried her over the threshold.

"Home," she breathed against his lips as he kissed her.

Within days they were hard at work on plans to make Haversham Square their own, though neither Miranda nor Reed had consciously chosen that goal.

Reed had removed the French-made centerpiece from the dining room table, and there he spread out his papers and drawings.

"You see, my darling," he said, pointing with a pencil, "here we'll add two rooms on the lower floor. We'll build them out over the back terrace. And then we'll extend the terrace itself."

She had smiled to herself. Those two rooms were not immediately necessary but she hoped that soon they would be.

"And you can see," Reed went on, "these other changes I plan. The windows enlarged here in the morning room. Do you agree?"

"Oh yes, of course. It will make for a light airy feeling."

"And new marble on this fireplace," Reed said.

"It will be lovely," she told him.

"It will be when it's done," Reed answered.

Soon the house resounded with hammering and banging. Plaster dust drifted in the air, and the smell of lumber, and paint was everywhere. There was not a room untouched, no place for quiet conversation by day, no spot for entertainment by night.

Miranda savored every discomfort of the work, and did not count the weeks nor care how long it took.

But Stacy, who no longer lived at Haversham Square, came and sniffed and complained. "Will there never be an end of this?"

Miranda only smiled. "I'm content."

When she and Reed returned from abroad, they found Stacy ensconced in the Van Eward mansion on Massachusetts Avenue, and Mary Van Eward departed to assuage her sorrows at Saratoga Springs.

Carlton Van Eward firmly believed that what had happened was all his own idea, and his own plan. Stacy, if she cared to, could easily have disillusioned him.

He had called for her one evening at Haversham Square, not long after Miranda and Reed had departed.

She remembered, as she dressed carefully that night, the sweet scent of the white rose petals that had fallen on her when she was Miranda's maid of honor. Remembering that, she had chosen a gown with a decolletage even more daring than usual, which meant that it was very daring indeed. She had perfumed herself with a lavish hand, and done delicate labor over her face. She and Carleton would be going to the Barrington sisters for a small dinner party. She suggested first, since the evening was so exceptionally warm, and the moon so exceptionally silver, that they might have a drive out the Canal Road near the river.

Pudgy Carleton was amenable. He was amenable, too, when she nestled close to him behind the driver's rigid shoulders, and allowed her breasts to touch his arm with each jostle of the carriage.

By the time they reached the Barrington house, it was quite late, and his thin white hair was tousled into an unsenatorial pompadour, and his round cheeks were very nearly flushed. They paused just a moment before the open drawing room doors and she, carried away, he thought, by some sweet though clearly embarrassing impulse, rose on her toes and planted a warm kiss on his mouth.

Mary Van Eward, already present, rigid as a tree trunk in gray silk, gasped audibly and spread her withered hands over her withered face.

Erna Barrington giggled and immediately looked both embarrassed and helpless.

Dorothea had the presence of mind to rise, to hurry forward, crying, "My dears, how nice to see you both," though there was a small question in her tone.

Carleton's face went from flushed to flaming. His plump arm settled protectively around Stacy, though she, in fact, needed no such support. There was, clearly, nothing to be done in his view but what he did, and what he did most happily.

He cleared his throat and announced, "My friends, and Mary, my dear sister, I should like you to know that Stacy has just now, after much persuasion on my part, finally consented to become my wife."

It didn't matter that his ringing tone belonged more properly on the Senate floor in discussion of fiscal matters.

Mary Van Eward sat frozen, but Dorothea quickly called out for fresh champagne, and Stacy's heart's desire was accomplished with a single well-planned and well-planted kiss.

Stacy chuckled. "Plainly you are content. I think all this confusion is but an excuse for you and Reed to prolong the privacy of your honeymoon."

Miranda threw back her head and laughed. "Privacy?" she cried. "With workmen underfoot from dawn to dark?"

Slowly the new rooms took form, and the back terrace was completed. The plaster dust was cleared away, and the paint dried.

The furniture was reupholstered and new drapes were done, and everything was in its place.

Even so, there were boxes, crates, and barrels still to

come. Two graceful urns done in Italian marble to join
the fawn near the lily pond. A pair of benches for the
conservatory. Sets of china from Wedgewood, and more
sets of Waterford glass.

One late afternoon in early March Reed and Miranda
were in the morning room.

He held over the mantel the painting by the young
Claude Monet. "Here, do you think?"

"Yes," she said. "Just there. Where I can look at it and
remember the day we bought it."

The light of the fire seemed to glow in her eyes, to
flicker on her cheeks.

Reed fixed the painting to the wall, adjusted it carefully, and then went to stand behind Miranda.

"Perfect," he said, and turned to her, his hands at her
shoulders. He looked into her face for what seemed a long
moment, and then drew her down to the hearthrug with
him.

FIVE

"I would say ten yards, Miss Miranda. Eight for the
skirt, one for the bodice, and one for trim," Mrs. Bannion said. She paused for breath and went on, "I do hope
you did buy ample. It would be impossible to find such
fabrics here, you know. And those French patterns . . .
well, Miss Miranda, I'll do my best, but . . ."

Her voice continued on, but Miranda suddenly no
longer heard the words. She had been in the act of mount-
ing the steps. Mrs. Bannion was hopping anxiously at her
side, and tripping repeatedly on the hem of her gown.
When they reached the top, Miranda saw the golden slant
of light across the brown of the floor covering, and in the
wide, gold-framed mirror, she saw the reflection of the
wide open door.

It was the door to John's study. The heavy drapes had been drawn back. Chill March sunlight came streaming through the bared window and across the room to lie here at her feet, a sudden chasm at which she halted.

A shiver touched her. The path of golden light seemed to spread at her feet. It was not a chasm now. It was a road, a road into the room that she had not seen for a long time. Since John's death, its door had remained firmly closed. She had heard Abigail and Lena speak of what they had found there, the blood on the chair and desk, the torn head above stony eyes glaring from the gray face.

Miranda closed her mind abruptly. "Mrs. Bannion, I must stop here for a moment. Would you go up to the sewing room and wait for me? I'll be only a little while."

The thin older woman nodded her head and trudged slowly up the next flight of steps.

Miranda moved to the threshold of the room John had called his study.

It was just the same as it had been when she first came to this house. Hanging lamps made pools of light on the green floor covering. There were the same bookcases lining the walls, and the windows were still draped in dark green silk.

She did not know what she had expected to see, but the sight of Reed, seated at the familiar big desk, his dark head bent over some papers, absorbed, unknowing, and frowning, was somehow a shock to her.

At last she spoke his name softly.

He looked up, the frown dissolving, his lean brown face alight with a sudden smile. She could not have known what effort it had taken for him to settle himself in that chair. How he had forced himself to claim this desk. She could not have known from his expression that he had determined he must exorcize the demons that inhabited this place.

He had sensed, under the brightness of the redecorated house, the brightness that Miranda herself brought to it, a thread of darkness, some faint lingering shadow. Though John was gone, these remained. And these were what Reed called demons in his mind.

"Miranda, I'm sorry. I didn't hear you. But come in. Come in and sit down."

"Are you sure that I don't disturb you, Reed?"

"Disturb me? I'm delighted for the distraction. I have a lot to learn, I'm discovering." He flicked at the papers with his fingertips. "Not the least of which is that this business is very nearly as dry as the law itself."

She, having forgotten that Mrs. Bannion would be waiting, advanced slowly into the room and across the thick carpeting that reminded her of the meadow behind the cottage in Dealeyton. She sank into the chair beside the desk. She allowed herself no more than a glance at the mahogany case that held the two dueling pistols John had always kept there.

Reed leaned back in his chair, observing her. She was oddly pale, the smooth curve of her cheeks almost the same shade as the heavy woollen cream-colored gown she wore. Her straight brows and the fringe of her lashes looked black as pitch, standing out against such background. A small line, more dimple than frown, marred her forehead. He decided that if a phantom seemed to hold sway in this place for her, then that phantom must be dispelled at once. And in the same way as his own demons must be. He said, "What is it, Miranda? You look troubled. Is something wrong?"

She answered, "I hadn't expected to see this room open and in use. We never discussed it. Do you think it necessary, Reed? Wouldn't it be better . . ."

He gave her a long gray glance. Then asked gently, "Does it bother you so? Do you think that we must keep this place closed away, an awesome secret, never to be seen or thought of again?"

"No," she said quickly. "No, not that. But . . . somehow."

"There are no somehows to this, Miranda. This is a room. No more than that. Walls, windows, furniture. A good hearth. A sound floor. This shall be my study henceforth. I have work to do, and it shall be done here."

That he already knew he despised the work he did not

say. He had determined that it must be done, and that he would do it.

"But Reed, I had planned that the downstairs library would be your study."

"I think not. It would be inconvenient."

Even as he said those words, she knew what she would do. If he would use this place, sit here hour after hour, day after day, then she would transform it. It would be no longer John's. It would be Reed's. That was somehow important to her. But she said nothing of that to him. "I think Abigail and Lena may be troubled by this," was what she suggested.

He grinned suddenly, "Miranda, you mustn't use them as a means to gain your own ends. And even if that were so, I would consider it very wrong to encourage them in childlike fancies."

"Very well," she answered. "I'm certain that you're right." But she noticed then that the golden path had disappeared from the window. A grayness hung there instead, and was not touched by the pale light of the hanging lamps. She forced herself to look away, to say lightly, "I do hope that you don't plan to work at those papers through tea. I've asked Stacy and Carleton to join us, and they'd be sorry not to see you."

"Of course I'll come down. Just send Lena to inform me when they have arrived, will you?" That he was relieved, glad to have an excuse for turning away from the labors he had set himself, he did not tell her. He was ashamed to acknowledge how much he would have preferred almost any activity to this scanning of rows of meaningless figures.

She rose, giving the bookcases a thoughtful look. She already saw how she would manage it. But the bookcases were a problem. How could they be transformed? She told herself that she would think on it. There would be a way.

She hurried up to the sewing room, suddenly remembering that Mrs. Bannion was waiting for her. They would have an hour before it was time to change.

All the while Mrs. Bannion chattered at her, and measured cambric against pattern, and pattern against Mi-

randa, Miranda asked herself why Reed had decided that
he must use John's desk, John's chair, and allow to be
before him, where he could see it daily, the mahogany
box that contained the dueling pistols. And, as she questioned the important without success, she resolved the
unimportant. She would send Mrs. Bannion to buy leather.
The bookcases would be covered and transformed. The
room would no longer be John's. Just as Haversham
Square was no longer John's.

"I do believe it will greatly become you," Mrs. Bannion said at last.

"Thank you," Miranda stroked the length of blue cambric. "You must have a meal before you go, Mrs. Bannion. Abigail will have it ready for you when you go
down."

Mrs. Bannion withdrew the pins from between her lips,
thrust them into the pin cushion tied to her wrist, made
her farewells and left the room.

Miranda lingered for a moment. There was, on the top
of the chest, a great rack of sheerest white lace, French
made, and very fine. There was a bolt of silky linen in
blue, another in pink. She smiled as she touched them
both, her flesh warmed as much by the symbol they were
as by the sensuous feel of them.

No one knew yet, and she was not even certain herself,
but she had the feeling that very soon now Mrs. Bannion
would begin to cut tiny patterns in those linens. She had
discerned a new fullness in her breasts. Within a few days
she would have Doctor Porter come to see her.

"I'm nearly frozen," Stacy cried. "I long for spring and
warmth and softness."

There was a high flush on her cheeks, and her eyes
sparkled with the embers that filled their dark depths.

Carleton, in the act of handing her ermine cape to
Jefferson, looked at her adoringly.

Jefferson took the white cape, and Carleton's fur-
trimmed greatcoat, and retired.

Miranda led the way into the morning room, and Stacy
sank into a deep chair done in pale tan brocade. She

stroked the plump arms lightly and nodded her approval, then preened herself as if it were a throne upon which she sat.

Plainly matrimony became her, Miranda thought, with hidden amusement.

She said, "Why, Miranda, what have you done with Reed? Surely he's at home to us?"

"Lena will fetch him directly," Miranda answered. "He's been working at his desk. I suspect from his frowns that our affairs have been greatly neglected these last months while we were settling in. But now, of course, Reed will arrange them."

Stacy made a pretty moue. "Carleton has been working as well, and too hard, I tell him. I don't want him to go rushing off each morning to the Capitol building. I want him to stay home with me. We've so much to do, to talk about."

Carleton sighed placidly. "But my love, these are such difficult times." He glanced at Miranda. "The Senate is positively harassed, you know. Last year there was an organization formed, the Ku Klux Klan it's called. It makes a name for itself, and that name is seeping like slime across the Senate floor. Men can be fools at times. There's the Reconstruction Act coming up. And the Senate is at loggerheads with the President. We don't know which way it will go. We must do what must be done. He stands stubbornly on one side, and more than half the Senate on the other. That half is determined that the North shall have won the war, regardless of what problems are created for the future."

This, to Miranda, was fascinating talk. Here, in her own home, sat a man who moved through the inner councils of one of the world's greatest nations. "And where do you stand?" she asked.

He shook his head sadly and pulled his lips firmly against his false teeth. "My dear, I am with President Johnson, of course. He's right, you see. Martial law will serve no real purpose but to deepen bitterness, which must be forgotten and outgrown. But these terrible tales of the Ku Klux Klan and the Knights of the White Camellia, such tales are inflammatory as are the acts reported, and the constituencies become angry, and this hardens the attitude of those in power."

"But what do you think will happen?" Miranda questioned.

Carleton opened his mouth to reply, but Stacy cried, "Oh, must we continue this awful conversation? It does try my soul. I hear nothing but politics day and night."

"You're in Washington, my dear," Carleton said fondly. "That's what we talk here. Politics, and not much beyond it." His eyes twinkled at her. "Now tell me, is there anything else to discuss?"

"There is indeed," she retorted. "And I've only been waiting an opportunity to do so. I've heard of a new gambling establishment on Connecticut Avenue."

Carleton gave a pained, "Oh, my dear . . . a Senator's wife . . . like Caesar's . . ."

She raised her voice slightly. "I hear that it's perfectly respectable. And decidedly fashionable. And if it isn't now, then it shall be after the four of us visit it."

Reed, entering at that moment, asked, "What will be fashionable, Stacy? You sound very heated over your proposition."

"Now I have an ally," she crowed. "You've heard of it, I'm sure, Reed. The Obermeyer establishment. Carleton has just tried to inform me that it isn't respectable."

Reed seated himself near Miranda, taking her hand. He grinned at Stacy. "And I think I'll remain quite neutral in this business."

He was neutral, and uninterested, too. He would have much preferred that Stacy and Carleton hie themselves to wherever they wanted to go and leave him alone with Miranda. He could never get enough of her company, though he knew that men married longer than he might find such a thought amusing.

Carleton, having seen the storm signals in Stacy's eyes, was asking in a serious tone, "No, Reed. What do you truly think? Would it be such a place to take our wives?"

"I daresay," he shrugged. "Who could say 'no' to us?" He glanced at Miranda, "Do you like the idea?"

"I do," Miranda told him. "I've never been to a gambling establishment, and think it might be enjoyable to see one."

Just then Jefferson brought in the tea tray, and Lena helped him arrange it on the marble table.

Miranda poured deftly, the sapphire ring sparkling like a bright beacon on her hand.

Carleton made a change of subject and discoursed solemnly at Reed.

But when Stacy finished her tea, she sat back and said, "Very well, Carleton. I take your meaning clearly." She turned to Miranda, "Have you heard the funny story about the Smithsonian Institution? It seems that the money came from a man named James Smithson, who was really the bastard son of the Duke of Northumberland, or one of those dukes anyway."

Carleton put in quickly, "James Smithson was a distinguished mathematician and a great philosopher, too. Regardless of the details of his birth."

Miranda took pity on him. She said, "Stacy, would you like to come upstairs and see some new fabrics I'm considering? Perhaps you can help me make up my mind."

Stacy giggled. "No, dear. I would not. I fear you can't lead me astray in that fashion." She rose to her feet, grasped the fullness of her skirt in both hands, and raised it as if preparing to run. "Carleton, my love, if you and our good friends the Havershams don't accompany me to John Obermeyer's, then I shall go there myself."

Johnny Obermeyer's gambling palace was a red sandstone castle squatting on a corner lot, with a short driveway that circled in from Connecticut Avenue.

Obermeyer himself welcomed the Van Ewards and the Havershams. He had long curly black hair and shuttered brown eyes, and a great round body that seemed to exude an earnest honesty. With exquisite manners and cordiality he led the party to the roulette tables, bowing and wishing them luck when he left them.

Reed sipped a drink, watching while Stacy, well supplied with chips denoting various denominations, made daring choices, squealing both when she won and when she lost. Reed himself saw very little in the game to attract him, though when he had been in school, he had played roulette, and poker, too, with some interest.

But soon Stacy cried, "You must join me, Reed. And you too, Miranda. Oh, Carleton, don't be such a stick. Do try your skill."

"Or your luck." Reed grinned.

"Either one," she retorted. The low-hanging lamps cast a flickering light that danced within the depths of her eyes. She bent her dark head to watch as the shining and polished wheel went around, and within its circle the bright ball spun until slowly both settled to a stop.

Reed placed his first wagers casually enough, but as the wheel turned, he found something hypnotic in its motion. A deep hard thrill burned through him as he won, then won again. He played on, choosing numbers and colors with care, yet setting his chips out more and more quickly.

Stacy, her stake gone and with it her interest, wandered away to chat briefly with acquaintances. Carleton trailed after her, proud of her beauty, and certain now that she had been, despite his doubts, right all along. Only the best people of Washington came to Johnny Obermeyer's. And it was amusing. For a little while.

Miranda would have agreed, but as she stood with Reed, playing each spin of the wheel along with him, she, like Stacy, began to tire of the game, and more importantly, she felt a certain stir of unease at his intentness.

Finally she said in a gentle undertone, "Reed, have you not yet had enough of this?"

He did not seem to have heard her. His face was concentrated, his eyes narrowed. His body was tense as he leaned forward, almost urging the wheel on with his own force.

She smiled mischievously, touched his arm. "You're fascinated, aren't you? But look, Stacy is already bored."

"Then let her be," he answered absently.

The wheel stopped. His tightened lips suddenly flexed in a grin. He raked in his winnings, counting them in his mind. It was a substantial amount, well into the thousands. He reached to set up a series of quickly decided upon wagers, in the grip of a hot and hungry elation. There was here, for him, a real challenge, and an unexpected excitement.

Miranda's long slender hand covered his chips. She smiled up at him through the heavy fringe of her lashes. "Shall we go, Reed?"

His fingers closed tightly around her wrist and firmly thrust her hand aside. "Stop it, Miranda. Don't interfere with me now."

He sounded as she had never heard him before, as if he were suddenly a stranger. From where had come that curt cutting edge to his voice? She saw that the croupier's glance was quickly averted from her.

A faint flush touched her cheeks. Her eyes glowed with hot yellow fire. But she said coolly, "Of course, I shan't interfere with you, Reed," and left him to join Stacy and Carleton.

He remained intent on the wheel until, much later, when he had tripled his original winnings, he took the chips to the cashier and pocketed the thick stack of paper money, and accepted John Obermeyer's restrained congratulations with a grin of intense satisfaction.

She went quickly into their bedroom. Angry tears blurred her vision, tears she had fought back and hidden until Stacy and Carleton had deposited her, with Reed, at the front door only moment before. Angry pulses pounded in her throat and temples. She could not forget the look the croupier had given her when Reed refused to finish his game. She could also not forget that Reed had, while concentrating on the silly spin of the silly wheel, become a stranger to her.

She undressed herself quickly, having told Abigail that she wanted no assistance that evening.

She was at the dressing table, brushing her hair with quick hard strokes and biting her lip, when Reed finally came in.

She caught a look of wary amusement in his silver eyes, and that made her own anger even more intense. She found herself trembling with it, mustering words. Yet he was plainly relaxed, unconcerned.

He said, at last, "You're so quiet, Miranda."

She flung the brush to the dressing table and spun on her bench. " 'Do not interfere with me,' " she cried, quoting him. "That's what you said. How could you speak like that to me? That man was listening, the one with the rake. He heard. He smiled."

Reed undid his cravat, tossed it aside. "The croupier, which is what he is called, is no one to be concerned with."

"I am concerned with myself," she retorted. "And with you."

He sat at the end of the blue chaise and stretched his long legs out before him, and took up a small satin pillow, turning it in his hands. He said, with a faint smile, "Miranda, I'm a grown man. I know when I wish to stop my game."

She rose in a swirl of white, her eyes flashing. "But did you know that you embarrassed me?"

He straightened up, the pillow between his hands. He said softly, "My love, I didn't mean to, you know that."

And, as she opened her mouth to reply, he batted the satin pillow toward her. "Catch, Miranda. Quickly, catch!" And then, softly, "Remember that I love you."

The pillow hit her at the waist, and she seized it, flung it back at him. Whatever she had begun to say was gone into astonished hilarity, for he caught it, threw it back at her, and as he did, it burst, and white down suddenly spilled in a trailing snow shower across the room, and they fell, laughing, into each other's arms.

SIX

"They've been back for five full months," Jake Rooker said with sour impatience. " 'Mr. and Mrs. Reed Haversham have returned from their wedding trip to England and the Continent, and they are now at home in Haversham Square.' " He pointed with a gnarled hand at the ragged clipping on the bare table.

"Why, you know it by heart, don't you? You needn't even look at that," Nan Cunningham told him admiringly. "You took the ink in through your skin and it ran up in your veins and got lodged in your brains." Burned there, she thought privately, with a modicum of sympathetic amusement. She went on irrelevantly, "And I suppose our Miranda is now collecting great stacks of visiting cards."

Jake did not answer her. He took a stiff pace away, his shoulders bunching.

They were in the garret room, the small fire sizzling on the hearth, the wind sending cold breath through the cracked window. There was a mug of neat rum next to the well-fingered clipping on the table, and a half-eaten and soggy beef pie.

Nan glanced at the rum, and decided against it with regret. Instead, she turned the brush in her hand and smiled. "Now then, if you don't stand still, how do I clean all that awful lint off your nice blue coat? You could have been rolling in a feather bed in it!" With that she gave him a sly, still-admiring glance.

"Could have, but haven't," he answered sourly.

"Then it was surely your own choosing." And after that, "Poor Jake, you are in sad spirits, aren't you?"

The wind blasted through the cracked window to burn at his cheeks and lift the thin red hair on his forehead. He found himself shivering inside his new warm coat. He was wary of opening his mind to her, knowing how much malice there was within the fat she carried. But he was alone, and there was no one else to talk to. "It's not poor spirits," he said. "It's a bind. I'm stuck, and I see you enjoy it. I don't like that. And I see no way out, and I like that even less."

"Which is why you're going to see Senator Hurley at the Barclay Hotel. Which is why you ought to be pleased with yourself, and pleased with me, too, instead of scowling at the both of us. If you weren't you, and if I hadn't set Mary Bennett after the Senator—"

" 'If . . .' " he retorted. "You and your small schemes. For all the good they'll do me. I ought to be in California where the gold is. Or almost any place else but this."

"There's gold here, too," she answered. "And plenty of it. And my small schemes might lead you to it." She flicked at his shoulders, then lovingly drew the brush across his chest, standing close to him, much closer than he liked.

She could, and he knew it, gather him in to her soft hot body and near smother him with it, and make him forget, as she had before, that she was a good ten years older than he was, if she told the truth, which he considered unlikely, so added five years on his own.

But he stared down at her, and finally asked curiously, "What's in it for you, Nan? What are you up to? Why do you bother?"

"Oh, a bit of a poke for my old age. We all need something to see us through, don't we? And how do we get it, if we don't work for it? So I'm working for it. Maybe it's that. And maybe it's something else."

"What else?" His flat blue eyes had a suspicious gleam. The sweeter her tone, and it was as sweet as molasses now, the less he trusted her.

"And maybe it's just that I aim to have a few small pleasures along the way." She stepped back, suddenly brisk and business-like. "There now. You'll do well enough, but you must stand up straight and not shuffle. You must behave as if you expect to be called Mister Rooker, which indeed you do deserve."

He gave her a twisted grin. "On the say-so of an old trollop like you?"

"Since there's nobody else to say it, perhaps my say-so will have to do."

He did not relish the coming interview, and he would have liked to find some way to avoid it. He grumbled, "It's a fool's errand, Nan, and I think you know it, too."

"It's no errand at all," she retorted. "You're on a fishing trip, and no more than that. I expect you'll come back with information, all right. But only if you go after it properly. Josiah Hurley knows, though no one else may, at least not quite yet, what has happened to the land that John Haversham left."

"And once I know that?" At the mention of John Haversham's name, Jake's eyes had begun to gleam. He was free, his own man, as he had not been since the age of seventeen. He dropped into a rickety chair and sprawled out.

"Here," she said, alarmed at his look of comfort. "What are you doing? You're supposed to be on your way."

"I'm waiting for an answer to my question. And if I don't like it, then I don't go."

She gave a deep gusty sigh. She sat across the table from him, bracing her fat elbows on its edge. "All right, Jake. Let me go over it one more time."

His mouth tightened and his eyes went dull. His big fists bunched on his knees.

She gave a throaty chuckle. "And don't get your bristles up. I'll go over it ten times, if need be. It's not that you don't see what I have in mind. It's just that you want to savor the joy of hearing it and talking of it. Do you think I don't understand that?"

Her small black currant eyes studied him slyly. She saw his body slowly relax. The technique worked once again, she was pleased to see.

"John Haversham's land went to Reed, of course. But he seems unaware of what its value could be. We surely wouldn't like to call it to his attention."

"No reason to. He's been busy playing bridegroom all

these months, I don't doubt. And I know for a fact that he never knew much of what John was up to."

"Now then," Nan went on, "if Josiah Hurley had dealings over that land with John, then Josiah would know its value. Were the two of you to join forces, you and Josiah . . ."

It was suddenly difficult for Jake to concentrate. He had a picture in his mind of Miranda's slender young body welded to Reed's, and his working over her . . .

He forced his attention back to Nan, and said, "Why should the likes of Josiah join forces with the likes of me? I've nothing to offer him. He can go to Reed, buy the land, and sell it as he will."

"He can," Nan agreed. "On the other hand, suppose you were to offer your advice to him, instead of to Reed . . ."

"When Josiah has no need of my advice?"

She repressed a sigh and forced a chuckle instead.

"True, Josiah does not. But Reed does. And if Reed had your advice, then Reed would profit, and Josiah lose. So if you and the Senator were to become partners . . ."

"All right," Jake agreed. "Now that I've heard it again, I agree. It's worth a try." He drew a deep breath. "But what I want is all of it, and not just some. I'm not after only a bit of blackmail to draw on."

"I shouldn't need to tell you we've no money for that," she said firmly. She pulled the rum jug toward her and filled a small glass, and thrust it into Jake's hand.

He emptied it. Then, "We'd have more money if you worked Mary Bennett harder."

"She does what she can, poor soul. It's not her. We need more than one working the street, you see. There's just not enough in that. If we had six—"

"And no place to put them," Jake said sourly. "Without a house—"

Nan suddenly sat back, frozen, her mouth open, and her small eyes wide. "What was that? What did you say?"

"Now what's got into you?" Jake demanded.

"A house," she cried. "But that's just it! A house. Dear Heaven, that's what we need."

Jake shook his head in mock sadness. "Poor old cow. She's finally gone and done it. I knew she would one day."

"Oh, have I?" she cackled. "The Kayhome Arms, you fool."

He was instantly on his feet, leaning over her. He caught a fold of flesh between his fingers and pinched hard. "Damn you, old cow. Don't call me names."

She didn't even seem to notice that he had hurt her, he saw. That stopped him as nothing else could have. She simply pulled her arm away and started wheezing with laughter.

He allowed her to get it out of her system before he demanded, "All right. Now tell me the joke."

"The Kayhome Arms. There it stands, going to wrack and ruin for more than a year. John bought it back from the bank. Now it belongs to Reed. But he knows nothing of it, I'll wager. And I wager he knows nothing of me either."

"What's that got to do with it?" Jake demanded. He saw what she was driving at, but again, he wanted to hear her put it into words.

"Do you realize what a real gold mine that would be? A real house . . . And we could do it up right and pull in the folks with the money."

She closed her eyes, and let her imagination paint the picture. A carriage driving up and stopping. Four men alighting. Big men, with gold watch chains across their ample paunches, and thick moustaches on their upper lips, and fat wads in their pockets. The white door opening wide to welcome them . . .

"With a gambling room on the first floor," Jake said softly.

"But of course," she agreed.

"And possibly other sorts of rooms, for other sorts of tastes besides the usual, up the steps, too," he told her. And then he had a sudden blinding picture of Miranda leaning at the railing of the old house, whipping her hand out to slap his face.

"Of course," Nan said again. "And I know just the thing."

"I'll bet that you do," he told her sourly. The triumphant joy, so heady and sweet, was suddenly gone. "How do we get that house, I'd like to know? Reed Haversham wouldn't sell it to me."

"In the first place, it's the bank that handles it for him. I'm sure of that. So he'd probably know nothing about it. But in the second, it wouldn't be in your name."

Jake gave her a hard look. "Oh sure, you pig. I see it now. You get the house, and in your own name, and you hoot me clear to Fort Reno out the Rockville Pike!"

"And why would I do that?" she asked softly. "We've had some good times together, haven't we? When there was naught in it for me, I stayed around, didn't I? Why wouldn't that give you some reason to trust me?"

He ignored the plea in her voice, not trusting that either. He had seen her act before and was convinced of her skill at it. "And what of your name? Miranda knows it, and you."

"She'd never hear about it," Nan assured him. "She's Mrs. Haversham now, and that should engross her."

He accepted Nan's assurance, but there was still the biggest question of all. "And how would you get the house from Reed, or from the bank, without any money?"

Her pudgy face was suddenly firm, the black eyes small and veiled. "You go and see Josiah Hurley and leave the rest to me."

Jake got to his feet, and she surveyed him up and down. He stood straight. There was, she thought, something to the saying that clothes make the man. She'd never thought so before. But here was living proof. Jake— gangling, shuffling, hangdog Jake—suddenly straight and strong-looking. She felt a quick hunger for him, but repressed it and savored pride instead. She needn't worry to send him off to the Barclay Hotel.

"You know what to do," she said softly. "All you need is a chance to do it, Jake. And you can make that."

He responded, without realizing it, to the pride in her

eyes. He straightened his shoulders even more, and grinned. "See you later."

The wind tugged at his round, low-crowned hat. It was dark blue and velvety soft, but it seemed a vise at his temples. It was the same with the coat and trousers, and the shirt with its tight collar. They had been Nan's choices, and she had paid for them. With what cash, and how come by, he didn't know or care. He felt bound and burdened in the outfit, though he much preferred it to John's hand-me-downs. But he knew he must look right. Otherwise, he would not be allowed to cross the threshold of the Barclay Hotel. This was not like that time when he had gone to Greenleaf Point with John towering beside him. He was on his own now.

Small diamonds of frozen sleet glittered on his shoulders and melted there soon after he settled himself in the horse car that trundled along the Georgetown Bridge Road and Pennsylvania Avenue to Capitol Hill.

The doorman at the Barclay Hotel did not challenge him but instead opened wide the door and stepped back with a murmured, "Good afternoon, sir."

On the fuel of that, Jake strode to the desk where the one-armed veteran's bitter glance reminded Jake that he still wore his hat. He yanked it off, smoothing his wispy red hair, and asked for Senator Hurley's suite.

The information received, he went slowly past the dusty palms and then up the steps. He kept an eye peeled for Mary Bennett, but didn't see her. She was, he supposed, still abed, resting for the night's labors.

The door to the suite was open. As he crossed the threshold, he heard the clink of hard money and the rattle of chips. These men who came over from the Capitol building to spend their time here enjoyed their games. They could be lured to a house in Georgetown. Especially if all entertainment was provided on the spot. He saw wheels spinning, dice rolling. He saw stacks of gold pieces growing high. That brought a certain confidence to his long jaw, a hardness to his shallow eyes.

Josiah Hurley sat in his favorite chair, boots up on the sill under the closed window, a crumple of drape caught under one heel. The spittoon was at his side, and he had used it liberally but not accurately.

He grinned at Jake and sent a brown stream into it, and then said, "Hello, Jake. How are you? I haven't seen you for a long time, have I?"

Jake knew exactly when they had last met. It had been a hot July day. Four bodies had danced on a sudden breeze. John Haversham had been alive then.

Jake sat down without being invited and unbuttoned his coat, and set his hat on the floor beside him, but carefully well away from the spittoon. "A lot's happened since then," he said finally.

"So it has," Josiah said. "And it appears to have done well enough by you, whatever the lot has been."

Nan had been right, Jake thought triumphantly. If he'd come here in work pants and collarless shirt, he'd have had to sneak up the back stairs, and once here, he'd have been thrown right down them. But now Josiah sat relaxed, chewing his cud of tobacco with a curious light in his cold blue eyes and the faintest of smiles splitting his black spade beard. "So it has," Jake agreed, with an equally faint smile.

"Then we'll have a drink on that," Josiah answered.

He bellowed for service, and when the white-coated attendant appeared, he gave his order, and then amended it quickly, "Make those large ones."

Jake allowed himself an approving smile but said nothing.

Josiah complained of the weather in the small interval before the drinks were served. When he had his in hand, he raised it, said, "Your good health, Jake," and tossed it through his beard and into his mouth.

Jake drank, too, wondering where Josiah had kept his tobacco when he swallowed.

Josiah put down his glass with a suddenly brisk air. "And now," he said, "you might as well say what you're here for. I've a feeling it's not just the pleasure of my company."

"Not exactly," Jake admitted. "Though I enjoy it."

"Kind of you," Josiah retorted. "But . . ."

"It's a bit of a story, but all of it's important."

"How about getting on with it, man?" Josiah answered. "I'm listening."

"Summer before last I did a job for John Haversham," Jake said. "It wasn't easy, and it took me quite a long while. Longer than he had patience for, at least. And considering how it all ended, I guess I can excuse him his hurry. Anyhow, I did it, and brought the information to him that he wanted. It concerned a parcel of land, quite a large parcel, in fact." He paused, his shallow gaze fixed on Josiah's face. He read nothing there, but he noted that the Senator's hairy jaw had suddenly become still. Nan's guess had been right then. Josiah Hurley *did* know what John had had in mind. But would he be interested to hear that Jake knew something of it?

In the face of the Senator's silence, Jake went on. "Squatters hold that land now, but it could be right valuable, couldn't it?"

"It might be," Josiah agreed cautiously. "Not right away, of course. But someday it's very like that the man who owns it would find himself with a fortune on his hands."

"Reed Haversham owns it now, doesn't he?"

"I expect so," Josiah said.

"You know so, don't you?"

"Maybe I do."

Jake grinned. "I'll bet you haven't told him what he's got though."

"Why should I? It's nothing to do with me what he owns or doesn't own."

"But it might be something to you. That is, if he *did* know, and if he decided to do something about it without cutting you in."

Josiah took his boots down from the sill and straightened in his chair. "Like what?"

"Like hold on for the highest bidder."

Josiah didn't answer that. He considered the window, which had grown purple with early dusk, and the lights of the Capitol beyond. He considered the gathering shadows in the room. Then he yelled for the attendant again and ordered a new set of large ones, and demanded the gas be lit and the fire, too. He waited in silence until all these chores had been performed, and the drinks downed, and then he said thoughtfully. "You worked for John Haversham for years, didn't you?"

Jake nodded. He kept his eyes carefully on the empty glass in his hand, hiding the heat of triumph he knew must burn in them.

How he wished Nan could see him now. Then let her smirk at him.

"You must have proved yourself over and over," Josiah said. "Else John would have gotten rid of you."

Jake nodded again.

"And now poor John's dead and gone," Josiah went on. "I assume that means you're no longer employed."

"That's right," Jake agreed.

"I need a good man off and on, you know. I think John's recommendation would suit me just fine. What do you say, Jake?"

"It'll be an honor. Any chore you have for me, just let me know."

"My first one is that you keep your mouth firmly shut," Josiah told him.

Jake nodded, and said, "I could do with a retainer now. Times are hard. Prices are going up. Have you noticed the cost of potatoes lately?"

"I quite agree," Josiah answered. "The inflation of war has become the inflation of peace." His blue eyes narrowed. "You may be sure that if you're faithful to me I'll reward you well."

"But you *will* take my word for it, won't you? For the moment, that is?"

Josiah put several large gold pieces into his hand. "Of course, Jake. We're both gentlemen, aren't we?"

Nan sat in the chair beside Tad Layton's desk, her black bombazine skirt spread neatly around her. The small black bonnet on her head was placed at a most respectable angle, and the veil which fell from it covered her mournful face.

"It's so good of you to see me, Mr. Layton. A busy man like you. The president of this big bank. I'm a widow. My dear husband died at Bull Run, and my oldest son at Chickamauga. My youngest fell at Gettysburg and lay mortally wounded for months, the useless medicines he needed taking the last of my resources, and then he, too, left me. Such as I expect little consideration and receive just what we expect. So I'm very grateful, more grateful than you can imagine."

She paused for breath, and to judge the effect of her words as well. She was not deterred by what she saw.

Tad took advantage of this first opportunity to ask, "And what can I do for you, Mrs. . . . ah, Cunningham?"

Plainly the name was not familiar to him. Then she had not been wrong in believing that none of the Havershams, excepting Miranda herself, would ever have heard of old Nan Cunningham, who had once lived at the Kayhome Arms and had every intention of living there again. But not as a boarder this time. And Miranda, just as plainly, had had no cause to mention that name, nor even, most likely, to think of it. And why should she?

Nan sighed heavily, her huge melon breasts straining against her bodice and against the plump hands she held to them. "Old as I am, alone as I am, I must live. It's God's will. Else I would already be dead. From grief, you see. From an excess of unbearable pain. But I am here, and here I remain. So I must live, eat, have a roof over my head."

She cautiously lifted back the veil. Her small black eyes regarded him dolefully. Her rosebud mouth turned down sadly.

"And that is what brings you to me," he said in a dry tone.

She sighed. "Yes, indeed, yes. And I hope, I pray, that you can help me."

"If there's any way . . ."

"But there is, you see," she murmured. "Believe me, if you have within you any spark of human feeling . . ."

"I am a banker, Mrs. Cunningham, but I hope I am also an understanding human being. Now, tell me, what is it that you ask? I have another appointment very soon, and surely you have, too."

"I have no appointments, not in this life. Not anymore. Who cares for an old woman, a widow alone?"

"Mrs. Cunningham," Tad stroked his blond beard, and then adjusted his cuffs, urging her on to explanation.

She restrained herself. She saw that she had set the stage as well as was needed. But she was careful to keep her voice slow and sorrowful. She said, "I have in my lonely wanderings seen a house, windows and doors boarded. A firm enough place it looks, but plainly abandoned. I inquired in the neighborhood and heard that the bank owns that house. I come to ask that you sell it to me."

"The bank does not own the house you refer to," he answered. He thought of John, but only briefly.

"Then someone must. Perhaps you know who."

"I do know," he agreed thoughtfully.

"You must understand that I have but very little money. If you were merciful, you would accept a small down payment as an expression of my honesty. And then, monthly, I would—"

"Since I don't own the property, I can make no arrangements. I could, however—"

Nan rushed on, "As it stands, it will simply fall to ruin. Or burn to the ground one cold night. But I . . . if I thought I could someday own it, would clean it up, you see, and have in boarders. I'm an exceptional cook. I'm good at a woman's chores. I would soon have every room full, I assure you. And then, each month . . ."

Tad considered, glanced at his clock, then rose to his feet. "It's not impossible that we may do business, Mrs. Cunningham. If you'll allow me a week or two."

"Of course. I'll return a week from today," she said eagerly.

"I'd suggest that you just leave your address, and I'll write you a note as soon as I know."

She lowered the veil over her face and heaved herself to her feet. "I can leave you no address, Mr. Layton. I told you. I am alone. I stay with a friend here, a friend there. But always on sufferance, you see. I move on when I see the frowns gather and the eyes measure my small cup of tea. So if you will permit me, I will return here a week from today."

"Then let us say in two weeks, Mrs. Cunningham," Tad suggested. And, "You realize, I hope, that I can promise you nothing. I have no authority over that property. But I will inquire. And if it is possible, then I will do what I can for you."

"You are more than kind. If a widow's prayers mean anything in Heaven, then you are blessed." She took her leave with a bob of her head and a creaking half-curtsy.

She moved slowly through the bank and into the street, where her joy shook her full body with silent laughter. Warmed, expectant, and already planning ahead, she made her way through the icy wind to the Union Hotel.

Behind her, Tad seated himself at his desk and drew a stack of papers toward him. He had been impressed neither by her piety nor her grief. But he knew the Kayhome Arms had been vacant since John had determined, in what seemed to Tad a foolish whim, to buy it. It was property, and must be used to be kept from decay. His banker's heart ached with the thought that it brought gain to no one. Surely Reed had no use for it, and never would have. Why not sell on a small down payment? Why not extend a series of notes that the lady, who was, he felt certain, not nearly as old as she made herself out to be, could pay off? If she failed to meet them, well, the house would still be there, and in better repair surely than it was at the moment.

And, all banker's considerations aside, what harm was there in helping a woman who had lost two sons and a husband to the sorriest of all wars?

SEVEN

The heat was oppressive that day, the air singed with the fiery breath of July. It lay in a visible mist colored bronze over the green of the lawns, and hung, shimmering slightly at the tops of the tall trees. The sun of noon burned through it, a single red eye glaring angrily at earth and never blinking.

Miranda moved her pearl-handled fan languidly past her face, causing a brief stir of turgid warmth. She sighed and closed the fan, and put it on the marble bench. Her black curls drooped on her neck, an uncomfortable damp mop. Her cheeks, slightly fuller now, were beaded with perspiration. A small hot rivulet ran down between her swollen breasts. A swarm of gnats buzzed hungrily around her. She was, she thought wryly, apparently more appetizing to them than she was to herself.

Obviously Abigail had been right. It was cooler within the house.

"Oh, no," she had said, her dark face taut with consternation, on seeing Miranda slowly descend the stairs. "Oh, no, you're not going out. Not now. Not in this heat."

It had been, since the older woman knew of Miranda's pregnancy, a daily battle to keep herself from being wrapped in cotton wool, wrapped as tightly as an Indian papoose, Miranda felt.

If Abigail had her way, Miranda would lie on the blue chaise in her room, eating three huge meals a day, nibbling in between, while she stuffed herself for two. If Abigail had her way, Miranda would rise at noon and go to sleep at dusk. She would look at paintings, read poetry, listen to piano music. She would think only high-minded thoughts. All this to ensure that the child within her had exposure only to the proper influences, and could somehow absorb them.

All this was, no doubt, the same advice that her grandmother would have given her, too.

The trouble was that as her body grew ungainly, her
stomach swelled against the laces until Abigail simply
refused to permit her to wear the garment.

She grew restless. Her long legs and her arms remained
slim and supple, obedient to every command. She felt
well, brimming with energy and expectation, just when
her activities were more and more curtailed.

Doctor Porter had pronounced her fit and said she
could go about as she pleased. But there had come a time
when no matter how adroitly Abigail adjusted her gowns,
the great mound of Miranda's belly went proudly before
her. She found herself more content to stay at home then,
but not content to sit and contemplate only.

Heavy as she was, she wanted to walk, to float, to fly
and dance. Something within her needed to.

But Abigail, mothering her as she would Lena, and
Doctor Porter, and most of all Reed—they all were determined to thwart her. They had formed an alliance that
was to protect her against herself. She must eat and rest
and think fine thoughts. She did, she believed, all of those,
though she considered such simplicities could be over-
done. But the alliance refused to account for her basic
nature. It was not in her to accept so placidly her condition.

That was why she had come so carefully down the
stairs, ignoring Abigail's strictures, and gone out onto the
back terrace. And then, allowing her own feelings to lead
her, she had walked slowly along the shell path to sit on
the bench at the lily pond.

She did not know how other women were in their
pregnancies. She supposed that all had these odd fancies
that she had had in past months. She would be borne high
on waves of elation. She would imagine the image of her
son, and tingle with delight. Then, quite suddenly, she
would find herself sinking in apprehension. Would life
treat this coming child kindly? Would she and Reed be
able to protect him from vicissitudes about which she
would not permit a conscious thought? Then, just as sud-

denly, she would be carried high with certainty that fate would provide only joy. She was a Haversham. The child would be a Haversham, too.

She never allowed herself to discuss with Reed these fancies. She did not want to plant in his mind any seed that might grow to shadow his joy and pride. She knew that he waited as full of hope and excitement as she did herself for when the baby would be born.

Now she took up the fan again, waving it before her face. Beyond it, she saw the thick green leaves of the floating lilies. She saw the bright clean flowers.

Her golden eyes widened as one of them seemed to become before her gaze a shadowed face. She gasped and turned quickly away, noticing now a heavy and hushed stillness. She remembered, but refused to remember. Perhaps Abigail was right. How could one tell? She could not chance that her baby be scarred by stray recollections.

Why had she come here?

How was it that she had allowed habit to lead her along the shell path, past the clump of rhododendrons and the marble fawn?

She forced herself to her feet, briskly disposed her crumpled gown around her, and over it the light veil that drifted from her shoulders, and went quickly over the grass to the path.

It was for the child, she told herself, that she fled from that place. For the child only. She had nothing to fear there.

But she was relieved to see Abigail trotting down the terrace steps.

She was relieved to hear Abigail call, "Miss Miranda, you've been out there long enough. I tell you it's not good."

Miranda answered, "I'm just coming in. It *is* too hot. You're right as usual, Aunt Abigail."

Abigail peered into her face, then carefully looked her up and down. She pursed her lips. "Do you feel anything, Miss Miranda?"

Miranda laughed. "What do you expect me to feel besides heavy and too warm?"

"You get off your feet and you won't feel so heavy. I'll bring you a nice cold lunch. Milk, and chicken salad."

The suggestion was not particularly welcome, but Miranda knew better what she herself said. Abigail would stand over her until she managed to choke down everything put before her.

As they went slowly up the steps, side by side, Abigail looked her up and down once more. "Miss Miranda, are you sure you don't feel anything?"

In truth, Miranda's gown, loose as it was, seemed to constrict her. She found it an effort even to breathe. Her body felt strange, full of sudden movements and pulses and twitches. These were, she supposed, to be expected, and hardly worth describing.

"I feel nothing unusual," she told Abigail.

"Maybe you don't." But Abigail was dubious. She had her own system, and her own knowledge. She said, "I believe your time has just about come, Miss Miranda."

"Then you and Doctor Porter disagree. He claims I have some three weeks still to go."

"Doctor Porter!" Abigail shrugged. "Well, I suppose he's a good man. But he *is* a man. What does he know about having a baby?"

Miranda laughed softly. "Aunt Abigail, please. I do hope he knows a great deal about it. I shall be relying on him for his assistance."

"He'll talk," Abigail retorted, "and you'll do all the work. But don't worry. I'm going to be right there with you."

It was cool in the house, and quiet, too. The air hung heavy with the scent of the roses that Timoshen had put in every room.

"Yes," Abigail said briskly. "I'm definitely going to get ready. You look ripe to me, Miss Miranda."

"Aunt Abigail!"

"Well, you do. Ripe to bursting. Ready. I've seen the signs before. I ought to know them. Now you go upstairs and leave everything to Lena and me."

Miranda slowly mounted the steps. It was even cooler in the upper hallway, but a strange languor was upon her.

As she passed by Reed's study, she saw with some surprise that he was there, standing at the window, and looking out.

He had approved the changes she had wrought in the room, but she had noted more than once that he spent very little time in the place.

Now the light before him, bronze and glaring, made of his body a tall lean silhouette, broad straight shoulders, dark tilted head.

She suddenly wished that she knew what he was thinking, what he saw when he looked out onto the sloping lawns of the estate.

Did he picture his son romping amid the carefully pruned yews?

Or were his thoughts elsewhere?

Though she neither moved nor spoke, he turned, and his solemn face warmed with a smile.

"I wonder if it's wise for you to go out in this heat, Miranda."

"You and Aunt Abigail," she retorted. "Still, I must admit I begin to wonder, too."

She sank into the big golden chair near his desk.

"Are you all right?" he asked.

"Of course. Why not?"

"You look . . . well, I don't know. A bit tired perhaps."

She laughed softly. "I think I'm simply tired of myself, and it does feel good to sit down. But Aunt Abigail is determined to prepare for the event. She sees signs, she says, that I am ripe for bursting. I confess, when I look down, I consider that she may be right."

"But Doctor Porter was quite definite, Miranda."

"Doctor Porter, according to Abigail knows nothing and less than nothing."

"I hope that's not so, and if he's so certain . . ."

There was an anxious expression on Reed's face now, and Miranda suddenly guessed that he must be thinking of Caroline. Caroline, who long before had had several pregnancies but no surviving child to show for them.

A shiver touched Miranda in spite of the heat. But then, suddenly, all was well again, and fleeting memory gone.

She felt a hard thrust at her side, a reassuring kick of active and hungry life.

She laughed, and her face took on a special glow. She found Reed's hand and drew it to the full curve of her body. "Your son, Reed. He has just told me, and you, too, that you mustn't worry. All will be well. Here, Reed, feel your son's movement."

He felt the warmth of her slender hand, and of her rich flesh, and then, beneath that, there was the kick at his fingers, the flutter of a strong pulse. It was awe-inspiring, even frightening, almost more than he could bear. He had a fleeting impulse to snatch his hand away, lest when life touched it it might damage itself. He found, as the movement subsided, that he was holding his breath. He expelled it in a long sigh.

"It's real, Miranda."

"It is," she said. "Or it soon will be." Her lips curved in a smile. "And then perhaps I shall be myself again."

A wave of tenderness rose in him. He took into his arms and kissed her gently.

A hot wet wind billowed the drapes and sent the ruffled blue canopy rippling like small waves.

Miranda watched them and counted softly to herself.

She had come awake suddenly, her legs cramped and an ache in her back. She lay very still, waiting for the discomfort to subside. It was not the first time she had had such experience, and she supposed it would not be the last. But the ache had become a deep stabbing pain. It was that that alerted her. She counted seconds slowly, waiting to see if there would be another such deep stabbing pain, and how long before it began.

She had almost decided that there would be no more. She had almost composed herself again for sleep.

Then suddenly the pain gripped her, hard and deep. She caught her breath and smiled into the dark, and began counting once more.

Reed stirred restlessly beside her, turned his face on the pillow, and then was still.

There was a tightness in her, an awareness of change. Some deep alteration was taking place within her. But slowly the pain faded away.

She sighed in disappointment. She had been almost certain . . . Of course, it would be soon. If not that night, then soon. But she had been looking forward for nearly nine months to holding her baby in her arms. She was feeling impatient now.

The pain lanced through her. It was strong and compelling. It brought from her an involuntary gasp.

Reed stirred, opened his eyes. "Miranda?"

She waited until she could speak, and then, when she had breath, she said, "Reed, I'm sorry to disturb you, but I think that our Abigail is right. I think you had better get up, and help me to the room down the hall, and then send Benjy for Doctor Porter."

She opened her eyes and squinted through odd mists into bright sunshine.

Abigail was instantly beside her. A familiar scarred hand dabbed at her cheeks and forehead with a cool cloth. "You're doing just fine, Miss Miranda. You're just fine."

She looked at the peak formed by her raised knees covered by the white sheet. She asked, "Aunt Abigail, will it be soon, do you think? Will it last much more?"

"Not much more, believe me," Abigail smoothed damp hair from her forehead.

"And Doctor Porter?"

"He's downstairs, having himself a cup of strong black coffee. Instead of a catnap. That's how soon he thinks it's going to be. Just don't you worry, Miss Miranda. Everything is going all right."

"All right," Miranda mumbled, squinting through the mists into sunlight again. It seemed so long since she had first awakened in the dark, with the drapes billowing at the window and the canopy rippling overhead.

"You just try," Abigail said. "When you feel it, then you push and push as hard as you can, and if you want to, then you yell. Don't be afraid. I'm right here with you. You just yell."

The soothing voice crooned on.

Miranda no longer heard it. Pain caught her and flung her high on a cresting wave. Her belly heaved, and her hips struggled, and her legs writhed.

She panted and cried out.

Abigail jerked her head at Lena, saying silently, "Doctor," and seized Miranda's hands.

"Just so, baby. Hold hard, and push and you're going to have a beautiful son."

She sank into dimness, drifted there for a little while.

She heard Doctor Porter's voice, and Abigail's. But hardly understood their words.

She was intent on completing the task before her. All her strength and will were concentrated on the one goal.

The life within her was struggling to make its way into the bright world. She must give it every aid. She must start now to send it on its way.

She imagined a long golden road in her mind, and a small boy walking there. The boy was suddenly tall and straight, with dark hair and a slow smile. Oh, Reed . . .

The pulsations within grew stronger and spread. There was pain, ever increasing. She panted with it, gasped with it.

Doctor Porter leaned over her and smiled. "You're fine, my dear."

Abigail's dark hands massaged the moving mound of her belly. "A deep breath," she whispered. "I know how it hurts, but just breathe deep, so deep. Now, baby, now try . . ."

She obeyed and found more strength still, and some soft flexible thing gave way within her. She felt a sudden thrust and heard Doctor Porter murmur, and gave herself to it, and then heard him say, "Oh, yes, here we go."

She screamed once, harshly, and heard the raw and terrible sound with surprise. She had not imagined that she could make such a noise. The thought was fleeting. She sank into dimness again. The room was misted in gray.

Doctor Porter and Abigail were no more than distant shadows.

She braced herself, expecting that there would be more. She would be caught, shaken, very soon.

Then she heard a sharp slap, and a sudden shrill cry.

She raised her head from the pillow.

Doctor Porter said, "Look at your beautiful son, Miranda."

When she opened her eyes, Reed sat beside her. He took both of her hands in his, held them tightly. He had heard her scream, the sounds of her struggle. He asked, "Miranda, are you all right?"

"The baby? Have you seen our Reedie?"

His hand cupped her cheek gently. "He's a real Haversham. But I believe he has your eyes, though Doctor Porter insists it's too soon to tell."

"He must be like you, Reed," she said. "I want him to be like you in every way."

Reed did not reply to that. He had his own reservations, but he could not voice them aloud.

"The baby?" she asked. "Where is he now?"

"Abigail is fussing over him. She'll bring him to you soon."

Miranda slept, Reed watching over her.

She awakened when Abigail put the tiny, blanket-wrapped figure into her arms. She insisted on stripping away blanket, gown, and even diaper. She touched the tiny rosebud lips, examined the ears, admired a fuzz of black lashes. She counted fingers and toes, and studied the small lump of belly button. Only then could she rest content. Reedie Haversham was perfect.

The end of that week, Miranda lay on the blue chaise, tiny Reedie soundly sleeping in the curve of her arm, and received her friends.

Erna and Dorothea peered at the baby and pronounced it the most beautiful one in Georgetown.

Stacy agreed, but then looked impatiently at the door. "Now where is Carleton? Where is Tad? Where is Reed?

There'll come a time, and it won't be too long, I assure you, when this ridiculous affair of leaving the men with their cigars and drinks will be abolished. It is uncivilized. It is primitive."

"But that's how it's done," Erna protested worriedly. "Why, no one would dare . . ."

Stacy grinned. She withdrew from her pearl-banded reticule a small, very black cigar. She thrust it into her mouth, relishing Erna's startled stare. "I shall celebrate young Reedie's birth, too. And now, if any of you happen to have a match?"

"A match?" Dorothea repeated helplessly. "But why on earth . . . I've never carried . . . Really, Stacy, you do go too far."

Stacy shrugged. "You see? That's what comes of leaving the gentlemen alone. My dear Carleton always has a match somewhere about him. And I shall have one, if I must go and obtain one myself."

She was having more fun than she had imagined she would when she planned this. It would be even more fun when the gentlemen joined these boring females to offer their felicitations to Miranda and found Stacy herself puffing away on her cigar. The small delay she had created came to an end when she considered the time right. She found at the very bottom of her reticule, wrapped in an elegant lace handkerchief, two heavy matches.

When the men came as a group into the room, they found the ladies, instead of chattering among themselves, standing silently in a circle around Stacy and watching her carefully while she nonchalantly demonstrated for them the proper handling of a small black cigar.

Two months later, as Miranda nursed the infant at her breast, Reed brought her a necklace of small, perfectly matched diamonds.

He did not tell her that the night before he had returned again to Johnny Obermeyer's gambling palace.

EIGHT

Nan Cunningham, wrapped in black silk with three gold chains at her neck and long dangling gold bells at her ears, was firmly ensconced, hips crowding the curves, in a deep soft red velvet chair. She leaned happily against the white lace antimacassars which Mary Bennett had crocheted for her in some idle moments.

With pleasure a warm wave in her ample flesh, Nan contemplated the thick red drapes at the windows and the golden tassels that hung from the brass knobs of their rods. The pleasure increased when she moved her small black eyes to the white mantel on which was disposed a treasury of small knicknacks, carefully chosen and not easily come by. A two-inch woman, nude and kneeling. A four-inch man, equally unclothed but standing tall. A long lithe lion of suggestive proportions in certain areas. A set of monkeys—see, hear, speak no evil monkeys, in fact. Yes, she sighed. They were right. It was all of it right and as it should be.

Outside, close by the door of what had once been the Kayhome Arms, there was a small neat brass sign. It had been suggested by Jake, but the name engraved on it, *Bon Chance,* had been chosen by Nan, in a flight of fancy not unlike Susanah Kay's so many years before.

Bon Chance. It had a sweet ring to it.

Nan smiled to herself and nodded, and her heavy chins rippled. She didn't quite remember how she had come by the name, but it suited her. Bon Chance. And that was what it had been, too, and what it would continue to be. The house was by far the finest on the lane, both within and without. There was, beside this comfortable reception room on the first floor, a pleasant little drinking room, and a large gaming room, where Jake had set baize-covered tables and wheels, and all the accouterments necessary to thrill the daring and take their money away from them at the same time. On the second floor there were rooms, pleasant little retreats, where fat cupids laughed down from the walls and dainty shepherdesses forwent attentions to their flocks for other pleasures. There were huge mirrors in some ceilings, and others on some walls. Nan was especially pleased with what she had done with the back room that had been Jake's own. It had now become a lush nest. On the third floor there were further rooms, and on the fourth, once the dismal attic where mice scampered, there was a sumptuous apartment. She had designed it with the thought that she and Jake would share it when they gave up their cold garret. He, however, had taken up lodgings at the Union Hotel, though he would, on certain occasions, make his way up the narrow flight under the pink-globed gaslight to her own little place.

But now he jerked open the door of the reception room, and demanded, "Well, are you ready? You want to see her or not?"

"What's your opinion?" Nan asked. "Tell me that much first."

"She'll do. If you take her in hand," Jake said.

"Then send her in."

Jake looked over his shoulder and stepped back from the door to propel a slim young girl before him. He closed the door, leaning against it with his arms folded.

Nan looked her up and down expressionlessly. She was perhaps sixteen. Her body seemed trim beneath the not very full but very well-worn dress that covered her. Her eyes were a sharp hazel, mixed green and brown, a combination that Nan found intriguing, and they were bright with anger at the moment. Her hair was red, wavy, and allowed to hang free to her shoulders. It looked well on her that way, but wanton, which was what she intended.

She shifted her weight from one foot to the other and moved her mouth, but said nothing.

Nan beamed at her. "Good morning, my dear. And how are you today?"

"Hungry," the girl retorted. "He said you'd give me

breakfast if I came along with him. But I've not seen a bit of it. And I had no supper last night, nor dinner at noon. And I—"

Nan raised a pudgy hand. "Jake, dear friend, wouldn't you like to ask our Dessie to make up a tray at once? Surely she can provide an egg or two, perhaps a slice of meat with it." She saw, as she spoke, that the young girl moved her lips again, and then swallowed. "And Dessie's bread, Jake. It should be from the oven by now."

He grunted, but there was a grin in his eyes as he left the two women alone. Nan knew what she was about. He'd always thought so. He thought so now.

"Men are thoughtless, dear," Nan said. "How do you expect them to understand? Now, do sit down and tell me about yourself." She added, as the girl lowered herself into a nearby chair, "And you might begin with your name."

"I'm Prunella Dalton," the girl said sullenly. "And you needn't laugh at me. Nor pretend either. I know what that man is, and I know what you are, too."

Nan smoothed her hair off her broad brow. It was no longer gray but black, a smooth and perfect black with no light in it. She had devised the formula herself.

"I do know," Prunella said once again.

"Indeed," Nan murmured sadly. Then, "We can always change your name, my dear. Prunella. No. I think not." Her small avid eyes gleamed. "Joy." Then. "Yes, I think so. How do you like that?"

"I don't care what you call me, as long as we get it settled. I'm dead broke, see. And I'm hungry." Her bright hazel look went to the door. "And if he don't come back with the tray pretty soon, then you're going to have a girl flat out on your fancy rug."

"It's been known to happen before." Nan smiled. "But be patient. My Dessie is a finicky cook. She'll want to do it up right and it'll be worth the wait." Then, "Meanwhile you might tell me where you're from and where you're bound, and how it comes about that you're out of funds."

"I'm from Middleburg to the south, and I'm on my way to New York. And I'm flat broke because I've run away from home. My father is a terror and my stepmother worse, and I've had my pocket picked of what I've saved for three months. It happened in the train depot this morning. Can you imagine the nerve of it? To pick on somebody like me, so down and out? Can you imagine such a scoundrel?"

Nan could well imagine it. She wondered if Jake had gotten much when he attended to that small chore, having decided that this particular girl would do. She concluded with regret that she would not ask him about that.

"So evil," she murmured placatingly. And then, "And your age, my dear Joy?"

"I'm seventeen," the girl responded after a blank stare. "Joy, hunh? Are you serious?"

"I am indeed."

"Okay. You can call me Joy, if it makes you feel any better." She drew a deep breath. "As for the rest, well, you don't have to draw any pictures for me. I understand."

"And how is that? Perhaps you can explain?"

"I was in Baltimore City for a while," Joy told her harshly. "You know what I mean?"

Nan nodded. This much, at least, she believed of the girl's glib tale of herself. She had, no doubt, been in Baltimore City. The rest did not really matter to Bon Chance.

What Prunella Dalton, newly named Joy, did not say was that she was fifteen years old, and two years off her parents' farm in southern Maryland. She'd had a lasting interest in men since she turned eleven, and arrived with much enthusiasm at a Baltimore City house at the age of thirteen. She had left there with her savings only because the jealousy of the other girls had become open, active, and dangerous.

Jake pushed the door open, brought in the tray, and set it on a small round table.

Joy quickly fell to.

Nan smiled approvingly. She *did* like to see a woman eat well. "It's all settled between us," she told Jake. "Joy will settle in today, and after we have a small private discussion upstairs, she'll be ready to begin."

Jake gave Joy a slanted smile, but said to Nan, "You have yours first. Then, after *we* have our small private discussion, she'll be ready to begin."

Nan nodded brightly, but she thought of Jake's big gnarled hands settling on Joy's pert breasts and his hips thrusting against hers, and she folded her thick thighs together under her black gown, wondering if that place down there ever gave up and admitted defeat and went to sleep forever.

NINE

Impeachment!
First it was a whisper.
A question.
Then it became a shout.
A demand.
A full three years after the signing of the surrender terms in Appomattox Courhouse, a new war began on the floors of Congress. In this one, the weapons were words. At issue was whether President Johnson, elected by the people, held office only at the pleasure of the Senate. The debate was on narrower grounds. The question arose when the Northern victors had to determine what was to be done with, for, and to the Southern defeated. Its climax came in May of 1868, when Washington was abloom with early roses, and Georgetown was scented with late lilacs.

A quickened tempo breathed along the broad avenues and the narrow lanes, spreading out from Capitol Hill in all directions. It was a pulse that touched and teased. A silent music to accompany the fearful drama that had been unfolding and was, that day, approaching its denouement.

That morning Stacy said, "Oh, Miranda, do hurry. We mustn't be late. They've been hawking tickets all over for days. The visitors' gallery may possibly be all filled up, just as it has been these past months. No one wants to miss the show. And surely this is the big day."

Miranda calmly tied on the small pale blue pancake edged with a frill of silk that was her hat. She carefully adjusted the smoky blue veil. "We'll be in good time, Stacy. Don't fret yourself. And I want to stop in the nursery before I go."

She had regained her figure within weeks of Reedie's birth. Now her waist was as tiny as ever, her skin glowing, her eyes brilliant.

Stacy sighed, but made no other protest. That, she knew, would be useless. Miranda could not be called a doting mother precisely, if for no other reason than that Abigail would not permit it, but she would not, no matter the urgency, leave the house without having a last look at her son.

Now the two women went down the hallway together. The nursery was aglow with the sun.

Lena, folding diapers, looked up and smiled. "He's trying to talk. You wait and see. It won't be long now. He's trying to say something."

"Ten months old and talking?" Stacy protested. "Lena, your imagination is astounding."

There was a rattle and a bang from the crib. Then a small dark head appeared, and plump dimpled fingers clutched the oak bars. Gray eyes beamed excitement across the room.

Miranda laughed and bent over to kiss the pink round cheek. "Reedie, if you're trying to talk, then say something now. Aunt Stacy is such a disbeliever."

"Not at all," Stacy protested, impatiently twitching her gown.

Miranda picked the baby up and hugged him. "You're a good boy, and beautiful," she murmured. Then she held the baby out to Stacy. "Take him for a moment."

Stacy stepped back quickly. "Miranda! Since you're his mother you may not mind appearing in the visitors' gallery of the Senate of the Congress of the United States with a blob on your shoulder, or a stain on your ribs. But

I, for one, as the wife of Senator Van Eward, who'll most probably speak today, certainly do not intend . . ."

Her haughty voice faded as Miranda thrust Reedie into her arms, and he grinned at her, beaming a warm loving light from his eyes. "All right," she told him at last. "You're a charmer. But you're too young for all that. Wait a year or two and then we'll be fine friends."

He burbled wordless approval and was still smiling when Stacy returned him to his crib, and then set about straightening her undisturbed hat and unstained gown.

As she and Miranda left the nursery, she asked, "And Reed?"

"He's gone ahead," Miranda said. "He had an errand in town, and said he would stop before going to Capitol Hill."

But Reed, even then, was in the Capitol building.

He went into the smoke-filled Senate cloakroom in search of Carleton, hoping to learn Carleton's most recent judgment of what the day's proceedings would bring.

Carleton's pudgy face was more flushed than ever when he said tiredly, "Reed, I don't know. But I think . . ."

What Carleton thought, Reed did not learn. For the Senator was drawn away to huddle with a group of his anxious colleagues.

Reed was making his way to the door when Josiah Hurley stopped him, saying, "Reed, I'm glad to see you. It's been a long time. We've many things to discuss now that these trying events are nearly behind us."

"Things to discuss?" Reed asked.

"John and I did a good deal of business together," Josiah said. "You knew that, of course."

Reed nodded.

"There were many services I could perform for him." Josiah smiled. "I'd be glad to do the same for you, Reed. If, for instance, there's information you require, I'm prepared to deliver it."

"I don't know what you mean, Josiah."

"My contacts are extensive, Reed. And expensive as well. But John considered them worth the while."

"How so?" Reed asked.

"My network reaches into every concern and every bureau . . ."

"Aside from your other interests, you spied for John? Is that what you mean?"

"That's hardly the word."

A cold disgust settled in Reed's chest. This was John's business. What had been before a disinterest to be overcome now became revulsion. Color rose in his face, then receded, leaving him white. He said, "It's my word, Josiah."

"Your brother—"

"My brother is dead," Reed retorted, coldly furious, and walked away.

Timoshen halted at the foot of the broad steps to the Capitol in a long line of other carriages.

They waited as each one rolled away, until he stopped and handed them down. Then Miranda and Stacy mounted the stairs and went through the doors, and down the long dim hall to the gallery.

It was already crowded, but they easily found seats.

There was some socializing, bobbing of heads, and nodding and smiling. Representatives of all the foreign legations stood about in their elaborate uniforms, or bowed elegantly over proffered hands. The highest-ranking members of all the armed services were there, each in full-dress uniform. It might have been, for this little time, a gathering in search of pleasure.

But below, under the gaslights, an expectant bustle seemed to echo from the walls. Young pages, secretaries, managers, and assistants of all description ambled to and fro, creating an underlying hum of sound that was peculiarly ominous.

Stacy leaned back and drew out a silken fan, relaxing now that she knew she would miss nothing. She scanned the galleries briefly, then said, "I've been so happy, Miranda." She dropped her voice to go on. "I know what people think. And what they sometimes say behind my back. When they dare, that is. But they don't really understand. Carleton loves me. He truly loves me. And I love him for that. It doesn't matter that he's an old man, and not very handsome. It doesn't even matter that he can give me so much, though that's important, too, and it helps me love him. The main thing is that he loves me and I love him."

"Of course. I know you do," Miranda said gently, somewhat taken aback by Stacy's unaccustomed seriousness. And then, as the bustle below seemed to increase, she leaned forward. "Are they about to begin?"

At that moment, a breathless hush fell over the chamber. The clerk of the Senate took his place. He looked over his glasses at the door, where Senator James W. Grimes of Iowa, having suffered a stroke only two days before, was being helped to the floor by four young men. When that small sad commotion faded, the clerk looked at Ben Wade, President pro tem of the Senate.

He rose, banged his gavel, and said in solemn tones, "The Senate is now in session."

Seated before him were the men who held in their hands a fateful decision. They were big and small, dressed in the neat fashion of the East, or in the frontier clothes of the West. They were bearded and clean-shaven. They wore hair flowing on their collars, or clipped straight at their ears, or they had no hair at all. But each knew his importance in that moment.

And each knew, too, that Ben Wade was so confident that the President would be found guilty of all charges, and that he, as next in line of succession, would soon himself be named to that august office, that he had already chosen his cabinet, which included Ben Butler, general of the Union Army as Secretary of State.

But nothing of that showed on his face as he went on to say that the Senate was sitting that day as a court, and its business was to consider Article XI of the impeachment charges against Andrew Johnson, and asked the secretary of the Senate to read that article.

The secretary did as requested, his sonorous words falling one by one like heavy stones into the lake of stillness that was the Senate floor.

Then, Chief Justice Chase, presiding, asked, "Is the respondent, Andrew Johnson, President of the United States, guilty or not guilty of high misdemeanor as charged in this article?"

Stacy gave a small gasp.

Miranda's eyes burned. She held her breath, remembering that the Chief Justice himself had administered the Presidential oath to Andrew Johnson in Kirkwood House just three years before.

The clerk began the roll call. There was, then, an unbearable hush, the flaring gaslights seemed to leap higher as his voice droned on and on, and the Senators responded one by one.

"Guilty."

"Guilty."

"Guilty."

Miranda had counted off twenty-four in a silent tally. Then Senator Edmund G. Ross of Kansas rose to say, in what was nearly a whisper, "Not guilty."

There were others to follow. Some spoken loudly, defiantly. Some spoken softly, nervously. "Not guilty. Not guilty."

Stacy gasped again and leaned forward, a small frown between her brows, when Carleton leaned on his desk to say, "Not guilty," and then seemed to fall back into his chair.

The count went on. At the end of it, the clerk gave the totals. They were 35 to 19, and President Johnson was vindicated by the one vote which would have met the two-thirds majority requirement.

The session was immediately adjourned for the next ten days because of the Republican National Convention to be held in Chicago, though behind the scenes, the impeachment managers made plans to continue.

But to all intents and purposes the historic proceedings were concluded as Miranda and Stacy made their way down the steps, through the bedlam of relief and regret.

They had begun to move toward the outer doors when Miranda saw Reed's dark head towering over the others and realized that he was fighting his way to them.

"Will you come with me?" he asked Stacy gently, as

soon as he managed to reach them. "And you, too, Miranda."

Stacy's dark eyes widened. "What is it?"

"Carleton, my dear. He's in the Senate cloakroom. I fear he's not well. We must see what we can do."

Stacy's oval face turned white. It shrank so that there were hollows in her cheeks. She suddenly became a fury, battling her way with elbow and shoulder through the crowds around her.

Miranda, trying to keep up, left a trail of murmured apologies in her wake.

Carleton lay on a divan, his face waxen. His collar was open, his cravat undone, and his waistcoat, too. His pudgy hands, withering now, lay folded on his breast.

A circle of solemn men surrounded him.

Stacy pressed her way through, fell on her knees, sobbing, "Oh, Carleton, no, no!"

He didn't answer her. She screamed and buried her face in her hands when she realized that he never would.

TEN

Stacy was disconsolate after Carleton's sudden death. She remained in seclusion in her Massachusetts Avenue mansion, alone but for two servants, and was seen, swathed in widow's weeds and tearful, by only a few intimates until Reed and Miranda took her back to Haversham Square with them. For three months she moved silently through the big house, spending hours alone in the lush heat of the conservatory, or sitting near the lily pond, always impeccably gowned in black, with her eyes red and swollen and her dull gaze haunted.

The first sign of recovery that Miranda observed was at the time that Ian Haversham arrived for a visit.

It was then the end of August.

Before that day, however, Reedie's first birthday had been marked by a gala celebration, in which he had received a red-and-green rocking horse, an Indian drum, and a silver spoon, the handle of which was set with an emerald. By then his gray eyes had turned silver, his dark hair curly. He knew many words and spoke them nicely, and since he experienced only love, he was loving to all. On that day, too, Reed gave Miranda a bracelet of gold set with fine rubies. He did not tell her that he had paid another exhilarating visit to Johnny Obermeyer's.

At midmonth there was another celebration.

It was the two years' anniversary of Miranda's marriage to Reed. For that he presented her with a pin of pearls and rubies, the whole of it larger than a robin's egg. Of equal pleasure to Miranda was the moment when, late that night and alone, he said, "You're everything to me that I hoped you'd be."

When Ian came, the sloping green lawns that surrounded the house were as smooth as velvet, the plantings full and sculptured, the roses grouped in masses of brilliance where hummingbirds hovered. Mockingbirds nested in the oaks at the driveway, and mourning doves sent their sad cries through the summer stillness.

Into the oasis of contentment and peace that was just slightly tinged with Stacy's sadness, Ian brought with him a lusty exhilaration. His bronze hair was always slightly rumpled, his blue eyes hot and piercing. His perfectly cut clothing seemed strained by his shoulders, by his stride itself. He was part of a mission to discuss American claims against the British for indemnities against losses incurred when English-built Confederate ships sank Northern merchant marine carriers, among them the *Alabama,* during the war.

His impact on Stacy was immediate. He smiled at her and bowed when they were introduced, saying, "I'm sorry for your trouble, Mrs. Van Eward."

She said, in a suddenly happy tone, "Oh, I'm very glad to meet you at last. You're just as Miranda described." Her eyes, beginning to burn with the familiar embers, swept him up and down. "But I fear that she hardly did you proper justice, Mr. Haversham."

Within days she had discarded her black veilings, and within the week she had Mrs. Bannion busy in the sewing room with the creation of a whole new wardrobe for her.

It was as well that she had done so, for very soon after Ian's arrival, Carleton's young nephew, Edward Farnsworth, returned to Washington from a tour of duty in the West. Stacy had inherited everything, which was much. But blond, moustached Edward did not seem to mind. And besides, Stacy was very generous. She settled a satisfactory yearly sum on him, as she had on Mary Van Eward, and soon Edward, with a number of his friends, was available to take her on long rides through the Oak Hill Cemetery, where they would stop to leave fresh flowers on Carleton's grave, or for quiet picnics along the Potomac River.

Meanwhile, Ian, who spent only a few hours each day on his mission, rode with Reed in the tree-shaded acres behind the house.

One day he spoke of Haversham affairs and asked about the railroad. When he saw the withdrawal in Reed's face, he sought to probe the reason for it. "You don't think of taking over John's affairs. Is there some reason why?"

Reed answered in a low hard voice. "Taking over John's affairs and dealing with his associates is a corruption. It's like a boil, Ian. A rot beneath the skin, soiled and spoiled and festering. I want none of it."

"Then you needn't have it," Ian cried with lusty zest. "You must lance it, if you prefer it that way. Lance the boil, man, and let it spill over into the good sunlight of the day."

In the rhythmic hoofbeats Reed heard John's voice in impatient mockery. *"You are a romantic, my brother. You must grow up and see we Havershams for what we are."*

He sat back in the saddle and drew up his knees, assaulted by a sudden cramp, a blow low in the belly that left him breathless.

In Ian's words, in the echo of John's, he heard Miranda herself speaking. What he saw as a stinking cesspool in which he could not bring himself to force his hand, she saw as a sweet lake on which she would launch herself as regal as any swan. Even with all her concentration on Reedie, and of late on Stacy, Reed felt that Miranda counted the hours he passed within his study. His only surcease from the knowledge of her yearning and hope was at Johnny Obermeyer's, and when he took it, he brought her a bauble to assuage the guilt of his deception.

As they continued on, his gray eyes were fixed on a tall tree. Around it was entwined the sturdy sumac vine. Its beautiful green leaves were shiny and innocent-appearing. But those same leaves were covered by a film of poison. He thought then that he was that tree, and if he but weakened once, the poisonous sumac of John's world would overwhelm him.

Aloud, he told Ian, "I must send Timoshen out to destroy that vine. Reedie might come this way some day."

With Miranda, Ian prowled the streets and alleys of Georgetown, fascinated by its combination of houses that reminded him of some sections in London yet were set in fields where chickens pecked, or were backed by cow pastures.

Miranda had suggested on their first expedition that Timoshen drive them.

Ian had thrown back his head and laughed, "Ah, well, if you think it necessary, we'll do that. But as for me, I'd rather go afoot so I can really see."

She agreed and gathered parasol and gloves, and set out to show him the sights. He was saddened by the canal, saying, "The time for such things is done. It'll be railroad from now on. Faster, cheaper, you know. And it can go where there's no water to take it. Some day this will make a pretty playing ground for children, but nothing more than that."

That same day, as they were walking on the Georgetown Bridge Road, just past the Union Hotel, she saw a tall drunken man bang a small boy on the top of his head. She thought instantly of Reedie and winced, not knowing quite what to do but feeling her fingers tighten on the parasol handle.

Ian did know what to do. With an oath he lunged across

the cobblestones, shouting, "Here you! This is how that feels!" He delivered a like blow to the adult, while the child stood wide-eyed and shivering.

The drunken man swore at Ian and wandered off.

Ian bent his bronze head to the boy and put a coin in the child's hand. The child bit it, and then ran down the block, crying, "Papa, wait for me! Look what I've got, Papa!"

Ian returned to her, his face alight with laughter. "It appears that I may have taught them a new game, Miranda."

But she was still thinking of Reedie, and pleased that Ian had done precisely what she had wanted to do herself. She told him so.

He shrugged, "I'll not see a child brutalized. Suppose it were my Rory." And then, "Do you know? I worry about him. He remains frail. I thought these two years at school would help him. But they haven't."

"Two years isn't very long, Ian. I'm sure all will be well with him."

"I'd be more confident if Grace didn't pamper him, Miranda." Ian's blue eyes were solemn now. "It can't be good for him. Yet she will not understand."

"He's her only chick, Ian."

Ian said gently, "And what of you, Miranda? You've only the one chick yourself."

"I hope for more and soon," she said with a smile. "And Reed does, too, of course."

"Ah, well," Ian answered, "I ought to have guessed that. It's in the blood, you know. We Havershams are dynasty-minded. In the old days we would have dreamed of being kings." He chuckled. "Or at least chieftains. Now we do what we can."

His words filled Miranda with a deep excitement. They seemed an echo of her own thoughts, feelings. What he said was what she had believed for as long as she could remember.

By the time Ian left after a three-week stay, the bonds of blood, and friendship as well, had been strongly forged. Miranda and Reed were certain that they would see him soon again, and they had his promise that he would bring Grace with him on his next trip.

With his going, Stacy became even more restless. Early in December, she sat in the morning room with Miranda, watching while Reedie proved that a fifteen-month-old boy can fall as well as rise. He did both within a single moment, and then sat back to beam. "Mama, I walk," he said, and rose and took four steps, and fell laughing to the floor.

When Lena came and carried him off to the cooking quarters for an early lunch, Stacy said, "I'll move home tomorrow, Miranda. You've been good to me, you and Reed. I'll not forget it, believe me." A repressed giggle choked her. "I fear that I've been a trial to you. But I'm over it now. And see it all quite clearly. Why, Carleton would scold me, if he could, for such behavior. It's the last thing he would expect from me. He'd want me to be gay, to be happy." She drew a deep sigh. "We must go on, Miranda. Whatever happens. That's the fate of each of us. To go on."

"Of course you're right. But we love having you with us," Miranda told her. "Why not stay a little longer? There's no need for you to return to that great empty house, you know."

"Oh, it won't be empty long, I assure you." Stacy smiled. She leaned back in her brocade chair at ease within herself. Her mourning was done. "I suppose that you and Reed will take Reedie to the children's party President Johnson is giving to celebrate his sixtieth birthday."

"We plan to. We want him to see the President. He'll only be in Washington a few months longer."

Two days later, Stacy's great trunks were brought down and loaded into a cart by Jefferson and Timoshen.

Edward Farnsworth drove her away through the lightly falling snow.

The day of the President's birthday party dawned bright. Reedie's cheeks were pink, his eyes silver, as he held both his parents' hands, and trotted between them up the steps of the White House and into the gaily decorated party room.

President Johnson bent down to greet the children, bowed and spoke to the adults, and led the way to the festivities. He plainly enjoyed the games and preferred to immerse himself in these rather than in conversation with the grownups present.

Miranda saw that there was more gray in his hair now, and deeper lines in his handsome face, and knew what strains he must have suffered while he waited for the Senate to decide his fate. And then, having been vindicated, what strains there must have been during the campaign.

Reedie had a wonderful time, managing to get into three fights and to win all three, but on his return home his cheeks were scarlet, and his eyes glittered like bits of glass.

Miranda thought him overtired and put him to bed.

The next day he was himself again but listless, and toward afternoon, she found him curled up in a corner of Reed's study, alone and sound asleep.

She picked him up, cradling his small body against her, and carried him to the nursery without awakening him. But he seemed cool enough, and she supposed he had simply interrupted his nap, slipped out to look for Reed, and then dozed off. She covered him carefully, pressed a kiss to his cheek, and left him.

ELEVEN

Corcoran Riley was a small debonair man with an open, engaging smile and candid brown eyes. He was dressed neatly in a brown suit, an expensive gold chain across his waistcoat, and his boots were brightly polished.

"It is very good of you to see me, sir," he said genially. "I know what a busy man you must be."

"Not at all," Tad Layton responded.

"My card." It was offered with a flourish.

Tad accepted the expensively engraved card, and read it: *J and R Land Investment Company*. He commented, "I've not heard of this before."

Corcoran Riley chuckled. "Oh, but you shall, sir. Though we are newly formed, we have great plans. Which is why I'm here."

Tad waited.

"The other reason I'm here, and not in some other bank, has to do with Mr. Samuel Ward." Corcoran paused to allow that name proper weight.

But Tad said, "I know of Mr. Ward, of course. But I don't know the man himself."

"Yet he knows you," Corcoran smiled. "And so I'm here. The J and R Land Investment Company has some interest in property owned by Mr. Reed Haversham. It lies south of Pennsylvania Avenue, and is occupied by squatters. Were the price reasonable, we would be glad to take it off his hands."

"I see," Tad said, wondering why this company should concern itself now with such property.

"You could convey an offer to the owner, no doubt."

"I could, though I've reason to think he has considered a sale."

Corcoran Riley rose, smiling still. "But it's surely worth some discussion?"

"It may be," Tad conceded, accepting the proffered hand and giving it a single brisk shake before releasing it.

"Then I'll be in again," Corcoran assured him.

When he was alone, Tad examined the card again, then dropped it on his desk and leaned back to consider.

He had never heard of the J and R Land Investment Company, a fact of not much consequence, since such businesses were proliferating with miraculous speed in those days. But he had heard of Mr. Samuel Ward.

Puzzled by this interest in that part of Reed's property, Tad considered a few moments longer. Then he put on his greatcoat, took his hat and stick, and set out for Haversham Square.

TWELVE

Miranda had just closed the nursery door when Abigail came up the steps to say, "Mr. Layton's downstairs. He asks can he see you for a few minutes."

"Why of course he can." Miranda paused. Then, "Aunt Abigail, tell Lena I want her to sit with Reedie the rest of the day. I found him a little while ago in the study, sleeping in a corner. I want to be certain he doesn't climb from his crib again."

"That child," Abigail said admiringly. "He's a walker and a wanderer already. That's what he is. He's going to do big things in this life. That's what that means." She paused, frowned. "But I'll skin Lena if she left him before he was asleep. She knows what he does. She knows he'll get himself out, no matter how high you set the bars."

"Just make sure she stays with him," Miranda answered.

Jefferson had taken Tad into the parlor. He rose to greet her. "Miranda, how well you look," he said. "A feast for the eyes."

Accepting his compliment with a smile that warmed him, she waved him to a chair. "Will you have tea? Or perhaps something stronger?"

"Something stronger, if you don't object, my dear."

He smiled back, relieved and pleased with himself. His guess that Reed would not be at home had been correct. He was certain that Reed would not approve one whit of what he was going to talk about. Tad knew that Reed would never be another John Haversham. There was something missing from the younger man. Perhaps a deviousness of mind, which, while it might make him a better man than his brother had been, made him less of a man for certain affairs. Reed would do his accounts, pay his bills off income, and continue on. But the Haversham fortune would not grow. That had become clearly evident in these two years. Miranda, he felt, was of different mettle. Tad knew that if there was information to be gained, she would have it, and soon.

She rang the small brass bell for Jefferson. When he appeared, she asked for a whiskey for Mr. Layton, with plenty of ice since it was yet early, and for a small sherry for herself.

"It's snowing," Tad told her. "Not very heavily though. I doubt there'll be anything left of it by morning."

"I hope not," she said. "I should hate to wallow through snowdrifts to your New Year's Eve affair tomorrow night and then again to Stacy's reception on New Year's Day. You *will* be at Stacy's, won't you?"

"I plan to be, yes," he said absently. Then, with his eyes on the huge Christmas tree that still gleamed in the corner, though its needles had begun to spread in a veil on the carpet, he asked, "Reed's not at home, I gather?"

"Why, no." She paused to allow Jefferson to serve the drinks. When they were once more alone, she went on, "Was it he that you came to visit, Tad? Or was it me?"

He grinned and stroked his blond beard. "I don't like to disturb you with business matters, but I wonder if Reed has run into a man named Samuel Ward, the brother of Julia Ward Howe. Since the election of General Grant in November, his name has cropped up several times. I don't know him."

Miranda shook her head. "I've not met him. I can't answer for Reed, of course. But he has never mentioned the name."

Tad went on, "That Ward is quite . . . well, quite a debonair person, I'm told. With a small white beard, an imperial, and a big domed bald head. They say he wears a huge sapphire on his right hand."

Miranda wondered just what this description must lead to. It was almost as if Tad expected, or hoped, that she would recognize Mr. Samuel Ward if she saw him. She asked, "What about this man, Tad?"

"I think," Tad said with a sigh, "that he'll be a man of some influence in the next few years. And that, of course, concerns us all."

Her interest quickened, but she said, "Naturally."

"We should like very much to know him."

"I quite agree."

"And, in particular, we should know him fairly soon. It is, after all, just three months until the inauguration." Tad looked as if he had just made up his mind to speak freely. He drained his glass and set it aside, and asked, "Would you mind if I smoked?"

"Of course not."

He lit up a cigar and blew out a plume of thick gray smoke. It made itself a perfect round ring and drifted away toward the high ceiling. With his eyes on it, he said, "There's a new land company formed just recently. J and R Land Investments, it's called. Their representative called on me, expressing some interest in property Reed owns. His name is Corcoran Riley. Have you ever heard of him?"

He paused while she shook her head, then he went on. "Mr. Riley referred to Samuel Ward several times, implying that Mr. Ward had sent Riley to me."

Her interest quickened even further. This was the kind of talk she enjoyed. If only Reed would sit with her like this and discuss these affairs. She no longer expected that he would ever do so.

"The property I refer to," Tad was saying, "was once owned by Caroline. She left it to John, and John to Reed, of course. It brings in little or no income, and is held mainly by squatters."

"Then it can't be worth much to anyone, I suppose."

"Not as it stands. Which is why I'm so curious to know why the J and R Land Investments Company should express an interest in it. And that is where Samuel Ward comes in. He might know better than anyone else."

Miranda made up her mind quickly. "What you must do, I think, is to speak to Stacy at once. I'm certain that you can suggest to her that an invitation to Mr. Ward to her reception would not go amiss."

"I'd sooner not say why, you know. So even if she did invite him—"

Miranda smiled. "But Tad, I shall be there, too, with Reed. I shall talk to Mr. Ward myself, you may be sure."

"Good, Miranda. I think that will be of help to Reed. It's important we know what's behind this company, and who."

"Will you have another drink?" she asked.

Tad rose. "I believe not. But thank you. I'll see you to-morrow night."

"Of course," she agreed. "I'm looking forward to New Year's Eve with you."

When she had seen him out, she returned to the morning room and sat thinking of what he had just told her.

She sat before the cheval glass, brushing her hair. The black waves crackled and sparked. As alive, she thought, as her beating heart. She knew that Reed watched her every move, admiration in his eyes.

She gave him a flirtatious look from under the dark fringe of her lashes, saying, "You missed Tad today. He was here with me for a little while."

Reed grinned. "And you entertained him, I suppose?"

"That I did. He had a cigar and I gave him a whiskey. And he entertained me by proceeding to do what you never will."

Reed tensed imperceptibly.

"He spoke of a problem he has, a business affair. Or perhaps it should more properly be called a small and strange curiosity, and no more than that. It has to do with a man named Samuel Ward, in a way. Do you know of him?"

"I don't. And I see no reason for Tad to trouble your pretty head with such things."

She deliberately widened her eyes. "I'm in no way troubled. I'm very interested. And you must know I would be." She hurried on, "His name, Samuel Ward's, that is, was mentioned by a man called Corcoran Riley, who represents a land company that inquired about property you own."

Reed shrugged, said nothing.

She had the sudden feeling that some invisible barrier was between them, an unseen veil behind which he had retreated. But she pressed determinedly on. "Reed, tell me, why hold the land if it offers no income?"

"Why, not? It costs little. If it did, I would see no reason to do so. No matter where it came from." He stretched, then went on. "I think it's too early for me to go to bed, Miranda. I'll work in the study for an hour or two."

"I see," she said softly. "But you mustn't think I intended to drive you from your bedroom."

He turned back, crossing the room swiftly. "Miranda, love, don't speak so. Not even in jest."

"But I think you were retreating from my conversation," she said lightly.

"I'll never retreat from you, and I never have, and I want you to remember it."

But he was glad her questions were over, and he cursed Tad for arousing them. He was already troubled enough. He wanted only the best for Miranda, for Reedie, and he would provide it. But that did not mean he must engage in the plans and promises, the trades and the trusts on which the Haversham fortune had been built. It did not mean he need employ Josiah Hurley's services. He would not add to the foundation already not clean. And he would not see Miranda soiled by it. He would not allow her to be even touched by it.

And now her warm firm body was snuggled against him. She buried her face in his neck, whispering, "All I want is to be everything to you, Reed."

He picked her up and carried her to the bed, but even as their bodies were made one in love, and she felt his strength against her own and his warm breath gasping at her breasts, she was aware that their conversation had gone unfinished.

She awakened suddenly, not knowing what it was that had caught her attention, caught it surely even through the blankets of sleep.

The room was very still, so that the sudden crackle of embers on the hearth seemed overloud and startling.

Reed was beside her, unmoving, his body exuding a

warmth that touched her own flesh. His arm was flung up, covering his face, but she could see his mouth, the lips curled in a smile of surcease.

She felt a deep tenderness well in her and bent to kiss him yet again. At the same time, she heard a soft coughing.

Reedie!

She rose and drew on her peignoir. Within the instant, she was moving down the hall.

Lena was already bending over the crib.

Her eyes flashed up, gleaming whitely in the dark room. "He's coughing something terrible, Miss Miranda. Had I better do a steam kettle? That's what my mother always says."

Miranda took Reedie's small convulsing body into her arms. "Yes, Lena, please. And then get your mother. She'll tell us what else to do."

Reedie cuddled against her breast, panting, then raised his dark curly head. His mouth spread in a wide grin. "Mama," he said. "Mama, no." And then he coughed again.

THIRTEEN

Abigail's remedy worked within the hour. Reedie's breathing eased. The cough gradually softened, and then stopped, and he sank into a sound sleep. He awakened the next morning to eat hungrily the thin gruel Miranda gave him. Though his small nose was pink and required continuous wiping, he played happily enough before the fire while Miranda, working at needlepoint, sent him anxious glances.

It was quite apparent that he was recovered when Doctor Porter, summoned earlier, arrived.

With a crow of delight, Reedie rose up, hurled himself

across the room, and climbed the doctor's legs to pull his beard.

"And this is the patient, Miranda?" the doctor demanded. "He seems hale enough to me."

"He does now," she agreed. "It was different last night." She went on to describe what had happened, and the doctor listened while Reedie settled himself on the older man's shoulders, and shouted, "Horsie, run!"

After a quick gallop to the hearth, the doctor set the boy down. He examined him carefully while Miranda watched.

At last the doctor said, smiling, "There's nothing wrong here, Miranda. Surely you see that for yourself. I hear a small wheeze in the chest. The remains of last night's congestion of course. But it'll pass within a day or so."

She let her breath out in a long sigh.

"Still, he may have another onset, you know. These things do happen. But it's nothing to be alarmed about. Should there be some small weakness in the lungs he'll soon outgrow it."

The clock struck midnight, signaling the advent of the year 1869. Miranda and Reed stood, arms linked, at Reedie's crib and listened to the gentle sound of his breathing.

They had promised to see the New Year in with Tad Layton and a group of others at a dinner and evening to be held in Willard's Hotel, but she had, after discussing it with Reed, sent Timoshen with their regrets.

Now she said, "He's well, Reed, but I'm glad we didn't go."

"I, too."

Later, sitting before the fire in their bedroom, they shared the small supper of caviar on toast points that Abigail had left for them, and drank the champagne Jefferson had chilled.

Reed looked at her soberly and said, "I'm glad we're alone, Miranda."

"To see the New Year in," she answered softly. "Yes. It's better that way."

Still, he wondered if she concealed any small pang of wistfulness that she had not made a grand entrance in velvet and diamonds to Tad's entertainment.

He forgot that when she came into his arms.

The relief after the uneasiness, the unity they felt in their spirits, lent a special poignancy to their lovemaking that night.

He could not get enough of her mouth, nor she of his, and when, finally, she took his weight to her body in a joining prolonged and tempestuous, and then peaceful and full of a dreaming sweetness, the concerns of the past few days were completely forgotten, and they slept, bodies entwined, into the bright sun of the first day of the New Year.

That night, for Stacy's party, Miranda decided on black velvet, and the whiteness of her bosom and arms glistened against it dramatically. The dress, gathered into a fullness at the back below the waist, and with a round train, was in the newest fashion from France. The pearl eardrops she wore were those Reed had given her as a Christmas gift before they were married.

She dabbed a touch of perfume on her wrist from the tiny glass flacon on her dresser, and saw that it was empty. There had been enough, though, to leave lingering traces of patchouli and roses about her.

She gave herself a last look in the cheval glass and turned away. Reed would be waiting for her, he had said, in his study. She caught up her pearl-trimmed reticule and went to tell him that she was ready.

He was seated at the desk. He looked up, smiling. "And now you're waiting for me. I apologize." He got to his feet, and her heart seemed to clench with love for him. He wore formal attire, black broadcloth, the cutaway trimmed with satin lapels, the small black cravat satin, too, and secured with a diamond pin, the shirt white and finely tucked. His black trousers were narrowed, and the black satin trim was repeated in a stripe down the outside seam.

They paused for a brief moment outside Reedie's door

and heard him rattle the bars of his crib, and then heard Lena whisper to him.

Miranda went in.

Reedie immediately rose to his feet, holding out his arms. She bent to kiss him, and Reed did too.

"I go," Reedie suggested, laughing.

"Not tonight." Reed grinned.

As they turned to leave, the baby cried, "I go, too, Mama! Papa, I go!"

Reed stopped. "What do you think, Miranda? Is it all right to leave him?"

She hesitated briefly, then said, "Doctor Porter told me he is well. And though we shall be careful, we must also be careful not to spoil him." She smiled, "It's so easy to do, Reed. He's so lovable."

They heard him call after them until Jefferson had closed the double doors behind them.

Lamplight shone from the windows of the lowly taverns. Gaslight glimmered from the windows of the luxurious clubs. Here and there were still the flickers of Christmas candles now burning at their stubs. Sounds of hilarity and celebration echoed through the snowy streets. New Year's Eve was past, and New Year's Day nearly done. It was as if every moment until the morrow must be filled with the expectation of joy.

It was the same when Timoshen drew up before Stacy's mansion and helped them alight. Laughter and brilliance flowed into the tree-lined driveway.

"We shall be ready to leave about one, I suppose. You may wait," Reed instructed the thin-faced young man before they went inside.

Stacy wore dark blue satin and a diamond tiara in her chestnut hair. Her oval face was aglow with delight. She was surrounded by a group of young men who hung about her like hummingbirds over a single juicy hollyhock. Small embers burned in her black eyes as she introduced each one of them to Miranda, with Edward Farnsworth looking on.

Tad, watching, saw Miranda's eyes move over the

crowd. He went to her. "Is Reedie recovered? I'm sorry you couldn't be with us last night."

"I, too," she said, "but Reedie's well now," and she gave Tad a questioning look.

He knew at once that she was remembering what he had mentioned to her before. In spite of the alarms of the past few days, she had not forgotten their conversation. How like her that was, he thought. He turned, gazing at where Samuel Ward stood in a small group. He was certain that she would understand.

She did, and not long after she contrived to be at the side of Samuel Ward when she saw that an acquaintance of hers was speaking to him. The acquaintance made the introduction, and Mr. Ward bowed gallantly over her hand, his small white imperial jaunty, and his broad beaming smile full of admiration.

The acquaintance soon drifted off, but Miranda remained, engaged in that sort of conversation so usual to such affairs in Washington.

She said, "I'm happy to meet you, Mr. Ward."

"I assure you that I've been looking forward to this with much interest, Mrs. Haversham. Your reputation, fascinating though it is, hardly does you justice, I should add."

She instantly saw that he was adept in the ways of the city, and instantly understood Tad's interest. But she smiled. "Have you been here long, Mr. Ward? I mean that you've already heard of me."

"No, not long," he answered. "But I hope my stay will extend itself. And I plan to see that it does. I find this a charming place." He made her another bow. "And now the more so, for having met you."

"And what do you do? Are you in the government? Or do you expect to be?"

"Not quite that. No, I'm a man of business, you see. That is to say, a man of several different businesses." His glance slanted away to where Reed stood, talking with Tad. "Much as your husband is, I should say."

She moved a bit closer, smiling into his eyes. "Oh, then you're in railroads and property?"

"To an extent." Mr. Ward paused. Then, "But, dear lady, surely you're not interested in such affairs. These are the concerns of men."

She might have stamped her foot in annoyance but knew that would not do. Instead she laughed prettily. "Oh, but I truly am. And not only interested, but attempting to inform myself." She leaned close to him now and saw that his eyes were fixed hungrily on her bosom. She leaned closer still and playfully took his hand. "There are so many new people these days in the city. I hear names I do not know. There is a Mr. Corcoran Riley, for instance. Surely you can tell me about him, Mr. Ward."

The elderly man said, "Corcoran Riley," and twined his fingers through hers. "My dear, I don't know the man."

"Is that so? How strange. I am certain I heard that he was somehow associated with you. At least," and now her eyes became wide and innocent and even more flirtatious, "he goes about using your own name as a reference."

Mr. Ward stroked her fingers. "My dear Mrs. Haversham, I've not been in this city long enough to know everyone. But I don't know him. Whatever he might say."

"You're certain," she cooed.

She did not like the touch of his hand, nor even the quality of his smile, but this was for Reed. She would do anything for him.

"I'm quite certain," Mr. Ward was saying.

"It's a quality of this place," she said, sighing. "Acquaintances become intense friends, and a glance across the room becomes a formal introduction. When there's reason for it," she added.

"A perfect example now follows," Mr. Ward murmured wryly, as Josiah Hurley made his appearance.

He bowed over Miranda's hand, and said, "I'm delighted to see you. And you, too, Mr. Ward. I hadn't known you were friends with Mrs. Haversham and Mrs. Van Eward."

Miranda, at that moment, saw that Reed's gray eyes were fixed on her, and that there was a strange cold look on his face.

She did not know that seeing her small flirtation with

Samuel Ward had sickened him. The hand-holding, the exchange of smiles, the warm glances . . . That she had blithely, and openly, pursued this man set anger burning hotly within Reed. It was all he could do to contain himself.

Miranda was saved from the embarrassment of having to in some way detach herself from Mr. Ward and Josiah by the appearance of Edward Farnsworth. The young man's eyes were bright, his moustache unruly.

He seized her by the arm, saying, "Mrs. Haversham, allow me to lead you to the buffet," and swept her off.

She went with him gladly, knowing that further conversation with Mr. Ward would be to no purpose. She caught a glimpse of Tad across the room, and determined that she would speak to him as soon as she could.

But now Edward put into her hand a dish of crayfish with cole slaw and slices of ham, and said, "I'm happy this evening, for Stacy's sake. She's herself again, and that's good."

"Yes," Miranda agreed, her eyes still on Tad.

Soon he came to join her. To Edward, he said, "My boy, you must have this waltz with Erna Barrington in my place. I'm not up to it."

Edward grinned, saying, "Mrs. Haversham, I'll be back for the next one," and left her alone with Tad.

She said, "It's odd, I think. But I believe your Mr. Riley is quite unknown to Mr. Ward, and if his name was used as a reference, it was without his authority."

"Mr. Ward said that?"

"Plainly, Tad."

Tad nodded. "Then we'll have nothing to do with the J and R Land Investment Company, nor with Mr. Riley."

Reed, standing alone near the hearth, drew a deep breath as Josiah joined him, and said, "Good evening, Reed. And how are you?"

"Very well."

"I've just been talking to Miranda and to Mr. Ward."

"Yes?"

"Your wife is a charming woman, Reed." Josiah smiled within his beard. "No man can resist her."

Reed slid a glance at him but said nothing.

"Certainly Mr. Ward didn't want to. And he'll make a good friend in days to come."

Reed's eyes grew colder. Color touched his brown cheeks. He said, "We've no need of such friends," and turned away.

The music continued.

Miranda was claimed for a waltz by Edward, then by Tad. She rested briefly, surrounded by certain of Edward's young friends, laughing at their sallies and approving their stories.

Edward drew her away when the music began again.

Her slender white arms were lifted, the sapphire gleaming on her hand. Her feet were in position. Her head was back, and she was smiling at Edward because she was happy and having a good time.

Reed, holding her sable-trimmed cloak, came to her side. He said, "Miranda, I fear we must go." He did not look at Edward.

"But can it be so late already?" she asked.

Stacy cried, "Oh, but you mustn't leave. The party has only just begun."

But by then Miranda had recognized the barely controlled rage in Reed.

She trembled with a rage to match it even as she made her farewells, drawing her cloak closely around her, and hurried across the ballroom and into the cold out of doors.

He had no right to spoil the evening. He had no right to stare at her with such coldness. He had no right to humiliate her before her friends and his. It was because she had spoken to Sam Ward, of course. Well, he had known beforehand that she would. Of course she would. It was for him. For him, for Reedie. They were Havershams!

Her thoughts boiled within her as Timoshen helped her into the carriage, his dark face hardly hiding his bewilderment.

She could not contain herself. She demanded, "Reed, what's the matter with you?"

"Not now," he said thinly. And to Timoshen, "Hurry, we want to go home."

She fell, shivering, into the seat, her hands clenched in her cloak, Reed stiff and silent beside her.

The horses went at a run through the midnight empty streets, under the white clouds condensed from their heaving breaths. The only sound was the jingle of their harnesses, the creak of the wheels, the thud of their hoofs. They sped through the wide-open gate to rock and jolt up the snow-rutted driveway, and jerk to a stop before the stone steps.

Reed handed her down and waved Timoshen away.

Unspeaking, he preceded her up the stairs and into the house, where Jefferson took their wraps, as bewildered as his son had been at their early return, and bade them good night.

They went up the steps together, the barrier of angry silence firmly between them.

She paused outside Reedie's closed door, then opened it to look in.

The boy's breathing was slow and easy.

She yearned to touch him for a moment, but refused herself the pleasure lest she disturb him.

Lena blinked sleepily from her pillow, and whispered, "He's been just fine."

Miranda closed the door, then went into her own room.

The flames burning on the hearth seemed to leap up at her entry, to cast small shadows on Reed's face.

He leaned on the mantel, and said in a jeering voice, "So you took a moment to look in on Reedie! How good of you to show such concern for our son now."

She flung back her head, "What does that mean? I'm always concerned for Reedie!"

"Always?" he raised his dark brows. "You were not so concerned a few hours ago that you would miss Stacy's party."

"You wanted to go, too," she answered. "And Reedie was perfectly all right when we left. He's sleeping soundly now. Do me the favor of being honest in your displeasure."

"Very well. I did not like your behavior with Samuel Ward."

She sat before the mirror, beginning to remove the pins from her hair. Her hands still trembled, and her eyes burned. She tasted an angry bitterness on her tongue, as if it were a bile rising up from within her. But when her hair hung to her shoulders, she said quietly, "I don't enjoy being humiliated in this way, Reed. How could you act so? Suddenly demanding that we leave, without even an excuse, an explanation. You seized me and dragged me away, so obviously angry."

"I could have been much more obvious," he said coldly.

She turned on the small satin bench. "Oh, could you indeed? Well, it wasn't necessary. You announced your total displeasure with me to everyone present. And why? For what reason? Because I did what you yourself refuse to do! Do you think I'm totally blind? Totally a fool? Do you imagine that I don't understand?"

He stiffened, frowning.

But Miranda went on. "You spend a few hours in your study just a few days a week, and pretend to yourself and to me that you're working for our fortunes. Pretend! Yes, that's what it is. For I know there are opportunities abounding, and I know, too, that Tad thinks you don't take advantage of them. Why don't you?"

"If you want for anything, you must say so," he told her through clenching teeth, while a surge of red came into his face. "I can't imagine what it might be, but if you feel a lack, then tell me now. I shall see it fulfilled if it's in my power."

"I speak of no lack and no need. And you already know that." Her voice dropped. "Reed, Reed, we're Havershams. We have a . . . a destiny. Whatever you may think of my efforts, they are always in behalf of that. On behalf of you."

"But I don't want these efforts of yours," he said thickly. "You allow your ambitions to drive you too far. Samuel Ward. Josiah Hurley. I tell you I don't need your assistance, nor expect it. This whole thing disgusts me."

"But I'm not a poppet to be cosseted and dandled and set aside," she cried. "I'm a grown woman!"

"So Samuel Ward must have noticed when you thrust your breasts at him and smiled into his eyes and held fast to his hand!"

"Reed!"

"I find it ugly, unseemly, and distressing to see my wife sell her wiles and charm to such a man."

"What do you accuse me of?" she asked hotly.

His gray eyes were shuttered, bottomless. He answered, "What is the name for a flirtation which is to be the basis for some damnable business deal for me?"

"I'll not allow you to speak to me this way," she retorted.

"Then leave my affairs to me," he answered. "I'll provide for you. Believe me, I'll do what needs to be done. But it will be in my own way, and my own way alone. And nothing you do, nor scheme, nor pretend, will change that."

The fire was cold on the hearth now, and the lights gone. A faint chill crept slowly across the silent room, and its breath seemed to invade the very recesses of Miranda's being.

She lay on her back, her eyes wide open, and stared at the shadowed blue canopy overhead.

Hours before she had sunk to these pillows, exhausted and stiff with anger, every fiber of her body prepared to rebel and reject Reed. She'd have no love from him that night, she vowed to herself. She'd not allow him to heal the wounds caused by his ugly words with sweet kisses. No! Not this time.

She would not even permit herself to tell him that one thing which would wipe away the whole of his anger and make him regret it with all his being. She believed she was pregnant again. Within days, she would be certain. But she would not tell him so. Not now.

He had stretched out beside her, close as always but

with his flesh not touching hers, and he had not turned to her, and now she knew that he would not. He would not turn to warm his hands at her breasts, nor put his lips to them. He would not throw his lean thighs over her and hold her captive until they were both forgiving.

Slowly, her rigid body eased, loosened, warmed with yearning, and then ached with it.

Slowly her golden eyes filled with tears until they overflowed and ran silently down her cheeks and into the ruffles of lace at her throat.

FOURTEEN

There was peace, and the promise of spring, in the clear yellow sunshine in the lane. A worn dray horse, tethered to a hitching post, stamped his hooves as though yearning for high green pastures, and flicked early April flies from his mangy back. A spotted black and white dog dodged under those hooves and then attended, with intense concentration, to a small withered bush. Two tiny boys with fishing poles over their shoulders ambled by, scuffing up dust on their way to the canal.

All the windows on the first floor of Bon Chance were open, and at one of them, Joy, *née* Prunella Dalton, leaned out and yawned and sniffed, and then swung back into the room.

"It's all very well for you," she said sulkily. "You've got something to show for it. But look at me, will you? I'm nowhere."

She wore a gown of sprigged muslin, tiny rosebuds surrounded by spring-green leaves. It was ruffled at the throat and wrists and hem, and sashed in white. A white bow was tucked into her shoulder-length red hair. Her small high breasts made hard peaks under the fabric, and her slim boyish hips were made bonny and curved by its gatherings above them.

Nan looked her up and down and smiled tightly, though there was a glint of anger in her black eyes. "You've certainly become an ungrateful baggage, it would seem to me. Why, the day Jake brought you here from the depot you went at your breakfast like a starving kitten going for a bowl of warm cream. You didn't have a decent gown to your name, nor even a name worth having, for that matter."

"And look at me now," Joy muttered sarcastically, resisting the urge to crown the fat woman's head with the chamberpot near the bed. "I've a full belly, I'll grant you that, and a full wardrobe, too. But I didn't get either for nothing. I worked for them. And how I've worked for them. And it's taken me a year to get them all the same."

"Well, of course you've worked. This isn't a charitable institution. Whatever made you think so? If you should prefer the workhouse, you're free enough to try it. Nobody's keeping you here. But I warrant they'd have you work there, and then you'd have cause for real complaint. First scrubbing on your hands and knees and emptying slops. And then maggoty bread and wormy porridge three times a day. My Dessie does better for you than that, doesn't she?"

"Sure, but I still say I earn it."

"Then I think you ought to make your complaints to Jake," Nan said softly. "He'll be interested. No doubt you can talk him around to seeing it your way. Though the other girls may object, of course."

Joy needed no hints about that. She'd been through it before, made it happen before. But she was determined to have what she considered her due. She had her own cherished ambitions. Her hazel eyes narrowed. She tightened her lips and flared, "Why, damn you for a fat old troublemaker! You know perfectly well that you'll turn Jake against me first. If you haven't already."

Nan shrugged her round shoulders. "Do as you please then. But that was the agreement. You get your room and your board, and your pay for every man, but the tips belong to the house. And they hardly cover your keep. It's twice now you've held back, and I've been more than patient with you. You can't say that I haven't."

"Only because you had to be," Joy muttered, stung by the false tone of sweet reason.

"Had to be? Oh, is that it? And do you imagine that you're really the only whore in the whole of the city?"

"You know Jake likes me," Joy snapped. "That's why you had to be patient." She thought, but carefully kept back from saying, that there was the reason Nan Cunningham did *not* like her. Because Jake did. The fat old fool was jealous!

"Well, then do as I tell you," Nan answered. "Make your complaints to him, if he likes you so much. But just remember this. I've warned you. Not once but twice. If you hold out on your tips, you're going to face trouble. The other girls are satisfied enough—why aren't you?"

Joy looked her up and down, and then grinned tightly. "For the same reason, Nan Cunningham, that you've never been satisfied with what you had."

"Are you so sure?" Nan asked. "Do you think, in this short time, that you've grown to know me so well?"

"I've known a madam or two in my life," Joy retorted. And learned from them, she thought triumphantly.

"That so?" Nan asked with a small smile. "And I thought you were from Middleburg, and running away from your mean Dad and meaner stepmother. I thought you'd just lost your way and been robbed when Jake found you, and I fed you, and even gave you the only work you're fit for and like."

"I never lied to you," Joy said, knowing she was caught but ready to brazen it out. "I really didn't. It was all true. Everything I said."

"Of course," Nan agreed. "It was that. In the beginning, I suppose. You changed the time around some."

Joy didn't answer that, but her smile suggested that Nan had the truth. For all that it mattered. And it didn't matter much.

"One way or the other," Nan went on after a moment,

"just turn over your tips, and don't stand there and hand me a bare-faced lie like you did last night."

"It's still not fair," Joy said sulkily.

"Do you know," Nan said with admiration, "I think I respect you even more after this little talk we've had than I did before? Do you know I like your spine and sense?"

That should have warned Joy, but it did not. She cried, "Then if you do, let me keep my tips!"

"Oh, I will," Nan said. "I'll be glad to. But it's not up to me. You must speak to Jake about that. He's my manager, and I give him full authority. I'd never go against his decision, whatever it is. So talk to him. He may make an exception for you. Since, as you say, he does seem to like you well enough. Though it would cause trouble with the other girls, and I'd surely have problems to keep them in line. Still, he may just think you worth it." She shrugged her shoulders. "Just ask him when he comes."

"All right," Joy retorted defiantly. "All right, then. I will."

She sounded less defiant that same afternoon when she approached Jake in his downstairs office.

He leaned back in his big chair, one exactly like the one that John Haversham had used, though he did not fill it as fully as John Haversham had, and stared, shallow eyes unblinking, while she carefully stated her case, more as a plea than a demand.

When finished, she stopped with a small gasp of relief, and he said, "So that's what it's come to, is it?"

She ducked her red head, and muttered, "I didn't think it would hurt to ask. I've got a right to ask, haven't I? And Nan said I should."

"It doesn't hurt," Jake said thoughtfully. "At least not much."

He wore a new suit. It was light in weight with a yoke at the back of the hip-length jacket, and cuffed sleeves. His shirt was striped, with a turned-down collar, in the same blue as his cravat. His trousers were tapered to narrow at the ankle over his pointed black boots. His hair was no longer wispy but smoothed across his forehead and held firm by application of a pomade that Nan had obtained for him. His sideburns, thicker and longer now but very well trimmed, seemed to accentuate the gauntness of his face.

Joy watched his fingers caress the gold watch chain that hung across his waistcoat. "Then you'll do it?" she asked eagerly.

"No."

"But you just said——"

"I said it wouldn't hurt much," he answered, his mouth slanting in a grin. "I wouldn't do it. Why should I? You've got a roof over your head, and the best food and drink, and more clothes than you know what to do with or have time to take off and put on. Why should you need more than that?"

"Because I'm not planning to stay here forever," she said softly. "I've got things to do and places to go."

"Is that right? Well, you can be on your way today if you like. I expect Nan will be glad to help you pack up what you came with, if you've still got it, that is."

"Now wait. I never said . . ." She didn't really think he would send her away. She was by far the best girl he had. So many men liked to play with her. And she was his youngest girl, too. Even younger than he knew. But somehow she wasn't sure. You could never really be sure of what Jake Rooker would do.

He said reasonably, "And how could I do it anyhow? What about the rest of the girls? If I make an exception for you, then there's them to think of. They've got their rights, you know, the same as you."

"Never mind them," she retorted. "They don't matter. And besides, they wouldn't even know. I wouldn't tell. Do you take me for a fool?"

"You are one, Joy, if you thought to talk me around." He grinned at her. "Keep on with this and I'll set you out in the street in Cow Town. Then you won't have tips to complain about, but something more."

She said, suddenly paling, "All right. If you won't see it my way, then you won't."

"That's right. But there's something else for you to consider. I've got good plans for you, if only you'll prove you're worth them. Show some good sense and some patience. And prove I can trust you."

"What plans?" she asked.

"You'll know when it's time." He added softly as she went toward the door, "And don't try it again, Joy. Because I'll know, I assure you that I will, and then you'll be sorry. I assure you of that, too."

She thought, as she climbed the steps to her room, that she wouldn't try it again. She had not liked a certain grim note in his voice. But, at the end of that week, when a plump out-of-town drummer had had a particularly good evening with her, and sought to impress her both with his gratitude and importance by handing her a ten-dollar gold piece, she was tempted to hide it away in her bodice.

She mentioned it to no one, of course. And she was sure that no one could have seen it. She had been alone, the door closed, the light dim. It was her own little secret.

Yet the next morning, while the girls chattered, and Nan presided over the breakfast table, Jake stood in the doorway and called her out.

When she asked what he wanted, expecting that she already knew and preparing to grumble that it was her time off after all, he jerked his head toward the end of the hall and went before her to his office.

She trudged after him angrily, but she was already beginning to be afraid.

He was not dressed in his gentleman's clothes now but wore a blue work shirt and blue trousers, and heavy, mud-caked boots that beat the floor when he walked.

He allowed her to enter, then closed the door behind her, closed it with a firmness that increased her fear. She reminded herself that he couldn't possibly know about the gold piece. He just couldn't. There was no way.

He just stood there, staring at her for a long time, before he said, "Take your wrapper off."

"What? Here? Now?" She looked at the fireless hearth and the open window, and added, "What for? It's too cold."

But she decided that she wouldn't grumble after all,

time off or not. There was something not quite right about
his eyes.

"Take it off," he told her in the same even tone.

"But why? What are you after?" Her face paled, and
she felt the gold piece burn between her breasts, but she
forced herself to offer him a coquettish smile. "I mean, if
you want to, Jake, we can go upstairs where it's warm
and nice, and make ourselves comfortable, and maybe a
drink wouldn't go too hard on either of us, and—"

His mouth slanted sideways. "That's not what I have
in mind. Take the wrapper off, Joy."

"Well, listen . . ." She knew with certainty that she was
discovered, but she couldn't imagine how. No one had
seen the plump and well-satisfied drummer hand her that
gold piece, and no one had seen her tuck it into her
bodice. She couldn't accuse any of the other girls because
there was no way for them to know. Yet surely Jake was
after that piece. It couldn't be anything else. She sighed
and prepared to admit to her folly, and to promise to be
good thereafter. But then it occurred to her that she might
possibly distract him. He was, after all, a man. Even with
that funny look in his eyes. And if there was one thing she
knew, then handling and distracting a man was it.

She changed the submissive sigh into a lewd little laugh,
and slowly, very very slowly, undid the wrapper. She let
it fall open to reveal the full-length but diaphanous gown
she wore beneath it. When she slid a look at Jake, she saw
that he was watching her, his face expressionless. She
opened the wrapper wider and held it as a drape around
her. Then she slipped it off and let it become a floating
cloak before she dropped it to the floor. She posed in the
gown, thrusting her breasts forward, and saw, delightedly,
that her nipples were hardening and rising. She began to
walk toward him, swinging her hips languidly.

He stopped her with a wave of the hand. "The rest."

She made slow and graceful work of the row of buttons,
sneaking an occasional look at him, but seeing no response. Oh, damn the man! He was usually fast enough
to come to it! Why wouldn't he now? The gold piece was

like a bit of fire between her breasts. But she still hoped to save it.

Beneath the gown she wore a white, ribbon-trimmed chemise. Her fingers fluttered suggestively at its bows.

"Come here," he said.

She ambled toward him again, her confidence renewed. She swung her hips insouciantly, and wet her lips, and blinked her eyes at him.

When she was close to him, leaning forward expectantly, he said, "Now, reach into that whore's bank of yours and give me that gold tip you got last night from your fat friend."

"Damn you!" she yelled in disappointment and fury. "Then why did you let me go through all that?"

"You enjoyed it," he returned, and put out his palm. "Set it there, you dumb little doxy."

"Get it yourself, you ugly ape," she flared.

He did not move nor speak. His wide open palm, marked with hard gray calluses, remained before her. Yet she found herself backing down.

She reached between her breasts and brought up the gold coin from where it burned her flesh. She threw it on the floor at his feet.

He didn't look at it. Instead he stuck his fingers into the cleavage at the front of her chemise and pulled hard, just once. The fabric split in half, revealing her nude body.

"You didn't have to do that," she wailed, and swooped to gather her wrapper as she made for the door.

He allowed her to get it halfway open before he said, "Hold on a minute. I'm not finished with you. What made you think I was?"

When she turned around, he held a thick leather belt in his hand. She sagged against the door, and it closed under her weight. Her eyes widened. She said, "Hey, Jake, you've got the money. I won't do it any more. You can have all the tips. I promise."

He did not really see her as he stepped forward. He saw a tall willowy girl with flashing golden eyes and glossy black curls. He saw her hands rise up to whip out at his face.

He doubled the belt in his fist and brought it down hard, slashing across her breasts.

Joy screamed, "Damn you, you'll mark me. Don't, Jake! No, please."

He brought the belt across her body again, savoring the loud slap it made against her bare flesh.

Joy screamed again and dropped to her knees, groveling.

But he hardly heard her cries, and finally, her moans. He saw the bowed back laced now with red streaks, and felt his power. He lashed at the quivering body again and again, until suddenly his vision cleared, and he saw Joy, Joy herself, and the white skin bruised and already swelling, and heard Nan pounding at the door.

Then he dropped the belt, feeling the sweat cold on his own body, and said, "You do that one more time and I'll put my hands around your neck and break it clear in two. And if you don't believe me, then just try me and see for yourself."

"I won't be able to work," she whined. "Look at me. Just look at what you've done."

He hauled her to her feet and shook her. "It won't do you any harm not to work for a couple of days." His grin slanted. "Maybe Nan'll be good enough to feed you anyhow, though I don't see why she should."

"You ugly ape! I still don't know how you knew," Joy wept, as he opened the door and thrust her into Nan's consoling arms.

Jake felt exceedingly pleased with himself when he climbed into the gig and set out that same afternoon for the Barclay Hotel. He wore his new outfit, and his hair was pomaded and smooth. Gray gloves covered his big callused hands. He was sure there would be order in Bon Chance for a long while to come. The other girls had certainly heard Joy's screams. They would see her bruises, and hear about his belt. There would certainly be order. And that was what Jake liked. He wouldn't admit to himself that he liked using the belt as well.

The J and R Land Investment Company that he had

established four months before, using his initials for the
name, was doing well. It had sent out its first feelers
through Corcoran Riley, whose special talents Jake had
discovered when they met in a West Street tavern. It had
been mention of Samuel Ward, merely in passing, by
Josiah Hurley that had led to the use of that important
name as a reference for Tad Layton's bank. Now that
Layton had refused to do business, Jake was more determined than ever. Reed Haversham would soon be persuaded to sell, and it would be not to Josiah Hurley, as
Hurley himself supposed, but to the J and R Land Investment Company, through the person of Corcoran
Riley.

Hurley had been helpful, but Jake owed him nothing.
Hurley's generosity had been to serve himself. Now Jake
knew that he would himself be served. It was what he was
waiting for.

It was of no importance to him that President Johnson
had pardoned Dr. Samuel Mudd, exonerating him of the
charge of complicity in the murder of Lincoln. It was of
no importance to Jake that President Johnson had refused
to participate in the inauguration of the new President,
nor even that this man was now installed in the White
House, and that its doors had been opened wide to new
faces and new aspirations. He had his own aspirations to
consider.

None of these showed on his gaunt face when he joined
Josiah over the dinner table. There were two tall tapers
burning between them, and a huge flagon of red wine.
There were platters of small roasted potatoes, and green
peas and carrots, and a great slab of fried steak.

The two men ate well and heartily, and the conversation was jovial and did not concern business affairs until,
over brandy, Josiah said, "I expect you've come again for
your cut, Jake."

"It's about that time," Jake answered, his smile slanting
to show a rim of teeth.

"And you expect to receive it, do you?"

Jake helped himself to more brandy and sipped it ap-
preciatively before he replied. "It's not my fault that you

haven't yet bought the land in which we are both interested."

"I haven't yet tried to," Josiah retorted. "It was at first not the right time. I knew I must wait until President Grant was in the White House."

"Now he is," Jake answered.

"Yes." Josiah stroked his black beard. "Do you see anything these days of Reed Haversham?"

"No," Jake said. "Why should I?" And he wondered uneasily just what Josiah was getting at.

"He's completely inactive," Josiah went on thoughtfully. "I've tried to talk to him several times and only made him angry."

"So much the better," Jake observed.

"Perhaps. In any event, I think it's still not quite a good idea to approach him about the land."

"I'll be patient, if you are," Jake grinned.

"It takes patience to do what you want to do."

"And what you want to do as well," Jake answered, doubting now that Josiah Hurley had any inkling of what Jake's own motives were, and having no intention of enlightening him. He would hear when Reed sold.

"As you say, we're in business together." Josiah reached into his pocket and slid a draft across the table. "But spend it charily, my friend. I've a feeling that I may see no great need for giving you many more of these."

Jake grinned. "I'm content."

"I doubt that," Josiah returned dryly. "But never mind. Tell me, how is Bon Chance?"

"You should come by sometime and see for yourself."

"Oh, I shall, one of these days."

"Or do you prefer Obermeyer's?"

"It's a fine place, Jake. Not only for gaming, but for seeing the people of the city."

Jake grinned even more widely. He needed to be told nothing about Johnny Obermeyer's. He had spent hours there, playing at small stakes, observing while he had planned with Nan the decor of Bon Chance. He had not had the resources, even with Josiah's unknowing help, to do so fine a job, nor had the Kayhome Arms been as fine to begin with as the Connecticut Avenue mansion in which Obermeyer had opened his gambling palace. But Jake was well satisfied with what he had. The house was owned in Nan's name, of course, but he had no fear of her. His other plans were ripe. He would end up with a fortune the likes of which Johnny Obermeyer would never see.

Before Jake's eyes there arose the vision of Haversham Square. The high iron gates, the ivy-covered brick walls, the tree-lined driveway beyond. And, hidden until approached, the house itself, windows alight with welcome for him.

Josiah misunderstood the expression on Jake's face, and said, "I see you *do* like Obermeyer's. Then perhaps you'd like to join me there later." He did not add that Reed Haversham was known to gamble there, and so successfully that the owner had been heard to remark that he would not be sad to see the end of Reed at his wheels.

Jake answered, "No, thank you, Josiah. Though I appreciate the invitation." He more than appreciated it. He cherished it. It was a sign of how far he had come so soon. But he went on, "I've a few chores, and then, to tell you the truth, I'm tired. I think I'll make an early night of it. Tomorrow's another day."

But Jake did not return to his quarters at the Union Hotel until very late.

When he left the Barclay, he stopped at Willard's Hotel for a short drink. There he mentioned to the Negro bartender that he'd heard a rumor about the Swampoodle area and Louse Alley, and about Cabbage Alley, too, and he asked if the man had heard it as well, by any chance. "Did you know that the man that owns it is going to burn the whole area out?" he demanded indignantly. "At least that's what I've been told. Can you imagine that? Just burn it out, and all those people there, a lot of them ex-slaves. Where are they to go, do you suppose? What will they do?"

The barman polished a glass carefully and shook his head, muttering, "Who knows? Who knows?"

"Have you heard the same thing, from your own people, I mean?" Jake asked. "Do you suppose it's true?"

"Haven't heard a word. Not yet," the man replied, and walked away to serve another guest.

From Willard's Jake went to the Metropolitan, and then on to Brown's. In both places, he mentioned the rumor he had heard to the Negroes that served him. In both, the men shook their heads and stared thoughtfully at him before turning away.

His last stop was in the Union Hotel to spend an hour with Corcoran Riley, who, dressed in coarse black, hardly looked the same man that had visited Tad Layton to mention Samuel Ward and the interest of the J and R Land Investment Company.

Jake said quietly, "It's a good thing you stayed downstairs. Is the stuff all ready?"

"Of course it is," Corcoran Riley answered disgustedly. "And been ready for weeks, as you well know. What's been holding you up, I can't see. I've got a date in San Francisco when my job here's done, and I want to keep it sometime in this life."

Jake grinned. "You'll keep it, and with gold in your pocket as primer, if you do what I say."

"I will. That's what you hired me for, and you can't claim I haven't delivered with satisfaction so far."

"Then get those things out tomorrow. Go down to Swampoodle before dawn, and just leave a stack of them sitting there. Then go over to Cabbage Alley and do the same, and in Louse Alley, too. And mind you don't get caught in either of those places. I'm warning you now. You'll be sorry if you do."

"Don't worry about me," Corcoran said grimly. "I know how to take care of myself."

Before dawn the next morning though, he had begun to have his doubts. He made his way across the Tiber, and down a dim lane, where rubbish skittered and slid underfoot and announced his coming with all the force of a trio of trumpeters. Still, he managed to drop a stack of the broadsides near some sagging shanty and to hurry on.

When he bent over to leave a handful more at another place, a rock suddenly spun past his head and banked into the wooden wall. He scrambled to his feet, bursting sweat, and beat a hasty retreat through the darkness.

As he ran, he heard the shrill cry go up. "Night doctor! Night doctor sneaking around. Ho, man, night doctor here!"

He fled from the stinking place, wishing he dared set a torch to the place and burn the whole thing to the ground.

FIFTEEN

Just below the long slope of the White House grounds, where President Grant now slept, the grumbling discussion went on.

It had continued for nearly ten days, rising up in heated anger, then sinking away to smoulder, only to flare anew. Some days it was mentioned in whispers edged with fear, some in pained and bewildered disbelief, some in shouts burning with rage.

There were not too many who could read the broadsides found scattered among the shacks, but a few could.

One of that few was a tall man, very dark of skin, and with a bald head deeply scarred. He had gone over it carefully by candlelight and by sunlight, word by word, saying each to himself until by now he knew the thing by heart. "The owner of this property is Reed Haversham, Esquire, of Haversham Square in Georgetown. You have been permitted to live here by his sufferance. He now orders you to depart from his property within the next two weeks."

Now he said the words again into the night, his voice rasping.

"Where for?" a voice yelled from the group before him.

"It's all we got," another cried.

"There's no place else. What he mean get off?" a thin man muttered hoarsely.

"Who do it say?" an old lady whispered, but her quiet question was lost in the general sullen growl.

A jug appeared from somewhere and was passed from hand to hand, and passed again. When it was empty, another took its place.

A skinny twelve-year-old recounted for the hundredth time how he had seen the man crouch at the shanty, and had thrown the rock that had sent him skittering away, and had cried out, as loud as he could, "Night doctor!" to offer warning.

No one listened to him as the smouldering embers flared up suddenly.

"He going to have to move us, one at a time, body by body, and fighting all the way," someone yelled. "We not going nowhere."

The roar of agreement was loud enough to awaken sleeping children, to chill their anxious mothers.

The tall man, dressed in the rags of what had once been a cavalry uniform, listened and nodded.

"And we'll go and tell him so!" someone at the rim of the group shouted.

The tall man nodded again, and took up his club, and started walking slowly. Others fell in behind him. First one, then a second. Suddenly there was a troop of more than twenty at his heels, and more coming with them.

A slender young woman reached out and caught the arm of a burly man, and cried, "Seth, no. Not you. You better not go." And he, jerking free, answered, "Why not? What I got to lose?"

The troop grew quickly. Young men, and old ones, in worn and patched working clothes. Skinny boys with ropey arms. Women with kerchiefs on their heads, and girls with perky bows. They moved together and crossed the stinking open sewer that was Tiber Creek, and set out along Pennsylvania Avenue.

They trod quietly, dark as the night itself, silent by common consent, past the White House and then Washington Circle, along the Georgetown Bridge Road, keeping together with stragglers hurrying after them, until they massed at the tall iron gates and pressed against them in a stubborn black tide. Now they were silent no longer.

Mutters became shouts, tearing the fabric of the night. Clubs were brandished, and whipped the bars in frenzy. Torches, gathered along the way, flared up, casting a grim and eerie light upon the scene.

Benjy came out of the gatehouse, pulling on his trousers. He took one look and started in a loose-kneed scurry up the driveway, epithets following and spurring him through the dark. Lena, meanwhile, slipped away into the shadows and around toward the back of the house.

The doorpull sent a wild clamor through the building, but by then the clamor outside had awakened Miranda.

It came through her sleep as an animal roar. Some deep and distant and ominous thundering. She continued to hear it as she sat up and swung her feet to the floor.

The dark room seemed to spin around her, full of quick-moving shadows and long slim spears of flaring light. Her heart began a hard drumming against her ribs, and her breath came shallowly. The infant in her belly seemed to stir, and she placed both hands protectively and caressingly along the full curves.

The ominous roar continued. She drew on her wrapper, slipped on night shoes.

Reed was already up and gone, she saw now, which meant that he had awakened before her.

She went directly to his study. He stood at the window looking out, but he turned when she asked breathlessly, "What is it? Can you tell what's wrong? Is there a fire, do you think?"

"I'll see," was his answer, as the doorpull clamored wildly again. "You'd better stay up here, Miranda." He hurried into the hall and then down the steps.

She went into Reedie's room. He slept soundly, his plump arms and legs outflung, his coverlet trailing on the floor. She tucked him in and then went to the window.

From there she saw below the trees licks of red flame that marked burning torches. She saw the shifting swelling outlines of something dark and menacing. And then, high above the trees, she saw the moon, red-misted and red-circled.

She gasped and caught her breath as she heard Benjy's shrill voice. Then, deeper, questioning, Reed's.

She gave Reedie a quick look and ran back to the bedroom. She wrapped herself in a heavy cloak and hurried into Reed's study. The dueling pistols were on the desk. She snatched one from the case, found cartridges, and held the pistol tight against her side with the cloak shielding it.

As she went down the steps she felt the baby stir again within her.

Reed had told her to stay indoors. But she could not. She could not allow him to go out alone into that dark night under the red moon. She would help him, against whatever the threat. She would protect what was her own. For a fleeting instant she thought of John, his hand curled around the pistol where her own hand was now clasped. Had it been this one? She shrugged the fleeting thought away. It was the present that mattered. Only the present.

By then, Jefferson and Timoshen had come from their own quarters at the back of the house and were running behind Reed and Benjy down the driveway.

Abigail and Lena stopped some angry argument between them when they saw Miranda. They concentrated on trying to keep her from going beyond the steps, from following the men.

"Miss Miranda," Abigail said sternly, "that's men's business, whatever it is. You can't go down there. Not in that cloak, and not as you are now. It's not right, and it won't be good for you. Go inside and sit down. Just sit quietly and catch your breath, and don't listen. It'll all go away, believe me. Mister Reed'll see to it. You go in, and—"

But Miranda could not stay within, not knowing what made that terrible roar of sound in the night. She could not wait until someone came to tell her what threatened. She pulled her cloak more tightly around her and clutched the pistol under it, and went down the steps.

Lena cried, "Listen, listen, you don't know what's going

on. But can't you hear? Don't go down there, Miss Miranda."

She neither paused nor replied.

Abigail set out after her, grumbling under her breath at Lena. "She won't listen. No more do you. And I'll talk to you later, see if I don't. I won't forget. I'll talk to you about where you've been."

But Lena only sobbed, "What *is* it, Mama?"

The clamor at the gate was a long rising howl. Torches lit the angry faces pressed against the bars. Shouted curses fouled the sweet spring air.

Reed stood before the gate with Jefferson.

The older man said nervously, "You'd better go back to the house, Mister Reed. You can't talk to them. They're too riled up to listen. Just go inside for now. After a while out here, and with dawn dew falling, they'll cool down. They'll go away."

But Reed shook his head. He was determined to know what it was before he retreated. He would discover why this mob had come here, to Haversham Square, and what it intended.

Behind him, Miranda fumbled at Timoshen's sleeve, drawing him close so that she could whisper. "Isn't there some way you can ride out to summon the police?"

"The back road, by horse," Timoshen answered. "I can do that all right."

Miranda glanced briefly at him. Then, "Try. Mister Reed will talk to them meanwhile."

"Better not to," Timoshen answered, and then he faded away into the dark and was gone.

Reed did not seem to notice. He stood still, staring at the torches, at the dark faces beneath them.

There passed through Miranda's mind then the memory of the night Lincoln was shot, and another angry crowd stood massed and raging, a dangerous animal in the dark. A night when torches burned, and men's voices were shrill on the sweet spring air, and the moon was red. She clenched one hand at her lips to keep from crying out. But the other hand held the pistol tightly.

Reed moved, raising his dark head. "All right, speak

up," he yelled. "What are you doing here? What do you want?"

A wordless howl of anger answered him.

"That tells me nothing," he shouted. "Say your piece now, or else go away. It's up to you to decide."

Another howl, blended of many shrieking and swearing voices, was the reply.

But then, as it died away, a shower of crumpled and dirty broadsides came down through the gate, littering the lawns.

Benjy swooped to seize one, to thrust it at Reed.

Reed smoothed it flat, stared at it. He read it through once, then again. He found it hard to understand the words. Hard to believe what he saw in black print before his very eyes.

He had not thought of that piece of land, once Caroline's and then John's, since it became his own. Only once Tad had mentioned it to him in passing in some connection he no longer remembered.

He had certainly not had these broadsides printed. Who had, then?

There was a restless movement in the crowd, as if a storm wind were gathering there.

Reed said loudly, "I did not put these things out. I have not even thought of such a thing. This is impossible to believe."

Miranda, having scanned a second crumpled sheet, clenched it in her hand and flung it down and kicked it angrily away.

"Tell them," she cried. "Make them believe you, Reed. Make them listen to you."

Reed tried. He put up his hands for silence, but the shouts rose louder and louder. He yelled, and his yell was echoed by a hundred maddened voices.

Miranda moved to stand beside him. She held the pistol tight against her body under the cloak. She threw back her head and screamed, "Who's your leader, if you have one?"

Her shrill demanding cry cut through the other sounds.

It was suddenly so quiet that she could hear Abigail draw her breath in in fearful protest.

But the tall dark man with the bald scarred head put his hand through the bars of the gate and shook his fist.

"It's a lie," Miranda cried. "Do you understand me? A lie. Mr. Haversham knows nothing of it. He is not planning to put anyone off that ground."

Reed said, his voice low and hard and very angry now, "Miranda, be quiet. Go indoors at once." He walked down, said to the tall dark man, "We know nothing of it. It is a false rumor and no more than that."

"It says so," the tall man retorted. "I read it for myself. I can do that much. I can do that much, I tell you. I can read. It says—"

"But it's a lie," Reed told him. "Take your people and go back to your homes. You can do no good here."

"But we have no homes," the tall man yelled. "Can't you understand? It says so right here. We have no homes anymore."

There was a great shout, and a dozen torches came sailing over the wall. At the same time there were thudding hoofbeats in the lane, and a warning yell and shrill whistles, as four mounted police began a galloping run.

The crowd before the gates suddenly melted, a receding black sea, a sea that disappeared into the shadows.

There were curses and the jingle of spurs, and hoofbeats, and then, quite suddenly, there was silence again at Haversham Square.

The torches burned out, leaving great scars on the sloping lawns. A breeze sent the crumpled broadsides dancing along the ground.

There were tears on Jefferson's face, and his hands shook as he made his way back to the cottage with Abigail, while Lena sullenly trailed after them.

But Abigail did not stay with her family for long . . .

Mrianda moved one foot before the other. She was suddenly more weary than she had ever been in her life. If she did not hurry, she thought, she would fall here on the path, and lie there. If she did not hurry she would not be able to go on.

The broad white steps loomed above her, endless and forbidding.

How many of them were there? She had traversed them innumerable times, and never counted them. Nor had she ever noticed that they were so steep.

Reed walked slowly beside her, silent, his face shadowed and forbidding.

She would have spoken, questioned. But she had no breath. She held the pistol against her body and forced herself to go on.

She had reached the top step and halted just before the wide open double doors when the pain struck her. It exploded brutally, low in her back, and tore a gasp from her throat. She staggered under its blinding force. The pistol dropped from her suddenly limp fingers and clattered noisily on the stone at her feet.

"Miranda! Miranda, what are you doing with that?" Reed demanded angrily. He scooped the pistol up. "What did you suppose you would accomplish? Will you insist forever on swinging your skirts about me whether I want them or not?" His words stopped abruptly. His anger was just as abruptly gone. He saw the faded whiteness of her face, and how she wavered on her feet.

"Reed," she gasped. "The baby. I'm afraid for the baby."

He gathered her into his arms and shouted for Timoshen to go for Abigail, and then to ride immediately for Doctor Porter.

Miranda was just barely conscious when he laid her carefully on the bed, and went down on his knees beside her, his lean face lined with terror.

The gaslight laid pale fingers against the blue canopy. A small fire whispered on the hearth, and the gray of dawn edged the big window.

Miranda was just faintly aware of this. It existed for her beyond the rim of consciousness, a periphery blurred by pain. Fire swept and blazed upward from a small central core in her side. It spread from that place where the pistol had touched her flesh, and consumed her in slow waves. Her body convulsed with it, and her jaws froze tight, and her thighs clenched, trying to contain within her that which was attempting too soon—oh, much too soon, impossibly before God's own time—to free itself from safety and into death. It was from the core where the pistol had touched her flesh, John's pistol, that the awful waves came.

Now she heard hard, heavy, and slow footsteps sounding in the hallway beyond the door.

John, she thought. John walked that way. His very step had been the signal of his soul.

Her jaws unwillingly eased, allowing a moan to cross her lips.

Abigail stroked her cheek, and whispered, "He's coming," gently, reassuring, even while she was certain it was useless and too late that Doctor Porter was arriving.

But Miranda answered, "No, no. He's dead," still thinking of John.

The scars on Abigail's face stood out against the gray of her skin. By her own means of knowing, she suddenly understood. She grabbed Miranda's hands in hers, and squeezed them hard, and cried, "Baby, no, listen! Doctor Porter. Look up and see. He's here."

But Miranda did not hear her. The thunder of pain, hoofbeats over her heart, deafened her. She sank under it, but she never allowed her clenched thighs to open. She would retain the life within her. Let John come. Let him come, she screamed in her mind. She would defeat him. She would save herself and hers from him.

She sank into darkness, and when she rose again, the doctor leaned over her.

He spoke for a long time, quietly, reasonably.

She shook her head on the pillow. She would not allow herself to understand his words. She would retain the baby.

Reed leaned over her. There was a pallor in his cheeks, and his eyes gleamed with tears held back, and when he touched her, she knew that his hand trembled. He said, "Miranda, please, please . . ."

And she closed her eyes and turned her head on the pillow again. She would retain the baby.

She drifted in darkness for a while, and then, quite suddenly, she was split by agony. A stake of fire laid her apart and ripped her asunder. What was within broke through the walls of clasping flesh, the tendon and muscle that was its protection. It burst through in a thick hot gush of what should have been the fluid of life. Her thighs could not dam it, for all their effort, and the effort of her mind. Nothing could stop it.

It came, and the feel of it, the knowing, the loss, tore a scream from her throat.

Doctor Porter held a spoon at her lips, whispering, "Miranda, child, swallow. It will ease you. It will help you."

There were no footsteps now, but Miranda thought of John. He had walked that way. And Caroline had listened, perhaps, as she suffered through this losing, suffered through it more than once, with her body maimed, her heart destroyed.

Miranda turned her head away from the spoon. "I'll not have it," she moaned. "No, take it away. I'll not have it, I tell you."

Later, while the doctor worked over her, tried to stem the flow of blood, Reed once again held the spoon to her lips. "Miranda," he begged. "Please, take it. Just now, this once. It will help you."

But she remembered Caroline, and she remembered a night when she had had such stuff as this by John's design. She whispered, "Never, Reed. Never while I live." She heard him gasp, and went on, "But don't be afraid. I will not die."

She kept her promise. She survived the bleeding and the cleansing. She found the strength somehow to bear knowing that the child, had it developed to full term, would have been a girl. She cuddled Reedie's uneasiness away, and smiled steady reassurance into Reed's desperate eyes.

In that week, she took her first faltering steps, leaning

hard on Abigail's arm and ignoring the older woman's anxious protests.

At the end of that same week, Jefferson awakened during the night, heard April rain on the cottage roof, and took Abigail's hand in his. He saw the shadows sink around him, imagined that he saw torches flaring against the sky, and heard threatening shouts from beyond high iron gates. When dawn came he was dead.

In the next week, Reed, against Tad's advice and Miranda's pleas, sold the squatters' land to the J and R Land Investment Company, which had once offered a bid for it. He told Tad that he wanted no more to do with it, and was glad to have it done. Tad unwillingly followed the orders given him, accepted the moderate payment from Corcoran Riley, handed over the deeds, and tried very hard not to think of Caroline and John.

But Jake, sitting in his suite at the Union Hotel, thought very deeply of John, and smiled when he received the deeds from Corcoran Riley, and paid him off and sent him on his way to San Francisco.

Jake smiled when he thought of John, and of Reed. The damned Havershams. He knew that he was a man on the road to making a fortune, though no one else knew it yet. On the road to making a fortune, on the backs of the Havershams.

SIXTEEN

Ulysses S. Grant had been President for six months when pandemonium suddenly struck on Wall Street in New York City. It was September 24, a Friday, and was known for years after as Black Friday.

In the Gold Room of the Exchange, Jim Fisk, chubby, fair-haired and self-confident, bid up the price of gold, until by noon, he had bought some sixty million dollars' worth, while all those forced to pay too much for the metal necessary to their transactions were wiped out. Fisk and his partner, dark-haired and cold-tempered Jay Gould, had cause, through a variety of their own actions, to believe that the government would not move to stop this. But it did. The Treasury began to sell gold, and within minutes, market prices began to fall. In hope of avoiding further panic, the Gold Room was closed.

Jay Gould apparently escaped with few losses.

Jim Fisk declared himself a bankrupt, though in the years that followed he hardly appeared to be in want.

Many others, however, were financially destroyed. Even more were brought close to the brink. Among those was Josiah Hurley.

He had too optimistically accepted the information passed on to him that the White House would not permit the Treasury to interfere in the free price of gold. He had expected to make a huge amount, and had heard too late to withdraw and save himself. In the weeks that followed the disaster, he considered the various ways and means by which he could reestablish himself.

By then, of course, he had learned of Jake Rooker's duplicity, though he could hardly prove it. He knew that Jake's land company had bought the property that Josiah had considered virtually his own, held in trust by Reed until that time it would be ripe for resale. Now Josiah saw that Jake was cleverer than he had thought, and would bear watching in the future.

Meanwhile, all that Josiah held securely were the shares of the stock in the Haversham Railway, given him so long ago by John.

Josiah thought long and hard before he saw the means by which he could further profit from those shares. He would, first of all, need more of them. That could best be accomplished as it had been accomplished before. But this time, Reed, rather than John, would be the donor.

What he had neglected to do before, in spite of false assurances to John, he began to do now. He mentioned, at first casually, to his colleagues the need for more transport into Washington, and described his idea of the new trestle bridge, and his certainty that the Haversham Railroad would bring the line in if only the government would build the bridge. When, in gradual stages, over a period of months, he saw that he had stirred his colleagues' various interests, he decided to move.

A few weeks after the New Year, approximately nine months after the catastrophe of the April night, Josiah paid a call at Haversham Square.

It was the first time he had been there since just after John's death, but he did not even think of that. He was concerned only to attract Reed's interest, to determine how best to deal with a man who plainly did not wish to deal with him.

He brought a huge bouquet of white tulips for Miranda, and a box of fine cigars for Reed.

He was taken aback to find Stacy ensconced in the morning room. She, of course, he had seen, even joined in her home for large receptions. But he had not thought her capable of any deep sympathies. He did not know that she had come, each day since the infant's premature birth and death, to sit with Miranda, to play with Reedie, to tease Reed.

She greeted Josiah with a gay smile and a brightening of the embers in her dark eyes.

"How kind of you, Josiah, to call during the dullest hour of the day," she said. "And it has been too long since we've had the opportunity for private conversation."

She began with that and soon had him purring within his spade beard.

Miranda was quiet but pleasant, and even more beautiful, Josiah thought, than she had ever been.

Reed did not put in an appearance that day, but Josiah was not disappointed. He indicated carefully to Miranda that he was anxious to speak with Reed. It was a matter of business already too long deferred.

She nodded and promised to mention it to her husband. She thought, as Josiah passed on to other things, that she would mention it to Reed, but there was no guarantee that he would even consider a meeting with Josiah. Still, if he would . . . She felt a spark of interest begin to glow in herself. Perhaps Josiah's visit was important.

Stacy was not troubled at all by such possibilities. She remembered Josiah's bony arms clasping her body when he helped her from the carriage, and his demanding hands at other moments, and smiled happily to herself. How correct he had been after she married Carleton. How difficult that must have been for him.

Once she saw him purring in his beard, she set out to accomplish more. She did it easily.

When, after a pleasant forty-five minutes, Josiah prepared to depart, he said first to Miranda, "I hope you'll relay my message to Reed. If he would visit me at the Barclay at his convenience . . ." Her gracious nod reassured him, and he turned to Stacy, "I should be delighted to see you home, my dear."

"You? See me home?" she asked. And then, as if catching herself, "Oh, but thank you. No."

"Perhaps you'd dine with me tomorrow evening?" he suggested.

"Tomorrow evening." She pretended to consider. Then, regretfully, "I'm so sorry, Josiah. I'm engaged tomorrow evening. Miranda is going to give me a lesson in . . . in checkers. Yes. In checkers."

"Then may I suggest next Saturday night?"

Again Stacy appeared to consider. She was determined to extract every ounce of grim satisfaction from these moments. But at last, with a regretful shake of her dark chestnut head, she said, "Josiah, I think not. I'm sorry. Indeed I am. That will be the evening for another lesson in checkers for me."

He knew what she had done, of course, and nodded politely. His disappointment was not as deep as Stacy would have liked. He had come on an errand of business, and he hoped he had been, or would soon be, successful in that, a matter more important in his priorities than Stacy's charms.

It was a few days later.

The January afternoon was gray. Sleet polished the

carriage and creaked under its wheels as it drew up before the Barclay Hotel.

Reed climbed down, told Timoshen to wait, and took a deep breath of the cold damp air. It was, he thought, clean and pure. He would need a good supply of it to last him through the next half hour.

He was here only because Miranda had wanted him to be. It was for no other reason, and nothing short of that could have brought him to see Josiah. She had told him of Josiah's visit, and relayed the Senator's message. Reed had seen the anxious look in her eyes as she did so. He would do anything to please her. He had immediately promised her that he would find out what Josiah wanted. That was why he was here now.

He made no such explanation to Josiah, but settled himself in the chair across from the Senator and observed the booted feet on the windowsill, and the not-quite polished spittoon, and waited. He thought that if Josiah so much as mentioned the spying system he had arranged for John, he would punch the Senator's nose and leave.

But Josiah said nothing of that. He ordered drinks, and when the two of them were alone again, and the only other sound in the room the hiss of the fire, he described carefully to Reed the favor that John had asked him to do years before, and how impossible it had been then to have the trestle bridge built. He went on to explain that it was now possible. If Reed were still interested, of course. He spoke of it to Reed, the Senator said, only out of a sense of obligation to John. It had been John's own idea. If Reed had no interest in it, then Josiah would like to know. For the Overland Seacoast Line, long envious of the Haversham rights of way, would perhaps be very well satisfied to do business.

Josiah did not think it necessary to tell Reed that the Overland Seacoast Line was a paper corporation, owning no rights of way of its own, no cars nor yards nor rolling stock, controlled by himself and a group of his associates. He also did not think it necessary to tell Reed that he was betting with himself that a man drawn to gamble at the roulette wheel could be tempted into gambling with stocks as well.

Reed, remembering his promise to Miranda and how she had looked, said he would think it over, and saw Josiah grow pleased.

Josiah grew pleased enough to suggest that Reed accompany him to Johnny Obermeyer's place.

Reed assented after a moment's thought. He already felt a surge of anticipation. To see the wheel spin . . . see the silver ball glide . . .

Timoshen drove the men there.

The gambler greeted Josiah with enthusiasm, and Reed with a sigh.

This Josiah noted. It was true then, he thought, that Reed won here, heavily and repeatedly.

He did so again that day. But this time he left the wheel without regret.

For all the while he stood at the table, making his bets, he considered what Josiah had said to him earlier. The Overland Seacoast Line would like to have the Haversham rights of way. To have the trestle bridge built by Congress would be of decided benefit to him.

He had two errands to perform before he returned home.

After he had Timoshen drop Josiah off at the Barclay Hotel, he had himself driven to Galt's. There he bought for Miranda a heavy amber stone suspended on a gold chain. He thought, as it was being packaged for him, that as brilliant as the stone was, it did not hold the luster of Miranda's eyes, but it would have to do, since there was no better piece to be found anywhere on the coast.

From Galt's, he went to a small red brick building at the corner of 19th Street and Pennsylvania Avenue, in which a fledgling company was attempting to operate a Washington Stock Exchange on the style of the huge one that did business on Wall Street in New York.

He had been there a few times before, idly buying and selling stocks in various enterprises, but in a small way. His experience there was not unlike his experience at Obermeyer's. There was the same exhilaration involved.

The same sense of certainty that he was relying on his own skill and nerve. Now he was interested only in the stock of the Overland Seacoast Line, its assets and principals.

He spent an hour reading what material he could find on it, which was not a great deal. But he did learn that it had shares for sale on the open market. He placed an order for a substantial number, and smiled to himself as he did.

When he returned home, Miranda eyed him anxiously, but she did not ask what Josiah had wanted of him. She waited, hoping that Reed would wish to discuss that with her, to explain it without any undue prompting or questioning.

But, having presented her with the amber stone, and receiving her grateful kiss, he withdrew to his study for several hours, during which he went over the structure of the Haversham Railway, and how it could be used to bait Overland Seacoast into his hands.

Later when he came down, more cheerful than he had been in months, with a gleam in his gray eyes, he said, "I heard Reedie shouting in the nursery and asked that Lena bring him to us."

Miranda set aside her embroidery hoop and smoothed the velvet of her brown frock, her hands slim and white and graceful against the sheen of the fabric. "He rides his wooden horse very competently, Reed."

"Soon he'll ride his flesh and blood pony," Reed told her. "Ian wrote not long ago that it's on the way."

"But you'll make certain—"

"My dear, of course," Reed answered quickly. "We'll stable the animal until the boy is ready for him. Don't worry."

Reedie had awakened several times more with a seizure of coughing since that first attack, and those had been nowhere as intense as the first one. Yet Miranda had learned to listen for him in the night, and knew it was the same for Reed.

Now he burst into the room at a fast trot. "Giddap,"

he shouted, grinning. "Horsie, horsie." He beamed a smile first at Miranda, then at Reed.

Reed scooped him up and swung him in the air, and watching, Miranda thought, At least we have him. We have our beautiful boy, and that was a comfort.

SEVENTEEN

An end of the winter snowstorm blanketed the swelling buds and froze the emerging March crocuses.

Snowflakes as big as goose feathers drifted slowly from the gray of the sky, and Reedie, perched on the window-sill where his father had put him, watched with fascinated eyes, chanting, "A snow man. A snow fort. A snow town."

These were what Reed had suggested they build when they went out of doors. Now grinning, he said, "We'll try them all at least, Reedie."

"We'll do them," Reedie answered. "A snow man. A snow fort. A snow town. All ours, Papa."

"Count the flakes," Reed said. "See how many there are."

"Too many," Reedie chuckled, hugging his knees. But then he sang, "One-a-flake, two-a-flake, three-a-flake, four-a-flake." He paused, eyed his father hopefully, and when no help was forthcoming, "Seven-a-flake."

Reed grinned through the steam rising from his shaving water. "Try again."

"One-a-flake, two-a-flake . . ." Reedie's song trailed off as Reed began stropping his straight-edged razor.

"One-a-sharp," Reed said. "Two-a-sharp . . ." And Reedie chimed in.

Miranda, pausing outside the door to listen, heard the blending voices, the clear treble of her son, the deep bass of her husband.

"Three-a-sharp," Reedie sang, "four-a-sharp . . ."

"Five-a-sharp," Reed bellowed.

Reedie giggling, cried, "Yes! That's right, Papa! Five-a-sharp."

Miranda smiled, and went on to her bedroom. How well Reedie was learning his numbers . . . how well Reed taught them.

Now Reed soaped his badger shaving brush, while Reedie hugged his knees and laughed and waited.

It took some time, that soaping, which was part of the ritual. Also part of it was the way Reed leaned close to the mirror over the marble washstand and drew his skin this way and that, making peculiar masks while he slid the razor over it.

Reedie moved to the edge of the windowsill and turned his small face up expectantly.

At last Reed took the badger brush and painted on the baby skin a heavy white moustache of lather, a thick dab of beard.

He held the boy before the looking glass so that he could admire himself, and Reedie, after a joyous moment, suddenly announced, "But when I'm big, I'll have a black moustache."

"You will," Reed said, and set the boy on his feet. "Go show Mama how you look."

Reedie raced down the hallway, crying, "Mama, see my grownup face!"

She admired him and said so, and bent to kiss him, and when she drew away, he burst into laughter. "Mama, you have a moustache, too!"

Later, all three of them, bundled in cloaks and wraps and shawls, went out to play in the snow.

They had a snowball battle, and Reedie proved to have a good right arm. He and his father built a fort, and then a snow man.

The snow man had a bucket for a hat, two black stones for eyes, a curled twig for a smiling mouth.

Reedie was so entranced by him that he darted indoors to find Timoshen, for whom such a wonder must be displayed.

Holding tight to Timoshen's hand, he drew him out, saying, "Timshen, look. My Papa made a man."

Timoshen agreed this was a man to beat all men, and admired the fort, already beginning to melt, and exchanged a snow shower with Reedie before he went inside.

Abigail, watching from the window, decided to start hot chocolate, and hurried to see if the gingerbread men baking in the stove would be ready in time.

They *were* ready, and so was Abigail.

She was at the doors when Miranda came in, Reed following with Reedie on his shoulders, singing, "The sun's out, the snow's melting . . ."

"And you, Master Reedie, you look like you're melting, too," Abigail said. "Run upstairs and tell Lena you need a drying, inside and out, and then come down and see what I have for you." She added to Miranda, "You need to be dried off, too."

A few minutes later, accepting the gingerbread man Abigail offered him, Reedie examined it with wondering eyes, and then looked up and said, "Aunt Abigail, I love you." And added hastily, "I love Mama and Papa, too. I love everybody. And everybody loves me."

To Miranda time seemed, in those days, to go quickly. August came, and Reedie was suddenly three years old, a tall boy losing his baby fat, with a mop of dark curly hair and silver eyes and a wide loving smile.

Reed and Miranda took him to visit Tad at the bank one day.

He stood between Reed's knees, rocking with the motion of the carriage.

Two small boys in ragged clothes, with long unkempt hair, scampered alongside the wheels. When Timoshen gave them a warning shout, they ducked aside.

But, Miranda saw, almost immediately they hurled themselves back into the road. They bent to sweep fresh piles of horse droppings into burlap sacks. In a few hours, she knew, they would present their full sacks at the market to be sold for fertilizer, and go away richer by a few pennies.

Reedie would never gather horse dung for pennies, she thought.

And he said anxiously, turning to look into his father's face, "Papa, will they get hurt?"

"No," she answered.

"I hope not," Reed replied, as Timoshen drew up before the bank.

Reedie looked thoughtfully up the road toward where he had seen the boys. "I hope not," he repeated, mimicking Reed's accents.

He whispered to Miranda, once the three of them had entered the dim interior. "Mama, do you smell it?"

She grinned at him, shaking her head.

But he widened his eyes mischievously, and suddenly he looked like a small replica of her. "Isn't it nice? The bank smell?"

Tad, overhearing this last, smoothed back the dark curls and swung the boy in his arms. "Reedie, I'm a banker, so I think it's nice indeed."

"Me, too," Reedie answered. "I think it's nice."

"He'll be a diplomat," Tad said. "At least that's where his talents lie."

"That remains to be seen," Miranda answered.

"Or you'll be a businessman," Tad went on to Reedie, "and come down to the bank and discuss your important affairs with me. You'll hand me my glasses, Reedie, and my cane, and help me up when I'm too old and stiff to rise alone."

"Tad, what are you saying?" Reed laughed.

Tad grinned into the boy's suspended face. "And, of course, you'll end up owning half the city and a large part of the countryside."

Reedie considered, then asked, "Is it a lot?"

"A lot," Tad informed him.

He took the boy into the counting room, and showed him the drawers of paper money, each filled with stacks of bills bound by denomination in red ribbon, and explained why that system was used. He showed Reedie the scales for weighing hard coin, and permitted him to deal with two stacks of pennies. He set the boy on a bookkeeper's high stool, and stuck a pen in his hand, and a clean ledger sheet before him.

Reedie was fascinated by it all, and when he left, he gravely shook hands. Then he threw his arms around Tad, whispering, "Unca, I love you, too."

That winter he had two small attacks of night coughing, and Doctor Porter examined him carefully.

But once again he said, "It's not important. He'll outgrow this minor weakness. In another year or two you'll have forgotten all about it."

When Reedie turned four, his birthday celebration was a trip to Jacob's Landing and a picnic on the banks of the river.

It was a hot day, the air heavy and still. The hum of the bees and the gentle sound of the falling tide filled the small clearing in which they sat.

They had Reedie's favorite foods, lovingly prepared by Abigail: beef sandwiches with pickle relish, and chocolate cake.

When they had eaten, Reed took the boy down to the water's edge, and asked, "Would you like me to teach you to swim?"

Reedie said wonderingly, "Can you?"

"Why not?" Reed grinned.

He stripped off the boy's shirt, took his hand, and waded in.

"Your boots, Papa. Your trousers," Reedie cried.

Reed laughed, and answered, "The sun will dry them, never fear."

Miranda sat watching, a blue parasol over her head, while Reed held the boy and showed him how to move his arms and kick his feet, and then moved him on the surface.

Later, when they came out, both dripping wet, Reedie hurled himself into his mother's arms. "Papa swam me! Did you see?"

Miranda remembered the joy of that day through the year that followed, and she decided that they would make the same trip again to celebrate Reedie's fifth birthday.

It was to be the following month, and he had already

wistfully inquired of Abigail if she thought he might have beef sandwiches and chocolate cake to take along in the picnic lunch.

He had become as competent on his pony as he had been on his rocking horse, and his vocabulary had grown even more quickly than his frame, which was, however, large for his age.

He would be a big man, Miranda thought, as tall as his father one day.

She leaned forward as he rose in his saddle, crying, "Can we go faster, Timoshen? Is that all right?"

Timoshen looked over his shoulder and grinned. "You can, Master Reedie. But I can't."

"It's fast enough," Reedie answered, sitting back, as Timoshen led the pony along the drive.

"He'll soon take the reins himself," Reed said, a look of pride in his face. "He'll be a wonderful rider one of these days."

"Yes," she agreed. And thought, but not too soon. He mustn't grow up too soon.

Reedie went with Timoshen to the stables, and Miranda rose to go indoors.

Reed seemed to linger on the steps, showing no indication of recalling their engagement for that night. She would have preferred that he speak of it, but when he did not, she finally said, "Reed, you do remember, don't you? That we're promised to go on the President's cruise this evening."

"I do indeed, but I've no stomach for it. We could stay at home, just the two of us, and do warfare over the chessboard."

"We can do warfare over the chessboard any night. And I've already accepted the invitation. It would be an intolerable rudeness not to appear."

He smiled down at her. "And besides, you're anxious to go."

"I would like to," she confessed. "And I think you're teasing me." She smiled up at him through her lashes. "I do think I'll begin to dress now. When you see me, you can decided whether I go alone and without escort, or whether I go with my husband."

He caught her by the sash, pulled her back, and held her tight against him. "I believe you'll appear with your husband, as a proper wife should."

She pressed close to the hard lean length of his body, burying her face in his shoulder.

They had met Stacy at church that morning, and Stacy had said she would be on the cruise with Edward. She had also, with a curl of her lip, announced that Josiah Hurley was expected to attend, and Sam Ward, and a host of other interesting people.

It would be good, Miranda thought, for Reed to be there, too . . .

Her gown was a soft lilac color, made of thin muslin. It draped itself to her figure and blossomed out into a full bustle at the back, and was girdled with a wide-swung band at the waist. The neck was scooped low, and the pearls she wore gleamed against the whiteness of her skin.

The hat she chose was only as big as her two hands together. It dipped down over her forehead and tipped up at the back, trailing long lilac streamers.

She heard Reedie chirping happily at Lena in the nursery and smiled to herself. Perhaps one day soon he would be moved down the hall to a larger room, and there would be another baby in the nursery. She had hoped that by now it would have happened. She ached to hold in her arms an infant to replace the one never cuddled, never nursed. But that had not yet happened. Still, she was sure that it would. She and Reed were both young, both healthy. Surely they should be able to have more than a single son.

With a final glance in the cheval glass, she caught up a lavender shawl and went into the hallway.

Reedie and Lena had gone down only moments before her, and she found them in the cooking quarters.

The boy grinned at her across the big table. He had a moustache of milk at his mouth and a chin bearded with cookie crumbs.

"You're beautiful, Mama," he said happily, and then coughed.

"Slow on the cookies," Abigail told him. "And take a sip of that milk."

He grinned, obeyed. Then, "Are you going out, Mama?"

"Papa and I are going for a ride on the President's yacht," she answered.

His silver eyes grew wide. "On the President's yacht," he echoed.

"And someday," Reed told him, coming in, "you'll do the same."

Reedie grinned. "I'll be captain and we'll go far away."

"You'll be the President," Abigail answered, "and stay right here in Washington City."

Theirs was the last carriage in line before the boarding pier.

Reed said, "It seems we're just in time."

He handed her down, thinking how beautiful she looked, and how he wished that they were alone now, the two of them, in some cool quiet place.

He simply did not have her taste for company, and he knew why. Just as he knew why she had her taste for it. The knowledge was always there, at the back of his mind. A silent reproach. They were Havershams, she said without words. They must live like Havershams. Which, to her, meant that they must live as John Haversham had lived.

Now Stacy descended from the carriage just before theirs, accompanied by Edward, and surrounded by her usual collection of young men. The sight of her—slim, her skirts billowing around her, her chestnut hair shining in the late sun—reminded him of those days at Haversham Square when she had drifted through the crowds of admiring men, teasing this one, flirting with that one, always somehow swimming on a wave of excitement.

She greeted Miranda and Reed at the gangplank, crying, "My dears, imagine! To keep the President and Mrs. Grant waiting! I'm horrified. I don't know how I can face them."

Her sweet carrying voice was surely audible on the reception deck, and it was, no doubt, intended to be. Stacy did very little by accident, though she often made it appear so.

She paused to plant a kiss on Miranda's cheek, to exclaim over the lilac of her gown, to sigh woefully that such was not her color. She kissed Reed, too, in greeting, received several narrow eyed looks from several ladies present, and then, with her coterie surrounding her, she sailed blithely up the wooden boards.

The President, in flannels and yachting cap, made her welcome, grinning around the black cigar he held in clenched teeth. Mrs. Grant spoke politely of Stacy's green gown. Stacy curtsied, offered her hand, and moved on, thinking that life would not, could not, be the same in Washington as long as this man and this woman remained in the White House. And remain in it, it appeared they would.

Miranda had followed her through the formalities with Reed, and when these duties were completed, moved to the railing as the yacht's engines began a steady thrum, and its whistles gave two long hoots and then a short one, and the hawsers were cast off. Slowly, unwillingly, it seemed, the ship moved into the thick brown turgid water of the Potomac.

Over the mast, there hung the American flag and the Presidential flag, and below them, the President's regimental banners.

The brasses gleamed, the paint was white and fresh, and the decks were glossy.

The banks were lined with wharves and warehouses and sheds, chimneys smoking black against the dimming sky.

An Alexandria ferry boat hooted as it passed.

Fishermen brandished skinned poles from the tree-lined banks.

"It's lovely," Miranda said. "I'm glad we came."

Reed nodded but did not reply. He was watching Josiah Hurley, the center of a group of men. Josiah's head, streaked with gray now, turned to observe Stacy pass by and then snapped back to nod in mock attention to what an acquaintance was whispering to him.

Reed had managed to keep his meetings with the Senator to a minimum in the past two years, joining him in conversation only to tell him the first time that, yes, Reed would be interested in having the new bridge built, and that he would assist Josiah in any way he could. Later meetings concerned only the number of shares Josiah believed he would need to persuade his subcommittee that the project was necessary to the city's expansion. The name of the Overland Seacoast Line was never mentioned between them.

Now Josiah appeared suddenly to notice Miranda and Reed, though he had, in fact, seen them the moment they boarded the yacht, and after a few moments he excused himself from the group with him and made his way toward them.

In the year before, the trestle bridge across the river had finally been voted by Congress, under the judicious pressure of Josiah and his friends, who had been well served by Reed's presentation of blocks of shares. Reed did not know that these were no longer individually held but were within Josiah's own direct control. The bridge was soon to be completed, and in a little while, the Presidential yacht would pass beneath it. He was certain that Reed, looking up at it, would think of the Haversham lines, expanded by ownership of the Overland Seacoast Railway Company.

What Reed could not know was that Overland Seacoast existed only on paper, that he had, as John would never have done, accepted the bait offered by Josiah, and walked blithely into the trap set by Josiah. He knew precisely what Reed was attempting to do. He was informed at the close of each business day about that day's transactions in the red brick house on 19th Street. He himself knew exactly how much Haversham stock had been used as security in purchase of Overland's shares, and manipulated the price of those shares accordingly.

But now he smiled with warm cordiality at Miranda

and stroked his spade beard. "My dear, how are you? And how is your young man? I hear such tales of him."

"We're well," she told him. "And Reedie is growing fast."

"As boys do." Josiah smiled. He turned to Reed. "Have you been much occupied lately? You've not visited me in some time."

"I'd not take you from your work unnecessarily," Reed said. "And with our arrangements completed . . ."

"You'll bring the line into the city, I suppose, as soon as the bridge is completed?" Josiah asked.

"I think so," Reed answered. "I'll keep you informed, of course." But the mild words were accompanied by a long look. Josiah sounded, somehow, as if he might know of what Reed had been trying to do, and might know, too, how dangerously he was operating. He had taken a series of risks with the Haversham Railroad, recognizing them for what they were, certain that the goal was worth it. Haversham Overland Seacoast would be one of the largest on the East Coast, and it would be something he had built. He, with his own nerve and skill. When Miranda knew of it, she would understand his long afternoon absences from the house, absences he knew had not gone unremarked but about which she had never questioned him. He felt sudden perspiration on his brow but did not allow himself to wipe it away. He gave a forced laugh, and told Josiah, "What I do depends on a great many things."

"Of course," Josiah replied smoothly. Then, leaning over the rail, he spat neatly into the river, tipped his straw hat at Miranda, nodded at Reed, and strolled away, well pleased with himself.

Reed saw the question in Miranda's eyes, but he ignored it. For two years he had planned this surprise for her. He would bring her the merger of the two railroads as a special gift. It would be something he had done, he alone, for her.

Then Stacy came and swept Miranda away, crying, "You must come and meet the Hollises. You'll like them, I'm sure."

Reed was seized by Erna Barrington who demanded,

"Reed, you must pay some gallant attention to Dorothea now. She fears she has slighted you, although on what grounds I cannot say, though I have my suspicions."

He forced a smile, but the muscles of his lean face had begun to ache. He braced himself to deal with the inquisition that he knew must follow. For Dorothea had seen him, only the week before, leaving the gambling house on Connecticut Avenue, and though she had shouted from her carriage and waved her parasol at him, he had foolishly ignored her and presented his back as he hurried away.

A panoply of stars gleamed in the sky when the lantern-lit Presidential yacht returned to its mooring. One star, brighter than the others, hung low and silvery over the mast.

Crickets sang, frogs croaked in the reeds, and wind stirred the shadow-touched trees.

Miranda was laughing as she came down the gangplank with Senator Sultz and Congressman Enderson.

It had been a good few hours. The company pleasant, and of the sort she liked. She had had a few words with Samuel Ward, a few others with Senator Hollis, and long conversations with older acquaintances. She had observed that Reed circulated nicely, charming Erna and Dorothea, as well as the President's wife, with his smile.

Now though, as she reached the firm footing of the torchlit dock, her laughter was suddenly stilled, soured in her mouth.

Timoshen waited there, and his dark skin was an odd dusky blue, his lips peculiarly pale.

She put out a trembling hand, but it was Reed who asked, "Timoshen, what is it? What's wrong?"

"It's Reedie. He got sick a little while after you left. As soon as I got back to the house, my mother sent me for Doctor Porter. He's been there all this time. And I came back to wait for you."

He had drawn the carriage out of line and right up to the dock itself, creating a jam of vehicles and receiving for that a barrage of disapproving looks. But he didn't care. He flapped his hands, urging Miranda and Reed to hurry.

Reed helped her up and dropped to the seat beside her. "What happened?" he asked, as Timoshen leaped up and beat the horses into a gallop that brought shouts from other drivers and more disapproving looks from the waiting crowds.

Timoshen's thin shoulders hunched under his dark uniform. He answered but spoke softly, and his words were blown away.

Miranda leaned forward, demanding shrilly, "Timoshen, tell me! Tell me, I say!"

"He was just fine, like always, after we left. That's what my mother said. But then, just before I got back, he had a coughing fit. It was no different from the other times. And my mother used the steam kettle like always. But then he started to shiver and shake, and it got worse. So when I got back I rode for the doctor." He hunched his shoulders again and fell silent.

The horses went at a dead run through the Sunday dark. Those few miles across the quiet city seemed vast as a continent to Miranda. She linked her hands in her lap to keep them from trembling. She breathed shallowly, carefully, to keep from bursting into tears.

At last they reached the gates. Benjy had them open and waiting. They rode through and raced up the driveway to stop before the house.

Doctor Porter's gig was tied there, empty.

Reed's face was touched with pallor under the rays of the two bronze lamps that flanked the white doors that finally swung open to admit them.

Abigail stood there, her hands clenched together. "The doctor's with him," was all she said, and there was a terrible and frightening anguish in her face.

Miranda nodded and ran up the steps, clutching her gown in shaking hands. Reed followed her.

Just as they reached the top, Doctor Porter came out of the nursery. He left the door open behind him and walked slowly and hesitantly to meet them. Then he put both hands out, one to Reed's shoulder, the other to Miranda's.

"I'm sorry," he said gently. "It's a sudden congestion in the lungs." He drew a ragged breath. "There's nothing I can do, nothing any of us can do, but wait and hope."

Miranda and Reed stared at him without comprehension but with a raw panic growing in their faces.

At last he repeated, "I'm sorry. Let's go in to him now. Let's stay with him. It's in the hands of God, you know. We must never give up our hope."

When Miranda reached the threshold of the dim room, she heard the slow struggling breaths and the long pauses between them.

She told herself that Doctor Porter was wrong. He must be. It wasn't true. Reedie would be all right. Soon he would stop that horrible rasping. Soon he would raise his head and smile. Doctor Porter was a madman, an incompetent. He didn't know what he said.

She sat close to the bed, leaning forward, her eyes fixed on the small pale face. It seemed, even as she watched, to shrink, to grow even more pale.

Reed stood just behind her, a hand on her shoulder, but she sensed his presence only dimly. All her heart and mind and strength were concentrated on the limp body of her son.

Breathe in. Gently. Easily. Fill your lungs, my love. Fill your lungs with good air. Breathe. Breathe.

Breathe, Reedie, but slowly, gently. Breathe . . .

She found that she drew air with him, expelled it with him. She found that her arms and legs convulsed when small jerking spasms shook his limbs. She watched him through a veil of unshed tears that made halos around the dim lamps.

Dawn had begun to creep into the hushed room. Dawn moved slowly across the floor, and finally touched his withering face. The curves and dimples were gone, the firm jaw, the pink flush. His rosebud lips fluttered against his teeth as he sucked in air and let it go.

Breathe, Reedie. Breathe.

She labored for him now as she had labored to bring him into the world. She fought for her own flesh as she had fought before.

Breathe. Rest. Breathe.

It will ease soon. Soon it will go away, and all will be well again. I promise, my love. All will be well.

His small hands, so competent with bridle and rein, so strong already, fluttered on the blue counterpane. His eyes opened wide, unseeing, staring, shining with a curious film of light. His mouth opened wide.

He took a long rasping breath, and suddenly his small dark head rolled sideways on the pillow. An awful silence filled the room.

Miranda did not understand. She held her breath, waiting. She held her breath, but she heard nothing. Nothing.

And still she did not understand.

Doctor Porter moved past her. He drew up the blue counterpane and straightened the small head on the pillow and closed the wide staring eyes. Then he drew the blue counterpane higher to cover the waxen face.

"What are you doing?" Miranda screamed, while Reed gave a gasp of anguish. "What are you doing, damn you? How can he breathe if you—"

Reed's fingers tightened into her shoulder. "Miranda, please . . ."

Doctor Porter said softly, "My dear, Miranda, Reed, I can't tell you both how sorry . . . It's happened. Your Reedie is gone."

She rose, feeling Reed's hands torn from her shoulders. She staggered and fell on her knees beside the bed. She screamed, "No, no, no! I won't let him go. I won't let him go, I tell you," and gathered the small lifeless body into her arms.

EIGHTEEN

The coffin was small, its blurred outlines a misty and shimmering white, streaked with hazy rainbows. Six faceless men carried it down the oak-shadowed lane beyond the chapel beneath trees that were bare. They set it on the winter-ravaged ground, and it became a glistening marble stone on which was cut by hand the words *Reed Haversham, Junior. Beloved Son. Four years and eleven months on this earth.* And somewhere in the darkest shadow, a familiar voice whispered, "I love everybody, and everybody loves me."

Miranda awakened, a sob rising in her throat, the last of the dreamed pain a part of her awakening. She reached out to Reed for comfort, but the place beside her was empty, cold.

She had not heard him rise. He had, as so many times before in the past three months, slipped silently away from her while she struggled with the grief of loss, and tried slowly to teach herself acceptance.

It was she who had gone, in the first few days after the pitiful funeral, to stand in the nursery, asking herself what she had done, what she had left undone. She wondered why her mother's heart had given her no warning, why her own instincts had not whispered to her. Had it been because she was not truly listening? Because she was thinking ahead to the cruise on the river, and imagining conversation with those important men who gave attention to her and defined the way in which she saw herself?

It was she who had finally whispered, into the sleepless night, "Reed, Reed, do you blame me? Is it my fault our baby died?"

He held her close, swearing that she had no stain of guilt, but when she looked into his eyes, she saw a shadow there, and it was as if a silvery veil lay between them.

She relived those moments when Reedie, laughing, raised his face to show her his lather moustache and beard. She had been through those moments when he grinned, "I'll be the captain and sail around the world." She had listened again and again in her mind to that small cough she had heard while he ate his cookies just before they had left him and returned to find him dying.

It was she who had finally, while Reed rode his big black horse through the trees, forced herself to go into the nursery. With her heart breaking within her, she had dismantled it, removing every sign of Reedie's presence. The rocking horse and crib had been wrapped, carried into a storage room by a red-eyed Timoshen. Abigail packed the small clothes. She, whose acceptance of Jefferson's death had been complete, broke down only once. Tears streamed down her face, and she moaned, "Oh, I know it doesn't do any good to cry. That won't bring our Reedie back. But it hurts, and remembering hurts, too."

Yet when the job was finished, and they left the room, she muttered with sad approval, "Yes, Miss Miranda, leave the door open. Yes. It's better that way." And then her eyes went to Reed's study, and some unspoken words hardened her lips.

Miranda agreed. She knew that the loss of Reedie would be a never-ending pain. There had been others in her life, her mother's early defection and death, her grandmother's passing, the infant girl. They had each left their scars. But this would leave an even deeper one, for Reedie had been of her body, of her love for Reed, and known, cherished, required. But she knew that she must bear it. She would bear it. For herself. She would bear it for Reed as well, if he would only allow her to . . .

Now she flung back the silken coverlet and rose. She wrapped herself in a blue lace peignoir, and went quietly into the hallway and then to the study.

No lamp was lit there, but the October harvest moon poured through the window, casting a silvery glow on Reed's bent head.

She went to stand beside him. "Reed, you must have your rest. You can't sit up like this night after night.

There's danger in such fatigue. It's weakening and depriving. You'll bring on the fever again in this way, and that surely will help none of us. Love, listen to me. You can do nothing if you sink into such a condition."

He said, not looking at her, his voice low and rough, "But there's no rest in staring at the canopy, in seeing pictures of what could have been. Our little girl . . . our Reedie . . . all that we hoped for, planned for."

She found a new reservoir of strength to fight back tears, to say, "I see the same pictures. But you must not give way. You must not look back, Reed, believe me."

"I know very well how wise you are, Miranda, so much so beyond your years, and beyond mine, too, I think. I know you're right. But I just don't know how to bear it. I can't."

Reedie was dead. He himself and Miranda had left him alone to face what had come to him.

Miranda leaned over him and slid her arms around his shoulders. "You have me, Reed, and I love you. I love you as much as life. Be grateful for that at least."

She felt his lean body shudder against her. He buried his face in her breasts and muttered, "You know that I'm grateful for it. There's nothing else."

But now he was remembering those long months after he had returned to Haversham Square from the hospital with his arm in a black silk, and his soul in invisible bonds. He had been able then to bear pain and illness, though his mind had been filled with a never-ending horror. Now something deep was gone out of him. Something for which he had no name. How could he explain it to Miranda?

She held him for a long silent moment. Then a mockingbird sang beyond the window. "Listen," she said. "How sweet his tune is. It means that tomorrow is almost here. You must come to bed now."

It crossed his mind that they two were differently made. Both blood and flesh and bone. But not the same. She heard the mockingbird's song and thought of the morrow. Of the future. He heard it and thought only of pain.

But he rose when she freed him from the circle of her

arms. He followed her along the hall, his face resolutely turned from the open nursery door.

She said softly, "I'm so glad that Ian is coming, although I am a little surprised. Did he say what was bringing him back this time?"

Reed answered without much interest. "The letter was a brief one. He wrote nothing beyond the date of his arrival."

She sank down on the edge of the bed under the blue ruffled canopy. "Perhaps it still has to do with the settlement of the *Alabama* claims."

"Perhaps," Reed agreed.

"I'm looking forward to seeing him so much, Reed. It'll be pleasant to have news of Grace and all the others we met when we were in London."

It was only six years since they had been there, but it seemed now a century ago to him, a lost age of happiness never to be known again. There had been the future then. He saw no future now. He stretched out on the bed, bent his arm, the one still scarred, across his face. He did not answer Miranda's remark. He felt that he should. He was being remiss, he knew, by holding to this silence. But he simply had no words in him. He had no thoughts in his head. He felt an emptiness there, the aimless emptiness of a dark and hidden cave.

She lay down beside him, snuggling close, offering to him the warmth and strength of her body. "Rest, my love," she whispered, while the image of the small white coffin rose again before her eyes and became a glistening white stone.

Ian drew a deep breath as the gates swung open, and the hired gig passed through and then rolled up the curve of the driveway. He watched the golden leaves swirl across the lawn and thought that he dreaded these next few moments to come as he had dreaded very few things in his life.

The news of young Reed's death had come hard upon the news of the unexpected, and frightening advent, of Grace's pregnancy. But for that he would have set out much sooner for America and Haversham Square. But for that, too, and the dangers of such a journey to her, Grace would be at his side now. She had wept over Miranda's letter, her small plump face showing her age as it had never before, and her light brown eyes showing an anguish that surprised him. The child stillborn . . . Reedie now . . . It had seemed to Ian and Grace that this was a time when Miranda and Reed would require the company of their only family. But now that he was here, Ian wondered. What could he say? What real help could he offer them? He determined in those few moments before the gig pulled up at the steps that he would mention nothing of Grace's pregnancy, or of the problems attendant on it.

Timoshen came running to pull the two small bags from the gig as Ian paid off the driver.

The door opened in welcome before the bell was touched, as if Lena had been standing there.

Indeed, she had been lingering nearby for the past hour, hopefully certain than Ian Haversham's arrival, his robust person, would bring a semblance of lightness to the big quiet house.

Ian greeted the girl soberly, gave her his coat, and then, hearing the rustle of skirts on the stairs, he turned expectantly.

Miranda stood there. Her dark head was high, chin lifted, and mouth firm. She wore a gown of black bombazine with no decoration, sleeves long and full, neck high, but within it her slender body was as erect and proud as ever. Still, as she hurried down, came closer, he saw that the curve of her cheeks, petal-smooth and pale, had hollowed, and shadows lay deep as bruises beneath her golden eyes.

He went toward her, and the usual restraints of courtesy became nothing. He opened his arms wide and swept her into them, hugging her close, hugging her as he would a hurt child, saying softly, "Miranda, I'm sorry. What else is there?" And then, "But all will be well."

She clung to him for a moment, offering wordless thanks, and then, as Reed hurried down, stepped back to smile.

His bronze hair was as tousled as always, she saw. His craggy face was still high-colored. The buttons of his waistcoat were strained, and his coat, too, as if he would any moment burst through his clothes, the power in him not to be confined by mere fabric.

The men clasped hands, and Ian once again felt the bond of sympathy forged with Reed in their previous meetings. The bond that made it possible for him to see, with a sense of alarm, that Reed had changed.

Reed said, "I'm glad you're here, Ian. We thank you for coming," and led the way into the morning room, where he took up the bell and shook it once. "Surely Ian would like a brandy and soda after his long journey."

"I've told Timoshen that we'd have tea," Miranda answered.

"Of course, it shall be tea in that case," Reed answered agreeably.

But after a moment he excused himself without explanation, and Ian wondered if he were off to secure the brandy and soda he had just offered his guest. Reed, Ian thought, would not be the first man who tried to drown his grief in alcohol, if that were so.

When they were alone, Miranda said, "I'm afraid this will be a quiet visit, Ian. Of course Stacy does come often, and Tad, but we don't have the heart to do much."

"But it's better to be busy. And to live as normally as possible," he told her.

"I agree," she said, resolution in her mouth, in the set of her chin. He could not see her eyes for her lids were lowered over them, her black lashes crescents on her cheeks.

That confirmed what he had already sensed. Miranda, even in this pain, would do. She was as stalwart as he had expected her to be. But what of Reed?

Instead of speaking of that, however, he asked, "And how is Stacy?"

Miranda smiled. "She's fine. She has her friends, many activities, but she comes each day to spend a little time with me, or to take me riding on the avenue."

Timoshen brought the tea, still nervous with tray and

service. Miranda poured. She filled three cups and looked expectantly at the door.

When Reed did not return, she said, "Perhaps we should go ahead, Ian," and served him.

He emptied his cup in silence, noticing how tensely she waited for Reed.

When he did rejoin them only a few minutes later, he seemed more relaxed, but that was the only sign that he had taken a solitary drink to assuage a pain that only time itself could blunt.

He asked about Ian's plans and projects, but Ian understood his interest was only a courtesy. When Ian attempted to speak of Reed's affairs, he said dryly, "I've not troubled myself much with business these past three months. I can't concern myself with it."

Ian saw that Miranda's slender white hands dropped to her lap. They carefully smoothed the folds of her gown over her knees, and then carefully pressed pleats into them. Her head was bent, exposing the vulnerable nape of her neck under her thick black hair. There was pain in every line of her body, and strength, too.

He quickly averted his eyes. He had, for a single unguarded instant, felt a longing to seize her, a longing to press his lips to her, to hold her. In that instant he had seen how much she was the woman that matched and met the man that he was.

He was determined to forget that instant, to wipe out the shocking recognition of his passion for her. His life was with Grace. He got to his feet, smiling now. He said, "I hope you'll both forgive me. I'm tired, you know. But tired only of being confined. I must walk and stretch these legs. If you don't mind, I'll go down into Georgetown."

"By all means. We'll speak more later," Reed answered, and left the room as if glad of an excuse to escape.

The impulse to escape had died out of Ian, however. He had no doubt of his control, and seeing Miranda's pale cheeks, he said, "Come with me, Miranda. The air will do you good."

She needed no persuasion. She knew that not only the

air, the walk, would do her good. But time with Ian would do her good as well. She took a light cloak, a veil for her head, and met him at the front door.

They walked slowly, hardly speaking but pleasantly companionable on the streets she had shown him before.

She saw his blue eyes shift and stare, study and fix, and knew that he was absorbing into himself the sense of the streets, of the shops they passed, and the faces, too.

They came upon an unfamiliar lane and took it, and found themselves at the foot of a crumbling clay bank. Above that place there was a house—big, old, and crumbling, too.

There were, sitting on its broken steps, ranks and ranks of children. Small children and large ones. Black-haired ones, and blonds and redheads. Fair-skinned and freckled and swarthy. They were in all colors and shades and shapes. But two things they had in common, Ian noticed; they were all skin and bones, and they were all listless, still, with none of the play of the healthy child in them. He knew immediately what the place was, and what the children were. He knew because he had seen such in London, in every city in England.

He looked at Miranda and saw instead of comprehension in her face a hungry yearning. A pain to which there could be only one answer, for which there could be only one cure.

He said softly, "These are orphans, Miranda. Do you know this place?"

She shook her head, and the black veil fluttered softly against her white cheeks.

"They are in need," he went on. "Do you see the rags they wear? Do you see the bones poke from the skin? Do you notice how quietly they sit, with no toys for playing? And no strength either?"

The hungry yearning burned in her eyes. She said, "Oh, yes, Ian, I see it all."

"Then shall we go in?" he suggested. "Perhaps, were we to discuss it, we might find the means to do what needs to be done."

She threw back her head in a gesture familiar to him, but not yet seen in the hours since his arrival. She said, "Oh, I need no information, Ian. I've already seen what needs to be done."

"And can you find this place again, do you suppose?"

"I'll find it," she promised him. "Don't be afraid that I'll never lose my way."

He allowed himself to be content with that, and went on with her. At the corner of Montgomery Street, he came to a full stop and rocked back on his heels, grinning suddenly.

Two young girls, bright heads wrapped in scarves, stood over a steaming pot.

"What's that?" he demanded.

No reply was required.

One of the girls, seeing his glance, cried, "Hot corn! Buy it here! Buttered, salted, and brought in by mule! Hot corn!"

"Before?" he muttered. "Or after, Miranda?" And, chuckling, he drew her with him. "We must try it."

She had not much appetite, but who could refuse his enthusiasm? They had a cob apiece, dripping butter, and salt and savory, while steam from the pot wreathed their heads with mist.

He had a second, and then, as they turned away, a shrill argument developed between the two girls.

"Give me my share," one screamed.

"Later," the other cried.

"Now. Or I'll never git it! I know you. You think I don't know you? Yesterday I had nothing for all my trouble. So give it here now."

Ian grinned and swung back. He was just in time to separate the two shrieking harpies, for they had lunged at each other, clawing for cheeks and hair.

He held them firmly by the shoulders and shook them into silence, and when they fell sullenly quiet, he demanded, "What's this? You'll drive your business away if you keep on so. Partners mustn't fall out. At least not on the public road."

The smaller and younger cried, "She'll not give me my money!"

The taller and older screamed, "I will, but later."

"Ah, well," Ian said. "I'll settle at least *this* disagreement in my own way." He pressed a second payment into the grubby hands of the smaller, and left both girls staring open-mouthed after him as he led Miranda away.

There had been another lesson for her here, and he wondered if she had learned it. He had his answer.

She said thoughtfully, "This is what becomes of children who have no one to care. They can't even trust each other. And with reason."

Ian was pleased at her understanding. But he didn't know what he had begun that day.

That same evening, he saw once more how little Reed had to say. They lingered alone at the table with brandy and cigars. It was a tense silence. They regarded each other over the tall tapers while Timoshen refilled their glasses, and then withdrew. Reed shrugged away each of Ian's questions, and offered none of his own.

Meanwhile, Miranda, waiting idly in the morning room with her embroidery needle in her hand, wondered if Reed would confide in Ian and relieve himself of the grief that so troubled him. Yet even as she thought of Reed, she remembered the old broken house with its rows of hungry and listless children.

A purple twilight filled the square of the big window until Lena came in to draw the drapes and turn the gas higher, and to light a tall slim lamp at the table beside Miranda.

"Miss Miranda," she scolded, "you oughtn't to work in the dark. It's bad for your eyes and makes lines, too."

"Yes," Miranda agreed briefly.

Lena completed her usual evening chores, but lingered. She did not like to see Miranda sit alone these days, something she did too often. Lena wished she knew what to say, but she had no words left. She had said them all the night little Reedie died, whimpering from behind clenched teeth that she wished it had been she herself rather than Reedie who was taken. Miranda had listened and patted her cheek, and said, "Lena, there's no need for that," and sent her off to bed.

Now Lena heard the men's footsteps in the hall, and asked, relieved, if there was anything else she could do. She was thinking that she would slip down to the gates to see Benjy. If only her mother slept soundly. If her mother did not, there'd be no chance. Abigail didn't approve of her interest in the small gatekeeper. But Abigail was old, and didn't understand. She'd never see that Lena needed somebody to belong to.

But she waited for Miranda to say that there was nothing more that needed doing, and then she made her escape.

Miranda, too, had been relieved to hear the footsteps in the hallway. But later, when she and Reed were alone in their bedroom, she saw the gray of his eyes darken when she said, "Now that Ian's here, we must do something for him, Reed."

His remote gaze touched her. "We can't, Miranda."

"But we can't ignore him either, Reed. He's our guest. And . . . you know that brooding is unhealthy and contagious as well. I'm not thinking of a party. He would hardly expect or want that. But Stacy . . . Tad . . . our good friends. Surely—"

"Whatever you think," he told her. "Whatever you feel you can do."

"I can do what I must do," she answered. And added more gently, "And so can you, Reed. So can you."

NINETEEN

It was a few weeks after Ian's departure.

Stacy sat curled on a couch in her drawing room, her skirts bunched up around her. She nodded emphatically, shaking her chestnut curls as Miranda spoke.

"They need so much. Everything inside and out of that awful place must be replaced," Miranda said urgently. "If you had seen them, the hunger in their tiny faces, the hopelessness . . ."

Stacy thought of Reedie gone, and knew that this feverish intensity of Miranda's was related to that. She gave Miranda a broad, bright smile. "My dear, I need hardly to see them to understand. I'll gladly give you a draft, and you already know that. But I'll give you a suggestion also." She paused, calculating how best to pose this. It was delicate, yet Stacy was convinced she could accomplish an aim here unknown to Miranda. Then, "As you say, there's so much involved. Suppose you do get a bit from me, and from Tad, who'll no doubt accommodate you. And add to that what you give yourself. Still, there must be more." Her eyes narrowed, embers sparkling. "You must do more, seek further. I propose that we make a day of it together. You and I. We'll visit Erna and Dorothea. We'll beard Senator Hollis in his office, and Josiah Hurley, and Congressman Sultz."

"Why, Stacy," Miranda said. "Would you do that for me? To drive all over the city asking for money?"

"For you?" Stacy giggled. "For the orphan children, Miranda. And, as for asking for money . . ." She shrugged her slim shoulders, "Why not? I enjoy receiving it." She rose to her feet, straightening her gown. "I'll order the carriage." She hoped that Miranda would not stop to think that she was in mourning, that crepe still bound the gates of Haversham Square.

But Miranda had already thought of it. She never forgot it, never for an instant. She dismissed the ritual of mourning. This was for Reedie. And she would do it wearing her black, wearing the veiling on her hair. She would do it.

She was at the door before Stacy, and smiling, with a brightness in her eyes.

They began their rounds at Capitol Hill, and were greeted cordially in turn by the various Congressmen they approached. They received moderate contributions, with moderate enthusiasm from each, except for Josiah Hurley. He promised to send a draft within a few days.

Miranda smiled prettily, "And if you forget it, then I'll return to remind you."

He bowed gallantly over her hand and grinned in his beard. He knew that within a few days he would be able to afford a huge contribution to the orphans of Washington. And this would be by courtesy of Reed Haversham. He knew also that Reed was not yet aware of what had occurred. Else surely Miranda would not be on this errand.

Miranda and Stacy, having paused for a light lunch at Willard's Hotel on Stacy's insistence, proceeded to visit Erna and Dorothea, and received a smallish sum from them. They were grateful for it, knowing that these two ladies lived on the memory of wealth rather than on wealth itself.

From Dorothea they also received a suggestion.

She said, "You must go to Obermeyer's. That gambler earns as much as the Mint fabricates. He owes these children something, I'd think."

Stacy crowed, "That's a lovely idea, Dorothea. How did you ever happen to have it?"

Miranda was not so sure that she wanted to go to the gambling palace. Still . . . if these children were to have proper beds, clothes, and food . . .

The fat gambler greeted them charmingly and gave them a substantial check, but his eyes seemed to evade their smiling faces, seemed, to Miranda, to linger nervously on the red damask walls of his private office. He seemed, too, to hurry them out, as if he was troubled to have them there.

Miranda understood, as Obermeyer himself accompanied them to the front door, when she glanced through the velvet drapes into the dim gaming room, and saw Reed standing at a green baize table, blank gray eyes fixed on a slowly turning wheel.

She could not go to him.

Though her body shook beneath her black gown, she continued on the rounds she had set for herself. She listened to Stacy chatter excitedly about their collections, and answered her questions.

Finally, Miranda returned to Haversham Square to find that Reed was not yet at home.

TWENTY

The hand-delivered letter was from the small stock exchange on 19th Street. It arrived only moments after Miranda had gone to talk to Stacy about her plans for the orphanage.

Reed read it carefully and disbelievingly.

It informed him that the huge numbers of Haversham shares he had used as security for his purchase of blocks of Overland Seacoast had, in the past four months, in the months since Reedie's death, decreased in value by half or more. It did not tell him that Josiah and his friends had, through their manipulations, ensured that this would be so, and had accomplished what Josiah had set out to do two years before.

The trestle bridge was ready for use. But hc had overextended himself. Even so, he did not yet know the worst.

He clenched the parchment in his fist and stared blindly at the dueling pistol case on the desk. He had been so certain that he would win. That he would have Haversham Overland Seacoast as his own. His own to present to Miranda. So certain, studying the figures, the lines on the tape as they came in, with a good hot feeling a-boil within him.

He got to his feet, his mouth hard with resolution.

The room had a dingy look he had never noticed before. The windows were fly-specked and uncurtained. The potbellied stove in the corner gave off ugly soot.

The ticker tape clattered uncertainly, and he did not even turn his head to look at it.

The man behind the desk said, unsmiling, "You received the letter then, Mr. Haversham."

"I did," Reed answered. "How much time do I have?"

"Not much."

"Name it," Reed told, him, noting the satisfaction in the man's voice.

"At four o'clock all your shares are forfeit, unless you've provided the difference due."

Reed had examined the figures he had been given. Some thirty thousand dollars was involved. He could raise it, and easily. But not in such a short time. It was not possible to turn land into cash with such speed. But . . .

He said, "I can give you fresh collateral."

The man shook his head. "We require the cash, Mr. Haversham. And perhaps I should point out to you what has happened to Overland Seacoast."

"And what has?"

"It's nothing," the man said. "Nothing."

Reed understood at once. He was wiped out. He had put all the Haversham line into this, and it was gone. But there were these shares, held on margin, still left. If he could cover them . . . "You prefer cash, you say?"

"Mr. Haversham," the man said, unsmiling, "it's all been a game to you, hasn't it? You played the stock market with your own shares and Overland Seacoast the same way you played the roulette wheel. Well, look at it this way. You win some and you lose some. This is the some you didn't win."

A cool wind stirred through the dingy room, and the potbellied stove hissed.

Reed said softly, "Don't enjoy yourself quite so soon, my friend. I haven't lost yet. I've until four o'clock, you said."

He would win it. He knew. He felt the excitement in his blood.

He drank deeply from the glass he held and placed his bets.

The wheel spun, gleaming before his eyes. The silver ball, a bright whirl . . .

The croupier raked his chips away, shrugged, waited until he placed his bets again.

The wheel spun, the silver ball flashed.

He lost, lost again.

Obermeyer accommodatingly cashed a sizable check for him saying, "Just this one, Mr. Haversham. I think your luck isn't good today, though I'm glad to win, of course."

Reed grinned and returned to the wheel. He played, and lost again. He drank, played, lost again.

He stood at the table, gray-faced. He did not stop, even knowing that desperation never wins. He played, lost once more.

Jake Rooker was suddenly at his elbow, saying, "Reed, I wouldn't. No more. This isn't your day. Not here in Johnny Obermeyer's anyway."

Reed ignored the words but nodded a greeting. There was, he was still certain, relief here. Soon he would feel the swift surge of confidence that came from gambling. Soon a hot elation would free him from anguish. He would have his thirty thousand, and he would go back to the place on 19th Street, and he would—

The wheel turned, and the bets were raked in by the blank-faced croupier.

The cash Reed had received from Johnny Obermeyer was gone.

"It's four o'clock," Jake said. "And they say you've been at it for hours. Why don't you quit, man? Why don't you give it a rest?"

Four o'clock, Reed thought. The Haversham Lines were gone. He was destroyed. Destroyed.

Jake said, "I've not seen you for a long time, but I heard what happened. I'm sorry about your boy."

Reed drew a deep pained breath. He glanced sideways at Jake. He saw that the gaunt face was filled out now, the wispy red hair neatly pomaded. He saw the big gold watch that hung on the checked waistcoat. Jake was prosperous now. That was what life was, Reed thought. Men rose. Men fell. Without comment, he turned to go to the bar.

Jake followed after him, determined to exploit what had not been precisely a chance meeting. He had visited Obermeyer's place once a day at the same time for weeks now, determined that sooner or later Reed would turn up there. That assurance had paid off, and he had no intention of wasting it.

He stood at Reed's elbow, drank with him, then sighed, "I like this place all right. But I'll tell you quite frankly that mine's much better."

"Yours?" Reed asked, remembering Jake as that shambling fool who had once worked for John.

"I should explain, I guess, that it's not really mine. Not in the proper sense. But belongs to a friend, which makes it homelike, you know. Bon Chance, down near the canal. Surely you've heard of it, Reed." He added, "Plenty of your group goes there, you know. Even Josiah Hurley."

"I know of the place," Reed answered. "I didn't realize you had an interest in it."

"I don't. As I explained, I'm friendly with the old lady that owns it. And I work there, too, sometimes. A manager, you'd call it, I suppose. I'm here on my own, seeing how things go. For her."

Reed nodded, hardly caring.

Jake knew that but said eagerly, "Listen, why don't you come along with me? I'm going now. I'll introduce you around."

A glint of amusement appeared in Reed's eyes. He had heard that almost patronizing note in Jake's voice. But what did it matter? He would not go home now, to face Miranda, to tell her what had happened.

He had lost the Haversham Lines. He was ruined.

So he went with Jake to the house in Georgetown in a rented hack.

Once there, Jake saw to it that Reed had another drink, made sure that he was comfortably disposed at a table, with a small loan to start him out. Then Jake excused himself, saying he had a few chores to attend to and would be back.

He found Joy in her room, dressed and ready for business, and described Reed by his looks. A tall man with dark wavy hair. Clean-shaven and a bit pale at the moment. And by his clothes: dark, flaring jacket, a silk shirt. Jake sent Joy down with a warning, "And don't push him. He's not that kind. You let him make all the moves. For if you don't you'll lose him, and if you do lose him, you'll be sorrier than you can imagine."

"All right," she said sullenly, tossing the wanton mass of her red hair. "I know how to manage. You don't have to push me, either. I'll hook him in just fine. You can leave it to me."

Reed had a drink with each pot he pulled toward him. Jake saw to it that both were doubles. The two that the house bought to celebrate his next two wins were doubles, too. Extraordinary, his luck had changed. It had changed, but too late. Still, he had four thousand dollars in chips when Joy whispered sweetly, "That's enough for now, dear. Save it for tomorrow. But be sure to play it all here."

He reached to push it on a new square. What if his luck changed? It was well past four o'clock now. And this was a trivial amount when he had lost so much. He would go back to Haversham Square with nothing. And the pull of the spinning wheel continued to hold its charm for him, offering surcease in challenge.

But Joy placed her small warm hand over his. "Please," she said. "I can feel your luck leaving you. I brought it to you, so you should listen to me. Sometimes it's like that. It goes from good to bad."

He agreed with her. It was like that sometimes, he thought with grim irony. When had his luck begun to go from good to bad? His heart clenched within him. It was when Reedie died. But he let that play go by, and found as he straightened up that his head was spinning. The big room was dim.

Joy said, "Why don't you come upstairs with me for a little while? You can count your winnings, and have a rest, and we can talk. Wouldn't it be nice if we had a talk?"

Her hazel eyes glinted at him through her dark lashes, and her red mouth was moist. He knew exactly what she was, and had known it ever since she approached him.

It did not matter. Her room, her company, appealed to him then. Anything that would keep him from having to go home, from having to face the recognition of his inadequacy in Miranda's golden eyes, would have appealed to him then.

Joy went ahead of him, up through the rose-colored shadows of the steps. She swung her hips neatly, trailing a musky scent, a scent that did not remind him of patchouli. She opened a door and went through the tinkling bead curtain, and let it swing back to dance against his cheeks. Her musky scent was stronger here, and the air was warm and sweet.

He found his way to the edge of the bed, a wide triangle of feather puff and satin cover that fit snugly into a corner.

She poured him a drink and put it into his hand, curling her fingers tightly around his, and crouching at his feet while she guided it to his mouth.

The whiskey burned its way down from lips past tongue to throat and on into his chest, where it spread like a liquid fire through his body.

She touched his shoulder and he fell back, and though the pink room spun around him, he knew when she loosened his cravat and opened his shirt and spread small silken hands, warm hands, on his bare chest.

She lay beside him and whispered against his cheek, and some time, though he did not know when, she asked him what troubled him so. What could trouble a fine gentleman like himself? So strong and handsome, and one who wanted for nothing.

When he began to speak it was as if he were thinking to himself, thinking out loud in a dull and wondering tone. He was not sure any more how it had happened, he told her, and himself, too. He had begun his gambling at roulette and ended it in stocks. The railroad was no longer his. The backbone of the Haversham fortune was gone. A desperate man never succeeds. Whatever he touches will turn to dust.

She suggested that perhaps he was not as ruined as he thought, and he groaned, "No, no. It's done."

Jake listened, and smiled, and watched, and smiled. The peephole he had devised long before, that same one through which he had seen Joy hide the tip that should have belonged to him, had become valuable now. He was repaid for his trouble and his foresight, too. There was a moment when he forgot that the man he observed was Reed. Jake called him John Haversham in his mind and heart. Jake repaid him then, in his silent thoughts, with a little smile and a great welling of angry pleasure.

Reed's tired shaken voice failed him at last.

Joy leaned over him, her small hard breasts exposed, to blow out the lamp. She was piqued by his indifference to her. What was he there for, if not to have a go at her? Men who paid for it were rarely indifferent. Besides, he was strong and handsome, and she was rather curious about him. With both professional and personal pride injured, she set herself to arouse him. She sent her light fluttering fingers to tickling and stroking, and grinned into the dark when he reached out and seized her, but her grin quickly faded.

He held her savagely, his hands hard and bruising, and buried his face in her throat and then her breasts. There was no tenderness in him, and she felt none. Only the hard driving anguish of guilt. She reached to kiss him, and he pushed her face aside. He took her quickly, brutally, and she, surprised at her own response, cried out and met him, raking her long nails along his back. He buried himself deep in her and hammered himself on the anvil of her body into the collapse of exhaustion. She had no way of knowing the guilt for which he so punished her and himself. But, as he lay still beside her, she began to consider the ways by which she could bring him back to her again.

Jake went down to Nan, and said, with a small hard grin, "That Joy's just proved herself. We've got him. It was just how I thought, Nan."

Nan leaned on her dimpled elbows and sighed, her black eyes glinting. "Poor man," she said. "Poor man." And then, with a chuckle, "What do you think to do now?"

TWENTY-ONE

Miranda sat in the dusk of the morning room.

Timoshen had just brought her a pot of tea and a plate of thinly sliced bread and butter, a token to tempt her appetite, she knew, that Abigail had hopefully added to the tray.

She smiled her thanks at the thin-faced man, and he handed her a letter on a silver tray.

She saw at once that it was in Ian's hand. She supposed that it was to inform them of his safe arrival home, and she sat holding it, thinking of the good he had somehow managed to do her.

It was he who pointed out the orphans in the yard of that old and broken-down house, and made her see what needed to be done. She had, within days after his departure, spoken to the matron there and seen the children again. It had gripped her heart, filled her with an aching yearning for what could not be. She had known the dizziness of refusal and fought it down. This would be her way of remembering Reedie. To help these abandoned waifs who knew neither love nor care. Today she had begun, and until the moment she saw Reed in the gambling house, it had been a bearable day, a day which taught her that she would, must, survive.

If only Ian had been able to help Reed, too.

She saw him once again in her mind, standing at the gaming table...

She carefully opened the letter from Ian and scanned

the brief words written in huge blue flourishes that had twice torn the paper on which they had been scrawled.

I must tell you, sorrowfully, my cousin, that misfortune has struck our family again. My Grace, pregnant and well enough when I left her, died two days after my arrival at home. My second son died with her. Rory will manage tolerably at his school. I stay now at Haversham Gate in London. I don't attempt yet to make plans. I hope you're both well, and trying to accept God's will. That's what we must all do now. Try to accept.

"Oh, God, dear God," she cried aloud. "Oh, no!"

She sank back in the chair and reread the note, her eyes burning with tears. Poor Ian . . . he was alone.

Alone.

The word echoed from the walls of the house.

She rose, went into the library, then the dining room. She wandered through the emptiness of the lower floor, and then slowly climbed the stairs.

Here, too, there was only stillness, a painful greeting, as she stumbled from room to room.

All whose lives touched John Haversham were doomed. All who knew him were destroyed.

The chilling recognition trailed her when she returned to the morning room to wait for Reed's return. It remained with her, even though she had composed herself, by the time she heard him speak to Timoshen and then heard his footsteps begin very slowly to mount the steps.

She went into the hallway, calling toward his back, "Reed? I have news of Ian. I must speak to you."

But Reed did not turn. He asked, "Now? Is it so important?"

"Now, Reed. And yes, it's important."

He turned and approached her slowly.

She saw that his cravat was askew, his coat wrinkled. His bloodshot eyes did not meet hers, and when he came close, he reeked of whiskey and of some odd musky perfume.

"What is it, Miranda? What do you want? I can't talk to you now."

She did not reply. She went into the morning room, willing that he should follow her, whether he could talk or not. How those words hurt her. Yet they were unimportant in this moment.

He did follow her, and he gently closed the door after him. "What of Ian?"

"It's Grace," she said softly. "Just two days after his arrival at home . . ." Her voice faltered and broke. She passed the letter to him. He leaned against the mantel, his back to her so that she could not see his face.

He read the words carefully and was still.

He could not talk to her, but he could think. Some dark and hideous shade lingered over all of them. Each would know it in turn. At last he said quietly, "So Ian, too, must feel the whip of Haversham misfortune."

The infant girl never known . . . Reedie . . .

His words echoed Miranda's own thoughts, but she would not allow herself or Reed to submit to that. She drew a quick deep breath. "The whip of life," she said firmly. "No more than that. Of life. And certainly not Haversham misfortune. There's no such thing."

Briefly, the memory of John was there between them.

Then Reed answered tiredly, "Call it what you will."

"It doesn't matter what name you put to sorrow, or what the cause is to be." She raised her eyes to his, her lashes beaded with tears held back. "I think we should go to him at once, Reed."

The beauty of her face, her dampened gaze, was like a blow to him. A glimmer crossed his mind of Joy's avid look and wanton hands and hips. He was soiled by her, and had come home to Miranda soiled.

But he said quietly, "I hardly think a visit from us at this time would be suitable, Miranda."

"It would be both suitable and helpful, I'm sure."

"It's impossible," he answered. "You mustn't even consider it. I couldn't get away."

"Ian came to us, Reed," she told him softly. "Couldn't we do the same for him?" She waited, then seeing the veiled and frozen look of Reed's bloodshot eyes, she added, "He left her alone when he came to us. Perhaps, if he hadn't done so . . ."

Reed refused to contemplate what Miranda suggested. He looked away, and said, "I can't go now. Maybe in a few months . . ."

"And why can't you?" she cried. "Is it because you refuse to pull yourself away from the gambling tables?"

"The gambling tables?" he asked dully.

"I saw you today, Reed, with my own eyes. Yes, you, at that place on Connecticut Avenue. I had gone to see Mr. Obermeyer for a contribution to the orphanage, and he gave me one and hurried me out. Because you were there."

"Yes," Reed answered. "I was there."

"And is that what holds you here? You, Reed Haversham."

"No," Reed said, and nothing further.

"That you should sink to such an occupation . . . oh, Reed, Reed, tell me, why do you do it?"

"You liked the baubles I bought you with my winnings, Miranda. You needn't be so contemptuous of the game itself. Only of the losing."

"Baubles?"

"The diamond necklace which you often wear, my dear. The big amber drop on the golden chain. The bracelet—"

"You bought me those with gambling earnings?" she cried. "Is that what you mean?"

"It's just what I mean."

She felt wrung out, bloodless, chilled. She said, "But, Reed, we are Havershams. You're no . . . no riverboat gambler who earns riches in such a manner. I'll not have you think of yourself like that."

"Even if it's so?"

She said quietly, "I shall never wear that jewelry again. Never. Never. Never."

He made a small bow. "I'm sorry. It does become you."

He walked from the room, and she saw that his wide shoulders were slumped, his gait unsteady.

He had been to Johnny Obermeyer's that day. But where else had he been? What else had he done?

She did not know and could not guess, and she would never ask him.

Instead, she brushed away tears. She settled herself at the table to compose a reply to Ian. She sat thinking of Grace, seen only on that brief visit six years before.

At last she put pen to paper to say that she and Reed wished they could be with Ian at this time, that they would, in the future, come if it could be arranged, that they were sorry, and only hoped he would keep himself well and busy and allow time to do the work that it must do. It was virtually the same advice he had given her. She prayed he would accept it.

With the letter done, she sat back. A chill had invaded her body. Her face seemed carved of ice. Even the blood in her veins ran cold as winter sleet.

She looked at the empty hearth, but saw before her eyes Reed's anguished face.

TWENTY-TWO

The saloon was dimly lit and over-warm.

Its only concession to decor was a strategically placed potted plant, its wide leaves making a small alcove of darkness.

It was filled to its swinging doors with the eight o'clock drinking crowd.

Reed sat in the shadows. He had wandered in off the street hours earlier, exhausted by a miles-long prowl through the misty city. He stayed when he saw how unlikely a place it would be for him to be seen by anyone he knew.

There was some relief in anonymity. He need force no smiles, make no pretense to pleasantness, nor engage in empty conversation. He could devote himself to the reexamination of what had happened. He could study it over in uninterrupted silence, applying thought to it as a tongue is applied to an aching tooth.

Step by step, he considered. Josiah Hurley . . . the Haversham shares required to have the trestle bridge built by government funds. Overland Seacoast's interest . . . His own determination to acquire Overland Seacoast . . . The manner in which the price of its shares rose and fell as he accumulated them . . . The risks he had taken, gambling that he could recover, and always successful . . . And then the months after Reedie's death when he had forgotten Overland Seacoast, and the red brick house on 19th Street, and all else beyond his pain . . . The day when he learned that his holdings of Overland stock did not cover the Haversham shares he had used for security . . . The day he had learned that the Haversham Lines were gone . . .

Josiah Hurley . . .

If the name had not already been in his mind, he might not have heard its mention in the murmur of conversation just beyond the shadowed alcove. But he did hear it.

"Josiah Hurley's brought himself back. Have you heard? You've got to give the crusty scoundrel his due, I suppose. I thought Black Friday had finished him for good."

The voice was deep, drawling, and unfamiliar to Reed. He carefully put his glass on the small oak table, then remained still, waiting.

"Three years ago he was on his way out, and there he is now, sitting pretty as you please."

This, too, was an unfamiliar voice, but Reed was curious now. He leaned forward, determined to miss nothing, and the murmured conversation continued.

"I might have made a bit myself. If only I'd known in time. One day the Overland stock was worth nothing, and five days after it was worth a fortune."

"You'd never have been able to buy, my friend. The Senator played the price of those shares up and down the way a puppeteer dances his dolls. And if you'd bought in those days when the price was down, you'd have had nothing. Overland Seacoast was nothing but paper until it acquired the Haversham Lines."

"Then John Haversham is turning in his grave, if he knows."

"If he knows," came the reply.

Josiah Hurley . . .

Reed got to his feet, and by the time he was out of his chair, he had forgotten the murmured voices and remembered only their words.

The men who had uttered them stared after him as he shouldered his way through the crowd and left the saloon.

It was dark. A cold misty wind stung his face and pulled at his coat. He paused on the corner, looked both ways along the road. He saw no hacks about.

He walked east along Pennsylvania Avenue toward the gaslit dome of the Capitol, his long legs covering the ground in quick, hungry strides.

Josiah Hurley . . .

He would find the man. He would learn if what he'd heard was true. He'd shake it out of him if need be.

The side entrance on the lower level was open. As he went through it, a cold wind at his back urged him on. On along the long corridor, with the sound of his boots echoing back from marble floors. On with the heat of rage feeding on itself for fuel, spreading within him.

The door was closed, locked.

Josiah Hurley had gone for the day.

Reed went out into the street again, eyed the lights of the Barclay Hotel across the way, and headed for them.

The suite was crowded. There was the tinkle of glasses, the rattle of poker chips. There was the rumble of voices.

Reed scanned the rings of faces. Josiah's was not among them.

The attendant hurried toward him.

"Senator Hurley?"

"He's not here, sir."

Reed went down into the street again. Now he walked west along Pennsylvania Avenue. Gigs and hacks for hire rattled by, but he no longer thought to ride. He walked through the dark in dogged pursuit of Josiah Hurley.

At Willard's Hotel, there was warmth, light, soft laughter. The air was perfumed with the sweetness of luxury.

Reed breathed it but did not notice.

He paused at the desk, and was told, "The Senator's not in," but went directly to Hurley's apartment. Here, too, the door was closed, locked.

The cold white moon followed him like a watching eye frozen in a scornful wink as he went toward Connecticut Avenue.

Johnny Obermeyer offered the usual courtesies, but with a certain restraint.

Reed brushed by him.

He circled the tables, briefly noting the dark shining wheels, the silver flash of the balls, but carefully examining each intent face that hovered there. None was Josiah Hurley.

It was the same in the bar.

But there, as he had a quick drink that burned his throat, he thought of Bon Chance. Bon Chance . . .

Georgetown Bridge Road was empty and dark except for a candle burning in the window of a small house.

A mule brayed in the night, and a bargeman cursed as Reed knocked at the door.

Nan opened it, peered out at him, then welcomed him in.

The moment he stepped into the dim light of the foyer, she was sorry. There was something in his gray eyes tonight that spelled trouble. She nodded her head, agreeing with herself, and the golden bells at her ears sang out.

But there was nothing to be done.

Before she could speak, he went past her and into the gaming room.

She hurried down the hall to Jake's office.

Reed saw the dark head in profile, the jut of gray-streaked black beard.

Josiah . . .

Reed's hand fell on Josiah's shoulder. It swung Josiah to face him, and held him there.

"You . . . I want to know . . ." His voice was low, hard, hot with the fire that burned within.

Alarm flashed in Josiah's blue eyes. However he said with smooth cordiality, "Why, Reed, how good to see you . . ."

Then Jake was there, moving quickly but surely between the two men. With a hand at the elbows of each, he drew them away from the table and into the hall. "I've a small private room for conversation," he said, and guided them to it.

"Wait," Josiah was saying. "Listen . . ."

But Reed pushed him inside and closed the door as Jake hurried away.

There was a table set up before the heavily draped window. A bottle of whiskey and two small glasses were there. Light flickered from two wall sconces.

The breeze from the partly opened window was colder now. A train whistled as it crossed the new trestle into the city.

Reed heard it and raised his head, a hard grin twisting his mouth. "That's it, Josiah. That's what I want to talk to you about."

The Senator eyed the door anxiously. "Now, Reed, there can be no hard feelings between us. I did only what I had to do."

"Then it's true," Reed said.

Josiah answered hastily, "No, no, not quite. And I don't know what you mean besides."

"You know. Overland Seacoast . . ."

Josiah cast a frightened look at the door, then motioned to the bottle on the table. "Let's have a drink, Reed. Let's talk it over."

"You ruined me," Reed said softly.

"It wasn't a personal thing," Josiah cried. "Be reasonable, man. I was ruined by Black Friday. I have many expenses. Two households. My wife and children in Illinois. My own here. And political expenses as well. You wouldn't believe—"

Reed gave a short laugh. "Oh, I believe that you have expenses."

Josiah hurried on, "As for you, why surely we can work out something."

The house was still now, so quiet that its night sounds became audible. The steps creaked, the walls whispered. The lamps hissed.

"You'll work something out for me?" Reed asked softly.

"Why, of course, man. Why not?" Josiah went on, "But you've no reason for concern. Within months you can restore your fortune. You've an asset, you know, in your clever and beautiful Miranda. Go into the marketplace, and she'll do for you what you can't do for yourself. She will, if you let her. It's what John would have done, you know."

That Reed knew this to be true only made it more unbearable.

Something hot and painful boiled up in him. Boiled up, and then exploded. It moved him on its own volition. It was the same force that had sent him through the city searching for Josiah, but it was at its crest now.

He responded to it mindlessly, with all controls gone.

He leaned forward and swung his doubled fist in a hard slashing blow.

Josiah cried out and threw himself at the door.

But Reed seized him and swung that doubled fist again. It caught Josiah at the side of the neck. He crumpled and fell backwards. He slammed his head on the jutting windowsill on his way to the floor.

Reed dragged him up, held him at the wall, and slammed his fist again and again into Josiah's face.

He wanted to pulverize that face and flesh, to drive away the ugly words and beat them through the broken teeth and into the convulsing throat.

Josiah made a small choking sound. His eyes widened within slit flesh that spilled blood down his swelling cheeks. His head tipped forward. As Reed let him go, he sagged to the floor.

Reed stood over him, fists clenched, waiting for him to move, to rise.

But Josiah did not rise.

His body was still. His torn face shrank above his beard.

There passed several long, heart-pounding moments before the mists of rage receded, and Reed's mind cleared, and he realized that Josiah Hurley was dead.

TWENTY-THREE

Reed stood hunched over Josiah's body.

He did not know that Jake, having been engaged in one of his favorite pastimes, had seen all of what had happened. He did not know that Jake, with his lips parted in a soundless whistle, now withdrew his eye from the peephole and crossed the adjacent room as silently and as quickly as a shadow.

Within the instant, the door behind Reed opened only inches, then immediately closed.

The gaslight jumped higher, flickered, sank lower, and then a floorboard creaked.

Reed heard the sound but could not move.

He was frozen in shocked disbelief. His mind was too paralyzed for thought.

Jake came close, then closer, but with movements both brisk and cautious. Finally he knelt beside Josiah, touching his temple lightly.

Reed's legs weakened under him. He staggered and fell into a chair. His collapsing weight moved the chair inches, and it struck the table. The lamp rocked, and great black shadows raced up the walls and then subsided in a dark wave.

"What happened?" Jake asked in a quiet voice.

Reed was breathing hard. A sheen of sweat covered the gray pallor of his face. He gasped, as out of breath as if he had run ten miles, "We had words. I hit him. I didn't realize . . ."

He found that he could not go on. He could not put the horror into words.

Jake understood. He told Reed, "You *do* realize now, though."

Reed nodded slowly.

"A fine mess," Jake said. "Mrs. Cunningham will be fit to be tied. And I can't say as I blame her. You know what it does to a place once the word gets out. You know what happens. And this is the first trouble she's ever had. The first, mind you, in all this time."

Reed's long body shook with a muscle-tearing shudder. His mind was full of Miranda now. She would be waiting for him, wondering. She would have to hear what he had done. He got to his feet.

Jake said, thinking quickly, planning, "Better sit down again. Have a drink and wait right here. I'll see to the rest."

He didn't wait for Reed to agree. He went out and told Nan to get everyone in the house behind closed doors and keep them there until he gave the word. She understood quickly enough and said she would do it, small eyes burning with curiosity. He returned to Reed then, and said, "Go out front and get Josiah's gig. Lead it. Be quick and quiet about it, too, and attract no attention if you can help it. Lead it around to the back. You'll find a yard. I'll have the gate open for you. Tie up. And then come through. I'll probably need some help."

Reed followed the directions numbly. He found the gig and took it down a side alley, pulling the horse by its bridle to the rear of Bon Chance. He tied it there and stumbled through the blackness of the debris-laden yard.

Jake was waiting at the back door. "I thought right. I can't manage it alone. Come on."

Reed followed him into the nightmare room.

Between them, he and Jake raised up Josiah and walked him down the dark hall, his body limp and heavy in their bracing arms.

A door cracked open somewhere. A flicker of gaslight wavered on the wall.

Jake said, laughing loudly and harshly, "Well, there,

Josiah, you've surely got yourself a load on. Are you fit to drive the gig, do you think?"

And then, after a smallish pause, he hacked, and mumbled an answer, "Of course, Jake. Don't be a fool!"

Reed heard, and was sickened. His gorge rose, and there was more cold sweat on his brow. But he did not protest.

"Come along," Jake laughed. "No Mary Bennett for you this evening. And we've not got all night to settle you down. You hop in your gig, and get yourself to bed. I, myself, will see that Mr. Haversham gets back to Haversham Square."

The still body lolled between them. The broken head jerked from side to side, while the mouth hung open within the beard.

The back door slammed hard, and Jake's good-natured laughter became a hoarse whisper. "All right now. Let's get it done fast."

"What done?" Reed asked, still bound in uncomprehending numbness.

"You'll see."

They got the limp body into the gig. Jake took the reins, and at his direction, Reed walked alongside.

Jake guided the snorting and nervous horse down the alley, down the lane toward the canal.

A bugle trumpeted, and a lock-keeper yelled. Otherwise there was utter silence. The cold white of the half moon was still a watching eye, and part of the sky was black with heavy clouds. The air here was sour.

Jake stopped the gig at canalside. He looked long and carefully in all directions. He cocked his head to listen, his mouth slanting in a faint smile that showed his teeth. Then, with a muted grunt, he reached up and pushed the body from the gig. It fell flat on its back in the dirt and dung.

He stood back and surveyed the scene for a long moment.

Reed made an incoherent sound deep in his throat, and staggered and turned away.

But Jake caught his arm and held him. "Not yet. I'm not through yet."

Reed gave him a dazed and bewildered look, but soon knew what Jake meant.

Jake caught the unwilling horse by its bridle. He forced it, snorting and dancing, toward the prone body and then over it, and then the gig wheels followed.

Once, twice, three times, he led horse and gig to the frozen body, over it, and then back again. Once, twice, three times the sharp hooves beat down and the wheels ground.

A single hoof crushed Josiah's rib cage. A single wheel ripped his ear away. His jaw was smashed. A blue eye stared from his shredded beard. His face was gone into a red jelly.

Reed's gorge rose and overwhelmed him. He turned away and vomited into the canal. He vomited from his stomach and his heart, still hearing the faint creak of the gig, the snorts of the horse, the pulpy resistance of what had once been Josiah Hurley to the weight that pounded it into the dust.

Sweating, shaking, he turned back in time to see Jake survey the scene again. Then he slapped the horse's rump hard, and as it bucked and galloped away, the gig banged violently along behind it.

Jake turned to give Reed a narrow look. "Now it's time for us to go."

"Look," the small boy said. "Look, Pa, there's blood. An awful lot of blood."

"Jesus, Mother of God!" his father whispered. He pulled the boy to him, hid the young face against his chest. "Mother of God!"

Josiah lay where he had fallen and been crushed into the dirt, tall black silk hat to one side of him, his coattails spread around him like a dirty ruff.

The mules plodded past him, but shied and brayed, and the hawsers tightened, and the barge slammed sideways into the canal wall and dragged along it until the bargeman, swearing, released his son and gave the team a taste of the whip, while he stared, leaning forward to squint now at the thing on the towpath.

He said nothing to his small son, but when he reached Lock Three, instead of signaling he made fast and climbed up and had a few words with the keeper, and a little later a horse and rider went pounding into Georgetown.

Reed was still lying abed when Tad arrived, looking somber and wishing that he had not had to perform this errand. But he knew that the news would be in the Washington *Star* and in the *Gazette*. He had seen their men industriously examining the place where Josiah's body had been found. He had heard their eager conversation. He considered that Miranda and Reed should learn of the Senator's death, not by accidental reading of it but more directly than that.

He paced the library anxiously while Timoshen went to announce his presence, and hoped it would be Reed, and Reed alone, who came down.

Instead it was Miranda. She looked tired, he thought, tired, yes, but so beautiful that it seemed sinful to place anything sad or sordid before her.

He drew a deep breath. He had to do what he had come to do. There was no backing away from it. He told her, as gently as he knew how, of what had happened.

She listened, very still, her slender hands clasped in her lap. At last when he had finished, she said, "Oh, Tad, how terrible. How could such a thing be?"

"We none of us know, Miranda." He got to his feet. "I must go now. Give my regards to Reed."

"I will, of course." She hesitated. Then, "Do you yet know about the services, Tad?"

"Not yet. But I'll send you word," he promised.

When he had gone, she went upstairs.

Reed would have to be told at once.

She found him up, dressed in boots and habit. He stood at the window, hands clasped behind his back into a single big fist.

She went and stood beside him, stood close enough so that he could feel her warmth and her love, and looked up into his face while she repeated to him what Tad had said.

Reed's silver eyes darkened. He shook his head slowly from side to side in disbelief. "The way things happen," he said gruffly, while his heart quaked in his chest. "Who can imagine it, Miranda?"

By the bright light of day he saw clearly his error. He ought to have gone for the police. He ought to have claimed that he had struck in self-defense. For that was what it had been. Defense of what was his, and stolen away. Defense of Miranda, who was a part of him. But it was too late now. He was bound in this complicity to Jake Rooker.

By the next morning he had such a fever as he had not had for years.

He was in bed when the memorial services for Josiah Hurley were read on the floor of Congress. He was still in bed when the coffin, seen off by a small group of mourners, was shipped west for burial by Mrs. Hurley.

Miranda attended both ceremonials with Tad and Stacy, and at both of them, she saw a sober-faced and well-dressed Jake Rooker wearing a mourning band on his arm.

Jake, returning to Bon Chance from the train depot, dropped his round black hat on the table and unbuttoned his black coat, and lit up a Cuban cigar. He smiled through thick plumes of blue smoke when Nan brought him a whiskey.

"How was it?" she asked.

"Just what you'd expect. A lot of pious lies, and no tears."

"I wouldn't know what to expect," she retorted, a curious light in her small black eyes. "How could I? When I don't know what happened."

"Who does?" Jake shrugged.

"Somebody must." She went to the mantel. She ran a fat finger over the plaster statue of the nude woman, then of the nude man. She touched the three see no evil, hear no evil, speak no evil monkeys, and muttered under her breath that Dessie had better get busy with the dust rag or she'd get what for. Then, folding her hands in a prayer-like gesture against her melon breasts, she turned back to Jake. "He was here when Reed Haversham came in with blood in his eye."

Jake shrugged. He leaned back in the red plush chair and stretched out his long legs. His shallow eyes studied the shine of his boots.

"And that's why I went and got you. Because I saw the blood in Reed Haversham's eyes."

"So what? They had a talk, some drinks together. They hit Josiah pretty hard, as happens sometimes. That's why Reed and I took him out to the gig and sent him on his way." Jake paused, then added, "A man's a fool who drinks more than he can hold."

Nan grinned, "And a Senator, too. But what I keep thinking is, what happened after that?"

She knew that Jake was up to something. He couldn't fool her. She was determined to know what it was. Not that she would spoil it, whatever it was, for him. Just that she would like to know. As a matter of satisfaction.

"So would a lot of people like to know what happened after he went on his way," Jake told her. "But they don't."

"Still, Reed and Josiah did start out together, off down the hall, with the usual loud noises, and you helping, so why—"

She had the feeling that if she kept thinking about it, recalling the scene in her mind, she would learn something from it. She had heard Josiah Hurley talking . . . hadn't she?

Jake was saying, "Reed saw Josiah wasn't fit to drive too far and decided to save him the traveling extra."

"Was he at the Capitol Building yesterday? Was he at the depot today?"

"He has a fever," Jake said, unable to repress the smile that curled his mouth. "I expect he caught it on his walk home from here. But Miranda was there all right."

"Ah," Nan said. "Our Miranda was, was she?"

But Jake had had enough. He had been careful that no one in the house guessed what had happened. It was why he had sent Nan and Joy up to their rooms, and then required that he and Reed go through the mockery of assist-

ing a dead man from the house. Nan, of course, would
have peered out and listened. She would have seen what
she was intended to see. But she already knew more than
she needed to of his affairs. He said now, to divert her,
"Nan, I think you'd better go over the books once again.
I believe you're doing a deal on me."

She opened her mouth to protest, and then shut it hard
enough to make her teeth click noisily. She stared at him.

"You'd be sorry," he said, "if I caught you at it, Nan."

She unfolded her hands and planted them on her wide
hips. She shook her head so vehemently that the gold bells
at her ears sang loudly but without tune. "You know
better, Jake. The profits are all there for you to see."

"They'd better be."

"Then do the books yourself from now on. But we're
partners. Just try and remember that. We've been partners
for a long time."

"Oh, I'm remembering." His mouth slanted down. He
hadn't cared what she knew of him when they began together. He'd had nothing to lose then. Now he had a great
deal to lose. And soon he'd have more.

"Partners," she said. "The way we've always been." But
her eyes were narrow and hard, and behind them her
mind worked furiously. There was something here that
she didn't like, that threatened her. But she didn't know
what it was. At last she said, "One thing about Hurley's
dying that way . . . it loses you not one patron, but two."

"How's that?"

"Reed Haversham won't be back. Poor Joy. She'll be
angry when she realizes. She had him all pegged, you
see."

"He'll be back," Jake said comfortably. "And Joy won't
be disappointed."

Nan took a chair at the table and picked up a deck of
cards and examined it, turning first one card then another
between her pudgy fingers. "He's quite a gambler, isn't
he?"

"He has a certain pleasure in it."

"The sort that leads to profit for us, my friend."

"Perhaps," Jake agreed.

She drew a long thin hatpin from under the white collar at her throat, and tested its sharpness against her tongue. It was an unnecessary gesture performed only out of habit. She had kept it well-honed for years as a weapon.

Jake watched her, his eyes narrowed with amusement.

She touched the ace of spades at one corner, the ace of hearts at another. She took up the queen of clubs and touched that, too. "I expect you know what you're doing," she said at last.

When Jake left her, she smiled to herself. He might consider that he had fooled her, and maybe he had in one way. But, in another, he had not. She knew that he was up to something. Something that had to do with Reed Haversham.

In the week after Josiah's death Reed rode down the Georgetown Road. As he passed by the turn into the lane to Bon Chance, he reined in his big black horse and came to a standstill.

He would not wait. He must know. He must begin to live with it. Knowing Jake Rooker, he was certain there would be more. The week just ended had not ended it for him. Josiah's burial had not ended it for him.

He was sweating profusely when he tied up at the hitching post and looked at the blank windows, neatly shuttered in white. A sedate place this, or so it appeared from the street. He shuddered within himself and went to the door.

Nan opened it a crack and peered out, and then, with a grunt, she smiled at him. "You're too early, Mr. Haversham. Hours haven't begun yet, you know."

"Is Jake around?" he asked.

"Why, no. He's over at the Union Hotel, which is his home. But you can come in if you like, and I'll send one of the girls for him. It's only a step or two away, and I know someone who'd be glad to do any errand you want."

Joy. He felt color burn in his face. A sudden overpowering need surged through him, and then quickly withered. "No, thanks," he said. "I'll see Jake another time, I think."

"I'm sorry," she answered in a voice larded with false regret. "But you do understand. We must do our bit of cleaning. To keep the place nice. And the girls must have their bit of rest, too." Her grin was sudden, broad, and lewd. "For the obvious reason."

Some sick evil seemed to flow from her. It reminded him of a cold dawn when creeping across a secured field he had fallen head-first into a stinking cesspool, and thought he was drowning in it until he fought himself free.

He felt the same sour distaste as he nodded and turned away. He had told her he would see Jake another day, but when he passed the Union Hotel, he stopped. He could not wait. He had to see Jake now. He stabled his horse, and went inside.

Jake was still at breakfast, though it was well past noon. He occupied a big round table, near the front window. Near enough, Reed thought, for Jake to have seen his arrival and prepared himself.

There was steak, a huge platter of scrambled eggs shiny with grease, another platter of fried potatoes. There was a pile of hot bread. Small jars of jellies and jams were strewn about. Two large empty bottles of ale provided an inelegant centerpiece.

Jake chewed, nodded, pointed a thumb to a chair. The sun glittered on his gold watch chain, and in his reddish hair.

"I thought I'd come to see you," Reed said, already wishing that he had not, already seeing in the shallow blue eyes that satisfaction which warned him that he had made a gross error, another gross error.

Jake swallowed, wiped his mouth with the back of his hand, and leaned back in his chair. "Have some. There's more than enough. Just help yourself to whatever you want." His grin slanted his mouth. "The funny thing is, when I couldn't pay for it, I had an endless appetite. Now money's no problem, my belly has shrunk. But I expect you've no idea how hungry a man can be."

He himself had a very good idea. He had never forgotten hunger, nor forgotten, either, the day John had first beat him and then fed him.

Reed shook his head, refusing the offer. The sight of the food was repellent, and Jake's manners, too.

Jake asked, "Are you too fancy to eat with me, Reed?"

"I can't afford to be, can I, Jake?"

Jake grinned.

"You know why I came," Reed said finally.

"Do I?" Jake sliced off a large piece of steak, hooked it with his fork, and slapped it onto his plate. He cut it neatly into a small stack of bite-sized pieces, then crammed two into his mouth. Chewing, he said, with a glance around the empty room, "I didn't see you witnessing the eulogies, Reed. I was surprised. That was a mistake, of course. Miranda was there, I know. But still, you should have been."

"I was indisposed," Reed said coldly.

"I expect you were. And with good reason, I know. But you missed the send-off, too."

"It was several days before I was myself again. Only just yesterday in fact."

"But you are now. I'm glad to know that." Jake buttered a thick slice of bread and crammed it into his mouth. When he had swallowed it, he grinned. He was as pleased with the deliberate grossness with which he ate as he was with the flavor of the food. He said, "What we need is a drink. I'll bet you won't say 'no' to that, though you do to anything else I offer you."

"I wouldn't," Reed admitted. "If a waiter were to be found."

"That can be arranged, I assure you." Jake grinned again, then threw back his head, and yelled, "Hey, you in the kitchen, we want some ale in here. Hop to it!"

Reed winced, but said nothing.

"Never fear. It may not be your way, but it works. You'll see."

Reed soon did see. A small blonde girl arrived at a breathless trot to deposit two bottles on the table.

"And a couple of glasses, if you please," Jake ordered. "Mr. Haversham here doesn't drink it straight from the jug the way I do. More's the pity. It might help him if he did."

Reed resisted the urge to rise and walk out. He kept his face blank and noncommittal. He had come here for a reason. Now that he was here he must go ahead with it.

Jake said, "Here's to your good health, Reed," with a glint of amusement in his shallow eyes.

Reed nodded.

Jake leaned back, held a big wooden match to his cigar, and said, "Now then, what did you want?"

"I owed you some thanks," Reed answered slowly.

"Why, that's all right," Jake grinned. "We're good friends, after all. It's almost in the family, you know."

"The girls," Reed said. "Nan Cunningham. What did they see? What did they hear?"

Jake shook his head.

"You're quite certain?"

"You're safe. Nobody knows. Just me. I took care of that."

"How can you be sure?"

"I guess *you* can't be. But *I* can."

"They've none of them mentioned anything? None of them passed a remark when hearing the news?"

Jake replied in an indifferent falsetto, "What a pity! Can you imagine that? Nobody's safe on the street these days, and he was so alive last night! That's how it goes, poor soul." He went on with a wide warm grin, "And you mustn't think of avoiding us after this. We wouldn't like that at all. We must have a game of cards together soon, Reed. And remember, too, there's Joy. She's already been asking after you."

Reed knew he would have been in less danger from the police if he had called for them at once, than he might be from the man who sat before him.

He had thought he would never cross the threshold of Bon Chance again, never hide within the hot arms and hot flesh of Joy again either. But he saw now that he could not stop his visits too abruptly. That would create questions. He must do it gradually. He still believed, then, that he could.

TWENTY-FOUR

Josiah Hurley had hardly been buried in his hometown by his weeping widow when Jake Rooker made his first demand, although it had not been worded so.

He had said, very gently, "You know, Reed, I'm in a tight spot. Do you think you could tide me over?" and named a substantial sum.

Reed studied the shallow blue eyes intently, then answered with caution. "Surely there are better men than me to ask. Even Tad Layton's bank would accommodate you, I think."

"I doubt it. And why should I pay interest when I can ask you?"

Reed hesitated. This was what he knew must come ever since the morning he had gone to see Jake at the Union Hotel.

"Oh, yes, and Joy says to tell you that she misses you. She wonders why you don't come around. Surely, she says, you can't have forgotten her. And she doesn't believe you're superstitious. She meant about what happened."

There was absolutely no inflection in Jake's voice, yet Reed understood the words to be a threat. As Jake meant them to be, of course.

Reed said, "I'll get the money for you, but that's all, Jake. You'd better understand that now. That will be quite all."

Jake gave him a look of injured innocence. "I should hope it's all. I don't expect to get into another bind like this."

That was the first time.

Then there was another.

And another.

Four times in four months, Jake presented to Reed the bill for what had happened to Josiah Hurley in the Bon

438

Chance. Each time the price increased. Each time Reed paid it.

Meanwhile, it was as if an unseen hand guided him unerringly into failure. It had required a heavy sale of land and securities, too, to give Jake what he demanded, but as soon as he prepared to deal, the value of each immediately went down. Which meant that more had to be sold. He turned, in desperation, to the roulette wheel, and found again that luck had deserted him there as well.

Suddenly, frighteningly, there was nothing left.

And then there was Joy. He found himself going back to her. He went, in his shame, for the relief of her admiration and compassion. He could describe to her his losses and know that her eyes would not darken with fear. It meant nothing to her. He could think out loud, and he could be secure, because she could not understand. Nor did she try to. She would simply listen, then run her hand into his shirt and caress his bare chest. She would blow kisses into his ear until he stopped talking, and concentrated all his attention on her pretty tricks.

Her pretty tricks would tempt him into excesses he never imagined, and her wanton pleasure in them always surprised him. It was as if he were two men. One who wallowed in Joy's arms and buried himself in her flesh. And another who belonged body and soul to Miranda, and would scrub his body raw before sharing her bed and lie staring into the darkness of the night, listening to her soft breath and aching with shame. That it could be thus, he would never have believed. That it was thus was just as unbelievable to him.

Miranda sat in the morning room working at her embroidery.

"He's out there," Timoshen said. "And he wants to come in. First he said he wants to see Mister Reed. I told him Mister Reed was out. So then he says he wants to see Miss Miranda, and I told him Mrs. Haversham was busy. Too busy for the likes of him. But he says he wants to see her anyhow."

She carefully set the needle into the fabric, then asked, "Who's out there, Timoshen?"

He said the name as if he disliked it, even disliked the thought of it. "Jake Rooker, that's who."

"Jake Rooker," she repeated softly. "And what does he want? What business has he here?" Her hands were cold now for no reason. She folded them in her lap while Timoshen shook his head from side to side. "All right," she said finally. "Then show him in."

Timoshen was obvious in his disapproval. He stood rooted as if he hadn't heard her. When she smiled faintly and repeated the order, he opened his mouth and then closed it again. He was more than a little afraid of Jake. He backed slowly from the room. Soon he returned, and Jake with him. He ostentatiously remained at the door until Jake grinned at him, and Miranda said, "Thank you, Timoshen. That will be all."

Then he just as ostentatiously left the door wide open as he withdrew.

"It's been a long time, Miranda," Jake said, crossing the room to her.

He carried in hand a low round bowler with a curled brim and narrow black ribbon. It was pearl-gray, a velvety fabric. His suit was the same color, of fine and obviously expensive wool, the jacket waist-length and falling in square tails at the back. The trousers were fashionably narrowed. His shirt was white under his double-breasted waistcoat, and his cravat was a neat black bow.

He stood still under her slow, unresponsive scrutiny, and guessed that she must think he had come very far indeed.

At last she said, "Yes, it has been a long time." But she thought if she had never seen Jake Rooker again, it would have been sooner than she desired. She looked into his shallow eyes, and asked, "What do you want here?"

"Why, I came to see Reed on a bit of business, and when I found him gone from home, I was so tempted to see you that I could not forgo the pleasure."

"What business?" Her breath was quickened by uneasiness. His effrontery in coming to Haversham Square, in asking to see Reed, to see her, troubled her.

The Havershams must have nothing to do with Jake Rooker. Nothing. She remained undeceived by his fine clothes, his pomaded hair. He meant danger to her and to hers.

"I think you must ask Reed," he was saying. "It's his affair to tell you."

"We have no secrets," she said sharply.

"Oh, is that so?" Jake asked. He grinned deliberately. "Then you're a very rare couple, aren't you?"

"We are," she retorted, still sharp, and knowing that she lied. Much as she loved him, Reed was more and more estranged from her these days.

Jake straightened and looked approvingly around the morning room. "It's all changed, isn't it? You've done a job on the old place. I like it. I approve. You've got good taste, and I always thought so. I'll say that for you."

"Thank you." Her voice was dry. Though she would not permit herself to ask again what business Reed could have with Jake Rooker, her mind was completely occupied with that question.

Jake said, "And what about the study upstairs? John's room? Is that all changed, too?"

She said nothing to that.

"It's almost like old times. My being here again. It gives me a funny feeling," he told her. "But it's good, too. I like it. I like this house. I always have, you know. And now, with the extra rooms you put on, and the plantings, and your own sweet touch, of course, I must say I like it better than ever."

She still did not respond.

"Yes. Almost like old times," he mused. "Except, of course, that John is dead."

She stiffened and flashed Jake a cold look. It crossed her mind that if John were to walk now into this room, Jake would leap to his feet and shuffle and look hangdog. Or would eight years have changed that?

"Sorry," he grinned. "I didn't mean to rake up old troubles. No need to do that, is there, when there are plenty of new ones." He saw her eyes narrow and her hands clench her skirt. The blue sapphire she wore winked a warning signal at him. He knew that if he went too far, she would be on her feet, ringing for Timoshen, who would be delighted to show him the door.

"What are you talking about?" she demanded.

He would have liked to have said again, "Ask Reed," but he deliberately pretended to misunderstand. "John. You know. Your cousin John Haversham. Reed's older brother. The one who first brought you here. The one who—"

"That will do," she said forcefully. "We needn't speak of that." She had the sense of a chill in the air, even though there was a fire in the grate.

He was saying, "That's what's so fine about you, Miranda. You stay the same, except that you get prettier. Yes, that's right. Prettier. Though it would hardly seem possible. And the same fire is still in you, too. I always liked that fire, you know."

She rose to her feet in a quick lithe movement, her skirts falling smoothly from her hips, her bustle high-curved at the back. Plainly her body was what it had been when he first saw her, and her face was, too, except perhaps for some new strengthening of the tilt of her chin. She went to the door, and said, "I'll tell Reed that you visited."

Jake rose, his mouth slanted in mockery, his thoughts full of Joy and Reed together, though he said in a mild voice, "You still don't like me, do you? Though you should. I never harmed you, Miranda."

She said angrily, "I remember everything about you, Jake Rooker."

"Remember, yes," he agreed. "But that's from a long time ago. You don't know me now."

"I don't want to," she retorted. "I've no reason to. Please leave. Reed will be in touch with you, I suppose."

Jake gave her a long, unsmiling look out of shallow eyes. "Oh, I suppose he will." Then, "You're still playing the queen of the realm. You, old Tom Jervis' daughter. Well, I guess that's all right. You look the part, and you talk the part, and you're no lower born than some others doing the same. It's all right for now at least."

He made her a small bow and went into the hallway.

She stood at the door, her slender body rigid, listening as he spoke to Timoshen and watching as he cast an admiring eye upward at the chandelier.

She did not relax until the doors closed behind him.

What business did Reed have with Jake Rooker? she asked herself. What business could he possibly have with that man?

When Reed returned home, she was waiting.

She allowed Timoshen to serve tea and small sandwiches, and, restraining her impatience, she filled the cups and passed the plates.

Then she said bluntly, "Jake Rooker was here an hour ago," and saw Reed stiffen. "He said he had some business to discuss with you. I wonder . . . I can hardly believe him, of course." She drew a deep breath. "Reed, what can you be involved in with Jake Rooker?"

Reed hesitated, then asked, "Why, Miranda, what did he say to you? You're white as a sheet."

"You've not answered me, Reed." She sounded calm, but she was suddenly frightened. She saw a lack of candor in his gray eyes. She saw the yellow tinge in his face.

"I don't understand, love. What was the question?" He tried to keep the shame from showing, to mask his horror. Jake here in this house, alone with Miranda. Saying what? What?

She saw that, too, and her fear deepened, and at the same time, her heart went out to him. "Reed, he's an evil man. We both know it. Evil as sin itself."

Reed shook his dark head and gave her a small smile. "You're right, of course. But there's no real business with him, Miranda. The man is a natural troublemaker. He can't help himself, I suppose. It's just that . . . well." Reed forced himself to grin now. "I'd better confess it. Though I know you'll be angry. It's only a gambling debt. I gamed with him some and forgot to pay it, and I think he took that as the excuse to come to Haversham Square."

"A gambling debt?" There was contempt in her voice. "You associate with him?"

"It was by accident one day."

She remembered how bitterly they had quarreled the last time gambling was mentioned between them, and wondered if he remembered, too.

But she made no mention of that. She said, "I'll return in a moment," and hurried upstairs.

She found the small box in the back of her chest where she had put it. It held the amber stone on its gold chain, the bracelet, the necklace. All these Reed had given her to celebrate a big win at the wheel, though she hadn't known it then. She had worn none since she learned how she had come by them, and put them away so that she wouldn't remember. Reed had never questioned her about them.

Now she took the box in her hand, and returned to the morning room.

She placed it near him, and said, "Pay your debts to Jake Rooker with these. It seems fitting that you should." Then she went on, "Reed, I don't want him here. Not ever again. I don't want that man in this house."

TWENTY-FIVE

Early the next afternoon Miranda set out on a mission for the orphanage. She was determined to collect five thousand dollars. It was not an untoward goal. She had accomplished much the same on other days.

But peculiarly, for the first time her collecting did not go well. Twice she was refused even the smallest contribution, with expressions of polite regret but no explanations. At Hadley's shop she was subjected to many questions. Just where was this orphanage, Mrs. Haversham? Who ran it? What was the name of the matron?

How many children were dependent on it? Would Mr. Hadley be invited to have a look at it one day, since he had several times made contributions to it? She was pleased to answer the questions, but puzzled, too. Always before her name alone, the Haversham name, had been more than adequate reference.

She was glad when the carriage finally rolled between the tall black gates of Haversham Square. It was good to be home.

When she gave her cloak to Lena, she learned that Mrs. Bannion had arrived somewhat early for the fitting appointment set days before and was already in the sewing room.

Miranda smoothed her wind-tousled hair and hurried upstairs.

There was a fire in the sewing room, and all the wall sconces were lit, and the curtains were closed against the early twilight. But as Miranda slipped into the basted gown with Mrs. Bannion's silent help, the place seemed to lack its accustomed coziness.

Mrs. Bannion worked for some time without speaking. Then suddenly she plucked the pins from her mouth and looked up from where she crouched at Miranda's feet. "Mrs. Haversham, I am . . . I'm very sorry to have to mention it. I know it must be an oversight. But I have no money, you know. I've not been paid. Not for the past month."

"What's that?" Miranda asked. "What do you mean? Why didn't you tell me sooner that you hadn't been paid? I'd no idea of it. I'll remind my husband at once. I can't imagine how this could have occurred, but we'll soon put it right."

She felt the heat of humiliation stain her cheeks. Mrs. Bannion was a poor woman, and dependent on pay for her labors. How could Reed have been so remiss?

Mrs. Bannion breathed a sight of relief. "Oh, would you? If only I could have it . . . or some at least . . . you see, there's my rent . . . I just wouldn't know . . . I did so hate to ask, but—"

"Help me out of this gown," Miranda said quickly. "We'll leave the fitting for another time."

"Oh, there's no hurry," Mrs. Bannion insisted. "No, really, Mrs. Haversham, you mustn't think . . . I'd be very sorry if I've upset you. I never intended . . . but you see . . ."

"Help me, please," Miranda answered, concealing her embarrassment, and what were now the beginnings of alarm. It was so unlike Reed to be uncaring. Why hadn't he paid Mrs. Bannion? He must know as well as she herself that the woman needed the drafts she received for her work in this house. But he had been unlike himself for so long now. She had known that.

She was suddenly frightened, frightened of what he would say and do when she spoke to him.

Mrs. Bannion, clucking protests, unbuttoned the gown, drew it off, and helped Miranda into her green frock. Clucking still, she sat down to wait, her hands folded in her lap, while Miranda went down the stairs to Reed's study.

He was there, his dark head bent over papers. It was a familiar pose. She had lately seen him in that position many times. Yet now there was something ominous in the way he sat. He was plainly not attending to what lay before him.

She said, "Reed, dear, Mrs. Bannion tells me that she has not been paid for a month. You do have her schedule, don't you? I did leave the bills for you, didn't I?"

He regarded her silently, then gave a brief nod.

Now he would have to tell her, confess his failure as a man, as a husband. He could not face it. He had promised himself that he would care for her always. He had promised her that, too. How could he tell her that the fortune John had built was gone?

"Reed?" she was asking. "Have you simply forgotten that poor woman's money? You must know she'll starve without it."

"I'm sorry," he said finally. "I'll give it to you this instant." He drew a draft toward him, a pen. He managed to keep his hand steady as he wrote, knowing all the while that it would drive his bank balance dangerously low, and that he would have to act quickly to replenish it. But there was nothing left with which to accomplish that. Even the jewels Miranda had returned to him were gone, bringing only a pittance compared to what he had paid for them. All that remained to him was Haversham Square.

She accepted the draft and hesitated for a moment. He saw the troubled expression on her face, and it seemed to him that John's name hung unspoken in the air between them once again.

Then she said, "Thank you, Reed. I'll take this to Mrs. Bannion now so that she'll be frightened no longer. I'll be back immediately."

He nodded, and she left him.

Mrs. Bannion mumbled her appreciation, nearly in tears when Miranda put the draft into her hand. They made another appointment, and Mrs. Bannion went down to the cooking quarters to have the dinner Abigail habitually prepared for her.

Miranda returned to the study only to find that Reed had gone.

There was a chill in the room. Night had fallen, and it was dark but for a single gaslight near the cold hearth. Its small flame jumped and flickered, and threw an elongated shadow of her body against the leather-covered bookcases. She lit two more lights. That seemed better somehow. She went briskly to draw the drapes. The window was closed yet she found herself shivering. The cold March wind seemed to blow through the walls from outside.

She rang the bell, and when Lena responded, asked for a fire to warm the room.

Even when it blazed steadily on the hearth, she found that it did not affect the chill in the air. She shivered again, hesitating for a long moment over the desk. At last she sat down in Reed's chair. She pushed aside the mahogany case with its silver engraving and began to examine the papers in the various drawers.

There was a great sheaf of bills of sale. They meant

nothing to her. She was even more bewildered when she examined the red-bound ledgers. She could not follow the entries. But in a bottom drawer, thrust back out of sight, she found a clutch of papers—accounts due, bills, threatening letters. There were months old, from the greengrocer, the wineshops, the butcher, from Hadley's Department Store among others.

Hadley's . . . She remembered how oddly she had been treated there that afternoon when she went to plead for money for the orphanage . . . Her experiences at the other places she had been.

Color flooded her cheeks. Shame filled her like an evil poison. She understood that these people had supposed the collection for the orphans would go into Haversham coffers. They knew they were owed vast sums, and believed she must know it, too.

She sat over the clutch of bills, slowly making sense of the appalling figures, and a new coldness crept over her. What had happened? Why had Reed allowed such a horrendous accumulation of debt?

Tears burned in her eyes, but her mouth was firm as she shuffled the papers neatly together and put them back in the drawer.

TWENTY-SIX

The wind came out of the northwest laying cold whips across the city. The great sloping lawns of Haversham Square lay sere and brown under leaden skies. The air hinted of snow, and smelled of the smoke of firewood and coal and kerosene.

Miranda drew in a deep breath of it as Benjy shut the gate behind her.

These were city odors, and she was well accustomed to them. But she suddenly thought of the cottage in Dealeyton and the groves behind it lying still in a summer sun. She thrust the memory away and set out briskly.

Since the day before, when she had discovered the vast debts that hung over Haversham Square, she had thought of nothing else. She was determined to seek Tad Layton's advice, to learn if he knew what had happened.

She had decided to walk, and though Timoshen had protested, and Lena, too, that she ought not go abroad alone, even at that time of day, she had not heeded them, nor Benjy's reproachful eyes either. Aunt Abigail would have been more difficult to gainsay, but she had been occupied in the cooking quarters and had not seen Miranda leave.

So now she went briskly down the lane beneath the bare sycamore trees, her fur cloak wrapped warmly around her, her hands folded into her muff.

There was a millinery shop, its window crammed to unbelievable proportions with veils, flowers, and plumes, all lightly powdered with the fine dust of the road.

The glass of the barber shop was steamy, and peering through it, she saw that the pale green walls of the place were plastered with pictures of men wearing elaborate beards, elaborate moustaches, and combinations of the two.

A delivery boy darted across her path, and then stopped to grin an apology while struggling with the pack on his back.

She went on. When she reached the corner, three black crows suddenly rose up from the roof of the bank, swooped, cawing wildly into the road, and then set off, cawing still, in the direction from which she had just come.

She refused to think of them as evil omens, but she followed them with her eyes until they were lost to sight in the trees. Then she swept inside the bank.

The hot steamy air seemed unbearable, the odor of ink, and paper, and money distasteful.

The clerk came toward her quickly, smiling a welcome, "Mrs. Haversham, how are you? It's a nippy day, isn't it?"

She agreed that it was, and asked to see Tad Layton. She was immediately taken to his office.

He rose to greet her, his eyes lighting up. "Miranda! I had no idea you intended to visit me. What a pleasant surprise."

"If you're busy, Tad, I'll wait. I don't mean to intrude. But I must have a word with you, if you're able to give me the time."

Once Caroline had come to him here, sat in this same chair beside his desk, and trembled as she gave to him for safekeeping the deeds to her father's land.

Now Miranda sat in that chair. But she sat with chilled composure.

He said, "I always have time for you, my dear. But this is a dismal place. Let's go out. There's a quite pleasant tea shop. Where, I might add, we may have a good coffee, if we please."

"Only if you're certain that you're free to do so, Tad."

"I'm free," he assured her.

He was, in fact, delighted that she had come.

He had only a little while before he had an interview with the widow, Nan Cunningham. There was nothing in that to trouble him. She had, with much sighing, made the last payment on her house. She had received the papers and his congratulations with a simper, saying, "If God cares for widows, Mr. Layton, then you will be blessed, believe me." Why her jowly smile had troubled him, he did not know. But he was pleased to be diverted from the memory. He took his hat, and his fur-trimmed greatcoat from a cupboard, and motioned Miranda ahead of him. He paused while she waited at the door to say a few words to the clerk, who nodded and listened, but smiled sweetly at Miranda past Tad's shoulder.

The tea shop was, as Tad had said, only half a block away, and not overcrowded. When they were settled, and he had ordered coffee for both of them, he smiled at her. "Now then, what is it? Why do you look so serious, and how can I mend it?"

"You can tell me the truth," she said soberly.

Tad's blue eyes became veiled and thoughtful. "I fear I don't quite understand," he said.

"But you must. You know what there is to know of Reed's affairs. The bank handles his accounts."

Tad made a quiet protesting sound.

"Tad, what's happened? Reed is in trouble. Why? Why are there so many bills unpaid?"

Tad sat still as stone. His blue eyes sought first one corner of the room, then another. His hand shook on his beard, and he brought it down to the edge of the table. "I know less of Reed's affairs than you think, Miranda," he said finally. "Have you spoken to him?"

"I've tried, but I've learned nothing."

"Miranda," Tad said gently, "You must know it's very unethical for me to discuss—"

She shook her head firmly. Her amber eyes glowed. "Tad! Don't!"

He forced his gaze away from her face, relieved that the waiter interrupted to serve their coffees, then to present a trayful of *gateaux*. Although she shook her head, he chose one for each of them.

When they were alone, she said, "Tad, I'm sorry. I don't mean to embarrass you. But if you'll not help me, then to whom shall I turn?"

He had been in love with her for a long time. Since then he had ignored all possibilities of marriage. To whom indeed would she turn if he did not help her? He made his decision quickly, knowing her strength and trusting it.

"Miranda," he said, "I don't know everything. I'll tell you what I do know. I gather that Reed has said nothing, nothing to you."

"Nothing," she echoed, leaning forward.

He drew a deep breath. He said slowly, spacing his words as if to soften the blow, "Miranda, some four months back the Haversham Railway Lines were lost."

"Oh no," she gasped. She half rose, then fell back into her chair. She felt the blood rush from her head, and her heart begin a quick drumming. She cried, "Tad! What are you saying? How could it happen?"

"It seems," he answered, "that Reed was attempting to acquire a company known as Overland Seacoast. Its stocks were uncertain. He mortgaged too many of his own, and ended by losing everything."

"I can't believe it! I can't. Reed would never—"

"It's my own opinion that he was victimized," Tad said softly. He thought of Josiah Hurley, but forbore mentioning the dead Senator.

"But the railway was only a part of our holdings," she said. "Even though it was the major part, there must still be—"

Tad answered, "In the past four months, Reed has, for reasons known only to himself, and never discussed with me, sold off virtually all of the Haversham holdings." He looked briefly into her eyes, and then away. The light that burned far behind them was a light that hurt his own. "Miranda, it was all converted into cash money, for what purpose I don't know."

"But why? Why? I must know why, Tad."

"He must have needed it." Then, "You do understand that if money is only spent, then it's soon gone, no matter how much there was to begin with. It either works for you or it is lost. There's no other way."

"That's a banker's explanation," she said quietly. "I don't understand it."

"Capital, money, has no value except what it can do to reproduce itself. If it's not used for that purpose, then it has no value. If it's used for food and drink and shelter it's soon spent, though enjoyed. If it's used to buy things, equipment, buildings, then it increases itself. Once the Haversham Lines were lost, Reed began to sell the capital holdings . . ."

"Then we have at this time nothing working for us?"

He nodded.

"We are bankrupt," she whispered, the full horror of the thought overwhelming her. "Bankrupt, Tad."

He smiled reassuringly and shook his head. "No, Miranda. You forgot. You have Haversham Square and all its acres."

"I'll not give it up," she cried. "I'll not do that. Never. Never."

"I don't think it will come to that, Miranda. I'm sure Reed would never permit it."

"Do you see any way for us to retrieve what is lost?" she asked.

"I'll give you whatever money you need if you find your debts pressing. I don't see that Reed is making an attempt to recover. He never did engage in any actual business dealings. Except this disastrous one with the railway lines."

She said softly, "He felt that he could not deal in John's business, Tad. It was against his nature somehow, though I couldn't understand why."

"Perhaps," Tad agreed.

"And then, after Reedie died . . ." She stopped herself. "It's hard to believe that so much could go so quickly, Tad."

"It would be less hard, if you thought as I do, that Reed has had a great deal of help in disbursing what he once had."

"Help?" She folded her cold fingers into small fists. "What do you mean?"

"Miranda, I see a pattern of sorts. Do you recall that Reed would sell those tracts of land on the Avenue after those squatters appeared at Haversham Square? I tried to dissuade him. I believe that, ill as you were, you did, too."

She nodded, remembering the lost infant girl she had never held in her arms.

"But he was angry at what had occurred. He wouldn't listen to me. Nor, I suppose, to you. In any event, that land, now so valuable, was sold. And I've guilt in that. The first offer was made to me. I mentioned it to you, you recall. It was well before those squatters created that frightening scene at your gate. Since then I've wondered who put out those false broadsides which named Reed. I made careful enquiries. There's no such person as Corcoran Riley in Washington City, and wasn't then."

"There was a deliberate attempt to force Reed to sell?"

He sighed heavily. "It's what's in my mind. Then the railroad . . . And after that . . ."

A malignant presence . . .

The bright promise of her life extinguished . . .

The destiny she had always believed in a lie . . .

Shadows seemed to gather in the corners of the room. She tried to blink them away, to hold them off. But they thickened and grew darker and surged toward her. She could not see. She could not breathe.

Faintly, from far away, she heard Tad cry her name, then shout for the waiter, for smelling salts, for water. She became aware of whispers around her, and staring eyes, and Tad's arm at her shoulder, a support that kept her from falling to the floor.

She struggled and fought the shadows back. She breathed hard of the steamy air. At last her head cleared.

She whispered, "I'm all right, Tad. I'm sorry. I just . . ."

He patted her shoulder. "Rest a moment."

Rest? How could she?

"But I must find out from Reed," she cried. "What has happened? Where did it all go?"

"Don't think of it now. You've had a shock." He saw the glint of determination in her golden eyes. "But remember, there is much you can do, Miranda, together with Reed. The opportunities are there."

She nodded.

"And whatever money you should need . . ."

She smoothed her muff carefully and then looked up at him. "Tad, no. Not for me. But you see, I can't go about collecting funds for the orphanage, and it shall require such a lot. If you could—"

"It's done, Miranda."

She thanked him. As she rose, she suddenly imagined a dark hand hanging over them. A dark hand that moved first one way, then another, unseen, inexplicably evil, and determined to destroy.

She gathered her cloak around her, and said, "I'm grateful you were candid with me."

The waiter bustled over, bent a reproachful eye on the untouched coffee and *gateaux*. Tad apologized by leaving a large tip, and then hurried after Miranda, offering to hail a hack for her.

She refused, saying, "I'll walk back as I walked here."

"But, my dear, are you sure? You've been greatly upset by all this. And it's bitter cold, with snow in the wind."

"I don't mind. And I think well when I'm afoot," she answered.

He stood still, watching her after bidding her goodbye. He saw her tall figure move gracefully through the pedestrians and cross the road, head held high, the ribbons on her hat fluttering around her dark curls like small victory pennants.

He was depressed when he went back to the bank, and he did not work any more that day, although the papers on his desk were piled high and the ledgers required his attention.

Miranda, on her arrival home, stopped in the cooking quarters. She told Abigail that she and Reed would dine in the morning room that evening, with the table set up before the fireplace, and that they would have roast chicken and new potatoes and green peas. The white wine would be chilled, the cream cake iced with chocolate, the coffee black and strong.

She was determined that there be no interruptions and no opportunity for evasion.

She herself set the tall white tapers in their crystal holders and brought in from the conservatory a bowl of orchids. Timoshen had grimaced to see them plucked, for he had grown to love his work there, and considered each of the flowers that bloomed an extension of himself. Now they lay among silken green leaves, glowing richly against the white lace of the cloth.

She had changed to an at-home gown of dark blue broadcloth, decorated only by a row of small velvet bows that lined it from throat to waist, and again on the deep cuffs. A small net with a scattering of the same bows was fastened into her hair. She sat in the chair before the hearth, awaiting Reed's return home. The fullness of her skirt, pleated and puffed at the back into a bustle, would have kept her rigidly upright in any event, but she did not need that support. Her will, and her restrained impatience, held her that way. Her fingers went to the strand of pearls at her throat, and then, as the door opened, dropped quickly to her lap.

"Oh, Reed," she said. "I wondered what had delayed you."

His eyes went to the table, catalogued tapers and flowers, and then moved to her face. "It looks pleasant for such a night. I thought we had some engagement this evening, however. Am I mistaken?"

"You weren't. We did have an engagement with the Hollises. But I sent our apologies."

Uneasiness rang a quick alarm through him. He answered, "However you like, Miranda. It's all one with me."

She saw it was not going to be a matter of cozening him into a pleasant mood and then asking him her pointed questions. She dismissed any further attempt at guile, at womanliness. She drew a deep breath, and said, "Reed, we must talk. I beg you to be open and honest with me, and to trust me."

He did not answer her. He sat down, his body rigid within the soft arms of the chair. He leaned back, waiting. He knew, from the set of her mouth, from the directness of her gaze, that he could not put her off.

She said, and her voice shook on the words, "I learned today that we lost the Haversham Lines some four months ago. I learned it from Tad. Not from you, Reed. From Tad. Why didn't you tell me? Why didn't you explain?"

His hands bunched into fists. He made no response.

She jumped up, crying, "How could you? How could you allow such a terrible thing to happen? And then how could you keep it a secret from me? You promised me, don't you remember? That I would always be a whole part of your life."

"It was a foolish promise," he answered softly. And then, "A bridegroom's promise."

She clasped her arms at her waist, hugging herself. She paced the floor before the hearth. "You must explain now. You must tell me what's gone wrong. And what we're to do."

Again he retreated into silence.

She turned, took a few paces and stood before him, her eyes blazing, "Reed! Reed, I demand that you tell me. Where has it all gone? What has happened?"

"I intend that you live as you deserve," he muttered. "You needn't worry."

"Needn't worry?" she repeated, her voice rising. "Have you gone mad? Needn't worry! There's nothing left. Nothing. The railroad gone. The property, securities, real estate. All of it gone."

He lowered his head, his gray eyes fixed on the small flames licking at the coals. Then he shrugged.

"But that's no answer! We had so much, and only a short time ago. Only months ago."

"We had what John left us," Reed said softly.

"What does it matter where it came from?" she demanded. "Why does it matter? What you had was yours. And now—"

"Now it's gone," he answered, still in a soft voice. "All of it, that John made, it's ours no more."

He thought that were it not for Miranda he would find comfort in the thought. It was good to admit what had always been true. He had always wanted to be free of John's works.

She almost staggered, then gathered herself. "And you're glad. I can see that you're glad! How dare you? How can you be? What will become of us? The railroad lost, the property . . . everything, everything. Those bills in your desk . . . we are bankrupt and you sit in that chair and look at me sadly . . . Reed, I must know the truth."

But he thought he had never wanted the everything she spoke of. There had always been some deep repugnance in him against John's wants and ways. Miranda's wants and ways, too, he supposed. He said quietly, "I think you ought to have married John."

She stood over him. "What madness is this? How can you speak so? If I didn't love you . . . if you weren't my whole heart . . . if you weren't all that matters to me on this earth, would what you do concern me? Would I fear for you? Suffer for you?"

"Yet you've wished always that I emulate John," Reed answered.

She stepped back. She blazed. "He was a man."

He got up, and she thought that he might strike her. She almost wished that he would. Instead he asked quietly, "And does that mean I'm not a man?"

"You must decide that for yourself!" she retorted.

She was pacing again, pacing like some caged animal, and her eyes flashed over her burning cheeks. He thought that she had never looked so beautiful as she did at that moment.

He turned his head stiffly to watch her. There was a pallor in his face, a terrible shadow in his eyes.

She cried, "Reed, I will not allow you to . . ." And her words trailed away as she saw the depth of his torment.

"Don't ask questions of me," he said quietly. "It's enough that you know you'll not go hungry. You'll have Haversham Square."

"But it's not enough! How can it be? I must understand. I must know. We had so much . . . Now . . . now . . ."

Reed's mouth hardened, but there was the terrible sheen of tears held back in his eyes, held back tears of a pain unbearable to him. Even so, he caught her by the shoulders. He shook her head. "Miranda, listen! Listen to me. You insist that I tell you, then I will. But remember, it was you who insisted that you know." He paused to draw breath, to steady his voice, his fingers still biting into her shoulders.

In that instant she remembered that Jake Rooker had come to Haversham Square, had come to see Reed and spoken of business they had together, and that Reed had later named the business as an unpaid gambling debt.

In that instant, she was suddenly certain that Jake Rooker was involved in this.

Reed held her and began haltingly to describe his old dislike of John's ways and means and ends, and then the despair that had filled him after Reedie's death, and the sense he had that he could not do John's work nor walk in his footsteps. The sense that some dark thing inhabited them all, all the Havershams, as it had inhabited John, and that it would destroy them.

She listened, her heart aching for Reed, but she thought that it was not fate that had reached out to destroy him, and her with him. Her fate was otherwise, and his must be, too.

She listened while he told her about Josiah Hurley, and how he had died by Reed's own hand. He described to her how Jake Rooker had presented his bill for services rendered, not once but many times over.

Reed's tired voice faded away, "And so we've come to this."

"Jake Rooker," she said thinly, already knowing what she would do.

Reed let her go, but now she took him into her arms and held him tight. "Never mind, love. All will be well for us again. You'll see. All will be well," she promised him, and she rocked him in her arms as if he were a frightened child.

TWENTY-SEVEN

The next morning, when Miranda stepped out of doors, snow muffled the world, made its pulse soundless, made it secret and strange. The bare limbs of the trees at the driveway wore long ribbons of white where thick flakes had clung to them, and the driveway itself had disappeared under a wind-ruffled counterpane.

A small gray squirrel burrowed through the round white cone that hid a shrub and raced toward her, leaving tiny prints behind. It came straight to the steps and chattered and bowed, its arched tail looped high, its beady black eyes gleaming. Then the carriage wheels rattled at the side of the house, and the squirrel went streaking away.

Timoshen came down and opened the door.

She lifted her heavy brown skirt and put a foot on the step. "Timoshen, I want to go where I can find Jake Rooker."

He slanted a faintly embarrassed smile across her shoulders, shrugged, but did not answer her.

"You must know," she said softly. "You've taken Mister Reed to him. I know that. So please . . ."

"No, I haven't. At least not lately. He mostly rides out alone, you know. And I don't know where he goes. It's not my business to—"

"Timoshen," she said very firmly.

He sighed audibly. He was both disapproving and afraid. He was not sure that he knew why. He was sure that he could not take Miranda Haversham to the place now called Bon Chance. Finally he said, "I could drive you to where Jake Rooker lives. The Union Hotel on Georgetown Bridge Road. Maybe you know the place. Would that do you?"

"If he's there it'll do me. If not, then not."

"We can see," Timoshen offered hopelessly. For he knew Miranda well. When she had that set to her mouth, nothing would turn her back. If he dared, he would pretend he was ill, let himself fall over and wail. But he knew that she would instantly see through him, and order him up with a flash of golden eyes. She was not a woman to be fooled, not unless she allowed herself to be. This morning she would not allow herself to be.

She had meanwhile swung herself into the carriage, ignoring the folded buffalo robe on the seat as if she didn't feel the bite of the cold. He reached in and opened it and spread it over her knees before taking his place.

She looked back as the gates shut behind, and the carriage jolted into the silent lane. The ivy leaves were shrunken and curled, winter-touched and lightly veiled with white. The great lawns rose like smooth round clouds toward the rim of the house just barely visible through the leafless trees. She had thought of it, always, since the first day she saw it, as the most beautiful place in the world. As her own place, and where she belonged.

Now she turned away, and sank back, a worm of nausea

moving within her. She swallowed hard, and breathed deeply, fighting it down.

She supposed that Timoshen would insist that his slow pace was due to the difficult road. She knew it was an expression of unwillingness. He did not want to take her to the Union Hotel. Well, neither did she want to go there. But she would, she told herself grimly. She would allow nothing to stop her. She would go to the ends of the earth, to Hell even, to find Jake Rooker now.

They passed the snow-lined cottage on Prospect Street, and went on. Beyond a split-rail fence at the corner, a great mound of snow in a lot reared up, and developed black markings, and gave out a great doleful moo, which was immediately answered by the cackle of an unseen chicken.

Here there were two new houses, large ones, with mansard roofs and much decoration. They seemed unsuited to this street, raw and unfinished, so close to what was old and well-aged, seasoned and made beautiful by time.

The shops were just opening. One had a window display of antiques. Skillets and pots of the colonial era. A rocking chair in which a kitten sat. A small square commode. There was a bustle along the brick sidewalks. Men wielded shovels and brooms and shouted to each other. She saw the marks of their breaths upon the frosty air as ostrich plumes, and watched them rise and waver and fade.

Here and there a gaslight winked out suddenly, and a dog slinked from one barrel of garbage to another, pausing to bark half-heartedly as the carriage went by.

At the Union Hotel, Timoshen stopped and came back to open the door. He did not offer her help to get down, but instead he said, "I'll go in and see if he's there."

"Make sure," she warned him, and, eyeing the place, decided that it was proper to her errand.

Timoshen nodded. He would like to lie to her, but knew he wouldn't dare. He went inside, and was back in hardly a moment. "They say he's out." The announcement was made with relief.

She gathered her skirts and stepped down into the snow. "Then I shall wait for him."

"Miss Miranda . . ." Timoshen began. "Now, you know—"

"I shall wait."

Timoshen said sadly, "All right, then. You wait here. I guess it's safe enough. And I'll go and find him for you."

"Do you know where to look?" she demanded.

He saw his mistake, and muttered sullenly, "Not exactly. But I'll drive around. There are a few places . . . I maybe might . . ."

"Very well." She turned toward the hotel door, and saw him leap to the carriage seat, then wait for her to go in. She stepped into the steamy foyer, aware instantly of the two drummers who examined her from head to toe with bright-eyed interest. Still, she watched Timoshen start the horses briskly and make for the corner. When he reached it, she went outside and saw him two blocks away within moments and swinging into a certain turn toward the canal.

She knew, with an immediate intuitive assurance that could not be questioned, to what place he was going, and she knew as well that he would return without Jake Rooker, either because the man would simply refuse to come, or because Timoshen would not actually tell him that she was waiting.

She set out immediately, walking quickly. Now she saw nothing of the shops, nor of the people that passed her by. She walked straight by Tad Layton's bank without even a small glance of recognition. She reached a familiar corner and turned down it, and it was as if she were walking backward in time itself.

There were the sounds and the stench from the canal. The snow was already black here with soot, and churned with mud. Here was the first place at which she had inquired on that twilight February evening so long ago.

The Kayhome Arms was just where she remembered it. Timoshen's brown hand was on the gate in the fence. She saw his fingers tighten as she approached him.

"He's just coming out," Timoshen said. "If you'll get into the carriage . . ."

"I'll go into the house," she answered. "He need not trouble himself, now that I'm already here. I knew this place well once, every nook and cranny of it. I can find my way again."

"Miss Miranda! You can't go in *there*. You just can't!"

"But I can, and I shall."

He opened the gate unwillingly, and unwillingly escorted her to the door.

She gave the façade of the house a single glance and saw a drape move at an upper window. She dismissed that. The place was well kept, even better than that. It had a definitely prosperous look. It had even a small brass sign that gave its new name. Bon Chance. Nicely chosen, she thought, with some bitterness. She wished herself the same.

She had left there with never a backward look and barely a thought, expecting not to see the place again. Now she had returned. Once again a worm of nausea moved in her. For a second time, she fought it down by swallowing hard and breathing deeply. She could do what she had to do.

There was no need to touch the doorpull under the discreet sign that somehow reminded her of Haversham Square.

The door opened. Jake Rooker stood before her, his shallow blue eyes hooded, a smile on his mouth.

He said, "You shouldn't be here, Miranda."

"But I am, and I must speak to you."

His smile broadened with open enjoyment. "Then welcome home."

She gave him a cool look. "This isn't my home, and never was. But is it yours now?"

Joy stepped out from a room beyond into the dim hallway. Her red hair hung on her shoulders, giving her heavily painted face an oddly wanton look. She stared long and hard at Miranda, and then made a bored yawning sound.

Miranda did not know the girl's name, but she knew the musky scent that swept over her in a dizzying wave. It had done the same in her own blue and white bedroom at home, coming from Reed's discarded shirts. This was the girl to whose arms she herself had sent him.

Jake was saying, without turning his head, "Leave us alone, can't you?" to Joy, and then to Miranda, "No, it's not my home. But if you want to talk here, we can. I've a small office I use sometimes."

She nodded, and followed him, and behind her the door closed softly, sealing away the pale light from the street.

The room to which he led her had been a small second parlor when the place was called the Kayhome Arms. She remembered that there had been a thin narrow piece of carpet before the hearth, and two old and sprung black horsehair chairs and a scarred settee. There had been two wilted aspidistras on the grimy windowsill. Now it was something else again. The windows were heavily draped, and when he lit the gas sconces on the walls, she saw that the fabric was red velvet, and the thick floor covering red, too. Red, the color of fresh blood. Jake Rooker did himself nicely, and she supposed she knew to whom the bills for this luxury had been sent for payment.

Jake said, "Sit down, Miranda. You're pale. I'll get you some coffee."

She sank into a chair, loosening her cloak, then drawing off her gloves. What this place had been once didn't matter to her. What it was now didn't matter to her either. Although she was sure she knew. She understood why Reed had come here. Aloud she said, "I'll have no coffee, Jake," and damned him for his false solicitude.

He sat behind his desk, and she realized that he was no longer the awkward, gangling youth she remembered. His wispy red hair was neatly combed across his forehead, and his shirt was crisp and white, with a tucked front and starched collar. A small diamond flashed at her from his black cravat and from his hand, also. She had noted his prosperity the last time she had seen him, but now it struck home to her with special force.

"What do you see, Miranda?" he asked, in acknowledgment of her surveying stare.

She drew a deep breath, and answered softly, "I see

before me the man who has brought me and mine to ruin."

"Me?" His shallow eyes were blank and bright. "Don't accuse me of another's crime, Miranda. I had nothing whatever to do with what happened." He had known since Timoshen first spoke to him why Miranda had sought him out. He saw no reason to temporize.

She remembered the terrible April night when torches blazed across the city, and the moon burned red through rain-wet clouds, and the President lay dying, and Jake seized her, his hands unbearably intimate on her body, and she fought him with all her strength. Had that moment given birth to this one?

She fought down a surge of loathing. "Jake," she said, "I know the truth. All of it. You need not lie, or try to. Reed has told me."

"Told you all?" Jake sneered. "What makes you believe so?"

She said, "You've been blackmailing Reed. A tragic accident occurred and you took advantage of it. You've never let go of him, and now he's destroyed, through you. We're all destroyed. There's nothing more to give you."

"Tragic accident? How has it become that? Josiah bilked Reed of the railroad. Reed found out and followed him here, and Reed beat the man to death. Beat him to death, I say. You were never a fool, Miranda. But I begin to wonder if you've changed. How can you make that an accident?"

She said hotly, "Reed lost his head. He was driven to it. You must know that."

"I know I was here," Jake retorted. "I saw Reed. And I have witnesses that'll back me up."

"I know you of old," she said coldly. "You're cunning. You'd know how to suborn witnesses, having done it before."

"It wouldn't be necessary this time," he answered.

She waved that aside. "Then, even now, you still threaten him, Jake? Even now, when there's nothing left?"

"Maybe not," Jake said.

"And what do you mean by that?"

"I think I'm able to see what's in your mind, Miranda. You consider going to the authorities to accuse me."

She did not answer. She would neither affirm, nor deny. It had been one among several possibilities that she considered. Reed was, after all, a Haversham. He had a name, a position. He had entertained the chief of police in his home, and dined with Senators, and danced with Senators' wives. Who was Jake Rooker? Who would take his word? But these witnesses he claimed to have, though Reed himself had insisted there were none . . . what of them? And then she thought, Jake Rooker was a man to trust no one. She did not believe in his witnesses.

"If you do go to the authorities," Jake was saying, "it'll be the end of your husband, I assure you. He might have, in spite of the circumstances, gotten away with it, if he'd reported the thing that night. Instead he concealed his crime."

"*You* did that," she flared.

"I merely did a favor to a friend, and I had nothing to do with the killing," he reminded her.

"What do you want?" she asked coldly. "Tell me that much. Now that you have bled us dry, what is there left?"

He considered explaining to her that she still had something. He imagined describing what his price would be. But he held himself back. There was only one thing he desired, and he would have it. To forewarn her would not be wise. And he had time. It was on his side. He had that, and his knowledge of Reed as well.

She read malice in his mouth and eyes, and guessed the truth. She gasped, "It's Haversham Square! That's what you want." She rose to her feet, her voice husky with rage. "You'll never have it, Jake. Never. Never. Not as long as I live. I'll not let you. I promise you that."

He rose, stepped around the desk, and grasped her violently by both arms.

But she swept him with a look of contempt and shook herself free of him, and said in a raw whisper, "Jake Rooker, if you ever touch me again I'll kill you. I'll kill you with my own hands."

She turned on her heel and went to the door. She jerked it open, and stepped into the hall. She brushed past the redheaded girl who stood there, arms folded around her beaded kimono, one long white leg revealed in its opening. She did not notice Nan Cunningham, who stood like a thick black stump in the shadow of the stairs.

Timoshen waited outside, his face anxious.

She said, "We'll go back to Haversham Square."

TWENTY-EIGHT

The firelight cast small shadows on Reed's face.

It was that which seemed to make his expression change, not the movements of his muscles nor flesh. It was that which gave him the look of an aged and hollowed skull, eyes gone from their sockets, and sweet lips gone, too.

She had once more carefully considered the possibilities of going to the chief of police, going to all those others who had power and could use it. In the end, she had reluctantly decided that she could not. What was in Jake's hands was irretrievable, and could not be regained. To have the truth known, which would surely happen, would only hurt Reed more.

Now she looked away from his anguished face. She folded her hands together in her lap, and said softly, "Reed, it's no use to keep thinking back. We can speak for a year of how it happened, even of why. But that no longer matters. It can't help us. I've considered carefully. I'm certain that Jake Rooker will not betray you. No matter what he swears, or says, or threatens. He'll not do that, for it would be betraying himself as well. And now he has too much to lose. He didn't before, but he does now. He's become a man of wealth. He sees himself as a gentleman. It's in his manner, his dress. He has that to lose as well. So he can't harm you."

"I studied the law, remember?" Reed asked dryly. "There's no statute of limitations on murder. I know what Jake can do and can't do."

"I'm not talking of the law," she said, struggling to hide impatience. "I'm talking of the man. Of the man Jake Rooker. Believe me, he'll not move any further against you. And you must refuse any demand that he makes. Do not go to him, do not see him, do not speak with him."

"If it weren't for you, it wouldn't matter to me either way."

"But there *is* me," she retorted. "Will you promise me that you'll no longer acknowledge the existence of Jake Rooker?"

"All right, Miranda. I will. For all the good it'll do."

She said quietly, "Reed, I know Tad will help us."

"Miranda!"

"No. I didn't tell him. Don't fear that. No one will ever know from me what happened. But he offered his help, and I refused it. Now I shall accept it." She saw Reed frown, and hurried on, "My love, you should have been candid with him long before this. He's our friend, only one among many, I promise you. He'll help us to recoup."

"It's too late," Reed said.

"It's not too late." Her voice was calm, the words measured, determined. "You've told yourself from the beginning, from the first time that Jake demanded money from you, that it was too late. But it's not so. You paid him to protect me as well as yourself. I understand that. He can't hurt me anymore however. And he'll not hurt you. We can do what we like. Tad promises to give us whatever we need. A loan only, of course. One he can well afford. We'll repay every penny of it. For, with that loan, we can begin to—"

"Begin what, Miranda?" He saw the glow in her amber eyes, the proud lift of her chin. What a woman she was! His heart seemed to turn over in his breast.

"The city is booming," she told him. "There's building

going on everywhere. Why, the Meridian area is being bought up for villas. Tad told me that. We sit and do nothing while all around us opportunities jostle each other."

"John's work," Reed answered softly.

"Not John's!" she cried. "Yours," And added, "Mine, too. We are Havershams."

Reed shrugged, then rose. She saw that his tall lean body was somehow bent, almost hunched at the shoulders. She saw the remoteness in his gray eyes. All brightness was gone, all joy became emptiness, when he was withdrawn from her. She told herself she would fight that, too. And win.

"Reed," she said. "I rely on you. You must help me with this. And you must let me help you. We are together. We are together, Reed. That's more important than anything. What we have lost are things, simply material things. They can be regained. We can do what we will together. Believe me. Trust me."

Reed did not answer. He walked from the room.

She sat before the fire, her hands folded into her gown. Sleet hissed at the window, but she did not listen. She considered and planned, her mind sorting and choosing. The bills must be paid at once. There must be no hint that the Havershams had a financial problem. There must be no whisper, though probably there were already some, that what she did was based on necessity. For men feared such necessity, and drew back from it. They feared failure as if it were a contagious disease, a pox transmitted from the stricken to the well. Once the bills were paid, all the entertaining she had done in the past would stand her in good stead. She could continue, gathering those men who could help Reed, and their wives. She must . . .

Later, when she went up to bed, she saw the door to the old nursery open. It was ajar on darkness.

Her breath choked her breath. She stopped, looked in.

Reed stood just inside, still as stone, frozen there as if he had been able to go no further.

He stood in what had once been Reedie's room, and

now she knew what was in his mind. He dreamed of what might have been.

She gave a small cry and ran to him, and buried her face in his chest, and she knew, as his arms folded around her, that he was weeping, too.

TWENTY-NINE

The Waterford chandelier of Haversham Square threw prisms of light on the white walls of the reception room, and the tall boughs of forsythia Timoshen had brought in that early April morning blazed like ribbons of sun in the corners.

It was three weeks since Miranda had vowed to Reed that they would regain what had once been theirs. Now she surveyed the scene with satisfaction. There was gaiety here, and laughter, and conversation spilled out in swift warm waves from cluster to cluster. Plainly all were of a mind to celebrate the end of winter, to look forward to budding and fruition.

Soon they would separate, and entering their carriages, they would form a caravan and ride out the Canal Road past Jacob's Landing to the place above the river called the Palisades.

She gave Timoshen a signal, and then Reed.

The two men began the shepherding into the carriages, and when the reception room was empty, she joined Reed in the first one.

Settling herself, then glancing back at the bright parasols of the women, the tall hats of the men, she said, sighing, "The sun is beautiful, Reed. Now, if only the weather does hold. And all has arrived and been properly set."

"Surely it'll be ready as you planned." He smiled at her wryly, "But you do make it difficult for yourself, Miranda.

You had all of Haversham Square at your disposal, and you decided you must have the Palisades for a picnic."

"But this is different, you see." She leaned her head back to look up into the pale green clouds of the blooming willows draped above them.

"And is that so important?"

"You know it is."

It did not take them long to leave the city streets and the shops behind, nor to go jolting along the road that paralleled the canal. Then they were in open country, passing only a few small farms, and throwing up a cloud of dust as they climbed to the place she had chosen.

It was all as she imagined it when she made her plans.

Bright throws lay scattered about on the new grass, and long buffet tables covered with matching cloths had been arranged. A fire blazed high in the open pit where the barbecued meats were being prepared.

Reed helped her down from the carriage, and she was swept away, her duties as hostess claiming her.

Later, seeing that all was as it should be—the food fine, the drink plentiful, the white-coated servants attentive—she allowed herself to relax and observe for a moment.

Stacy, gowned brightly in ruffles and frills, moved like a butterfly, swooping and spinning, from one man to another, and each fell in line to trail after her, hoping for a flick of her fan or a touch of her hand. She still displayed the same remarkable languid grace that Miranda had observed in her eight years before. And the men responded to it in the same way.

Reed charmed Mrs. Hollis with his smile and quiet conversation, and Senator Hollis and George Deilion were huddled together near the buffet. That alone was a sight to please her.

She heard Tad speaking of the politics of Washington, and smiled to herself as she moved on.

Erna Barrington and Edward Farnsworth were deep in discussion, and Edward was grinning teasingly under his moustache.

Miranda turned to find George Deilion at her side.

He had made a fortune in gold in California, and come

East from there to make a second fortune in Washington City. He was very tall and rawboned. He had a long black moustache that curved downward around his mouth, and his black hair hung well below his ears, brushing his collar. When she had first met him several years before, he had worn cowman's clothes and high-heeled boots, and an oversized hat, which he often forgot to remove indoors. He had been civilized since then, and now wore a fine suit of broadcloth and very correct linen.

He smiled at her, "A most pleasant affair, Mrs. Haversham. And the barbecued meats are equal to those I've known at home, perhaps even better. You've a gift for making welcome your guests, and for knowing their desires before they know them themselves."

"Why, you've a gift yourself, Mr. Deilion," she answered, her smile brilliant and her golden eyes aglow. "For making a lady feel appreciated, that is. Quite a gift, I think."

"You're never other than appreciated," he told her. "Believe me, I can see that with my own eyes."

"I hear," she said, smiling still, "that you manage to see all."

"At least some," he amended.

She looked down along the meadow. From where they stood on the heights, it was possible to see the river below. It was running white at the narrows, foaming and spraying over the slick black rocks. There would be good fishing on the morrow, she thought, and almost laughed aloud. That knowledge was a remnant of Dealeyton, and country wisdom. Who would have thought any of it remained in her?

"You must tell me what you see," she said, smiling up at George Deilion. Beyond his neatly tailored shoulder she saw that Reed was looking her way. He still spoke to Mrs. Hollis, but his eyes were fixed on Miranda.

He thought, while he spoke of inconsequentials, for that was all he could find to offer blonde Mrs. Hollis, that Miranda was more beautiful than she had ever been. Yes, this afternoon, while she did John's work, she was more beautiful than ever. Bitterness was sour on his tongue. He longed to escape from Mrs. Hollis' hopefully flirtatious gaze, from the backslapping, joyfully successful men with whom he was surrounded.

But he had delivered himself into this nightmare. It had been he who had constructed it. The guilt was all his, and he knew it.

He imagined John at the big desk from which he had ruled, a ruler no longer.

He imagined Josiah Hurley sprawled on the floor, his mouth a hole in his black beard.

The guilt was his that Miranda should smile so sweetly into George Deilion's predatory face, with the sure knowledge that her smile, and a few words, would soon bring to her what she wanted.

Now George Deilion's fingers touched her arm just below the lace of her sleeve, stroked her silken flesh. She did not draw back.

Reed turned sickened eyes away. It was he who had taken from her all that was her right. It should be he who would return it to her.

"Why, Reed," Mrs. Hollis chirped. "I do believe that you're not attending to me."

"Of course I am," he answered. "And I agree, I assure you."

Miranda was saying, "There's been talk, and I suppose I'm not the only one who has heard it, that the land near Meridian Hill will soon be valuable. I have some interest there. Do you suppose you could arrange a purchase for me?"

"If it were done quickly, yes," George Deilion said. "I say that because there is other interest, of course. Speculators, you see. It's necessary to move before the price goes up. Meridian Hill will soon be built over with the loveliest of homes, large and comfortable. There's an influx, you understand, people, like myself, who foresee fortunes to be made. But for you, though, my dear Mrs. Haversham—"

"I, too, believe in moving swiftly, Mr. Deilion. Would tomorrow suit you? If you'll just let me have the details, then my husband and I . . ."

"You'll have them tomorrow by noon. Then it will only be a matter of delivering the binding fee."

"Oh, my cousin Tad Layton will attend to that for us. And the finder's fee as well, of course."

"Then there's certainly no problem. By late afternoon, it will be settled. I hope we shall have a long and favorable relationship in the future."

She ignored the intent look in his dark eyes, the touch of his fingers on her arm. These didn't matter. It was for Reed. Triumph, sweet and heady, swept over her. This much was done. More would be done.

She chatted with George Deilion for a few moments longer, then allowed Stacy to draw her away and to engage her attention.

"Do you know?" Stacy giggled. "Mary Van Eward has found a medication which cures all her aches and pains. It's really quite amusing to see her go at the celery tonic or Hostetter's bitter. It dizzies her head rather quickly."

"Now Stacy . . ." Miranda began.

"And so both drinks should," Stacy cried. "Why, they're three-quarters alcoholic spirits. But never mind. I see you disapprove. What news lately of Ian?"

"Not much, I fear. Just his regrets when I wrote to ask if he would visit soon."

"A pity. I'd like to see him again." Stacy's laugh tinkled. "And besides, I think he could affirm or deny a rumor I've heard. Did you know that Mary Lincoln is supposed to be wandering about Europe, alone and quite mad?"

"Stacy!"

"That's what they say."

"Talk," Miranda answered. "But, if you like, when I write next, I'll inquire if Ian has heard this ridiculous thing."

"I'd sooner ask him myself," Stacy returned.

Finally, with careful effort, Miranda managed to separate herself from Stacy, to approach Reed. She was anxious to tell him about her conversation with George Deilion.

She had now so much to share with him. And this, just

concluded, was the least part of it. Though a major part
of it, too. Her two pieces of news together spelled out the
future. And it was good again. Oh, yes, it was gloriously
good, she thought.

That special radiance that so many had remarked upon
this afternoon, that melting luminousness which she herself
had seen in the cheval glass, had its own cause. She had
been uncertain for weeks, and fearful to affirm or deny,
but the day before, Doctor Porter had made suspicion fact.
Now she would tell Reed only what George Deilion had
promised. It would be a savory for what was to come.
And later, when they were alone, she would tell him the
rest.

But she had no opportunity to speak at all. For he
looked down at her, and said, "Miranda, excuse me. I
must talk to Timoshen for a moment," and walked away.

Her eyes followed him to the edge of the meadow,
watched until he disappeared.

She was to see him no more that afternoon.

He spoke to Timoshen first, and then climbed down the
cliff and sat at the riverbank. He remained there for a long
time, listening to the sounds of merriment that drifted to
him from above. Then he set out for town.

He was an odd sight as he walked along the dusty road.
He was hatless, his dark hair tousled by the spring breeze,
and by the frequent nervous tug of his hand as well. The
carnation in his buttonhole was wilting. His boots were
soon scuffed. His coattails were wrinkled, and his trousers
streaked with dirt.

But Nan Cunningham welcomed him at Bon Chance
when he finally arrived there as if all were just as usual.
There was, on her fat face, neither surprise that he had
returned, nor was there pleasure either.

She simply said, "Hello, Mr. Haversham, will you go
into the parlor? Or are you here to play?" and her black
eyes raked him up and down while she awaited his answer.

"Joy," he said, "Send Joy to me. And whiskey, too."

She nodded. "The parlor then, if you please. I must
see ..."

He followed her in to the chair she indicated, and accepted the whiskey she poured for him.

"It'll be but a moment," she told him.

When she left him, she went to Jake, and said, "You were right as always. Reed Haversham's in there now, asking for Joy. What shall I do?"

"Give him Joy," Jake answered. He went to a cupboard, took out a bottle. "And send this along with the girl. I think he's due a few drinks on the house. Tell her to make certain that he has them, mind you."

Nan tucked the bottle under her fat arm and asked, "And then?"

"Then nothing. Just tell me when he's about to leave her, no matter when that is."

Nan sighed gustily in wordless reproach. Why did he insist that she work in the dark? Why would he not trust her? But when his shallow eyes narrowed on her face, she left him.

He immediately stationed himself at the peephole he had used so often before.

Soon Reed followed Joy into the small dim room. He looked overlarge in that place of doll-sized dressing table and wardrobe.

Joy's hair seemed to blaze about her pouting face. "Oh, but it's been so many weeks, Reed. I didn't understand a bit. I did miss you though. You're my favorite person and always have been. It doesn't seem fair you'd go to somebody else."

"I'd thought never to be here again."

"Well, then, what made you come now? If that's what you feel?"

He did not answer that, but saw in his mind Miranda smiling through the fringe of her long dark lashes into George Deilion's face.

He gestured to the bed. "I don't want to talk. I'm too tired for it, and it's not why I came."

"I like that," she cried. "Aren't we at least to have a drink together? See, Mrs. Nan specially sent it up for you. A welcome-back gift. And I do want to taste it, I assure you. Even if you don't. I'm not bought a drink by the house, not ever, not under any circumstances. They don't give me a thing. So I shan't want to pass it by."

"A drink then," he agreed.

She brought him the glass, and twice refilled it when he had emptied it, though he did not seem to notice that, his mind seemed that far from her and the dim room. Of her own, she sipped, and spilled away what was left. He did not seem to notice that either.

Then, slowly, while he watched, she disrobed, making the game of it that she knew must excite him. But she saw, to her annoyance, when she bent over him, that his eyes were closed.

"Here now? Are you asleep?" she demanded, unbuttoning his shirt and sliding long fingers against his flesh.

"Douse the light," he muttered.

She held back an irritated sigh and turned the jet down.

He watched her walk back to him, swinging her narrow hips seductively. But it was not Joy that he saw move in the dark, nor Joy who joined him on the narrow bed. It was only faceless escape.

She bent to kiss his mouth, and her touch was fire.

He slapped her face away with an open-handed blow that brought tears to her eyes. When she yelped a protest, he caught her by the hair and jerked her head around, and said through his teeth, "Don't do that!"

But her hazel eyes brightened with triumph, and she laughed softly.

He could not bear those bright eyes, nor the gleam of triumph. He could not bear that laughter.

The fire raged through him, its flame his strength and passion.

He turned her, pressed her face into the pillow. He mounted and rode her, stallion-fashion, galloping wildly toward escape. He buried himself in it, buried himself deeply, sinking, drowning in it, and finally into the escape of the temporary death that is sleep.

He awakened much later to renewed laughter.

Joy's mouth was at his ear, and her hand held a drink at his lips.

He swallowed it quickly, fighting down a rising bile, and

got up and dressed. He left silver coins on the table, and did not reply to her when she asked how soon he would return, with her mouth wanton and her eyes hungry.

He was at the downstairs door, giddy now, and wavering on his feet, his eyes burning and a haze of hot drunkenness churning in him, when Jake stopped him, saying, "Come in for a minute, Reed. I'll give you more of a chance than you deserve. If you're smart enough and brave enough to take it, that is."

Reed knew no caution then. Where caution might once have been there was no more than self-hatred and despair. There was the image of Miranda smiling into George Deilion's predatory face, and Joy smiling into his cwn.

He sat sprawling in the chair near Jake's desk, chin on his chest, and stared at the blue-eyed man. "What chance do you give me?"

"We're done, just about. I've all that I want of you," Jake said.

"So?"

"Play a short game with me," Jake answered in a voice hardly more than a whisper. "You can win back all that you gave me. Take my word for it. If you win, I'll hand everything over to you with no argument."

"Why should you want such a game?" Reed asked, but already he felt a flicker of interest, some sense of life suddenly stirring in him.

Jake grinned. "Why would you think? Because I'm a gambler. A gambler at heart. Just as you are."

The flicker of interest was stronger, becoming a blind hope in Reed. But he was still cautious. "I've nothing for stakes, more's the pity."

"Of course you have."

"Then name it, if you're so certain."

"You've something and more than something. You gave a big entertainment this afternoon at the Palisades. The *Gazette* has described what it would be for weeks. Do you think I don't know? And many of your debts have been paid off already. The money came from somewhere, so that's what you have."

Reed closed his eyes. A red flush crept into his face. "It's borrowed from Tad Layton."

"Borrowed, is it? That won't do."

"It won't," Reed answered. But the sense of life in him was stirring harder. If he had a stake . . . if he could find one . . .

Jake asked, "And if you agree, it will all be on the turn of a card? I get it on the high one? Or you do, whichever way chance serves us?"

Now Reed could think only of Miranda. If he were to win everything back she would be free again. She would not need to shame him by doing John's work. It would be as it had been in those golden days that he remembered with such hopeless yearning. He would bind her to him, enchain her within the fragile strands of her silken sash. She would nestle her head against his shoulder, and kiss the fading scars on his arm. He could see her laughing proudly at him, her head high, her slender form so straight, saying, "We are Havershams, Reed."

It was all he could do for her. Suddenly he saw very plainly that he could not lose. He would win. Of course he would. His heart told him so, pounding against his ribs now. His blood, hot and pulsing through his veins, told him so, also. It was fate that he should win. Just as it had been fate that he first know despair before he returned to hope again.

His voice was calm when he asked, "What stakes do you have in mind then?"

"Surely you already know that."

He looked into the shallow eyes, and now, for the first time, he did know. "Haversham Square," he said softly. And then, "Against all that you've bled me of, Jake?"

"And more," Jake said hoarsely. "Even more than that. I'll throw in a piece of land I had from you a long while ago. What's on the Avenue and growing more valuable by the minute. Then you'll have from me everything I've ever had from you."

Reed did not think. Or consider. He did not ask himself what would happen if he should lose, because he knew that he could not lose. He did not ask himself why

Jake desired to play so dangerous a game. He thought he knew. The same fire burned in both of them. That was what Reed believed then.

He could do it after all. For Miranda. He would do it for Miranda.

He nodded.

Jake pushed paper and pen toward him. "Write the note down. The transfer."

He gave Jake a crafty stare. What did the man think he was? "Then you must do the same, Jake."

"I will." Jake took a second pen, a second sheet of paper. His hand moved busily across the page.

Reed read over the words. The land on Pennsylvania Avenue that he had sold away after a fiery night and a terrible loss at Haversham Square. The sums of money. Yes, yes, it was all there. The Haversham fortune nearly intact. He was so enwrapped in the dream of the great gifts he would bring Miranda this night that he wrote the transfer just as Jake directed it. If he lost, then Jake Rooker would win the grounds, the contents, and all of Haversham Square.

"Five out of six?" Jake asked softly.

Reed nodded, his mouth suddenly dry, though his blood beat with the hot promise of victory.

"Here then." Jake drew from the desk six packets of cards. They were wrapped, the seals unbroken. He passed them to Reed, who turned each of them in his hands and then passed them back.

Jake opened one, thinking of Nan and her pin and her adept fat fingers marking the cards. He put the deck down between them. He rose, adjusted the light so its flame leaped high. Then he returned to the desk. "Go on."

Reed drew, and laid the card aside.

Jake drew, glanced at it, and did the same, and then passed Reed the fresh deck.

The gaslight flickered and jumped, and shadows momentarily rushed in from the corners of the room.

A carriage squeaked by outside.

A drunk roared a wordless song.

Six times in silence, each chose a card.

Then it was done.

Jake had Haversham Square.

Reed rose without a word. He stumbled into the chill of the spring night. He noticed neither the scent of lilac nor the stench of the canal. His senses were numbed. He was no longer a man of flesh and blood and bone. He was a lurching mechanical thing, strung together of broken parts. His plodding feet beat out a slow tattoo as he returned to Haversham Square.

There were no carriages in the driveway now. The company would have returned from the picnic, and scattered to its various homes. The house was in darkness, but for a single gaslight burning at the top of the steps.

Miranda would be here. He hoped only that she slept.

He went up slowly, quietly, seeing the shadows gather before and behind him, closing in nearer and tighter.

Dawn broke as he went into his study. The long rectangle of the window became pink between the drapes. The floor became pink, too. It was as if the whole of the place were painted with diluted blood.

A mockingbird sang out its greeting, and a mourning dove cooed, but all around him the house was breathless, still.

It was still, yet he imagined that he heard John's heavy footsteps walking the carpeted stairs, coming now along the hallway. He imagined that John stood in the doorway, his huge body filling the frame, his head thrust forward on his bull neck, his eyes stony, accusing.

When he reached for it with numbed fingers, the mahagony box seemed cool, comforting.

He opened it slowly, and John seemed to nod his agreement, seemed to tell him that this was what he must do.

It was meant to be. Here was the dark legacy left behind in Haversham Square. And here it would end.

He straightened, and the chair creaked under him.

Miranda heard the sound and jumped to her feet. She had been listening with all her strength for Reed's footsteps, listening, waiting, willing him safely home. But she had not known that he was in the house until that instant.

She started for the study, her lace gown fluttering about her ankles.

The noise of the shot caught her in midstep. She hung on its reverberations, paralyzed, unable to move, for the space of a breath.

A second sound, and the dull thud of the dueling pistol against the rug released her.

She screamed, "Reed!" and ran into the hall, and the great distance that was but a few steps seemed endless. Endless those steps that carried her to him.

He lay back in his chair, the white of his shirt stained dark. His eyes were tarnished silver, aged and dull, but wide open.

"Reed!" she gasped. "Oh, no, my Reed!" She reached blindly for the padding behind him, and seized it, and pulled it free. "Reed!"

She made a thick wad of it, and pressed it against the great welling gout of blood that poured from him, and saw it instantly turn dark.

She ripped the flounces from her gown and made a new wad and covered the old one over.

Then his lips moved, and she bent close to him, feeling his faltering breath on her cheek.

"I love you, Miranda." The words were a hoarse whisper, a rattle in his throat. "Forgive me, Miranda. Forgive . . ."

His words faded. His breath was no longer on her cheek.

She caught him up and into her arms, screaming, "No, no. I will not let you go!" but even then she knew that he was dead.

THIRTY

Great wreaths of flowers filled the sunny room. Roses mingled in a profusion of yellow and red and white on the huge hearth above a drift of fallen petals. Lilacs dripped purple and white blossoms on the floor covering. Tulips and lilies and snapdragons mingled their perfume in the still air.

Miranda sat amidst this display, unnoticing and uncaring. It was two weeks after Reed's death and the black of her dress accentuated the pallor of her camellia-smooth skin, and the sheen of her amber eyes, but the small white snood that bound her black curls seemed a defiant gesture, and the set of her mouth was defiant, too.

She would not give way, no matter what effort of will was required. She would not give way.

These were her thoughts now as they had been earlier that morning.

She had passed the cheval glass, and her face caught her eye, and as she turned to look, she saw a faint and shimmering image through sudden tears. It was Caroline's face.

She heard Caroline's soft whisper, *Now, when you look in the glass before you, you don't see what you will see. And even if you could imagine it, which you cannot, you are still unable to imagine what it will lead to. Ten years take their toll, and you will learn how it matters by and by.*

Miranda turned away, saying fiercely, I will not give way.

Now Stacy, who had moved in within the same hour that she had heard the news, took a restless path around the room.

It was she, with Tad, who had made most of the arrangements, she who had sent an unknowing George Deilion away when he came with his papers ready, she who had cabled Ian. Thinking of that, she said, "When do you think Ian will arrive?"

"In the cable I received he said only that he would be here as soon as possible," Miranda answered. She tried to picture Ian in her mind, but found that she could not. The time since she had last seen him was not so long, but it might have blurred his image. Still, she thought, that was not so. It was the peculiar state in which she found herself that made her memory unclear. She felt adrift, unmoored. For the first time in her life she was unsure within herself. But she would not give way.

Stacy sighed, "Oh, I'll be so glad to see him. One needs a man about. Tad and Edward are such a help. But they require direction. One needs a man who does not require direction at such at time." The moment those last words were out she was sorry. She was relieved to see Abigail appear in the open doorway.

The older woman came in, her head tilted forward, leading her wiry body. She carried a silver tray on which she had set a tall glass of milk, and a narrow silver dish of dry toast. Lena had added an embroidered napkin, and Timoshen a tiny yellow rosebud.

Stacy's eyes moved curiously between Abigail's dark hopeful face and Miranda's tired one. Surely, she thought, the milk, the dry toast, meant something. Even in grief, that was not a respectable diet. Except in one circumstance. She felt a small frisson of knowledge. But she did not dare ask, or attempt to confirm it. Ordinarily she would have no fear of impinging on Miranda's reserve. But not now.

"It's time you had something," Abigail said. "You can't go a whole day and not eat."

Miranda looked at the tray with repugnance. "I'm not hungry, Aunt Abigail."

Abigail set the tray on the marble-topped table, pushed it close to Miranda, and then hovered nearby. "But you have to be," she said finally. She believed that life came before all else. Yes. Even before death. Certainly before death. If that were not so, then how was man made, and where was God?

She added, "And anyhow, you can eat, hungry or not."

Miranda smiled up at her. She took the glass of milk, sipped it slowly. Reed's child, she thought, aware of but ignoring Stacy's still-curious gaze. Would it have been different if he had known? Why had he determined to destroy himself when, together, they could have vanquished all their troubles?

In the short time since his death, it seemed to her that she heard those questions in her mind with every pulse of her blood. She heard them in the midst of tired dreams, when she reached out to Reed for comfort, and awakened to find him gone.

She dutifully finished the milk, and set the glass down just as Timoshen came in. His mouth was tight, and there was a lowering look on his thin face. His body seemed braced by anger within his neat dark uniform.

"Yes, Timoshen," Miranda said. "What is it? What's the matter?"

"He's out there. He wants to come in," Timoshen said plaintively. "He drove right up to the door, past the crape on the gates, just as bold as you please. Benjy didn't know better than to stop him, I guess. I told him you're not receiving, and he says he knows you're not. And he wouldn't expect it. Things being what they are. But you are receiving him, he says."

Abigail burst out, "What are you talking about? You go right out and slam the door in whoever's face is standing there. Haven't you any sense? Did I raise my only son to be a fool?"

Miranda lifted a hand to silence her. She studied Timoshen's face for a moment, and what she saw there told her what she wanted to know. Timoshen was not only angry. He was frightened. There was only one person to whom he would refer as "he" in that tone of voice. She said softly, "Send him in, Timoshen. It will be quite all right."

Stacy cried, "But you don't even know——"

A faint bitter smile touched Miranda's lips. "But I *do* know, Stacy. It's Jake Rooker, isn't it, Timoshen?"

"Yes. And I told him. I said he's not welcome here, and we don't want him, and—"

He did not mention that Jake Rooker had caught him by his arm hard enough to leave bruises, and given him a shake, and told him to shut up and do as he was told.

"But I shall see him," Miranda answered. "So do show him in, Timoshen."

If argument would have moved her he would have made it. But he knew the set of her mouth. He turned on his heel, and went slowly into the hallway.

Abigail dug her boots into the floor covering, and folded her scarred hands before her and prepared to do guard duty. There was Miranda to protect, and the coming child, too, and Abigail would see neither of them in jeopardy.

But Stacy said, "Whatever can the man want? At a time like this, surely he knows . . ."

"And I shall see him alone," Miranda announced, flashing a look at Abigail.

The older woman grunted disapproval and ground her hands together, but she finally left the room.

Stacy, however, was not so easily disposed of. She took a chair and braced herself, and immediately stood up, her eyes flashing hot embers. "I'll not leave you alone with Jake Rooker." She planted her hands on her hips, and drew herself to her full height. "I'll remain here, and be with you, and whatever he says, I'll—"

"I need no one as my witness," Miranda said coolly. "And I need no protection, Stacy. So . . . if you please . . ."

It was instinct alone that told her she must see Jake privately. She did not know whence the warning had come, but she heeded it with full confidence.

Now he stood in the doorway, his hat in his hand, a cane beneath it, an ebony cane with a gold head. He was unsmiling, and very still.

Stacy swung on him furiously. "What do you want?

Why are you here? You've no right to intrude now. This
is a house of mourning. How dare you?"

Miranda rose, though her knees felt weak under her.
She went to Stacy, and said, "Thank you, my dear, but
believe me, it will be all right." She pressed a kiss to
Stacy's cheek, and Stacy felt the trembling in her body.
"It will be only a few moments. I'll ring very soon."

Stacy sighed, defeated. She sent a scathing look at Jake,
went to the door, paused to stare at him again, and then,
grumbling, "I shall be close by, believe me. I shall be
right here, Miranda." She swished past Jake and disappeared into the hallway.

Jake advanced into the room. He stood very straight in
his fine clothes, and handled his cane with a certain jaunti-
ness, yet there was something about his eyes and mouth
that reminded Miranda of the Jake she had once known
at the Kayhome Arms. His glance seemed to strip her of
her mourning gown and touch her unwillingly exposed
flesh.

She said quietly, "You must have a reason for coming
here."

He shot a look at the chair near her, but waited.

It amused her that he had learned courtesy when he had
donned his fine clothes. She allowed a moment or two to
pass, motioned him to seat himself.

She had managed to control the trembling of her body
now. She reached for and found an impenetrable calm.
He was not here to offer condolences. He was here for
some purpose. She was already certain that it would not
be to her advantage. But how could he harm her any
further?

He sat down gingerly, wishing that he had not yet
come. He had allowed these two weeks to pass, fighting
an urgent impatience. He had dreamed of walking as
master in Haversham Square for so many years. But since
he had argued and threatened his way past the obstacle
of Timoshen's stubbornness, and stepped into this room,
since he had seen Miranda's face, all the impatience and
hunger had drained away from him. He did not know how
to begin. He did not, somehow, even want to begin.

She said dryly, "Well, Jake, what is it? Oh, you needn't look uncomfortable. I know that you must bring me bad news. I'm prepared for you."

What had been the uneasy stirrings of pity were gone just as the impatience had been gone before. He felt a sudden resurgence of triumph. He gave her a long shallow blue look, then shrugged. "So he didn't tell you, did he? I imagined he wouldn't have. I imagined he couldn't face you and say it."

She shuddered inwardly, shuddered as if she had taken a body blow, but nothing of her pain showed in her face. She said, "What is it that you believe Reed must not have told me? What more had you done to him?"

"I didn't," Jake said. "No. It wasn't me, Miranda. It was him. You couldn't keep him away from me and Bon Chance. You couldn't protect him against himself could you? It was him that did it. He *would* risk everything, and so he did. He came down to the place late that afternoon. Left your entertainment at the Palisades, and came to me. As he'd done before, which you already know, of course. I guess he was determined to try his luck again."

She was suddenly cold. The warmth of the room, the scent of the flowers, all sustenance and breath, was gone into an unearthly chill. Her hands shook again, and she folded them neatly together, pressing the fingers hard, so that she felt the nail crescents burn into her flesh.

"Tell me what you're talking about," she said at last.

He took from his pocket a sheet of paper. He passed it to her, and saw how carefully she arranged that their two hands should not touch, not even fleetingly. He smiled to himself, sure in his triumph.

She saw the familiar writing sloping across the page, the blot of ink, the long smear. She saw every mark of the unsteadiness of the hand that had written these lines. Through a blur of sudden dizziness, she read the words, read and understood them. It was all gone. Everything. Everything. Haversham Square was gone.

Now she knew where Reed had gone when he left the picnic at the Palisades, turned his back on the laughter, the friends, all that might have saved him.

She knew why he had returned silently, and climbed the steps, and gone into his study to await a final dawn.

She said nothing but raised her head and looked blindly around the room. She had believed with all her heart and soul that this place was to be her destiny. She had committed herself in love and faith to that life which was to be here. Now it was gone.

She rose and went to the mantel. She touched the branched candelabra with a finger that was steady. She looked up at the painting done by Monet that she and Reed had bought together on their honeymoon. She turned slowly, examining the dying flowers that was all that remained now of Reed.

With her back straight, and her head high, she went to stand behind the chair she had been sitting in before. She clutched its soft velvet in her hands, and leaned all her weight on it, and said in a harsh whisper, "You'll not have Haversham Square, Jake."

"Miranda, still playing the queen of the realm, are you?" he said. "Well, you're queen of this realm no longer. That paper is legal. I made sure it would be." He looked pointedly at the table on which she had dropped the note. "Read it over, if you like. You'll see there's no mention of how the conveyance came to be made. Just that it is made. Haversham Square, contents and acres, is mine."

She understood now what had happened in the room where John died. She saw very clearly how Reed must have felt, the depth of his despair, and what he had thought as he settled into John's chair, and took John's pistol from its case.

Jake said softly, savoring the words, "But, of course, for old times' sake, and because we were once friends, you can stay here for a while, if you want. I'd not put you out into the road, you know. Say a month or two? Then I'll need to take possession, I'm sorry to say. For I've plans. Big plans, Miranda."

She thought her heart would break within her, but she reminded herself that she could not give way. She said, in a cool dry voice, "You'll make Haversham Square a bordello, I presume?"

Somehow that hurt him. His mouth tightened and he struck back. "A bordello was good enough for your husband, Miranda."

She remembered the musky scent on Reed's skin, but Jake Rooker could no longer wound her. She brushed the comment aside. She said, "I'll not live here on your charity. Not for a day, for two months. Paper or no, this place is not yours, and you'll never have it."

He rose, gripped his cane in both hands. He stared at her for a moment, then answered, "Do as you like. But remember, this place is not for sale. Not all Tad Layton's fortune can retrieve it for you. Within two months I'll be back with an eviction notice and men to serve it on you. You'll be gone by then, or leave willingly, or else you'll be dragged out by force and thrown into the road." He turned his back and walked slowly from the room.

She was still standing where he had left her when she heard the outer doors bang open, and heard a lusty shout, and then there were quick, lunging footsteps in the hall.

She knew that walk, that voice. She drew a deep breath, struggling for composure. She lifted her head proudly.

Ian came in like a whirlwind, and Stacy and Abigail followed, leaves blown along in his tumultuous path.

He paused for a moment on the threshold, his bronze head thrust forward, and saw, painfully, the desperate hurt that she had endured.

He crossed the room to her and swept her into his arms. He kissed her first on one cheek, then the other. Finally he lifted her, swung her into the big chair. "Miranda, if ever a man wanted wings these past two weeks, then this was the time when he did. I was on board the day after I heard the news, and though I bribed the ship's master beyond belief, and he laid on the steam beyond belief, too, it could go no faster."

It was no exaggeration. His terror for her had driven him, his grief for Reed as well. But there was something else. Something he would not mention now, could not. Though, with time, perhaps he would. He had loved her for years and concealed it. He had never dreamed nor even hoped that there would be a time when he might allow the passion in him to flower, and had cherished it as a beneficence without expecting any return. He expected none now. Except that he be allowed to help her, to care for her. To lead her gently out of this morass of sorrow, out into the safe terrain of life.

She whispered, "Oh, Ian, I'm so glad that you've come." She realized that she had never forgotten what he looked like. He was the same familiar Ian, although some of the bronze in his unruly hair was silver, and there were new lines in his rugged face.

But he was still the same. His cravat was awry, his collar wilted, his coat wrinkled. The dear familiarity was too much for her. Her hard-won composure was suddenly gone even as she told herself that she must not give way. Sobs rose in her throat and choked her. Tears gathered in her eyes. She put her hands to her face, and at last, wept bitterly.

"Jake Rooker," Stacy shrilled. "I knew . . . I knew . . . he was just here . . . that beast . . . Jake . . . what did he say to you, Miranda?"

But Ian motioned her out of the room, and Abigail, too. Both women made as if to protest, but Ian was not a man to be denied.

"Hurry," he said. "Why do you stand still doing nothing? Hurry now, the two of you. Be quick, if you please. Have tea made, and bring sherry. You mustn't waste my time. There's too much to do."

He thrust a handkerchief into Miranda's hand, and said loudly, "All right. You may have five minutes for this. Just five. But be sure you'll have no more. I suppose you've yet to cry yourself out, so this may help. But I must tell you that we need to speak together, and I'll not attempt it while you weep. A mere male couldn't bear it. And you couldn't understand me, nor listen, in any case."

He stood over her, shaking his head, and muttering to himself, and waiting.

Her sobs lessened slowly. And then she wiped her eyes. When she raised her head, she was able to smile. She said, "I'm sorry, Ian."

"Now then, I want to know it all."

She protested, "You must be tired after your journey."

He interrupted brusquely, "Miranda, I'll not have you offer me a hostess' grace when your face is still damp from tears. Nor will I allow you to play polite games with me. I'm not tired. Except of my own thoughts. We must talk. And I'll expect candor from you."

It was just this firmness that she had always suspected in him. She was grateful to him for it. It made possible her own response as nothing else could have. She said, "You shall have candor from me as no one now living would ever have it."

He frowned at the doorway where Abigail appeared, unnecessarily assisted by Stacy. "Leave the tray," he ordered, and added, "And, if you don't mind, please go away again."

"But Ian," Stacy cried, pouting prettily and advancing into the room, "It's so good to see you. And we must have your advice. You must realize that there's so much . . . poor Miranda . . . you hardly know . . ."

"Not now, Stacy. I shall advise you, I promise you. But at another time."

She sighed loudly and disapprovingly, but she retreated as quickly as she had advanced.

When she was gone, Miranda said, "She has been so good to me, Ian. She came to stay at once, as soon as she knew, so that I wouldn't be alone. It was a great help somehow."

"I'm glad to hear it. I'd have expected no less. Stacy is a silly woman, I think. But she has a good heart." Then, "But we'll discuss Stacy, on another occasion. I'm concerned now only with you."

She looked down at her hands. The blue sapphire sparkled at her. The wide gold wedding band gleamed as if new. She said faintly, "Ian, I fear I simply do not know where or how to begin."

"Then let me begin for you, Miranda. And if I'm wrong in any particular, you must stop and correct me at once. You're alone now that Reed is dead. You don't know how to face the future. Your income is extremely small. If it exists at all."

"But how did you know that, Ian?" she gasped, and added, "There's no income. There's nothing. Nothing but debts."

He leaned back, and let a great sigh heave his chest. "Ah, well, my dear, I am your cousin. I believe that allows me certain rights. Tad Layton seemed to agree with me. I stopped to see him before I came here to Haversham Square. He told me what he knew. It only confirmed what I, myself, had feared."

"But why did you—"

"Miranda, it's no mystery, and I'm no seer. I knew Reed had no interest in adding to John's fortune. I am a self-made man, who learned a fortune does not stand still. It either grows or shrinks. When I heard of Reed's death, I feared for you."

"I see," she said softly.

"You see only that I'm concerned. And that's why I wish to speak to you of what I have decided will be best."

"Go on," she said.

He drew a deep breath. He did not quite know how to proceed. He was prepared to bully her, if need be. Or to bribe her. He would do anything to gain her agreement. Now, having seen her, he was determined that his decision, taken the moment he heard of Reed's death, was the right and proper one. He said quietly, "Miranda, you have no one, and I can't think of your being alone." He drew another deep breath. "Remember that I know what that is. I've been that way since Grace's death. I have my Rory, but I've been alone nonetheless. And I'm a man of many interests and freedom of action. For you—"

She said gently, "Ian, I have to believe that one is always alone."

It had been one of the great lessons of her life, she thought. Her mother, then her father, her grandmother —and now Reed. Each loss a terrible lesson in being abandoned and left alone.

"Listen to me," Ian said. "I can't allow you to stay in this room full of dying flowers and painful memories. It breaks my heart to see you so. Whatever you may think at this moment, you're only twenty-five years old. You're at the beginning, and not at the end." He paused, then went on, "I should like you to return to London with me."

She gave a start of surprise, of protest.

He put up a big hand. "No. Now stop. Just listen. I want you to return with me, to bring your whole household with you. I'll stay and help you prepare for the journey, and see to the closing of Haversham Square for you. I'm adept at that sort of thing. You needn't fear for Abigail and her family. We'll see to them. I'll give you Haversham Gate in London for your own establishment. You'll stay only as long as you like, as long as you find it comfortable. And when you tire of it, I'll suggest you visit Haversham Manor. The country would be fine for you for a while at least. And when you tire of that, you'll go where you please. Or even return here."

"I have nothing to return to here," she said quietly.

He raised his bronze head, rapped out, "What's that you said?"

"Ian, it's gone. Everything. And Haversham Square is gone, too."

He simply looked at her, his very bright blue eyes filled with disbelief that slowly became acceptance. "Ah," he said softly. "Tad Layton told me nothing of that."

"He doesn't know yet." She paused for a few moments. Then, in only a handful of words that expressed nothing of her pain, she explained to him what had happened.

"Reed . . . poor boy . . . oh, my dear . . ." Ian said. He bent his head and was silent for a long time. Then he looked up at her. "Surely you'll do as I suggest, Miranda."

She closed her eyes briefly. She saw in her mind her first vision of Haversham Square, when she had stood on the broad white stone steps and looked up at the big double doors, and the brass lamps, and the carved cornice. She saw in her mind the prisms cast like rainbows on the white walls below the sparkling chandelier.

Eight years she had spent in this place.

Here she had loved Reed with all her heart.

She had come near death at John's hands here.

She had learned pity here, and sorrow, too.

Reedie had been born here, and the infant girl never held in her arms . . .

Within these walls, the new baby she carried, whose being was still secret from all but Abigail, had been conceived. The new life . . . the future . . .

At last she said slowly, "Yes, Ian. I'll do as you suggest. And I'm very grateful to you."

Briefly she thought of Jake Rooker. Even then she knew what she would do.

Ian got to his feet, stood rocking back and forth on his heels. "It's I who should be grateful to you, Miranda. Now I shan't be alone anymore."

There was something in his voice that made her look at him quickly, but his face was all at once expressionless.

He knew that though he had almost given himself away, she did not guess his true feelings yet. He must learn to be careful, he thought, until she was recovered enough to accept the future, and him with it.

THIRTY-ONE

The private railway car stood alone on a siding in the busy yards. It was several hours before it would be coupled to the train that would haul it on its jolting trip through the quiet countryside to New York for the transfer to the ship that would take them to Southampton.

Miranda stirred restlessly and looked past the green velvet drapes at the falling dusk. Clouds of white steam billowed past fences and poles, and spirals of black soot drifted over sheds and stalls. A myriad of lanterns glowed red against the coming night. A steam engine racketed by, its whistle wailing. She folded her hands in her lap, and told herself to be patient. There was still time.

She had packed only what she considered to be hers. A daguerreotype of Abraham Lincoln, another, taken in the first year of her marriage to Reed, the silver-backed brushes engraved with the Haversham initial, her wardrobe.

She had packed, too, a small dried wreath of daisies, dandelions, and buttercups, presented to her by the children in the orphanage when she visited them for the last time. As she smiled down into their young faces, she savored the knowledge of Tad Layton's promise. They were not being abandoned. He would see that they were provided for and never forgotten.

She had taken only what was hers. Haversham Square, its contents and acres, belonged to Jake Rooker now.

Her hands became small fists. She unfolded them quickly and looked at the timepiece pinned to her gown. Again she told herself to be patient. There was still time.

She heard Ian's voice at the door, and then it opened. He looked in, smiled. "Are you comfortable, Miranda? Is there anything you'd like?"

"No, thank you, Ian." Her glance touched the box of candies on the table, the two books, the flowers. He had seen to those, as well as the closing of the house. "I have all I need. But I *am* a bit tired. I think I'll lie down for a little while. Would you send Abigail to me?"

"Of course," he answered. "And I'll be reading in the end compartment, if you should want me."

She was not in the least tired. The whole of her body beat with quick angry energy. She rose the moment he was gone. She went to the small, gilt-framed mirror. She wore black linen trimmed with white lace, a small tipped-forward black hat, its veil, black, too, tied over her face. She removed the hat. She took from her carryall the lightweight black shawl that she had put there earlier. She tied it over her head, and drew on black gloves.

She waited, tapping her foot, until Abigail came in. Then she said, "Aunt Abigail, I must go out for a little while. Go and tell Timoshen to find a hack that I can drive myself."

Abigail's face tightened with alarm. "You? Go out?

Now? Miss Miranda, you can't! We're about to leave.
You mustn't . . ."

"Don't argue, Aunt Abigail, just do as I say. And then
come back and stay here. If Mister Ian asks for me, you
must tell him that I'm sleeping."

"Miss Miranda . . ." Abigail wailed.

"Hurry," Miranda said. "Hurry, I tell you."

Moments later, she ducked beneath the window of
Ian's compartment, and saw the bronze of his hair gleaming under the lamplight, and the strength of his face. For
just a moment, she paused. He would be there. How
wonderful that he would be there when she returned. She
darted across the yards past flickering red lanterns to
where Timoshen waited with the hack, an anxious protest
on his lips.

He helped her into the seat, saying nothing when he
saw her set face, but as she took the reins from him, he
burst out, "You're going back to Haversham Square! And
nobody's there now. Lena and Benjy will have left for
Miss Stacy's. And the place closed up. If you forgot something, then I'll go. But—"

"Stand aside," she told him. "And don't say a word to
anyone. Do you hear me, Timoshen? Not to anyone."

He nodded mournfully and backed off.

She tucked the shawl more tightly at her throat, then
flicked the reins.

The drive through the quiet city did not take long.
Then the familiar ivy-covered walls rose before her, shadowed, dark. Gaslight burned in the two lamps that flanked
the gates.

She climbed down and opened them, and tied the horse
to a post.

Slowly, she walked up the driveway under the tall oaks,
walked through the hushed and breathless dark.

The house rose before her.

She climbed the white steps. The door was open, as she
had left it earlier.

Now she stood in the reception hall. How still it was.
How dim with all the drapes drawn, the jets turned off.

And how beautiful it had once been. The chandelier whispered to her as she turned away.

She made a careful tour of the lower floor, pausing to admire for one last time the painting she and Reed had bought from young Claude Monet in Paris. Reed had hung it himself, and then made love to her on the hearthrug. She adjusted slightly the position of the golden center-piece in the dining room. She touched the candelabra in the drawing room.

Then she walked slowly through the shadows, catching up a lamp as she passed the table, and then went even more slowly up the stairs, feeling through the fabric of her black gloves, oil from the lamp on her fingers.

She went past the sewing room where Mrs. Bannion had made her gowns for her, to the top of the house, and out onto the roof terrace.

Washington City lay at her feet. The Capitol Building was aglow in the night. The half-finished monument to George Washington, the White House and Pennsylvania Avenue, hotels, houses, and shanties were marked by the faint twinkling of lights that burned like distant stars.

She had been part of it once. She was no longer.

She felt a tremor of fear arrow through her. But it did not disturb her. It was always thus when she was faced with some new step. She had had it when she left Dealeyton to go to the Kayhome Arms, and had it again when she first came to Haversham Square. Now she was looking ahead to a new life, and saw faint glimmerings of the shape it would take. She had felt at home in London when she first went there. Surely she would one day soon feel the same again.

She allowed her eyes to linger on the panorama below for one final moment, and then turned away.

She went inside and down, swinging the lamp in time with her steps.

She paused at the room that had once been the nursery. Reedie had ridden his rocking horse and shouted with glee in this place.

She glanced through an open door. Caroline had once

wept here, and taken her terrible pills and dreamed her terrible dreams.

She moved past the blue and white room that had been hers. She and Reed had loved there.

She paused on the threshold of Reed's study, and then went in. She stood still, holding her breath. Tears spilled from her eyes and down her cheeks. Tears of anger and defiance. She did not even feel them. She did not even know she wept.

"He shall not have it," she said aloud into the unanswering silence. "He shall not have Haversham Square."

She turned the lamp slowly in her gloved hands and watched the oil drain out and spill across the floor covering, blotting the golden weave. She saw it soak in, and darken and spread.

She opened the window wide, and then took a match from the big desk.

She paused for only a moment longer, her eyes fixed on the chair that had been John's and then Reed's.

She had tried to remove every sign of John's presence. But he was still here. John was here, in this room, the dark stain that would never fade.

She struck the match and put it to the oil-soaked carpet, and saw small embers begin to flare and spread and smoke. She bent and blew on them, and they began to gleam like a hundred tiny eyes.

She opened the gas jets and went down to the lower floor. There, too, she opened the gas jets as far as they would go.

As she went out, she left the doors wide open behind her.

Midway down the driveway, she stopped and turned back to watch.

In Reed's study, the small embers grew larger and became deadly fingers of flame that spread slowly, eating their separate paths through heavy wood, sending up dim spirals of smoke. Gradually, they joined and crested as they licked at the big desk, and devoured the drape at the open window. They sputtered and hissed as they ran swiftly into the hallway, and from there, prowled upstairs and spilled down. They climbed the walls and sucked at the ceilings. They sank down in whispers of steam, and blazed up in smoky gusts, and fed on the flowing gas jets until, with a deafening roar, they burst through the roof spewing embers and fire, and spreading a wild red glow against the starry sky.

Miranda, watching from midway on the drive, saw first a faint glow at the windows that was like a summer dawn, and then the drapes came billowing out in flaming pennants, whipped in their own hot wind. A single tall black pillar of smoke rose straight into the night. The air suddenly shook around her with the rumble of muted and faraway thunder.

In the trees overhead there was a stirring, the flapping of wings, chirps and chatters of alarm, and then the birds took flight, sailing beyond currents of heat.

Somewhere a bell tolled.

A shout echoed wildly up and down the lane, and was answered by other shouts. The horse tied to the post neighed fearfully and backed and kicked and the wheels of the hack rattled.

A fire signal clamored strident warnings, and answers to it shrilled from all directions.

It seemed as if the earth had opened up, and hell poured through, reaching hungrily to fling itself at heaven.

The house was consumed in flame now. Its windows burst, and their glass spun through the pungent outpouring of smoke, agleam with light from within. Its walls wavered, became liquid and dancing fire. It shuddered from some inner pressure, and to the sound of muffled and distant thunder, it seemed to rise from its foundations in a thick and blinding spray of swirling embers, to rise and hang on red pillars over a great bursting blaze.

Miranda let her breath out slowly. Even where she stood, the heat burned her cheeks, the brilliance her eyes. She was seared, and purified, and made whole once more.

She returned to the horse, untied it and whispered soothingly. Then she drew her skirt up and climbed to the seat of the hack.

There was a crowd at the open gates now. A shouting, questioning, clamoring crowd.

Women in aprons and men in shirtsleeves jostled each other. Children yelled and dogs barked, struggling in the smoking air.

They all went surging past her and up the driveway under the trees, caught in an eerie brightness that burned the dark away.

"It's Haversham Square . . ." The first words were a disbelieving whisper.

And then the cry went up, "Haversham . . . Haversham . . . Haversham Square's on fire!"

The lane was suddenly full of carts and carriages. The fire wagons, bells wildly ringing, drove their way through, scattering everyone in their path.

"Haversham Square is burning! It's Haversham Square!"

Miranda picked her route carefully through the confusion, and finally escaped it altogether emerging into a quiet street. There she signaled the horse to a run.

She stripped off her oily black gloves and flung them away. She dropped her head shawl into the dust of the road.

Behind her, the sky was red with fire, bejeweled by wind-blown sparks that flared and faded, speckled by drifting ash. A thick pall hung over the trees and the air was heavy with smoke.

But Miranda didn't turn to look back.

There was, for her, no more to see.

It was done.

Within hours, Haversham Square had burned to the ground.

J. BARNICOAT
CASH SALES DEPT
P.O. BOX 11
FALMOUTH
CORNWALL TR10 9EN

Please send me the following titles

Quantity	SBN	Title	Amount
————			————
————			————
————			————
————			————
————			————
			————
		TOTAL	══════

Please enclose a cheque or postal order made out to FUTURA
PUBLICATIONS LIMITED for the amount due, including 10p
per book to allow for postage and packing. Orders will take
about three weeks to reach you and we cannot accept responsibility for orders containing cash.

PLEASE PRINT CLEARLY

NAME..

ADDRESS...

....